John Pentland Mahaffy, Victor Duruy

History of Rome

and of the Roman people

John Pentland Mahaffy, Victor Duruy

History of Rome
and of the Roman people

ISBN/EAN: 9783337381714

Printed in Europe, USA, Canada, Australia, Japan

Cover: Foto ©Andreas Hilbeck / pixelio.de

More available books at **www.hansebooks.com**

History of Rome,

AND OF THE ROMAN PEOPLE,

FROM ITS ORIGIN TO THE INVASION OF THE BARBARIANS.

By VICTOR DURUY,

MEMBER OF THE INSTITUTE, EX-MINISTER OF PUBLIC INSTRUCTION, ETC.

TRANSLATED BY M. M. RIPLEY AND W. J. CLARKE.

EDITED BY

THE REV. J. P. MAHAFFY,

PROFESSOR OF ANCIENT HISTORY, TRINITY COLLEGE, DUBLIN.

Containing over Three Thousand Engravings, One Hundred Maps and Plans,

AND NUMEROUS CHROMO-LITHOGRAPHS.

VOLUME VIII. — SECTION I.

PUBLISHED BY

C. F. JEWETT PUBLISHING COMPANY,

BOSTON.

TABLE OF CONTENTS.

VOLUME VIII.

———

FOURTEENTH PERIOD (*Continued*).

THE CHRISTIAN EMPIRE; CONSTANTINE TO THEODOSIUS (306–395 A.D.).

CHAPTER CIV.

ADMINISTRATION, ORGANIZATION, AND SOCIAL CONDITIONS IN THE NEW EMPIRE.

CHAPTER CV.

CONSTANTIUS (MAY 23, 337, TO NOV. 3, 361).

CHAPTER CVI.

THE RELIGIOUS QUESTION DURING THE REIGN OF CONSTANTIUS.

CHAPTER CVII.

JULIAN (NOV. 3, 361, TO JUNE 26, 363).

CHAPTER CVIII.

JOVIAN, VALENTINIAN I., AND VALENS (363-378).

CHAPTER CIX.

GRATIAN (367-383); VALENTINIAN II. (375-392); THEODOSIUS (379-395).

GENERAL SUMMARY.

APPENDIX.

LIST OF FULL-PAGE ENGRAVINGS.[1]

VOLUME VIII.

[1] Facing the pages indicated.

LIST OF COLORED PLATES AND MAPS.

VOLUME VIII.

— ◆ —

COLORED PLATES.[1]

COLORED MAPS.[1]

[1] Facing the pages indicated.

ALPHABETICAL INDEX

TO

TEXT ILLUSTRATIONS, INCLUDING MAPS AND PLANS.

VOLUME VIII.

HISTORY OF ROME.

FOURTEENTH PERIOD.

THE CHRISTIAN EMPIRE: CONSTANTINE TO THEODOSIUS (306–395 A. D.), *CONTINUED.*

CHAPTER CIV.

ADMINISTRATION, ORGANIZATION, AND SOCIAL CONDITIONS IN THE NEW EMPIRE.

I. — THE HIERARCHY.

UNDER Diocletian and Constantine, and especially under the latter, the Roman state passes into its last phase: the Latin spirit dies, and the Later Empire begins. In commenting upon the institutions of Augustus, we showed that an Oriental monarchy in the germ already existed in that republican royalty; what is usually called the Constantinian transformation is therefore the result of historic causes. Notwithstanding the vast difference existing between the two periods, the fourth century of the Empire is connected with the first by those mysterious ties which unite the present with the past, and sometimes with an extremely remote past. It is the forms which differ; the spirit remains the same: it is that of the *lex regia.*

We have delineated the principal change, — that, namely, in religious beliefs; we will now observe the new order established in the state, and the results that followed from it.

In all that concerned the court and the government, Constantine developed the administrative work of Diocletian; he by no means completed it: nor is it possible to determine in the *No-titia dignitatum*, — a sort of imperial directory prepared about 400 A. D., — what part is due to each of these Emperors, and what to their successors.[1] However, the laws of Constantine show that in this Emperor's reign the separation between civil and military duties becomes definitive;[2] that titles and privileges secured to functionaries, their wives, children, and grandchildren, are confirmed and extended;[3] that, finally, the hierarchy of court offices and administrative functions is definitely established, each having its special authority and its clearly marked position in the series of magistracies which rose one above another all the way up to the central functionary, the head of the department. "Constantine," says Eusebius, "devised a large number of titles, in order to be able to honor a larger number of citizens."[4] A similar expression is used by Suetonius when he represents Augustus as seeking to distribute all the citizens into well-marked classes.[5] Here, again, Constantine was faithful to the imperial tradition, which had developed rather than opposed the radically aristocratic character of Roman society. Let us briefly examine "the divine hierarchy."

At its head was the Emperor, midway between earth and heaven, addressed as Your Eternity, Your Divinity. He was the law embodied, and hence could do anything, and do it with impunity, since there was absolutely no public opinion, nor institution capable of speaking for it had it existed. All that belonged to the Emperor and all that he did was sacred, — his palace, his occupations, his edicts, — and these decrees were called "the celestial oracles of the divine will." He was never approached but with

---

[1] This *Notitia* is a description of the imperial administration at the time when it was prepared. In his *Breviarium*, Augustus gives the model of these useful tables of statistics, the last of which is the one now under consideration. — lacking, however, in its present condition, the schedule of the revenues of the Empire. In respect to the *Breviarium* of Augustus, see C. Jullian, in the *Mélanges de l'École française de Rome*, 1883.

[2] Contemporary with the *Notitia dignitatum* (*Or.* 26, sect. 2: *Occ.* 59), and doubtless in the time of Constantine, in some remote and disorderly provinces, such as Isauria, Arabia, and Mauretania, there was a union of the civil and military administrations.

[3] It has already been remarked (Vol. VII. p. 383) that a kind of restricted hereditary succession was observed as early as the time of Marcus Aurelius among the great personages of the Empire.

[4] *Life of Const.* iv. 1.

[5] See Vol. IV. pp. 105 *et seq.*

the attitude of worship; on his head was a diadem set with gems, and on his coins the nimbus which the Church later gave to the saints.[1] The members of his family had the title *nobilissimi*, with the purple robe embroidered with gold; and every one recognized his sons as the legitimate heirs of his power. The old and idle formality of an election by the Senate still remained; Majorian, in 458, speaks of it;[2] but facts show clearly what it was worth.

The Emperor was surrounded by the *consistorium principis*, which assisted him in the exercise of his legislative and judicial power. This high council was composed of those whom we should call the ministers, the great officers of the crown, and the heads of the principal departments of the Empire.

The ministers were as follows: —

The quaestor of the sacred palace, who may be called the secretary of state, since he receives petitions, prepares the laws which the council discuss, and countersigns them, after the Emperor "with his divine hand" has written his name in crimson ink.[3]

The master of the offices (*magister officiarum*), a sort of minister of the imperial household, who has under his superintendence and jurisdiction the innumerable officers of the palace, the *militia palatina*,[4] the *scolares* or guards, the *curiosi* or agents of police, whose duty it is to take note of current rumors and to arrest criminals or persons suspected of crime, the under-secretaries in administrative or judicial affairs, the workmen in arsenals, the corps of interpreters (*interpretes omnium gentium*), etc.

The grand chamberlain (*praepositus*), at the head of the imperial domestics, having under his orders the chief of the *cubicularii*, the count of the palace, the architects, the count of the wardrobe, the steward of the imperial residences, the *silentiarii*, the imperial

---

[1] Eckhel, viii. 84. He directed his mint-masters to give him on his coins the aspect of Alexander, with head thrown back and eyes raised. Eusebius considers this a sign of piety. Eckhel a mark of pride. I have little belief in Constantine's piety, and much in his pride; but is it not probable that he sought by this attitude to confirm the legend of the vision? Since the time of Marcus Aurelius the imperial family had been called *domus divina* (*Bull. des Ant. africaines*, fasc. i. Inscr. No. 3, p. 25).

[2] *Nov. Major.* l. 1.

[3] The forms of appointment to the great offices fill vols. vi. and vii. of the *Letters of* Cassiodorus.

[4] The word *militia* is applied to the entire service of the state, whether civil or military.

physicians having the title of count, and lastly the horse and foot-guards, the *protectores* and *domestici*.

The four praetorian prefects, who are now concerned only with the civil and judicial affairs of the four prefectures. However, in memory of their former power, they take rank above all the other functionaries, and no appeal from their decisions is allowed. They have charge of the *cursus publicus*[1] and of the commissariat, they provide for the publication of the imperial decrees[2] throughout the Empire, and they apportion the taxes annually among the cities and provinces. The entire civil administration is carried on in the *praetorium;* "thus," says an old writer, "from the ocean come all the rivers, and thither they all return."[3]

Attached to each praetorium were one or two advocates of the treasury; and except in their presence no case concerning the treasury could be decided.[4] Constantine even assigned to them the duty of prosecuting offenders, "to bring to an end the execrable race of *delators.*"[5]

The two ministers of finance: namely, the count of the sacred largesses (*comes sacrarum largitionum*) — or, as this population of mendicants called him, "the minister of public enjoyment" — and the treasurer of the private estate (*comes rerum privatarum*), the former the public treasurer, the latter the private treasurer.

Lastly, the two ministers of war, or rather, the two generals-in-chief, — the master of the infantry and the master of the cavalry, who divide between them the military forces of the Empire.[6] They have under their orders the counts and dukes commanding

[1] This is the modern post-office department. (Cf. Marquardt, *Handbuch*, i. 417.) It must be remembered that the persons who were authorized to employ the *cursus* in travelling were lodged and fed at the *mansiones*. See Vol. VII. p. 530, note 1.

[2] The rescripts, which must not be confused with the laws or decrees, were answers made to inquiries from officials or private individuals.

[3] Lydus, *De Magistr.* ii. 172 (ed. of Bonn). The cases which came before the prefect were so numerous that a hundred and fifty advocates were attached to the praetorium of Illyria (*Codex*, ii. 7, 17).

[4] Rescript of Marcus Aurelius (*Dig.* xlix. 14, 7).

[5] *Codex Theod.* x. 10, laws 1, 2, and 3, *annis* 313, 319, 335. This, however, di , not prevent him from encouraging, in 319 and 325, the practice of giving information (See *Codex Theod.* xv. 16, 1, and cf. our Vol. VII. p. 558.) Each president had in his court an advocate of the treasury. (Cf. Godefroy, *Paratitlon* to the *Theodosian Code*, x. 15.)

[6] *Codex Theod.* i. 7, and viii 7, for the years 359 and 372. However, i·) every expedition the two arms were united under one or other of the two chiefs. In this way, later, were created *magistri utriusque militiae*, or simply *magistri militum*, to the number of four, as there were four praetorian prefects.

the troops of a province and the frontier garrisons. The Romans not being accustomed to separate jurisdiction from command, these two principal officers decided in all military trials, and even in those where a civilian brought suit against a soldier; while the praetorian prefect took cognizance of cases where a soldier was the plaintiff against a civilian. This was the application of the principle, *forum accusator sequatur.*

Rome has not even that which the smallest cities possess, — a curia and duumvirs;[1] she is governed by a prefect whom the

CHARIOT OF THE PREFECT OF ROME.[2]

Emperor selects from among persons of consular rank. This prefect, supreme head of justice and administration in the city and suburban region to the distance of a hundred miles, decides in the first instance or upon appeal all cases, civil or criminal, even those where senators are concerned, as the presidents in their provinces have the supreme jurisdiction. The prefects of the *annona* and the *vigiles* are under his orders.

The old capital retains its Senate, over which the consuls preside; that of Constantinople has a pro-consul for its presiding

---

[1] Constantinople retained its duumvirs and its curia up to 359, at which time Constantius gave the city a prefect (Godefroy in the *Codex Theod.* vol. i. p. lx). It has been seen (Vol. VII. p. 444, note 3) that the municipal curia registered legacies and donations. Rome and Constantinople having no curia, this duty of registration was performed by *censuales,* or employees of the *magister census.*

[2] From the *Notitia dignitatum* (Böcking, i. 15).

officer. The Emperor selects these functionaries, and makes known his choice to the magistrates and the cities by sending out ivory tablets which bear the likeness of the consuls and their names; this it is necessary to do, since these names serve to date all legal acts, whether public or private.[1] These humble successors of the great consuls of the Republic still had their curule chairs, their

CURULE CHAIR, CALLED SAINT PETER'S CHAIR (CATHOLICA), LIBRARY OF THE VATICAN.

purple robes embroidered with silk and gold, their gilded slippers, their lictors and rods surmounted by axes which were no longer used; and on the 1st of January they solemnly entered upon their harmless office by going to the Forum, where they enfranchised a slave, and then to the circus, where they gave the signal for the games to begin. This duty fulfilled, their political *rôle* was ended: *in consulatu honos sine labore suscipitur.*[2]

---

[1] *Si qua edicta vel constitutiones, sine die et consule fuerunt deprehensa, auctoritate careant* (*Codex Theod.* l. 1, anno 322).

[2] *Pan. vet.* xi. 2.

The other great Republican magistracy, that which had begun the vast work of the Roman law, the praetorship, was also only a gilded idol. With the exception of a little unimportant civil jurisdiction, the praetors of Rome and of Constantinople had

GAMES IN THE CIRCUS.[1]

nothing wherewith to feed their pride but the memory of a lost authority. Their duties consisted in giving public games at their own expense. Symmachus later expended in this way two thousand pounds' weight of gold.[2] Many persons endeavored by con-

---

[1] Bas-relief found at Constantinople. The first section represents actors; the second, a machine by which seats are drawn by lot ; the third, the starting of the competitors ; the fourth, a scenic interlude ; the fifth, the arrival at the goal (*Revue archéol.* iii. 147–148, and pl. xxviii. and xxix.).

[2] *Letters*, iv. 8. At Constantinople, Theodosius instituted in 384 eight praetors. The first two were obliged to spend, jointly, a thousand pounds' weight of silver; the others much less (*Codex Theod.* vi. 4, 25).

cealment to escape this costly honor; in such cases the treasury
furnished in their stead the necessary funds. The religion of the
'State had changed, it is true; but manners remained the same,
the people must be

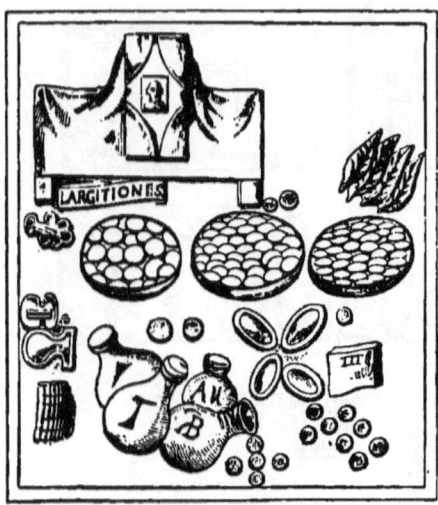

INSIGNIA OF THE COUNT OF THE LARGESSES.[2]

amused, and a *cla-
rissimus* had the duty
of taking charge of
the public entertain-
ments. As for the
treasury, it was sure
to recover the money
advanced ; in case
of need, the heirs of
the praetor designate
paid back the sum.[1]

Since the time of
Alexander Severus
there had been nei-
ther aediles nor tri-
bunes, the officials
bearing the latter
name at Rome and
at Constantinople
having no connection whatever with the Senate.[3] In memory of
the former patriciate, Constantine created patricians, who kept this
title during their lives, and took precedence of all persons except
the consuls in office,[4] — a last homage to that old Republican institution. Patricians and senators had no official duties, except
when specially assigned them.

The senates of Rome and of Constantinople were no longer

---

[1] *Codex Theod.* vi. 4, 5; Zosimus, ii. 38.

[2] *Notitia dignitatum,* Seek, p. 35, and Böcking, p. 41.

[3] Mommsen, *Staatsr.*, p. 459. The last tribunes and aediles mentioned in inscriptions are anterior to Alexander Severus.

[4] Zosimus, ii. 40. Two decrees of Valentinian I. (*Codex Theod.* vi. 7, 1, and 9, 1, anno 372) thus regulate precedence : the praetorian prefect, the masters of the cavalry and the infantry, are equals, and will follow the order of their promotion ; the quaestor, the master of the offices, and the two treasurers, have the precedence over proconsuls ; the latter, in their turn, over counts of the first rank and honorary masters of the cavalry ; the masters of registry over the vicars ; but says Godefroy (ii. 78), *Non unus idemque semper ordo fuit.*

anything more than municipal councils of the two capitals of the Empire, although from time to time they appear to be allowed to express their opinion upon ordinances prepared in "the sacred council."[1]

Each of the ministers, prefects, vicars, and presidents had his offices crowded with employees (*officiales*). The chief of these were appointed, according to the old custom, for one year;[2] but their lives were passed in the public service, and frequently in the same office. They received a salary in money, certain supplies, and when the public service required it, a permit to employ the horses of the *cursus publicus*, with the right of lodging and food in the *mansiones* established along the military road, a day's journey apart from each other.[3] These *officiales* formed a numerous *militia;* those of the palace were thus designated, *qui in sacro palatio militant.* Like the soldier under the standards, when these persons had completed their time of service they received honorable discharge, accompanied by various immunities, — exemption from municipal burdens and extraordinary contributions of all kinds. The *officiales cohortalini*, or inferior employees, were kept by hereditary title in this sacred *militia;* the *coloni decuriones* and *corporati* were excluded from it. We have seen that in the Early Empire the officials of the governors remained the same, being slaves and freedmen bound to their duties.[4]

Constantine maintained the twelve dioceses and the ninety-six

---

[1] Symmachus, *Epist.* x. 28, and *Codex*, i. 14, 8.

[2] Cassiodorus, *Var.* vi. 4–8, 18, 20, 21; vii. 4. In the time of Arcadius, the employees in the ten offices of the count of the largesses were two hundred and twenty-four in actual service, and six hundred and ten supernumeraries (*Codex Theod.* vi. 30, 15, anno 399). An *agens in rebus* asks, as a reward for a successful accusation, to be retained two years in his place. This was contrary to rule (*retita*), says Amm. Marcellinus (xv. 3).

[3] *Codex Theod.* viii. 6, 1; *Codex Just.* xii. 52. These *mansiones,* administered by the *curiales,* were at once taverns for travellers, stables for the post-horses of the imperial service, and storehouses where the food and provender of the *annona* were gathered. There must have been at least forty horses in each (*Codex Theod.* viii. 5, *Parat.,* and Law III.). The *annona* consisted of barley, corn, lard, salt, meat, wine, oil, and provender, and each man employed by the state had a right to one or more rations. The *domestici* had each six rations. On roads where there was no *cursus publicus,* the praetorian prefect on his rounds could make requisition on private individuals for horses and beasts of burden, and was lodged and fed by the inhabitants. The governor had a right to provisions for three days in each city where he stopped. Lodging must be furnished to officials in the *mansiones,* or if there were none, in the houses of the inhabitants (*Codex Theod.* i. 7, 4). Contributions of provisions, very burdensome to the people, were replaced, in 439, by a fixed sum in money (*Codex Just.* i. 52).

[4] See Chap. LXXXV. sect. iv.

provinces of Diocletian; but he divided the former among four prefectures, — those of the East, of Illyria, of Italy, and of Gaul; this was a new grade in the hierarchy.

Whatever name they bore,[1] the governors of provinces had the same duties with their predecessors: they were at once administrative officers, judges, and receivers of the tax, which they were obliged to make good out of their own property when the amount fell short.[2] A division of functions was a thing unknown to the Romans, except towards the close of the Empire, when the military order was strictly separated from the civil; and this ignorance they bequeathed to the Middle Ages. But that which had been an advantage in a small city where, the struggle for existence being the matter of prime importance, it had been needful to concentrate all powers in the hands of the magistrate, became an evil when, in a vast empire, the executive officer had the right as judge to dispose of the fortune and even the life of citizens, — a right all the more formidable since the change from the old methods had greatly increased the judicial authority of the presidents.[3] The Emperors themselves were conscious of the danger arising from this confusion of powers; one of them says: "It may be terrible."[4]

The provinces, meanwhile, still had their assemblies, for a decree confirms to the subjects of the Empire their ancient and valuable privilege of sending to the Emperor the expression of their wishes.[5]

---

[1] See Vol. VII. p. 386.

[2] *Codex Theod.* xi. 7, 16. All the employees shared with their chief in this responsibility: *judices et officia . . . de proprio cogentur exsolvere . . . quod debetur.* (Cf. *ibid.* 29, Law 5.) When the *praeses* was punished by a fine for the infraction of a law, his *officium* suffered a like penalty. In 365 Valentinian I. decided that for a tax unduly established, the *rector* of a province should pay double, by way of fine, and his employees quadruple (*Codex Theod.* viii. 11, 2). This tended to obviate the disadvantages of a frequent change of heads of departments. The employees, who were rarely changed, were in this way interested to keep their chief well informed as to law and precedent. This solidarity between the *officium* and the *praeses* (which later we shall see established among all the workmen in an imperial manufactory, and, later still, between a general and his soldiers) is one of the curious methods employed by this government.

[3] See, later, sect. ii. of this chapter.

[4] . . . *Potest esse terribilis* (*Codex Theod.* iii. 6, 1, anno 380).

[5] See Vol. VI. p. 31. . . . *Liberam tribuo potestatem ut condant cuncta decreta, aut commodum quod credent consulant sibi, quod sentiunt eloquantur decretis conditis missisque legatis* (*Codex Theod.* xii. 12, 1, anno 355). These requests were to be first submitted to the praetorian prefect, who then laid them before the Emperor, accompanied by his own views (*ibid.* 3). Constantine had thus decreed (*ibid.* 4): . . . *juxta legem Constantini.*

This ordinance of Constantine's son proves that the institution of Augustus still existed in the fourth century. Another, of the year 382, speaks, as of an ancient custom, of assemblies which at the will of the provincials could be freely made up of deputies from two or three provinces, even of those from a whole diocese; and this ordinance prohibits the governors, and even the praetorian prefect, from opposing this procedure.[1] Lastly, we know that Constantine, after the example of the Antonine emperors, sent eminent persons from his court into various provinces to exercise control over their administration. But when Trajan intrusted to Pliny an extraordinary mission to Bithynia, it was that he might reform abuses then existing; while Constantine only ordered his envoys to note the diligence or negligence of the governors in the public works which he had ordered.[2] We shall see that more thorough investigations were needful.

The tax was neither voted, nor was its expenditure directed; the Emperor alone determined the amount of money to be raised, and the use that should be made of it. The distinction between the *aerarium sacrum* and the *aerarium privatum* arose only from the difference of the sources whence these two treasuries were replenished; for expenditures the Emperor drew from either at will.

Throughout the Empire everything was a source of revenue: persons and property, agricultural and manufacturing labor, commerce, and even poverty were taxable.

Into the public treasury came, first, the product of the direct contributions, — the *capitatio terrena*, levied on all land-owners; the *capitatio humana*, levied on the rural population;[3] the *lustralis collatio*, a sort of license, for which all were required to pay who lived by traffic or handicraft, even the pettiest or the most disgraceful, — a burden which became intolerable;[4] the *follis*, or *gleba senatoria*;

[1] *Sive integra dioecesis in commune consuluerit, sive singulae inter se voluerint provinciae convenire (Codex Theod.* xii. 12, 9). The whole of this section xii., *De Legatis et decretis legationum,* should be read; it justifies what we have so often said on the subject of these assemblies. The meeting of the deputies of the seven Gallic provinces in the city of Arles in the reign of Honorius is famous in history.

[2] . . . *Ad diversas provincias diversos misimus (Codex Theod.* xv. 1, 2, under the caption *De Operibus publicis.* Cf. Chap. LXXIX. sect. iii.).

[3] See Vol. VII. pp. 399, 400.

[4] Zosimus, ii. 38. It was paid by beggars and by courtesans.

and the obligatory offerings made in certain cases by the decurions
and the *clarissimi*, — the *aurum coronarium*, which was, says Libanius, from one to two thousand pieces of gold from each city, and
the *aurum oblaticium*, which, for the *decennalia* of Theodosius, cost
sixteen hundred pounds' weight of gold to the Roman senators :[1] and
second, the product of the indirect taxes, or the revenue from tolls
(*portorium*), mines, quarries, and salt-works, carried on by com-
panies under the surveillance of a procurator of the government;
the tax upon sales; and the product of the imperial manufactories,
where the workmen labored as a matter of hereditary succession.[2]

The private treasury received the revenues from the domains
of the state and the Crown, the ancestral estates of the Emperor,
property falling to the Crown or without owner, and that of criminals; also fines, which later multiplied to an enormous extent.[3]

The *annona* and the *cellaria* — that is to say, the corn and supplies necessary for the government and the army — made part of
the land-tax; as did also the supplying of horses and military
clothing. The praetorian prefects had the superintendence of this.
They were also the army paymasters, for which expense their
treasury (*arca praefecti praetorio*) was supplied from "the sacred
treasury." Besides this they had no other share in the financial
service of the Empire, except that of transmitting to the vicars
of the dioceses the edicts fixing the amount to be raised by
taxes.

We may remark that the tax was payable in gold :[4] whence
it resulted that the burden of the tax-payers was increased by
the expense necessary to obtain the required metal; that in order
to prevent the fraud of tax-gatherers' paying into the treasury
solidi which they had clipped (*solidi adulterini*), they were compelled to convert the coin into ingots ;[5] that this obligation was a

---

[1] Symmachus, *Epist.* x. 26.

[2] *Monetarius in sua semper durare conditione oportet (Codex Theod.* x. 201, *ad ann.* 317).

[3] We have frequently remarked that in the Roman legislation the confiscation of property
was a consequence of capital sentences, which, in expelling a member from the community or
in putting him to death, deprived the state of a citizen and a fortune. In respect to fines, we
have seen above (p. 10, note 2) that this was an administrative penalty.

[4] Vol. VII. p. 81, note 3, *ad fin.* The *lustralis collatio* was to be paid in gold and silver
(Zosimus, ii. 38), and hence is sometimes called *chrysargyrum.* Certain fines fixed in silver
must have been paid in that metal (*Codex Theod.* xvi. 5, 52); the same was true in respect
to the didrachma of the Jews (Vol. V. p. 132, note 4).

[5] *Codex Theod.* xiii. 6, 15 (*anno* 367).

further burden to the state, which must have been obliged to
increase the allowance made to its financial agents as compensation
for the loss caused them by the conversion of the ingots into
coin ; that, finally,
regulations like these
greatly increased the
amount of coining
and the number of
mint-masters. Thus
we see them, under
Aurelian, capable of
making a great riot
and offering resist-
ance to the praeto-
rians.[1]

The Romans were
ignorant of a power
which the moderns
sometimes abuse ;
namely, credit. We
read in ancient times
of city loans, but nev-
er under the Empire
of a state loan ; and

INSIGNIA OF THE PRAETORIAN PREFECT IN ILLYRIA.[2]

with the habits of ancient communities in respect to usury, there
could hardly have been one. Against unexpected necessities, the
government had recourse to superindictions,[3] which, constantly

---

[1] Vol. VII. pp. 320, 321.

[2] *Notitia dignit.*, Böcking, i. 12. The portrait over the table is certainly that of the
Emperor. He is represented again, with the Empress, on the piece of furniture at the side of
the table. In the Empire of the East the praetorian prefects, the proconsuls, the count of the
East, the augustal prefect, the vicars, and the *consulares* of Palestine alone had the right, which
the military functionaries did not possess, of placing upon their insignia the likeness of the
Emperor. It was the same in the Empire of the West (*ibid.* p. 172).

[3] "Superindictions" were the additional centimes of the French tax. As to loans, they would
have been ruinous to the state, on account of the high rates of interest. In the ancient world
usury was an endemic evil. Brutus lent at the rate of 48 per cent. and Pompey ruined the
king of Cappadocia by his usurious demands. Between private individuals 12 per cent was
a low rate. At Pompeii, in the most flourishing period of the Empire, the banker Jucundus
lent at 24 per cent, and the legal rate in Egypt was 30 per cent (Revillout, *Rev. égypt.*, 1881,
pp. 134-138, and 1883, p. 64). At Athens the law fixed no limit except in the case of guar-
dians employing a minor's money (12 per cent), or in the case of a dowry kept by those who

increased, caused great distress, by exhausting the taxable material. Certain taxes also became very heavy, as under Constantius the land-tax paid by all the *possessores*, since Julian reduced the

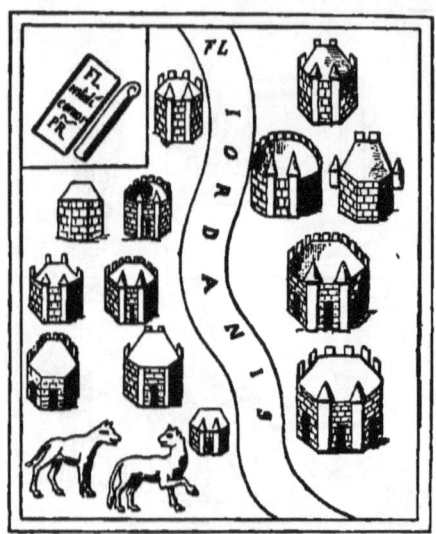

caput for Gaul from twenty-five aurei to seven.[1] Two sources of revenue seem to have been particularly productive, — the *gleba senatoria*, paid by the great provincial families when vanity led them to seek the title of *clarissimi*, or when the government, from interested motives, imposed it upon them;[2] and the *lustralis collatio*, which, by the testimony of all contemporaries, weighed heavily upon the lower classes. The

INSIGNIA OF THE DUKE OF PALESTINE (DUX PALESTINAE).[3]

statements of Libanius and Zosimus may be regarded with suspicion; but those of Evagrius, Cedrenus, and Zonaras cannot be impugned. Under pretext that the decurions were employed in traffic, Constantius later imposed this tax on all the municipal senators. Exemption from the *lustralis collatio* was granted only to those of the clergy who had charge of burials, and to such ecclesiastics and veterans as carried on a small traffic to support life. Finally, all these resources being insufficient, the Emperors drew at will from the treasuries of the cities: they shared with

had no right to retain it (18 per cent). In the Hellenic countries the praetor often required as much as 30 or 36 per cent (see Saumasius, *De Modo usurarum*); so that in three years the capital was doubled. Synesius borrows sixty aurei, receipts for seventy, and after a time returns eighty (*Letter*, 60).

[1] *Codex Theod.* XI. i. 1.   [2] Zosimus, ii. 38.

[3] Böcking. p. 76. Representation of thirteen cities in this military government.

them the product of the tax levied on provisions, and took two thirds of the remaining product of the municipal contributions.[1]

When the savage desires a fruit, says Montesquieu, he cuts down the tree that he may obtain it. Despotism does the same.

Then, as now, the heaviest creditor of the treasury was the soldier; and as dangers increased, it became necessary to increase the army, and also the pensions paid to the Barbarians. How large the effective force was under Constantine, we cannot say with certainty. He had

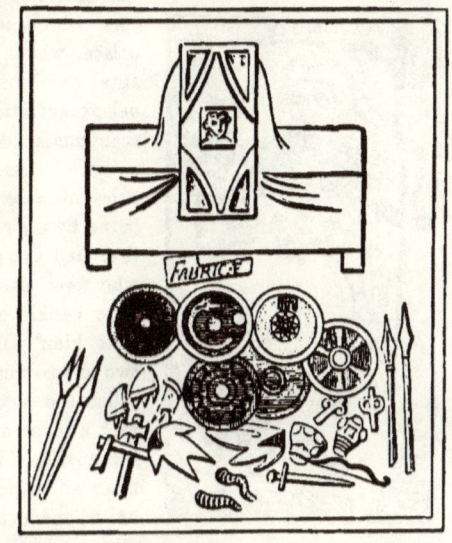

INSIGNIA OF THE MAGISTER OFFICIORUM IN THE EAST.[2]

three distinct armies, — the *militia palatina*, the army of the line, and the frontier regiments.

I. The "palatine militia" consisted of the horse and foot guards[3] (*domestici* and *protectores*), who, recruited from veteran centurions and young nobles,[4] had higher pay, numerous advan-

---

[1] *Codex Just.* iv. 61, 13.

[2] *Notitia dignit.*, Seck, p. 31. See the colored plate representing the insignia of the *magister officiorum* of the West.

[3] Service in the cavalry was more esteemed than in the infantry. (See Godefroy, *Codex Theod.* ii. 277.) This preference went back to the time when the knights alone formed the cavalry of the legions.

[4] In 354 a *protector domesticus* was the son of a former *magister equitum* (Amm. Marcell. xiv. 10.) This corps was a kind of later form of the *cohors praetoria* of the consuls of the Republic, which had been also composed of young nobles who formed an honorable and trusted guard to the consul. Jovian, at the time he was proclaimed Emperor, was *domesticorum ordinis primus* (ibid. xxv. 5); Ammianus also was a *domesticus*. These guardsmen were sometimes despatched on very important missions. Valentinian I. sent into Africa, to examine into complaints made in that province, a *protector*, the son of a count, and one of the *scutarii*, — soldiers who were allowed to bear the Emperor's arms (ibid. xxvi. 5).

tages, ten commanders who were called *clarissimi*, and two superior officers, " the counts of the domestics ; " and the *scolarii*,[1] under

the orders of the *magister officiorum*, who were the guard of the palace, where innumerable attendants were installed. The habitual exaggeration of the time caused their commanders to have the designation of "senators;" and from the titles of *ducenarii* and *centenarii*, borne by their officers, we see that they had extremely good pay : all who were placed near the Emperor were certain to derive advantage from him.[2] The soldiers of these two corps were more particularly called the *palatini*; but this name was also borne by the legions, by the auxiliary infantry, and by numerous squadrons. These corps united made up the reserve of the army, and accompanied the Emperor in all important expeditions.

SIGNIFIER OF A GALLIC LEGION.[3]

II. The army of the line (*comitatenses*) — that is, the infantry, cavalry, and Barbarian auxiliaries — were dispersed through the territorial divisions of the Empire, under counts or dukes, who also commanded the flotillas which had the duty, in their respective districts, of keeping order on the rivers and sea-coasts.

III. The troops which we should call the frontier-regiments were the *ripenses* and the *limitanei*, called also *pseudo-comitatenses*, because they never changed their place of garrison. They occupied, under the *duces*, the intrenched camps, castles, and fortresses built

---

[1] Procopius (*Historia Arcana*, 24) represents the *scolares* as numbering thirty-five hundred men, and says that the guard was less numerous. There seem to have been *scolares scutariorum* and *gentilium* in the time of Gordian III. and of Philip (Cedrenus, i. 451, and *Chron. Paschale*, pp. 501, 502, edition of Bonn).

[2] A rescript of 413 speaks of *praepositi et tribuni scholarum qui et divinis epulis adhibentur et adorandi principis facultatem antiquitus meruerunt* (*Codex Theod.* vi. 13).

[3] The nationality of the Barbarian legionary is indicated by the cock (*gallus*) placed at his side (G. Schlumberger, *Œuvres de A. de Longpérier*, iii. 355). Bas-relief from Strasburg.

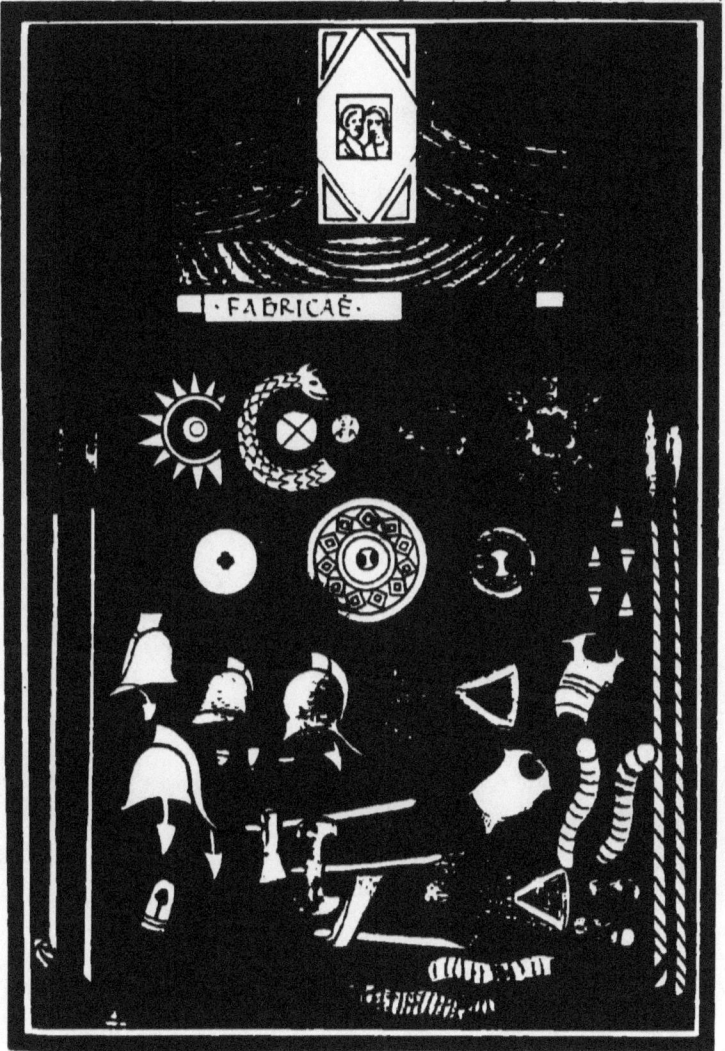

INSIGNIA OF THE MAGISTER OFFICIORUM OF THE WESTERN EMPIRE

(From the Notitia Dignitatum.)

along the rivers (*ripa*), or behind the intrenchments (*limes*), which were the boundaries of the Empire.[1]

In the civil order the *coloni* were but partly free; in the military order the *leti* and *gentiles* were, like the *coloni*, established permanently in the frontier provinces, upon small estates which had been given them under condition of military service.

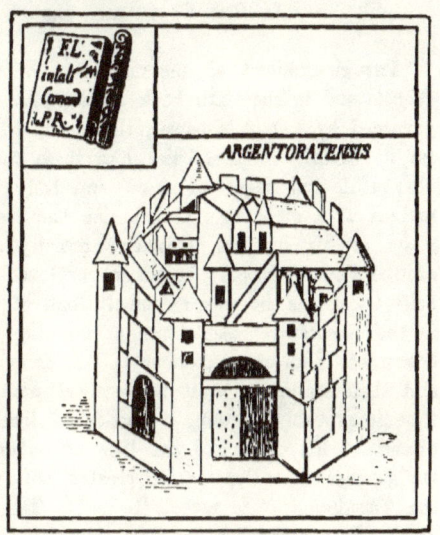

Lastly, whole corps of Barbarians (*foederati*) were in the Emperor's pay; and he bought, moreover, by pensions paid to the chiefs of the nation, the right to levy troops among them.

We pass rapidly over this administrative organization,

INSIGNIA OF THE COUNT OF STRASBURG (COMES ARGENTORATENSIS).[2]

which interests archæology rather than history; but it is necessary to show the consequences of the policy inaugurated by Diocletian, developed by Constantine, and carried to an extreme by their successors, for the reason that out of this policy arose the whole social system of the fourth century, — the last with which this work deals.

---

[1] The minimum height of the soldier was 5 feet 7 inches, Roman measure (*Codex Theod.* vii. 13, 3, *anno* 367), which, according to M. Aurès, is equal to 5 feet 5 inches. The minimum of height in the French infantry is 5 feet. The Roman standard gives a further proof that the greater part of the Roman army was composed of Barbarians, since soldiers drawn from the southern portions of the Empire would not have reached this minimum, — which, moreover, was not required of the *pseudo-comitatenses* (*ibid.* vii. 22, 8). In respect to all these corps, see Godefroy, ii. 286-287.

[2] *Notitia dignit.* Böcking (i. 284) explains the initials *F. L. intali Comord P. R.* in the following manner: Felicitati, Laetitiae, *I*mperatorii Numinis, Tutelae Augustorum Larium Civitates Omnes Majestati Obediant Regiae Domini Populi Romani.

II. The Court and the Nobility.

THE government, all the machinery of which is given in the *Notitia* and in the sixth book of the *Theodosian Code*, was itself governed by a higher power, the court, which had the Emperor for its divinity. Monarchies like these require the ruler to be always in full vigor of mind and body; and, without having arrived at a great age, Constantine had lost both. In the later years of his life his legislative activity slackened;[1] he rarely quitted Constantinople; he no longer loved war, but, if we may believe Zosimus, he was extremely fond of pleasure;[2] and Julian in the *Caesars* represents him as reposing to all eternity on the bosom of Indolence. Zosimus is an enemy, Julian an adversary, and their testimony must be received with doubt; at the same time it probably contains a portion of truth. One of the great officers of his court had the title of *tribunus voluptatum*. Shall we suppose that Constantine created this office whose existence the *Theodosian Code* reveals to us?[3] The first of the Emperors of the East perhaps ended like so many Oriental monarchs who in their declining years slumber upon the throne or shut themselves up in their harems. This is the moment when in absolute monarchies the reign of the courtiers begins; by the testimony of an old writer, this conqueror of so many kings was incapable, during the last ten years of his reign, of mastering himself: like a young spendthrift (*pupillus*), he had need of a tutor.[4]

Constantine had increased the pomp of costumes and the solemnities of etiquette,[5] and, as in the time of Elagabalus, the apartments

---

[1] From 312 to 326 we have, in the *Theodosian Code*, two hundred and sixty-one ordinances of his; from 326 to 337, there are but eighty-nine.

[2] Zosimus, ii. 32: . . . μείνας δὲ ἀπόλεμος καὶ τρυφῇ τὸν βίον ἐκδούς.

[3] *Codex Theod.* xv. 7, 13, *anno* 414. Reference is here made to *voluptates populi;* but this *tribunus voluptatum* was probably also the director of the court entertainments.

[4] The author of the *Epitome:* . . . *Decem novissimis annis pupillus ob profusiones immodicas nominatus.* Zosimus (ii. 38) adds: "He exhausted the treasury by gifts to useless or unworthy men, believing that such profusion did him honor."

[5] Synesius, *Concerning Royalty*, 16. See, in the commentary of Pancirolus on the *Notitia dignitatum*, the foolish display with which the praetorian prefects were to be sur-

of the palace were sanded with gold dust. When Julian, arriving
from Gaul, required a barber, a person sumptuously attired presented himself, whose employment gave him a great salary, twenty
rations for his table, and as many more of provender for his horses.[1]
A whole world, interposing between the Emperor and the Empire,
hid from the sovereign the truth which he no longer sought out
by prompt personal investigation in cases of difficulty; and this
servile and luxurious court soon had all the vices which are
developed in a situation so favorable to passions and intrigues.
Since the whole power of the Empire was in the palace, those
who approached nearest to the master by the humble character
of their duties, — slaves, eunuchs, servants of every grade, —
having his ear, had also his hand to write with, and his will to
command.[2] Their favor obtained what should have been given
to merit, and scandalous fortunes were amassed at the expense
of the treasury and of private individuals. The avidity of the
courtiers made them search for victims; calumny furnished these,
and wealthy families were ruined by false accusations. Amm. Marcellinus, who signalizes the progress of this evil under Constantius
II. and gives the proofs of it,[3] accuses Constantine of having been
its originator, — "the first to excite the appetites of his followers." [4]

The Constantine of Eusebius addresses paternal remonstrances
to his courtiers: "Will you put no bounds to your cupidity?" he
says to them; and marking out on the sand with the point of his
spear the six feet of ground, our last dwelling, he adds: "If you
possessed all the gold in the world, you would soon have nothing
beyond this space of ground, if that should be allowed you." The
Theodosian Code shows us the historic Constantine in a rescript

---

rounded. Honorius forbade all the *honorati*, under penalty of a fine of ten pounds'
weight of gold, to appear before the *vicarius* otherwise than in official costume (*Codex
Theod.* i. 15, 16).

[1] Amm. Marcellinus, xxii. 4.

[2] *Ibid.* xviii. 4, where he shows the *comitatensis fabrica* . . . *eamdem incudem, ut dicitur,
diu noctuque tundendo.*

[3] xiv. 5; xx. 2; xxi. 16; xxv. 4.

[4] . . . *Ut documenta liquida prodiderunt, proximorum fauces aperuit primus omnium* (*ibid.*
xvi. 8. Cf. Zosimus, ii. 38; Eutropius, x. 7). Eusebius himself (*Life of Const.* iv. 54) recognizes this evil. "I saw," he says, "an insatiable avidity plundering other men's property, and
hypocritical piety in the Church. The Emperor trusted in some whose lives were full of
artifice and imposture, and this confidence led him into great errors." Julian (*Pan.* i. 37)
praises Constantius for having on his accession repaired many acts of injustice.

which attests the excess of the corruption, and on the part of the
Emperor not quite so much Christian resignation. "Let the rapacious hands of our officers be stayed," he exclaims; "let them be
stayed, or I will smite with the sword!" and he enumerates the
many ways employed to extort money from those who have business with the government, or seek to obtain justice in the courts.
"If these men dare not complain," the Emperor says, "let others
make known what wrongs have been committed, that we may
punish such robberies with merited penalties."[1] The rescript contains good intentions, and threats in equal number; but we may
doubt whether it produced any change in public morals, since, a
century later, Valentinian III. repeats the same complaints, and
draws even a darker picture.[2]

Venality was an ancient Roman evil; but never before, unless in
the last century of the Republic, had it opened so many doors and
influenced so many minds. Constantine's innumerable agents were
not like the eminent persons sent by the sovereigns of the Early
Empire into the provinces, at that time few in number, where they
filled a very conspicuous position and were not called upon to
determine many trivial questions. These men of consular rank,
these imperial legates, whose houses held the statues of venerated
ancestors, were scrupulous themselves for the honor of their names,
or else were watched and held in check by the Emperor with
a care in proportion to the peril into which they might bring
him. The functionaries of the new government, on the contrary,
are only the men of low degree who swarm in every Oriental
court, — who, gliding everywhere in the darkness, with few scruples
and many intrigues, unnoticed advance from post to post, until
they reach the very highest; where arriving, they sell justice to
compensate themselves for having so long bought favor. During
a period of two centuries the inhabitants of the Empire had had
for judges in ordinary suits the magistrates their fellow-citizens,
whom they were accustomed themselves to choose. If the matter
came within the cognizance of the imperial officer, it was not his

---

[1] *Codex Theod.* i. 16, 7, *anno* 331. The small as well as the great at this time were dishonest. The *mansiones* and the *stationes* of the *cursus publicus* were the scene of endless
frauds. Cf. *ibid.* viii. 5, 21.

[2] *Nov. Val.* iii. tit. i. 3, sect. 2, *anno* 450.

duty to decide in the case, but to indicate the law applicable; and judges, who much resembled the juries of modern times, made the decision. Now there was one judge, more easily to be corrupted,[1] proud of the power conferred upon him by his official title, and with reason, since behind him stood the Emperor, whose direct agent he was. Accordingly he assumed an extremely arrogant tone towards the persons under his jurisdiction, and was approached with offerings as if he had been a god. Venality is the scourge of perishing nationalities, and Rome was in a state of decline.

Courts have sometimes been schools of elegance in manners, refinement in mind, and politeness in speech. Literature and art have received from them valuable encouragement. But at the epoch of which we are speaking, poetry and art — those social forces by which the soul is elevated — no longer exist. With an Asiatic government and a religion soon to become intolerant, great subjects of thought are prohibited. There is no discussion of political affairs, for the Emperor gives absolute commands; no history, for the truth is concealed or condemned to a complaisance which is odious to honest men;[2] no eloquence, for nowhere can it be employed except in disgraceful adulation of the sovereign.[3] The great Roman science, jurisprudence, has even lost its beautiful terse language; the rescripts are verbal and declamatory, and the words stifle the thought. Towards the close of the century appear three men, Symmachus, Claudian, and Rutilius, through whom Latin literature throws a dying gleam; the rest are of no value. Only the Church is to have mighty orators, — but in the interests of

---

[1] See, later, an ordinance of Valentinian I. forbidding judges to decide cases in their own houses with closed doors.

[2] An exception must be made in the case of the truthful Amm. Marcellinus; but how remote is he from the Roman authors! The works of Eutropius and Aurelius Victor are chronicles rather than histories. Eutropius bestows only a few lines upon Julian, although he accompanied that Emperor in his Persian campaign (x. 16).

[3] Three Greek rhetoricians, Themistius, surnamed εὐφραδής, Libanius, and Himerius, all pagans, had a great reputation in this century. Posterity, more critical, places them in the list of fine talkers, who die at once, because their harmonious and musical but empty sentences give nothing to philosophy and very little to history. The most interesting of the three, Libanius, understood at last the inutility of that rhetoric which turns the whole mental effort upon words; his last treatise is upon the worth of silence. For us the most important of the Greek authors of this time is the Emperor Julian. Later I shall speak of the Greek Fathers.

heaven, not earth;[1] and so, in this Empire now exposed to countless perils, the little mental activity still existing in civil society
will occupy itself only with court intrigues, the subtleties of philosophers aspiring to be theologians, or the petty literature of some
belated and feeble admirers of the early Muses.

The court extended itself throughout the Empire with a sort
of radiance of imperial majesty, separating from the mass of the
people those to whom it communicated, by honors or offices, something of its own splendor.

The great functionaries were called "the most perfect," or
"excellent;"[2] later, we find *illustres, respectabiles*, and in the two
capitals the senators are called *clarissimi*. But the senators of
the fourth century differ much from their predecessors. Through
causes which we have already explained, the evil from which Italy
had suffered was now extended to the provinces : the *latifundia* had
everywhere absorbed petty ownerships. "The poor man," says Salvianus, "cannot live beside the rich; he there loses his property, and
often his liberty." The same complaint is made by Saint Ambrose
and Saint Gregory Nazianzen.[3] It was difficult to arrest this economic development; Constantine made no attempt to do so, but
he sought to derive advantage from it. To create and multiply a
new class of tax-payers, he associated to the *amplissimus ordo* many
great provincial land-owners and subjected them to a tax propor-
tioned to their fortune, the *follis senatorius*.[4] In earlier times there

---

[1] In the Latin provinces, Hilary, Ambrose, Jerome, and Augustine; in the countries
using the Greek language, Athanasius, Basil, the two Gregorys, John Chrysostom; in
Syria, Ephrem; in the Cyrenaica, Synesius.

[2] *Perfectissimi vel egregii* (Lactantius, *De Morte pers.* 21), — ancient designations preserved by Constantine, like that of *clarissimi*. The other two seem to date officially only
from the reign of Valentinian I.

[3] Ambrose, *Hexameron*, v. 10, and Gregory Nazianzen, *Disc.* xvi. 18. The lamentable condition of certain Italian provinces, — the Basilicate, for example, — which is still
given up to *latifundia*, shows how much destitution the extension of this agricultural system
throughout the Empire must have produced.

[4] The senators paid besides, like the other *possessores*, the *tributum soli;* furthermore,
they had to offer to the Emperor every year new year's gifts, and in special cases the
aurum oblatitium. In 373 the senators offered to Valentinian and to Valens, on their
tenth year, sixteen hundred pounds' weight of gold (Symmachus, *Ep.* x. 26). When
the Emperor gave the praetorship to a senator, the latter was obliged to pay for public
games a sum amounting to 25,000 *folles*, and fifty pounds of silver (*Codex Theod.* vi. 4,
5). Zosimus (ii. 38) is wrong in complaining of the *follis senatorius*. It was proportionate
to the fortune, for to establish it Constantine had required each senator's fortune to be
stated, ἀπεγράψατο δὲ τὰς τῶν λαμπροτάτων οὐσίας: accordingly certain senators, having but

were no senators except in Rome;[1] now men could be senators anywhere. Those who had obtained by hereditary succession, imperial
favor,[2] holding of a magistracy, or service in the palatine militia,
the right to be called *clarissimi*, composed the senatorial order,
which soon came to include all the rich men in the provinces, and
the chief officials on their retirement from office.[3] This imperial
nobility possessed certain important privileges, distinguishing it
from the rest of the nation; and the senatorial dignity was hereditary, in law for three generations, in fact for as many as preserve
the necessary fortune, — custom, as well as the policy of the period,
retaining the son in the father's career.[4] "Between the senator and
the curial," says the law, "there is no similarity."[5]

The official residence of the senators was Rome and Constantinople (*sèdes dignitatis*);[6] but many of them were never there. As
early as Trajan and Marcus Aurelius there had been complaints
of absenteeism;[7] the case was much worse when the remotest
provinces had their *clarissimi*. The son of Constantine, during
his residence in the old capital in the year 357, vainly reminded
the senators in Greece and Macedon and Illyria that there were

little property, paid a tax of only five, or even no more than two, gold *solidi*, — *etiamsi posses-
sionem forte non habeant* (*Codex Theod*. vi. 2, 8). Lastly, an ordinance of 428 says: *Pro
suis viribus glebales fonctiones agnoscant* (*Codex Theod*. vi. 2, 21). The private domain of
the Emperor, *res privata*, paid the *follis*, because the Emperor was also the chief of the senators (*Ibid*. 19, and ix. 2, 1).

[1] In the time of Paulus a senator required special authorization from the Emperor
to live in a province (*Dig*. L. i. 22, sect. 6).

[2] *Si quis senatorium consecutus nostra largitione fastigium, vel generis felicitate sortitus.
. . . (Codex Theod*. vi. 2 and 8, *annis* 383 and 397).

[3] The *honorati*. Alexander Severus had already pensioned or subsidized these persons
in order to enable them to maintain their rank: *honoratos pauperes . . . commodis auxit*
(Lampridius, *In Sev*.). The diptych on the next page, perhaps of earlier date than that
of Flavius Felix (Vol. VII. p. 392), represents on one of its leaves a man who has been by
turns called Claudian, Ausonius, and Boethius. Wrapped in his philosopher's cloak, he holds
a *volumen*, and other *volumina* are unrolled at his feet; the second leaf represents a female
musician, — which strengthens the opinion of those who call the other figure that of a poet
(Gori, *Thesaurus diptychorum*, ii. 243, and *Trésor de Monza*, pl. iv.).

[4] On the privileges and obligations of senators, see Godefroy, vol. ii., *Paratitlon*, in
book vi. chap. 2. Symmachus (*Epist*. iv. 25) writes to a young noble: *Secundum natales
tuos honorum culmen indeptus es;* and Sidonius Apollinarius (*Epist*. i. 3) promises himself
the same honors that have been enjoyed by his father: *Adipiscendae dignitati haereditari
incumbam, cui pater, avus, proavus praefecturis magisteriisque micuerunt.*

[5] *Codex Theod*. vi. 3, 2–3.

[6] *Ibid*. vi. 4, 1.

[7] Atticus Herodes, a senator of consular rank, quitted Rome, but after having resided
there for a long time.

also agreeable residences near Rome, and that by establishing themselves there they would escape the long journeys now necessary before receiving the honors due to their rank ; it was for the purpose of avoiding these expensive honors that they resided out of Italy.

The nobles of the Republic and the first Emperors had in their train friends (*comites*) whom they classed in lists. These companions now took their place in the hierarchy. The appellation *comes* was, like decorations at the courts of modern Europe, a permanent honor to the individual, and not to the position; so that great functionaries, counts of the first degree, and simple decurions, or retired shipmasters,[1] counts of the third degree, could all appear in the *comitatus*, or imperial train, without offence to those of the higher rank. It was not the less a gratification of vanity, for each man had his title, and the neglect to use it in addressing him was punishable by a fine. A decree of 384, after having minutely determined the order of rank, makes such disrespect a case of sacrilege (*plane sacrilegii reus*);[2] and it was with all gravity that the Emperor, writing to his magistrates, addressed them as "Your Sincerity" or "Your Gravity;" and to him they made reply: "We shall obey the divine precepts of your Eternity." The pomp of formulas increased as men became more and more debased.

These titles and many offices of state gave privileges. Some of them were honorary, — a rank, a certain dress, the right of entrance at court or at the praetorium of the governors, the right of being judged only by the urban prefect or the Emperor, and the like. Others were extremely useful, — as exemption from cer-

---

[1] The *navicularii* who brought corn to Ostia composed, with the *mensores* of the port, corporations which, in 417, by the order of Honorius, made choice of masters whose duty it was to prevent frauds and thefts (*fraudes et furta*). These masters remained in office five years, and when they had faithfully performed their duties received the title of counts of the third order; but if they had acted dishonestly, their property was confiscated and they were condemned to labor at grinding corn, *ad pistrini munia revocatur* (*Codex Theod.* xiv. 4, 9).

[2] *Codex Just.* xii. 8. A decree of the year 412, when the order of titles had considerably changed, shows at what inequality this society had arrived. For a like offence an *illustris* paid fifty pounds of gold ; a *spectabilis*, forty ; a senator, thirty ; a *clarissimus*, twenty ; a *sacerdotalis*, thirty ; a *principalis*, twenty ; a *decurio*, five ; a *negociator*, five ; a *plebeius*, five (*Codex Theod.* xvi. 5, 52). In another decree, of the year 414 (*ibid.* 54), the fine is for a proconsul, a vicar, or a count of the first rank, two hundred pounds of silver ; for a senator or a *sacerdotalis*, one hundred ; for one of the *decemprimi*, fifty ; for a simple *curialis*, ten.

CLAUDIAN (?), UPON A DIPTYCH OF MONZA.

tain taxes, customs dues, municipal burdens, torture, etc.; and these advantages inspired pride in their possessors, and envy in those who were less favored. Immunities which had been very rare under the Republic and in the Early Empire[1] were multiplied in the third century in proportion as public functions increased, and the interference of the government in municipal affairs.[2] Constantine largely developed this system, which enabled him to make his nobles conspicuous, and to pay, with privileges which cost him nothing, for services which he was not willing to reward with money. From 314 to 328 five laws establish and extend the privileges of the *palatini*.[3]

Christianity, which, it has been said, brought equality into the world, made no attempt to combat the aristocratic tendencies of the society upon which it had just laid hold. The Christian Emperors are gods upon earth much more than ever the pagan Emperors were, and they organized a state nobility such as Rome had never before known.

As we count the successive grades which rise, one above another, from the people up to the sovereign, and notice the barriers which fence in so many of the citizens to the places and positions in which they were born, we shall be tempted to believe that the Empire at last is supplied with those monarchical institutions which ought from the first to have protected the ruler, by placing between him and any outbreak of people or soldiery a whole world of men, each interested in the maintenance of the imperial

---

[1] Livy, xlv. 26; Suetonius, *Oct.* 40, *Claud.* 25. In the time of Ulpian, the immunity ceased with the life of him who had enjoyed it (. . . *cum persona extinguatur*); but for regions (*loci*) and for cities, it was permanent (. . . *ad posteros transmittitur. — Dig.* l. 15, 4, sect. 3). Trajan had granted to the philosopher Potamon exemption from the *portorium*; Tyras had early obtained this exemption; and Brundusium received it from Sylla.

[2] See in the *Digest* (l. 5 and 6) and in the *Theodosian Code* (vi. 35), *De Privilegiis eorum qui in sacro palatio militarunt.* Law 1, which is of the year 314, says: . . . *Immunes eos a cunctis muneribus permanere cum universis mobilibus et mancipiis urbanis, idque beneficium ad filios eorum atque nepotes . . . pervenire.* Law 2 exempts from the *productio equorum* (anno 319); another, of the same year, says: *Nec ad curiam, vel honores, vel onera, vel munera municipalia devocentur* (ibid. 3).

[3] The law of 314 explains what is meant by *palatini: Tam his qui obsequiis nostris inculpata officia praebuerunt, quam illis qui in scriniis nostris id est memoriae, epistolarum libellorumque versati sunt.*

NOTE. — The engraving facing the next page represents the two capitals, Rome and Constantinople, personified. (Ricardi diptych, formerly at Florence, now in the Imperial Museum at Vienna. Gori, *Thes. ret. dipt.* vol. ii. pl. ix.)

authority. But these ramparts, which in modern Europe have
for centuries made royalty secure, are solid only when they have
sprung up of themselves. Powerful aristocracies are formed only
by religion and by war. The *noblesse* of Constantine arose neither
from one nor the other. Born of yesterday at the Emperor's
caprice, having land but not having arms,—which they at once
dread and despise,[1]—this was not a veritable *noblesse*, since under
all its titles, which were mere labels of classification modified by
the Emperor at his will, there was no special authority in those who
bore them. Their property, their lives even, were at the absolute
discretion of the Emperor; and this exact order, which hid the
confusion of a system as yet only partially projected rather than
perfectly devised, will not prevent slaves and eunuchs from being
all-powerful in the palace, or praetorian prefects being driven thence,
to be put to death with torture. The gilded menials of Constantinople had therefore nothing in common with the great aristocracy which had made the fortune of Rome. They fled from camps,
where they might have gained a virile confidence in the presence
of dangers bravely met; and when invasion came, they had
nothing to oppose to it but bodies enervated by indolence, and
souls rendered pusillanimous by servility.

The fundamental political principle of classic antiquity had been
election, and men had preserved the image of this after they had
abandoned its reality. During the whole duration of the Early
Empire the duumvirs had been always appointed by the popular
assembly; even as to the Emperors there had been a semblance of
election.[2] In the Later Empire, on the contrary, hereditary succession, established or encouraged by the law, was the dominant principle. We have already seen it accepted for the imperial dignity and
for the senatorial rank; we shall soon find it imposed upon *curiales*
and *coloni*, upon employees of the administration (*cohortales*) and

---

[1] *Militine labor a nobilissimo quoque, pro sordido et illiberali rejiciebatur* (Mamertinus,
Gratiarum actio, 20). *Honestiores quique civilia sectantur officia* (Vegetius, i. 7). Carrying arms
was forbidden, except when expressly allowed by the Emperor (*Codex Theod.* xv. 15, 1,
anno 364).

[2] As late as 458 the Emperor Majorian, chosen by the Suevian Ricimer, wrote to the
Senate: . . . *Imperatorem me factum, patres conscripti, vestrae electionis arbitrio,*—an old for-
mula which deceived no one, but which for centuries it had been considered proper to employ
(*Nov. Maj.* i.). Constantius appeared also to ask the consent of the army in making Julian
Caesar,—another formality (Amm. Marcellinus, xv. 8).

ROME AND CONSTANTINOPLE PERSONIFIED.

upon workmen in the imperial manufactories, upon corporations needed by the state and by cities, and even upon the great majority of soldiers.[1] But by this principle of hereditary succession and the hierarchy combined, life was, so to speak, suspended in this great body, and it was struck with paralysis at the moment when there was a general advance of the Barbarians to attack it. When the invaders arrived, the nation remained indifferent to the efforts of its government because it saw above its head and weighing upon it with all the weight of its privileges and its insolence, a mass of functionaries and titled persons who drew largely from the public treasury, while many of them paid but little into it. We can scarcely exaggerate the number of these privileged persons. Titles were sought with all the eagerness that has been shown in the countries of modern Europe in seeking patents of nobility. As early as the time of which we speak they were bought, and the number of tax-payers had diminished, while that of parasites increased.[2] A time came when in a single grade there were five classes of holders.[3] Hence the language of Lactantius, which is alarming, even with its evident exaggeration: "Those who live upon the taxes are more numerous than those who pay them."

[1] The *cohortales*, for example, cannot, without the Emperor's permission, abandon their employment or aspire to another condition (*Codex Theod.* viii. 4, laws 4, 18, 21-3, 25, 26, 30; *ibid.* viii. 7, laws 2, 3, 9), unless they have had twenty-five years of service (*ibid.* vi. 35, law 14; viii. 4, law 30), under penalty of being sent back to their position. Justinian subjects to the trentenary prescription the prosecution which might be set on foot against *cohortales* who had abandoned their employment (*Codex Just.* xii. 58, laws 12 and 13); their children could not withdraw themselves from the paternal condition (*Codex Theod.* viii. 4, *lex ultima;* and tit. 7, law 19), even those who were born after the expiration of the paternal term of service (*ibid.* vi. 35, law 14). "This prohibition of change of condition is one of the most characteristic traits of the imperial legislation. It is applied to so large a number of positions or professions that we may regard it as a general rule for the mass of the inhabitants of the Roman Empire" (Serrigny, *Droit public et administratif romain, du quatrième au sixième siècle,* i. 170). At the same time we should observe that while a man was attached as a matter of hereditary succession to the same branch of service, he was not held to the same position in it; thus he might rise from one grade to another, and in certain corporations he even obtained his liberty after a fixed number of years.

[2] Amm. Marcellinus, xxv. 4. Frauds became so numerous that many laws were made to send back to the lists of municipal tax-payers pretended nobles and veterans (*Codex Theod.* xii. 1, laws 24, 33, 36, 38).

[3] For instance, in the case of the *illustres,* — *Illustres in actu,* or on duty; *Ill. vacantes praesentes,* or unattached; *Ill. vac. absentes; Ill. honor praes.; Ill. honor abs.* (cf. Godefroy, *Code Theod.* vi. 18). For the *clarissimi* there were three grades, — the *cl. illustres,* the *cl. spectabiles,* and the simple *clarissimi.*

III. — THE PEOPLE: CURIALES AND POSSESSORES.

AFTER the nobles and the court let us observe the people, here, as elsewhere, divided into two classes, the rich and the poor. But wealth imposes upon the former burdens often intolerable, and poverty places the latter in a condition of semi-servitude.

In the days of their independence the citizens in the Graeco-Italian states provided for everything, — the keeping up of roads and public buildings, the maintenance of public order, the financial management, the administration of justice, the rites and ceremonies of religion, public festivals, etc.; and they did all this without complaint, because liberty compensated them for the sacrifices they made. But Rome had imposed her authority upon these little republics, and the Empire finally suppressed their municipal franchises. Only the burdens remained. These were rendered obligatory; and they became heavier for the notables of the city in proportion as the number of those excused from them grew constantly larger. Among persons excused were the state nobility, the veterans of the army, farmers and collectors of taxes, colonists on imperial lands, artisans whose work was useful to the court, and even ship-owners who transported corn to the points where distributions were made. We have seen that immunity conferred honor, because it was a privilege, — and profit, because it relieved from an expense which fell instead upon the mass of the inhabitants. It was therefore to the detriment of a class of the citizens that the government gratified the vanity of the nobles, and secured services for which it should have paid. A man was born a *curialis;* he did not become so except, in the case of the poor man, by a stroke of good fortune which brought comfort into a humble house, or in the case of a noble, as the penalty for an offence. Guilty persons, or those regarded as guilty, were condemned to the curia as to a penalty and instead of a punishment (*ob culpam, loco supplicii*).[1] Men were

---

[1] *Codex Theod.* xii. 1, laws 66 and 108. These two laws, of the years 375 and 384, forbid condemning to the curia *ob culpam*, showing that the practice had existed at an early period.

impressed, so to speak, for municipal honors. Thus, during the last persecution, Christians possessed of property were *addicti curiae*, so that their wealth might be at the discretion of the municipal senate. A law of Constantine provides that if a man appointed to the duumvirate flees the city, his property shall go to him who takes the office instead.[1]

Shut up in the curia as in a jail, the *curialis* was the prisoner of his *municipium*, the slave of his fortune.[2] He remained subject to the ancient *munera*[3] of the times of liberty, and the government imposed upon him actual state duties, such as the levying of part of the tribute. The *curiales* at their own risk and peril[4] must allot and levy this; and they were even charged with the recruiting, since military service was one of the taxes on property.[5] Also there were many legislative provisions, admitting to the curia the son of the decurion as soon as he was eighteen years of age, forbidding the *curialis*, under penalty of banishment, to alienate any

---

[1] Euseb., *Life of Constantine*, ii. 30, and *Codex Inst.* x. 31, 18, anno 326. Another law, of 319, condemns to the curia any veteran's son who is unfit for military service (*Codex Theod.* vii. 22, 1).

[2] . . . *Originalibus vinculis* (*ibid.* xii. 1, 82), and elsewhere: *curiales . . . serviunt.* The word which designates one of the forms of ancient slavery, *nexus*, is also employed to show the chain which binds the son of the *curialis* to the curia, *quem avitus curiae nexus adstringit* (*Codex Theod.* xii. 1, 64, anno 365). There was no special rule in respect to this slavery : . . . *per originem obnoxii curiis*, 13 ; . . . *qui statim ut nati sunt, curiales esse coeperunt*, 122. The *curialis* appointed by the governor or the decurions (*ibid.* xii. 1, 61, anno 365) could not be released from the curia till he had fulfilled all municipal obligations (57, 58, 65, 182).

[3] The *curiales* and their chiefs, the annual magistrates, administered the city's property and managed its finances; they built or kept in repair public edifices, streets, roads, bridges, and aqueducts; they inspected the harbors and markets, and were obliged, in many places, to superintend the administration of the public relief given to children, the sick, and the aged; they bought the corn for distributions, and the wood for heating the baths ; they gave games and spectacles; they visited the governor or the Emperor on matters concerning the welfare or interest of the city. The most serious feature of the situation was that all the acts of their administration involved responsibility, which was made very grave by heavy fines or large indemnities which they were often required to pay into the city's treasury. See, in respect to the obligations of the *curiales*, for the period of which we now speak, Godefroy's *Paratitlon ad Cod. Theod.* xii. 1, p. 355. A decree of the year 315 reserves to the Emperor alone the right to grant the *vacationem munerum* (*Codex Theod.* xii. 1, 1).

[4] The responsibility of the *curiales* in respect to the public treasury was not collective; each individual answered for that portion which it was his duty to collect: *nequis omnino* [*unusquisque decurio*] *pro alio decurione vel territorio conveniatur* (*ibid.* xi. 7, 2, anno 319). In respect to the financial responsibility of the *curiales*, see the *Theodosian Code*, xii. 6, *De Susceptoribus.* Law 1 belongs to the year 319.

[5] *Possessoribus indicti tirones* (Vegetius, ii. 5). The expense of equipment fell upon the land-owners. This was the system of Charlemagne and the Valois kings of France, and, until recently, of Russia.

part of his estate or to travel without authorization of the governor,[1] and denying him admission to the militia, the Church, or offices of state. If he died without children, the curia became his heir; if he left daughters only, the curia took a fourth of his property. From Constantine alone there remain twenty-two constitutions relating to the *curiales*, and the chapter *De decurionibus* in the *Theodosian Code* contains a hundred and ninety-two. A dangerous solicitude is this, for it is not the well-being of the cities which the government has in mind; it is only to secure the payment of taxes, the recruiting of soldiers, and the execution of public works, — a triple duty, which, with the administration of justice, falls almost entirely within the province of the state, — which, however, the Emperors shifted upon the municipalities. When we see the *curialis* flee from the city, or buy a title to hide himself in the classes that enjoy municipal immunity,[2] or descend willingly to the position of agricultural laborer, it is easy to understand why the old historians show us cities without inhabitants, and why Constantine has curiae without *curiales*. Hence so many efforts to arrest desertions, which the Emperor himself had occasioned by a false conception of the division of social obligations between the state and the citizens.[3]

These slaves of public business had their compensations, — first, municipal honors, a show of authority, the pleasure of feeling themselves raised above the crowd, and if they ruined themselves in the service of the city, the right to be supported at the public expense; moreover, exemption from torture, in a time when there was frequent recourse to it; lastly, exemption from certain dues, and whatever advantages — not very creditable certainly, but sometimes very productive — they could derive from

[1] *Codex Theod.* xii. 1, 9, *anno* 324.

[2] An ordinance of 383 condemns to be burned to death the *civitatum tabularii* who falsely inscribe a name on the list of those enjoying immunity (*Codex*, x. 15, 1). Constantius reproaches the *curiales* with buying *honores imaginarios* (*Codex Theod.* xii. 1, 25 and 27).

[3] Zosimus, ii. 38; *Codex Theod.* xii. 1, 6, and 13 : . . . *curias desolari* (*annis* 319 *et* 326). Constantine repeats it : *curias vacuefactas* (*ibid.* 25 and 27; cf. *Nov. Majoriani*, vii. *initio*). One of the epigraphic ordinances of Constantine, in the collection of Voigt, orders : . . . *Quibus studium est urbes . . . inter mortuas reparare.* (Cf. *Bull. de Corr. afric.* 1882, p. 84.) A decree of 340 (*Codex Theod.* xii. 1, 29) speaks of *magistratus* [*civitatum*] *desertores.* Accordingly, a new title of honor was devised for a man who, exempt by birth or condition from municipal burdens, consented to assume them; he was declared *pater civitatis* (*Codex Just.* x. 48, 3, *anno* 463).

the exercise of their functions. To place in the same hands the
apportionment and levying of taxes in money and in kind, was
a wretched system of administration. Some tax-payers were
rated too high, others too low. This man deceived as to quan-
tity, that man as to quality; and the deception was practised with
impunity, thanks to the connivance of the assessor-collector, whose
indulgence was paid for, or whose severity money could lessen.
By a natural retaliation, those whom the Treasury persecuted,
became in turn persecutors. Amm. Marcellinus shows this as
early as the reign of Constantius, and later, Salvianus says:
" There were as many tyrants as there were *curiales.*" [1]

But the government cared little for this. It appeared so
convenient merely to name the amount of the land-tax, and then
to stretch one's hand out to receive it, that the same procedure
was adopted in respect to the tax on trades (*lustralis collatio*).
These tax-payers collectively, by their delegates, apportioned and
levied the tax required of them as a body, *absque ulla aerarii
nostri deminutione.*[2] This method of collecting produced the
same evils as did that in which the *curiales* were the agents :
upon the assessors it laid a ruinous responsibility, and upon the
tax-payers annoyances and hardships. Thus this tax became
the most hated of all that were paid.[3]

The care of the aqueducts had been one of the chief duties
of the Republican censors and of the early Emperors. Constantine made the land-owners, whose territory the aqueducts trav-
ersed, responsible for keeping them in repair and for the
distribution of the water. As compensation, he exempted these
persons from the extraordinary taxes (which increased their
burden upon others), and in case of neglect he punished by
confiscation.[4]

---

[1] Amm. Marcellinus, XIX. ii. : *Nomina titulorum . . . per suscipientes exaggerata . . .
adusque proscriptiones miserorumque suspendia pervenerunt ;* and Salvianus, *De Gubern. Dei,* v.
4. To put a stop to these malversations, the Emperor Anastasius instituted, near the close of
the fifth century, official collectors (Evagrius, *Hist. eccl.* iii. 42).

[2] *Codex Theod.* xiii. 1, 17. This law is of the year 399, but makes reference to an old
custom, . . . *cum soleat,* it is said.

[3] The Emperor Anastasius calls it, in 501, *vectigal miserabile prorsus, Deoque invisum, et
barbaris ipsis indignum* (Evagrius, *Hist. eccl.* iii. 39, 41).

[4] *Codex Theod.* xv. 2, 3, *anno* 330.

IV. — THE PLEBS, THE CORPORATIONS, AND THE COLLEGIATI.

WHEN we consider the privileged classes as such, we find that the Empire had two grades of nobility, — that of the state, namely, the high officers and titled persons; and that of the cities, consisting of the *curiales*, and also of land-owners and merchants not included in the curia, who in certain circumstances were admitted to deliberate with the decurions.[1] Collectively, these privileged persons made up the class of *honestiores*,[2] or what would have been called in France forty years ago *le pays légal*, outside of which were those who may be regarded as the ancestors of the mediæval serfs, — in the country, the *colonus* or agricultural laborer; in the cities, the artisan, the freedman, and the petty tradesman, *qui utensilia negotiatur*.[3] This plebs of the city and country formed a countless mass of human beings who were the pariahs of the Roman world. As early as the reign of Augustus, he who was called *honestior* could not be summoned into court by the *humilior*. From the time of the Antonines, the penal law and the civil law clearly separated the citizens into two classes. The *plebeius homo* is excluded from the curia; and in the matter of punishment, for a like crime the rich man is banished, the poor man dies under torture; the former cannot be beaten with rods, the latter may be beaten to death.[4] From this time, whoever had municipal honors, any official position in the city, or a certain fortune in the state, was no

---

[1] Inscriptions often say : . . . *ordo possessoresque* (Orelli, No. 3,734), or *uterque ordo* (*C. I. L.* vol. ii. No. 3,745). The appointment of the municipal physicians was intrusted *ordini et possessoribus* (Ulpian in the *Digest*, l. 12, 1). A law of the Emperor Leo (*Code*, xi. 31, 3) required, to render valid the alienation of communal property, the addition to the curia of the *honorati et possessores*, as in France it was formerly the custom to join with the municipal councillors the heaviest tax-payers in voting extraordinary taxes. The *possessores* could not quit their city without exposing themselves to twofold taxation, since they remained subject to the *munera* of their native city, while also bearing those of their adopted place of residence.

[2] See Appendix to this volume.

[3] *Ab aedilibus caeduntur* (*Dig.* l. 2, 12).

[4] *Dig.* l. 2, 7, sect. 8. The exception ceased in cases of treason: . . . *Cum de eo crimine quaeritur nulla dignitas a tormentis excipitur* (Paulus, *Sent.* v. 29).

longer of the people: "Let the judge," says Constantine, "especially consider the testimony of the *honestior*." [1]

But how distinguish one from the other?

In the class of *humiliores* were all persons who had been inscribed upon the city registers as branded with infamy on account of their employment; also, all the poor, that is to say, citizens whose property did not amount to fifty aurei, — equivalent to about $173, but doubtless a much larger sum then than now. In France, where it is so easy to rise above actual poverty, the average value of a working-man's household goods scarcely exceeds this sum, and those who do not possess even this, form a third of the whole male population. Hence we must conclude that the proportion of poor was much greater in the Roman Empire, since the great majority of the inhabitants were not, in spite of Caracalla's decree, citizens *pleno jure*. The *honestior*, on the contrary, had the privileges which were enjoyed by the *civis Romanus* under the Republic.

In this mass of outcasts were, however, the producers, — those who by their labor supplied all the needs of society. The condition in which we find this class, at the beginning of the fourth century, had been prepared by previous ages; but Constantine determined it.

The idea of levying a portion of the tax in kind was so Roman, and had so long been in practice both under the Republic and the Empire, that it had been extended to everything. The treasury had undertaken to feed and clothe, with the supplies furnished by the provinces, the court, the officers of government, the army, and even those persons occupied with public instruction. Accordingly, perhaps half of the tax was paid in kind, with all the disadvantages attached to this method, which brought about numerous abuses and an enormous waste of the public resources. But in the matter of clothing and weapons, and those gifts of the Emperors to their servants of which we have elsewhere given the long and curious list,[2] luxury made demands which the tax-payers could not meet. Accordingly, imperial manufactories had been established for stuffs, dyeing, goldsmith's work, and the like,

---

[1] . . . *Ut honestioribus potius fides testibus habeatur* (*Codex Theod.* xi. 39, 3).

[2] Vol. VII. p. 190, note 2.

making use of the raw material furnished by the provinces; for weapons only, there were not less than thirty-five of these workshops. Artisans whose labor had been judged necessary for the cities or the government, formed also obligatory corporations.[1] Rome had two hundred and fifty-four bakeries. At the age of twenty, the son was required to enter upon his father's trade, unless he relinquished his right to inherit.[2] The charcoal-burners, lime-burners, teamsters employed in the transport of wood for heating the baths, and many others, were enrolled. A law compelled freedmen possessing thirty pounds of silver to enter the corporation of the unloaders.[3] Once registered, the laborer was, like the curials, bound for life.[4]

In return, these *fabricenses* and artisans were exempted from *munera*, — an illusive exemption, which they held from their poverty much more surely than from the law, for it ceased for those whose property, by any chance, became sufficient to enable them to provide for these charges.[5] In 337 thirty-eight liberal or scientific professions obtained from Constantine a complete immunity. This time a real advantage was conceded, for in these careers there was prospect of acquiring a competency, and all persons possessing a competency at once fell under the municipal yoke. But the favor was granted only "to permit these *artifices* to

---

[1] *Codex*, x. 47, 7: *Vestiarios, linteones, purpurarios et particarios qui devotioni nostrae deserviunt* (law of Constantine, undated).

[2] *Codex Theod.* xiii. 5, 2, *anno* 315, and xiv. 3, 5, *anno* 364.

[3] *Ibid.* xiv. 11, 9, *anno* 368.

[4] Symmachus, urban prefect, writes to Valentinian II.: "You are aware that the support of this immense city depends on the corporations;" and he enumerates those who bring in sheep, swine, and cattle; who transport corn, oil, and the wood required to heat the public baths; "who make ready, with industrious hands, the objects destined for imperial use; or who suppress fires when they break out. It would be tedious to name all, — to specify the keepers of public houses, the bakers, and the numerous classes who, under various designations, labor for the country, *patriae servientes*" (*Epist.* x. 27). And he adds: *Liquet privilegium vetus magno impendio constare Romanis. Jugi obsequio immunitatis nomen emerunt* (*ibid.*). Immunity from municipal burdens was the main fact in the privileges granted to these corporations; but there were many other advantages added to it, — for example, exemption from extraordinary taxes, and from certain taxes in kind. These advantages varied for each corporation, and we know but a few of them. Thus the *navicularii* received one solidus for every 1000 modii transported, and they were allowed four per cent of waste (*Codex Theod.* xiii. 5, 7, *anno* 334); each cargo of 10,000 modii excused them from the land-tax for 50 *jugera*, and they were exempted from customs-dues on their merchandise (*ibid.* 14). The corporations which levied the tax in kind received as indemnity an *epimetron*, or additional measure, which was as much as $\frac{1}{48}$ of wheat and barley, and $\frac{1}{72}$ of wine and bacon.

[5] *Dig.* xxvii. 1, 17, sect. 2, and l. 6, 5, sect. 12.

become more skilful in their professions, and the better to train their children to the same."[1] The legislator of the fourth century seeks, therefore, to establish, even in the professions which have remained free, the principle of hereditary succession, which he strives to put in practice everywhere. "The mint-masters," writes Constantine in 317, "must remain always in their workshops."[2] The *fabricenses* of the imperial factories, the *navicularii* who transport corn, oil, and supplies due to the state,[3] the *metallarii*,[4] officials, members of corporations serviceable to the state or the cities, are placed in the same condition, which is really one of servitude (*serviunt*).[5] In the imperial factories the workmen are branded on the arm or hand with a mark by which they may be recognized in case they escape,[6] and they are collectively responsible for one another; the reparation for one man's error or accident falls upon the whole corporation, as in an *officium* if the chief has been punished by a fine, the employees collectively pay another equal in amount, or even larger.

No mention has been made of the engineers, who at a very early date were attached to the legions, whom we find still thus

---

[1] . . . *Et ipsi peritiores fieri et filios suos erudire* (*Codex*, x. 64, 1).

[2] *Codex Theod.* X. 20, 1. Cf. *ibid.* xiv. 7, 1, and xii. 19, 2. There were ten imperial mints.

[3] *Dig.* iv. 6, sect. 5. Whoever had a vessel in the Tiber was obliged to put it, in case of need, at the service of the state (*Codex Theod.* xiv. 21, *anno* 364). To recruit the corporations of *navicularii*, crews were impressed, and sometimes owners (*ibid.* xiii. 5, 1, *anno* 369).

[4] *Sint perpetuo navicularii* (*Codex Theod.* xiii. 5, 14, and 19, *annis* 371 *et* 390); *Metallarii qui migrarunt*. . . . *ad propriae originis stirpem laremque revocentur* (*ibid.* x. 19, 15, *anno* 424). In his law *De Sicariis* (*Codex Theod.* xiv. 4, 1, *anno* 334, and in the law of 317 in the *Code*, xi. 7, 1) Constantine shows extreme severity towards those who sought to escape from their corporation. No honor can withdraw them from it; it even involves their lives (*salutis etiam periculum subituro*), if they attempt to escape.

[5] *Codex Theod.* xii. 19, 2, *anno* 400, and *Codex Just.* 7, 7, *anno* 380. Besides the advantages given them by the state in the form of indemnities or exemptions from taxes, some of these corporations were strongly guarded from competition. Thus all merchandise arriving at Ostia was to be unloaded by the government (*saccarii*). If the importer wished to have his goods landed by his own men, he was obliged to pay the treasury twenty per cent *ad valorem* (*ibid.* xiv. 22, 1, *anno* 364). These *saccarii Ostienses* remind us of the powerful corporation of porters at Marseilles. See in Vol. VL p. 107, note 2, the organization of the company of the mines of Aljustrel.

[6] *Ibid.* x. 9, 5; 22, 4; xi. 9, 3; and *Codex Just.* xi. 7, 2, and xi. 42, 10. In certain cases the death-penalty was attached to this offence. *Singulis manibus eorum felici nomine pietatis nostrae impresso signari decernimus* ... *ut militiae quodam modo sociati* (Rescript of Zeno). Those who concealed such fugitives were condemned to the same workshop (*Codex Just.* xi. 9, 3, *anno* 398). Shall we conjecture that the tattooing which the modern workman often has made upon his arm is a reminiscence of this custom?

attached in the reign of Hadrian, and whose number doubtless increased with the number and variety of machines which engineering science had multiplied; but there is no doubt that they shared in the soldiers' lot, and were from father to son attached like the soldiers to the army.

The corporations devoted to the public service included only a part of the artisans of the whole Empire. Those who had never belonged to them practised their trades freely, and, according to the Roman custom, united themselves in the different cities into guilds, whose formation the Emperors encouraged, and in some cases required.[1] Some of these *collegia* were rich and important, as had been, and doubtless still were, the boatmen of the Seine and of the Rhone, and many other corporations of trades or mercantile pursuits, — the last remnants of an expiring prosperity. But lesser ones, formed by small tradesmen and artisans, vegetated miserably in city hovels. Of the degree of esteem granted to these we may judge when we find, in a tariff of fines, that a mere decurion, or a man belonging by birth to the curia (*obnoxius curiae*), is worth five *collegiati*.[2] Upon them rested the *sordida munera*.[3] It is an old law, says the Emperor Majorian, that the *collegiati* be required to perform in turn, under the direction of the curials, all the servile work of the city (*ministeria urbium*);[4] and this became the legal penalty of being incorporated into a college (*collegiis applicetur*). Accordingly, the incorporated artisan sought to escape from his prison, as did the curial from his. On the subject of persons *qui conditionem propriam reliquierunt*, the *Theodosian Code* says: "The cities, deprived of the labor needful to them, have lost much of their prosperity, since many of the *collegiati*, abandoning their work, have escaped into the country, and live in remote and secret places; let them be seized wherever they can be found, and brought back to their former work."[5]

[1] *Codex Just.* xiv. 8, 1, *anno* 315.

[2] *Ibid.* xii. 1, 146, *anno* 395.

[3] The law of the *Justinian Code* (xi. 16, 15, *anno* 382) enumerates these base tasks.

[4] *Nov. Majorian.* vii. sect. 3: . . . *Quae praecedentium legum praecepit auctoritas.* Cf. sect. 4.

[5] *Codex Theod.* xii. 19, 1, *anno* 400; *ibid.* xiv. 7, 1, *anno* 397.

V. THE COLONI AND THE SLAVES.

FROM the city plebs we pass to the rural plebs, that which is subject to the *capitatio terrena*, which in the Middle Ages became so merciless a taxation. The *coloni* of the treasury had originally been excused from municipal burdens that they also might not be in any way distracted from the culture of the imperial domain.[1] They had the family relations; they might possess property to be inherited by their sons, and they were admitted to bring suit in the courts; but their condition became worse as the class grew more numerous, and Cato's frightful language as to the slave (*instrumentum vocale*) was used in respect to them. In the time of Ulpian they were reckoned with the ox, the plough, and agricultural implements, — attached to the soil, the *instrumentum fundi*.[2] The *colonus* was sold with the land which he cultivated. " If he makes his escape," says Constantine, " let him be pursued like the fugitive slave; "[3] and such was, notwithstanding his title of free man, the degradation of his position that the healthy mendicant, by way of punishment, was condemned to be a *colonus*.[4]

The greater part of economic labor, as performed by the artisan and the *colonus*, became, therefore, very nearly servile.[5] The feudal system used no harsher language towards the artisan than that employed by the sons of Constantine in a rescript: " Let them not dare to aspire to any honor, even if they might deserve

---

[1] *Coloni quoque Caesaris a muneribus liberantur ut idoneiores praediis fiscalibus habeantur* (*Dig.* l. 6, 5, sect. 11). On the formation of this class, see Vol. VI. pp. 14–18.

[2] *Dig.* xxxiii. 7, 8. *In instrumenta fundi . . . veluti . . . villici, boves domiti, pecora, stercorandi causa parata, vasaque utilia culturae, quae sunt aratra, falces,* etc.

[3] *Codex Theod.* v. 91, *anno* 332. Constantine forbade the dividing of families of *coloni* when the land was sold to different owners (*Codex Just.* lii. 38, ii. *anno* 334). This was the application to the agricultural laborer of the favor which had been granted to the slave (see Vol. VI. p. 4), or rather it was the renewal of a provision of the laws by which the *coloni* had probably been long benefited. The *coloni* could possess as their own a *peculium* gained from the products of their farms, and, consequently, land bought with their own money.

[4] *Codex Just.* xi. 25, *anno* 382.

[5] We have just seen (p. 34) that the professions which we call liberal, those of the physician, architect, teacher, painter, sculptor, etc., remained free (*Codex Theod.* xiii. 4, 1–4, and *Codex Just.* x. 64, 1).

it, the men who are covered with the filth of labor (*omni officiorum faece*), and let them remain forever in their own condition "[1]
Thus was prepared what alarmed witnesses of contemporary agitations have called, while wishing it existed still, "the solid gear-
ing of social conditions in the Middle Ages."

The great evil of the ancient civilization had been slavery.
The Church mitigated it in a 'fatherly spirit, for the reason that

THE CULTURE OF THE VINE.[2]

mercy is the whole sum of the Gospel; but inasmuch as the Church
does not propose to change either political organizations or social
conditions, the evil itself was permitted to remain. Saint Paul
assures the believers that they are all one in Christ Jesus;[3] but he
makes them no promise of earthly equality. Accordingly, the bishops themselves held slaves, even for their personal service. Those
belonging to Georgios, archbishop of Alexandria, copied so many
manuscripts for him that they made for him the valuable library

[1] *Codex Just.* xii. 1, 6: . . . *Si quis meruerit repellatur.* Theodosius, speaking of a
slave, calls him *servili faece descendens* (*Codex Theod.* xvi. 5, 21). The same expression had been used by Cicero. The *humiliores* were always objects of contempt to the
Roman aristocracy.

[2] Fresco dating from about the year 300. Painting from a *cubiculum* in the cata-
comb of Praetextatus (Parker, *Catal.* No. 1882).

[3] *Galatians* iii. 28.

of which Julian speaks with envy.[1] In his will Saint Gregory be-
queaths "to the Russian virgin" two maid-servants, who, after
her, shall belong to the church of Nazianzen. When, in the fifth
century, the body of clergy became the greatest land-owners in
the Empire, they had, as such, multitudes of slaves, whom they
treated mildly; but while they favored enfranchisements by pri-

A SHEPHERD AND A WOMAN DRIVING BULLOCKS.[2]

vate individuals, they did not enfranchise extensively themselves,
for they needed all these laborers to cultivate their vast domains.[3]

Softened in character, but still preserved by the Church, slavery was maintained by Constantine, who in certain cases increased
the rigor of the penal laws applicable to slaves as such;[4] and this

[1] Letter 9.
[2] From the Vergil of the Vatican.
[3] See on this point the learned essay by M. Fournier: Les Affranchissements du cinquième
au huitième siècle, in the Revue historique, January, 1883.
[4] See on this subject, Vol. VII. p. 550, note 2.

severity of the first Christian Emperor was not likely to inspire
more pity in the hearts of those masters who had not learned
compassion from the teaching of the gospel.[1]

A society in which existed so many forms of servitude, and
in which so many men were striving to escape from the condition
into which they had been born, was, indeed, sick unto death.
The ancient slavery had produced terrible distress; but at least
above it there was a class of free and proud men, capable of
great things, and doing such. Above the forms of servitude which
we have here depicted, what was there? Nothing. Liberty is
sometimes a stormy life; but under despotism is formed only the
stagnant marsh whence escape deadly miasmata.

VI. — THE ARMY.

BUT did Constantine at least save the oldest and best of his
country's institutions, that to which Diocletian had lately restored
its discipline and strength, — the military organization? In the
Early Empire the legion, with its cavalry, auxiliaries, and engines
of war, was an actual army-corps, complete in itself; and all these
corps, the praetorians alone excepted, were alike. In the time
of Septimius Severus there were thirty-three of these ranged along
the frontier; at the end of the fourth century there were one
hundred and seventy-five legions,[2] posted for the most part in the
interior. During eighteen years of civil war the Emperors had
gathered around themselves, for protection against rivals, the best
troops of the Empire, and had dismantled the lines of defence
without caring for the Barbarians, who, moreover, were kept
almost motionless outside the Roman intrenchments by the memory of the heavy blows with which they had been chastised during
the period of the tetrarchy. Of that which had been a need of
the moment, Constantine made a principle of government. He
did, it is true, intrust the protection of the frontier to corps per-

---

[1] Cf. Wallon, *Hist. de l'esclavage*, iii. 394.

[2] Marquardt, *Handb.* ii. 588, from the *Notitia dignitatum.* — *Legionum nomen in exercitu
permanet hodie, sed . . . robur infractum est* (Vegetius, ii. 3).

manently stationed there; but he divided up the legionary army among the provincial cities where it seemed to him most thoroughly to protect his personal safety. This was the overthrow of that system whose value had been proved under Augustus, Hadrian, and Diocletian; it was also the destruction of whatever remained of the military spirit. "The small garrisons destroy discipline," were the words of Trajan; and we repeat them after him. Read what an officer of Constantine thinks of these dissolute soldiers whose cup is heavier than their sword, who are insolent and rapacious towards their fellow-citizens, and cowardly towards the enemy because they have become so effeminate.[1]

ROMAN HORSEMAN (FROM TRAJAN'S COLUMN).

We have seen that the rule of the division of powers put in practice in the civil administration had been applied to the army, and that Constantine had four or five different classes of soldiers. The *domestici* and *scolares* were two splendid corps who guarded the imperial residences. When these soldiers appeared, on occasions of ceremony, standing in rank under the porticos or in the courtyards of the palace, their height, their gilded shields, their glittering armor, excited admiration.[2] All modern courts have also had these privileged corps, which seem to enhance the majesty of the throne and secure the safety of the sovereign. In reality, the *protectores*

---

[1] *Ferox erat in suos miles et rapax, ignavus vero in hostes et fractus* (Amm. Marcellinus, xxii. 4; Zosimus, ii. 34).

[2] Corippus (*De Laudib. Justini minoris*, iii. *versus* 157 *et seq.*) describes one of these ceremonies.

were only show-troops, as useless to the state as had been the
praetorians, their predecessors, but less formidable than they,
because less numerous.

The *comitatenses* were of more value; but the principle being
once admitted of dispersing the army through the cities of the
interior, it was necessary to multiply the corps, in order to
establish many small garrisons, reducing in each corps the number
of soldiers, so that the treasury and the people should not be
exhausted. Under Diocletian the legion still consisted of six
thousand men, — this at least is the number of the Jovians and
the Herculians according to Vegetius. Shortly after Constantine,
it was impossible to put in the field a force of that number
without calling out five legions; twelve were united for some
trivial expedition into the Caucasus, and seven shut themselves up
in the small fortified town of Amida, attacked by the Persians,
and were not able to defend it.[1] Five hundred years earlier, the
legions had sufficed to vanquish Antiochus and subjugate Asia
Minor; but at that time the legion was that strong and supple
body which has been an object of admiration to the great soldiers
of every age.

Nowhere, then, could there be found in the Empire of Constantine great masses of soldiers capable of encouraging ambitious
designs; and this dispersion facilitated the action of the *magistri
militum*, and even the indirect surveillance of the civil magistrates
and of the *curiosi*, who were able very quickly to discover and
denounce any project of sedition. To this we must add that, the
infantry and the cavalry having each its own special chief, an
army capable of efficient action could not be formed without the
Emperor's will or without an agreement between these two chief
officers; furthermore, that between these two there always existed
jealousy rather than any dangerous cordiality; and finally, that

---

[1] Amm. Marcellinus, xviii. 9; xix. 2; xxvii. 12 and 16; Zosimus, v. 45. Honorius, shut
up in Ravenna, was joined there by five legions, forming a total of four thousand men, and
seven corps, collected by Stilicho for a very important expedition, gave him only five thousand
soldiers in all. Upon which Tillemont remarks that the legions had at that time sometimes
twelve hundred men, sometimes even fewer, — seven hundred. (Cf. *Mém. de l'Acad. des inscr.*
xxv. 481, and Kuhn, *Verfass. des röm. Reichs*, i. sect. 140.) Procopius (*Hist. secr.* 24) gives
the most melancholy picture of the army. We have already seen that the nobles refused
service, and the notables of the cities were no less reluctant to enter the army. Aur.
Victor (*Caes.* 41) says of Constantine that he changed the military organization completely.

the commissariat, entirely separated from the command, was intrusted to a civil magistrate, the praetorian prefect, who was also the paymaster of the troops,[1] — and we shall see that, while the generals indeed had soldiers, they had not the means either to pay or feed them. The campaigns of Julian in Gaul show the dangers of these jealous precautions, as well as their inefficiency. In this system all possible provision had been made for the security of the Emperor, and very little for that of the state; an ancient writer attributes the ruin of the Empire to the military regulations of Constantine.[2] Zosimus might have added that palace-conspiracies were now to take the place of military seditions, while even the latter were not wholly to cease.

Unlike the legionaries, the *ripenses* were permanently established in the districts where they served. With them and among them were old soldiers who, having attained the veteran standing, received a little piece of land on the frontier; this was to be an hereditary possession, accompanied by the obligation for the son to take his father's place in the ranks, or else the land would revert to the state.[3] The same condition of military service was made to the Barbarians receiving Laetic[4] lands from the Empire, —

[1] Zosimus, ii. 33.

[2] Zosimus, ii. 34. Lydus (*De Magistr.* iii. 31, 40) deplores the unguarded condition of the Danubian frontier after the dispersal of the troops through Asia.

[3] Alexander Severus, Aurelian, and Probus had given the soldiers fields and farms, with the slaves and domestic animals necessary for agriculture, — a possession which became hereditary on condition that the sons, at the age of eighteen, should enter the service. Constantine made in 320 a general regulation of this matter. He decided that there should be granted to veterans new land, free from tax in perpetuity (*vacantes terras, perpetuo immunes*), 25,000 *folles* to buy what was needful for agriculture, one yoke of oxen, and a hundred bushels (*modii*) of grain and seeds (*fruges promiscuae*); the tax on sales (*lustralis collatio*) not to be levied upon them for products of which the price was less than 100 *folles* (*Codex Theod.* viii. 2, 3). A law of 366 gave them absolute immunity in buying and selling (*ibid.* 9). Under Constantine, and probably before his time, the soldier who had the right of citizenship enjoyed exemption from taxes for himself, his father and mother, and his wife (. . . *suum caput, patris et matris et uxoris . . . excusent . . . ita tamen ut . . . vere proprias facultates excusent*). He had this exemption for himself only if he served as an auxiliary. (See *Codex Theod.* tit. vii. 20, 4, and Godefroy, commentary on this title.) Accordingly, the sons of veterans who sought to escape from their father's profession were carefully sought for, that they might be compelled to return to the service, or that they might be subjected to municipal burdens (*muneribus atque obsequiis municipalibus.* — *Codex Theod.* vii. 22, 1 and 2, *annis* 319 *et* 326; and xii. 1, 15, *anno* 327; 18, *anno* 329).

[4] See Vol. VII. 571, note 1. These lands were not always of the best. Certain soldiers — in revolt, it is true — complained, as early as the time of Tiberius, that to the veterans were given only swamps and rocky lands (*per nomen agrorum, uligines paludum vel inculta montium.* — *Bull. épigr. de la gaule,* 1883, p. 1).

an official colonization which probably succeeded no better than that attempted by France in Algeria. A great modern state, Austria, having established a similar organization, abandoned it. It is not thus that this matter was handled under the Republic and in the first years of the Empire. Then, after a victory, it was usual to give to Roman colonists the half of a city and of its territory; and these colonies, rapidly becoming prosperous, latinized all the West, and the northern part of Africa.

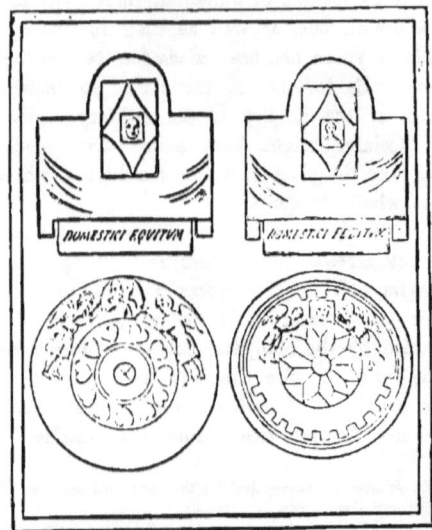

DOMESTICI EQVITVM

DOMESTICI PEDITVM

INSIGNIA OF THE COUNT OF THE DOMESTICS.[1]

While these *ripenses* were no very considerable force, the Barbarians received into the legions of the interior, into the corps posted on the frontiers, and even into the Palatine guard, were a danger. Still more imprudent was it to take whole tribes into the pay of the Empire. Constantine thus received forty thousand Goths, who served as a national corps (*foederati*). He believed it to be for the interest of Rome to show Salians and Alemanni and Bructeri in public office, and their rude fellow-countrymen under the standards, as if the Barbaric world had no other desire than to live within the great civilized Empire, or, as the Emperors expressed it, "In the bosom of Roman felicity." "Let the Barbarians supply soldiers," the courtiers said, "and then we can have gold from the provinces, instead of recruits."[2]   The tax was a lucrative one, for exemption from military duty cost

---

[1] *Notitia dignitatum*, Seek, p. 39.   [2] Amm. Marcellinus, xix. 11.

twenty-five, thirty, or thirty-six gold solidi.[1] But this gold,
levied upon Roman cowardice, went to the Barbarians; and
we shall see these dangerous auxiliaries warning their fellow-
countrymen, left behind in German forests, of the designs of the
Romans against them, and deserters from their ranks guiding
bands of German or Persian plunderers to the pillage of the
provinces.[2] In distributing the Goths through his cohorts,
Claudius II. had said: "It is a reinforcement that should be
felt, and not seen;" and Probus did the same, receiving into
his army but one foreigner to every ten Romans. But this prudent limit was no longer observed. From day to day the number
of Barbarians of every race increased in the Roman army; they
filled the auxiliary cohorts, especially the cavalry, and in the
streets of Constantinople their chiefs might be seen preceded by
the lictors and invested with the consular toga.[3] Gratian went
even farther than this: he took pleasure in wearing the costume of those whom the Emperors of an earlier day had represented on their triumphal columns as captives or suppliants; and

---

[1] *Codex Theod.* vii. 13, laws 7, 13, *annis* 375 *et* 397. Socrates (*Hist. eccl.* iv. 34) says
that Valens raised the sum payable for exemption to eighty solidi.

[2] A deserter from the Roman army guided the expedition of Sapor in Mesopotamia (359),
after having revealed to him the condition of the troops and fortresses in that province; it is
said that the representations made by another induced the Alemanni to undertake the great
invasion of 357. In 354, secret information transmitted to the Alemanni prevented Constantius from surprising them on crossing the Rhine; three Alemanni, who had the title of count
and held important offices at court, were suspected of this treason (Amm. Marcellinus, xiv.
10). In the reign of Valentinian I. a secret correspondence was discovered between certain
Alemanni serving in the Roman army and the king of this nation, whom the Emperor
considered his most formidable enemy (*ibid.* xxix. 4, *ad fin.*). We know how Gratian
was prevented from bringing aid to Valens after the disastrous battle of Hadrianople. In
respect to the great number of Barbarians serving in the Roman army, see the *Notitia dignitatum* and Richter, *Das Weströmische Reich*, pp. 219 *et seq.* Like all German authors, Richter
naturally finds this invasion very advantageous "for the rejuvenating of the world" (*für die
Verjüngung der Welt*). This is the old and false theory that the young, rich blood of the Barbarians renewed the impoverished blood of Gaul, — whence the Germans disappeared so quickly
that they left but a very small number of words in the French language.

[3] Amm. Marcellinus, xx. 10: *Barbaros omnium primus ad usque fasces auxerat ut trabes
consulares.* However, no Barbarian names appear in the consular *Fasti;* but almost all the officers mentioned by Amm. Marcellinus in the reign of Constantius have these names, and we
have also seen that the Barbarians assumed Roman designations; for example, two kings of the
Alemanni were called Ursicinus and Serapion (*ibid.* xvi. 12). Eusebius (*Life of Constantine,*
iv. 7) says that Constantine took pleasure in having them about him, that he loaded them with
gifts and raised them to public honor. These Barbarians, except in the case of individual
grants, had not the *jus connubii* with the citizens (*Codex Theod.* iii. 14, *anno* 370); but they
soon became so numerous in the Empire that Honorius was obliged to remove this disability
(Prudentius, *Contra Symmachum*, ii. 612).

two Germans, Magnentius and Sylvanus, after his
the purple in Gaul. If we except the count Theo
few other Roman generals, the great soldiers of th
the fourth century are Merobaud, consul in 377
count of the domestics, Bauto, Frigerid, Arbogast
Stilicho, Alaric, — whose names indicate their origi
mention those who, like the Sarmatian Victor, the
nentius and the Frank Sylvanus, concealed their Bar
under Roman names. Their presence in the great offi
strates the loss of the military qualities in the mass of t
Latin populations, as in the second century the adve
provincial Emperors had marked the decline of the Itali

Thus Constantine divides the army, but at the same
lowers its tone. He seeks to shelter himself from tl
whereby thrones are overturned, and in so doing he enfe
state; but he does not prevent revolutions. What, compa
the legionaries of the Republic and of the Early Empire, a
soldiers recruited among the Barbarians or from the lowes;
of Roman society, whom Constantine brands upon the arm
many criminal slaves,[1] and whose profits and honors incr
their military value diminishes? To the *ripenses* was allotte
two thirds the pay of the *palatini;* twenty-four years of
was required from them, instead of twenty;[2] and into these
were received those recruits whom insufficient size or st
excluded from the *comitatenses.*[3] To this refuse of the arm;
intrusted the guard of the frontiers.

A contemporary of Justinian writes that the army of
Emperor, which should number 645,000 men, consisted of
150,000,[4] — which does not mean that these were all that we
pay. A fraudulent absence from the standards was extremely
mon among the troops of the Later Empire; and this military cr

---

[1] *Puncturis in cute punctis* (Vegetius, i. 8; ii. 5). This had not yet become the cust
the reign of Diocletian. See, Vol. VII. p. 412, the story of Saint Maximilian, where or
entrance of the recruit into the service the putting a leathern string bearing his number a
the neck is all that is done. A jurisconsult, contemporary of Constantine, speaks of the
on soldiers as like the tax on cattle (*Dig.* l. 4, 18, sect. 3). See Vol. VII. pp. 188 *et seq.*

[2] *Codex Theod.* viii. 1, 10, and vii. 20, 4. The same difference had formerly exi
between the praetorian cohorts and the legions.

[3] *Codex Theod.* vii. 22, 8, *anno* 372.

[4] Agathias, v. 13, p. 305 (ed. of Bonn).

whose frequency is revealed by a law of the year 406, evidently began much earlier, for Libanius, a contemporary of Constantine, mentions it with indignation.[1]   The army had for many years fallen very low in public estimation: the Emperors, from jealousy, had banished the higher classes from it ; a long-continued prosperity had turned away the lower classes. The Roman army, formerly so renowned, was now so despised that a master of the cavalry did not appear worthy of any consideration from a provincial governor; that not one duke obtained under Constantius the title of *clarissimus*, of which the Emperors were so lavish ;[3] and that the *officium* of the soldiers employed in every district

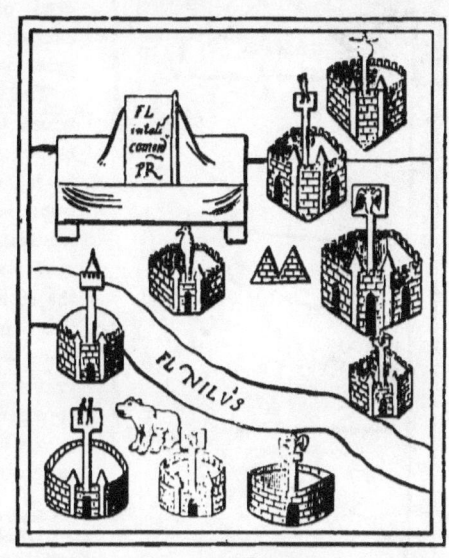

INSIGNIA OF THE COUNT OF THE EGYPTIAN FRONTIER.[2]

to pursue robbers (*stationarii*) was counted among the *sordida munera*. This contempt had produced its usual effects; feeling that he was despised, the soldier avenged himself by deserving to be so.[4] "We pay our troops," says Synesius later, "and we are obliged to defend them."[5] The army of Aurelian, of Probus, and of Diocletian was still a formidable one ; but from the time of Constantine, this mighty instrument of the prosperity of Rome was

---

[1] In his treatise Περὶ τῶν προστασιῶν. See Godefroy's commentary on the law of 406 (*Codex Theod.* vii. 4, 28 and 29) and upon the *stillatura*, a portion of the military pay left at the disposal of the government by the difference between the number of soldiers on the lists and the number present under the standards. Later we shall see with what small armies Julian defended Gaul and undertook to conquer the whole Empire.

[2] *Notitia dignitatum*, Seek's edition, p. 58, and Böcking's, p. 67.

[3] Amm. Marcellinus, xxi. 16.

[4] *Ibid.* xxi. 16.   [5] *Letter* 72.

but a worthless sword, ready to break at the first encounter.

CARPENTER'S TOOLS.[2]

When once the Barbarians should come, there would be need of no long-continued efforts to bring about the great destruction.[1]

The rigorous classification which the Roman world had undergone was not offensive to it; the Roman had always been gratified by having his place definitely fixed, even were it at the foot of the social scale. The artisan was never ashamed of his trade, — he had his tools engraved upon his tomb; the corporations had their banners, which they carried on occasion of public festivities;[3]

[1] See the sad picture drawn by Vegetius a half-century later. "The old discipline is lost. Our cavalry have borrowed the weapons of the Goths, the Alani, and the Huns, and our infantry are almost disarmed (*pedites nudatos*). They obtained from Gratian permission to give up *cataphractas et cassides*. *Sic detectis pectoribus et capitibus . . . multitudine sagittariorum saepe deleti sunt . . . ita fit ut non de pugna, sed de fuga cogitant qui in acie nudi exponuntur ad vulnera* (*De Re milit.* l. 20). In the next paragraph he adds: "We no longer even know how to fortify a camp, hujus rei scientia prorsus interciidit." As early as the reign of Gordian III. it had been necessary for Timesitheus to compel the army to resume the old Roman custom of fortifying a camp every night.

[2] Bas-relief from the tomb of P. Boitenos or Bertenos-Hermes, bedstead-maker (*cleinopegos*). On this bas-relief, of Parian marble, are represented compasses, a square, a plane, and a fourth implement, resembling that now used by carpenters in tracing irregular curves. A triangle surmounts the whole. (Museum of the Louvre.) See our Vol. VI. pp. 94 *et seq.*

[3] See Vol. VII. p. 168. The *Notitia* enumerates an immense number of legions, cohorts, squadrons of cavalry, in garrison, in the cities and provinces. It has been inferred that the Empire had a vast army, with millions of men in actual service. Upon paper the enumeration is very formidable, but history reduces these forces to very small proportions. With twenty-five thousand soldiers only, Constantine crossed the Alps to overthrow Maxentius; with even fewer, twenty thousand, he made his first campaign against Licinius. The Count Theodosius had but thirty-five hundred to re-take Africa from Firmus, which, in the time of Stilicho, five thousand re-conquer from Gildo. Julian has thirteen thousand when he drives back the great

provinces and cities had their emblems,[1] the soldier his decorations, the functionary his insignia, varying with the office, and

THE SPHINX, ONE OF THE EMBLEMS OF EGYPT.[2]

bestowed with it; the judge did not appear at the tribunal without his. A purple belt with gold buckle distinguished the official

Alemannic invasion; twenty thousand when he prepares to dispute the Empire with Constantius; in the expedition into Persia, for which he was a year in preparing, and withdrew nearly all the troops from the other frontiers, he took with him into Babylonia, to strike his great blow at the hereditary enemy, but sixty thousand men, of whom twenty thousand were employed upon his thousand vessels; and he says that when the war between Sapor and Constantine broke out, the Empire of the East was destitute of all military resources. Lastly, in almost all the wars of the fourth century we nowhere see, with the exception of the battle of Mursa, any great forces hurled against the foreign enemy or against the rebels.

[1] On many coins we see characteristic emblems of Africa, Egypt, the Cyrenaica, and other provinces. On other coins there are *vetera civitatis insignia*. Cf. Or.-Henzen, No. 6,850, inscription of the time of Constantine. For military decorations, see *ibid*. No. 6,850, and in the *Index*, p. 144. The *ornamenta consularia, praetoria*, are well known.

[2] This valuable cameo, in Oriental sardonyx, called the *Tazza Farnese*, is eight centimetres in diameter. The personages represented are believed to be as follows: seated on the sphinx,

in active service, ἔμπρακτος, from the mere titulary.[1] The person adorning himself with insignia to which he had no right was punished, according to his station, with death or banishment; and this legislation was ancient, for it is mentioned by Ulpian, Paulus, and Modestinus.[2] The more evidently the Empire tottered

to its downfall, the closer did the Emperors draw the bonds which they thought might retard the catastrophe; but these were only the wrappings drawn tightly around a mummy. Valentinian, Gratian, and Theodosius each promulgated many laws "for the maintenance of orders of rank."[4]

GOLD COIN.[3]

This classification of persons retarded the action of society. The relations which men naturally have with each other, in which a free activity is displayed and intellect developed, being replaced by artificial and constrained relations, each lived confined in his corner, so that the mental horizon was low and narrow. This *régime* had now been long in existence, and consequently pagan society had long been powerless to produce men of distinguished ability; and although now the other, namely Christian society, which was just beginning to make itself conspicuous, was capable of forming such, the state still gained no advantage, for these men who aimed at Heaven, were indifferent to the affairs of earth.

Isis, holding an ear of corn; near the fig-tree, the Nile, with cornucopia; at the right two nymphs, protectresses of Egypt; in the centre, a prince, with the attributes of Horus-Apollo; above, the Winds, whose breath, slackening the current of the river, favor the inundation, while Horus-Apollo, with his hydraulic pump, prevents it from being too much dispersed. The crocodile, hippopotamus, and Ibis were also symbols of Egypt. (See Vol. VII. p. 91, a coin of Caracalla.) We have some reason to believe that this cameo, which was found in the ruins of Hadrian's Villa, may be of the Antonine period. The two figures of the upper part recall by their pose the apotheosis of Faustina (Vol. V. p. 488). This cameo and the horseman of the Column of Trajan show, being compared with the designs given of the third and fourth centuries, how great and sudden was the decline in art. (From the Museum of Naples.)

[1] Lydus, *De magistr.* ii. 13.
[2] *Dig.* iii. 1, 1, sect. 5; xlviii. 10, 27, sect. 2; Paul., *Sent.* v. 25, sect. 11.
[3] Egypt holding a sistrum (reverse of a gold coin of Hadrian).
[4] . . . *Ut dignitatum ordo servetur.* Cf. Godefroy, *Paratitlon to Codex Theod.* vi. 5, 1; vol. ii. p. 69.

VII. — Summary.

THE reign of Constantine, lasting thirty-two years, was the longest the Empire had known since Augustus. Time, therefore, was liberally granted to this Emperor. How he employed it, we have seen; and we may now inquire what place it is fitting to assign him in the series of Emperors of Rome. A great place, assuredly. At the same time there was much "miry clay" mingled with the iron of his statue. His military fame is derived only from victories gained in the civil wars; his penal laws are atrocious;[1] and while he had upon his lips Christian words, he had never Christian sentiments in his heart.[2] His reign is full of murders, his palace reddened with blood; he put to death his wife, his son, his father-in-law, and many of his near kindred, including young children.

The organization of his army was bad, the policy of his later years imprudent, his financial system worthless, — although this, it is true, he inherited from his predecessors.

On the pages of the *Notitia dignitatum*, where the insignia of the praetorian prefects are represented, we see women personifying the provinces, and holding in their hands vases filled with coins. It is a faithful representation of this Empire, in which the art of governing was reduced to the art of making gold.[3] And this gold,

---

[1] He abolished punishment by crucifixion, ameliorated prison discipline, and made a law favorable to poor children; but he increased the number of offences punishable by death at the stake, condemning to it the Jew who should throw stones at a Christian Jew, the dishonest tax-gatherer, the scribe wrongfully inserting a name in the list of exempts, the aruspex who entered a private house, the slave who married a free woman, the accomplices in an abduction, the counterfeiter, those who had secret understanding with Barbarians, the creditor who seized for debt the oxen and agricultural implements of the debtor, and others. He decreed that melted lead should be poured into the mouth of the servant-woman who had aided in the abduction of a young girl; and workmen called *baphii* and *gynaecii*, who spoil the material on which they work, may be put to death . . . *gladio feriantur* (*Codex Just.* xi. 7, 2), etc. Lastly, for the poor of this world he was far from having Christian consideration, preserving the distinction in penalties between the *honestiores* and *humiliores* (*Codex Theod.* xvi. 2, 5, *anno* 323). His sons resembled him in severity; one of their laws decrees the death-penalty against a paternal uncle marrying his niece (*Codex Theod.* iii. 12, 1).

[2] Niebuhr (*History of Rome*, ii. 360, Schmitz's edition) says of Constantine: "He was certainly not a Christian." This is going too far; but we are justified in saying that Christianity made no change in him.

[3] Justinian (*Nov.* viii. chap. viii.) reminds the governors that their first duty is to collect

instead of being employed in works of public utility, maintained a sumptuous court, whose unbridled luxury recalls that of the reigns of Domitian and Nero.

In the religious order, Constantine considered the bishops as a

new kind of function-aries. The Byzantine Empire inherited this idea, and Oriental Christianity, with its Church enslaved to the civil power, was destined to remain al-most a stranger to the general work of civilization. Accord-ingly, we sympathize with Athanasius, who still demands only re-ligious liberty, against Constantine, who re-fuses it, after having for a time been par-tially aware of its ne-cessity.

MACEDONIA AND DACIA PERSONIFIED, BEARING VASES
FILLED WITH COINS.[1]

In the civil order, while the Emperor continued the work of the Roman jurisconsults in introducing more justice in the family relations,[2] and while, under the influence of the Church, he carried forward the chari-table measures of the Antonines in respect to poor children, he so completely established the odious principle of privileges and hereditary succession in the public service that he passed for its author in the eyes of succeeding generations.[3]

the taxes; he repeats this (*Nov.* xvii. chap. i.): . . . *Festinare primum fiscalia tributa exegi vigilanter.*

[1] *Notitia dignitatum.* O. Seek, p. 9, and Böcking, p. 13.

[2] According to the law of the Twelve Tables, the father was all, and the relatives on the father's side alone inherited. This rigor was early softened; and Constantine granted to the son, even in his father's lifetime, the ownership of the maternal property, and to the mother a third of the property of her deceased children.

[3] A law of 428, referring to the fact that the titles of the father were transmissible

It has been shown that the monarchy of the fourth century existed in germ in the imperial institution of Augustus.[1] To arrest its development or to put the Empire upon another road, it would have been necessary to give Roman society a mighty shock, and this Constantine did not do. It is unreasonable to expect a sovereign to be a great man ; the son of Constantius Chlorus was only a sagacious man. He had wit enough to die upon the throne, — a very unusual end for a Roman Emperor in those days : this was enough for him, but it was not enough for the state. He did not see that in chaining the laborer to his plough, the artisan to his work-bench, the soldier to the standards, and in obliging the son to follow his father's career in public office or in the curia, he struck with paralysis those forces which are destroyed when deprived of their natural action.

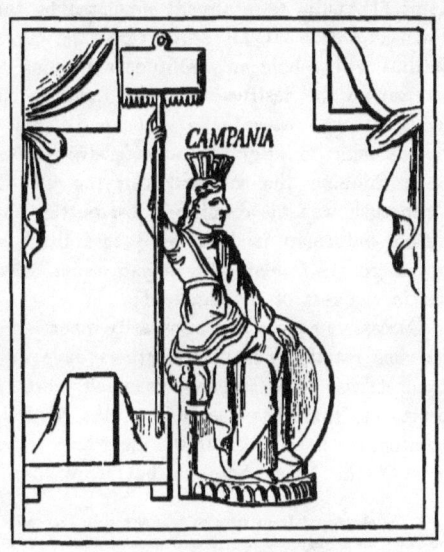

CONSULAR CAMPANIA PERSONIFIED.[3]

To bad administrative measures disastrous economic practices were added. The fourth century saw the greatest effort that was ever made to realize the dream of the organization of labor by the state. What was the result of this memorable experiment ? The impoverishment of the whole community. In Campania, that

to the son and grandson, adds. *Secundum divi Constantini constitutiones* (*Codex Theod.* vi. 2, 21).

[1] Vol. IV. chap. lxxi. pp. 362–400. We have sought to follow in the reigns of successive Emperors, especially from Hadrian to Diocletian, the slow evolution which transformed the empire of Augustus into an Oriental monarchy.

[3] *Notitia dignitatum*, Böcking, p. 123.

country favored of Heaven, whose soil had never been trodden by
a hostile foot, there will soon be more than a half million *jugera*
uncultivated; the eighth part of this fruitful province will be a
desert, where neither a man nor a hovel will be visible. The rich
plains of Apulia were already desolated by the pasturage of flocks
which crowded out all agriculture, and along the Tuscan coast
Rutilius will behold only solitude and ruins. It was the *mal'aria*
that caused the destruction of the Etruscan cities, once so flourishing. But who caused the *mal'aria?* They who had not been
wise enough to keep up the defensive works of the old inhabitants, draining the soil and carrying off the stagnant waters.
When such was the condition, just outside the gates of Rome, of
the old Saturnian land, formerly so fruitful in men and harvests,
magna parens frugum . . . magna virum, what may we expect to
find in the rest of the Empire?[1]

Successive generations necessarily inherit from their predecessors,
the sons reaping what their fathers have sown; and the historic
circumstances of a people have much more to do in social trans-
formations than has the will of the sovereign. We must not
therefore ascribe to Constantine the whole series of changes whence
emerged the Later Empire; but more than all his predecessors

---

[1] The abandoned lands were so extensive that Theodosius recognized ownership after
two years where they had been placed under culture (*Codex Just.* xi. 56, 8), and Honorius was obliged to relieve from all taxes 300,000 acres (528,042 *jugera*), *quae Campania
provincia, juxta inspectorum relationem . . . in desertis et squalidis locis habere dignoscitur*
(*Codex Theod.* xi. 28, 2, anno 395). The entire title 28 should be read. It contains
remission of arrearages and reduction of taxes in the provinces of Italy, Africa, and the
East. Cf. H. Richter, *Das Weström. Reich unter Gratian.* Under Constantine even, Lactantius laments (*Instit. divin.* vi. 20) the frequent abandonment of children, caused by
the extreme poverty of the parents, and advised the poor *ut se ab uxoris congressione con-
tineant.* It was the Malthusian doctrine fifteen centuries before Malthus. The evil was
so great that to save the exposed child or slave, Constantine granted to those who should
take up such children or slaves, the full right of father or master, subject to no invalidation
(*Codex Theod.* v. 7, 1, anno 331). But he gave permission to fathers to sell their new-
born offspring, with a reserved right to redeem them later (*ibid.* v. 8, 1, anno 329). In
the reign of Constantine, Amm. Marcellinus speaks of the "incurable wounds" made by taxation of the provinces: . . . *Insanabilia vulnera saepe ad ultimam egestatem provincias con-
traxisse . . . quae res . . . penitus, evertit Illyricum* (xvii. 5, and xix. 11). In the time
of Gratian, Symmachus (*Ep.* x. 42) shows a twofold result arising from the same cause, —
the value of gold coin prodigiously increasing, and the prices of commodities at the same
time diminishing (*auri enormitate crescente . . . et quum in venalium majore summa solidus
censeatur, pretia minora penduntur*), — which is to say that the circulation of gold had
diminished, traffic was declining, and the supply of commodities being greater than the
demand for them, prices had gone down.

together, he impelled Roman society to take that inferior form of political organism. Now, to every kind of government correspond in the subjects peculiar virtues or vices. With a social organization in which each citizen has his designated place and bears a label which in most cases he cannot change, it would seem that dangerous agitations were no longer to be feared, and that the most admirable order must prevail. But these men, who have no will of their own because they are no longer free, have no energy for good, and no protection against temptations to evil. Each man uses stratagem against the power that binds him, and seeks to regain by craft what he loses by submission. The *Theodosian Code* shows that in this new Empire there was neither thing nor person that could not be bought. Reduction of the census, relief from taxes, change of position, all was marketable. For him who pays, the collector has false weights, the judge has mitigated sentences, the executive officer and the recruiting officer have dishonest favors. The heads of offices live by their subordinates, the generals by their soldiers. The new comer in an office or a cohort must make his gift; a recruit in the corps of *domestici* is taxed fifty gold *solidi*.[1] It is the very reign of baksheesh: up to the governors of the provinces there is no man who does not pay it to the officers of the sacred bed-chamber; and even the Emperor himself demands it from those to whom he grants a favor.[2] At a later date Justinian, who professed to assign magistracies gratuitously, required of a man receiving office that he should send fifty pounds of gold to the "very pious Empress."[3] Originating in the Byzantine court, this contagious pest destroyed in the social body all that sense of honor which preserves public integrity, and spreading from man to man throughout the whole Eastern world, for fifteen centuries has undermined and ruined it.[4] The Emperors

---

[1] *Codex Theod.* vi. 24, 3, *anno* 394.

[2] . . . *Auri argentique collationibus . . . obnoxii* (*Codex Theod.* xi. 20, 1). This is a law of Constantius. These gifts were an ancient custom. In the first years of the Empire the soldiers paid the centurions for exemption from certain tasks, *vacationes* (Tac., *Ann.* i. 17); leave of absence was also bought to such an extent that a fourth of each maniple was absent from camp (*Id.*, *Hist.* l. 46). The Emperor Otho undertook the payment of the *vacationes*, — no doubt after examination of reasons; but there is no certainty that this ancient exaction did not re-appear after his time.

[3] *Nov.* xxx. chap. iv. sect. 1.

[4] When the French entered Egypt in 1800, a third part of all that was levied in taxation

themselves attest by their laws the reality of the evils which
their government caused. To one of them Synesius says: "Everything is bought."[1]

It will be said that Constantine founded the city of Constantinople, thus retarding for ten centuries the triumph of Oriental barbarism; that he caused Christianity to sit down with him upon
the imperial throne; that without intending to do it, he prepared
the way in Rome, deserted by her Emperors, for the pontifical
monarchy of her bishops; and that he thus stands midway between
two ages in the world's history, — closing one, opening the other.
These are great things, and we have already rendered merited
honor to the Emperor who, amidst animosities and ambitions
wrought to the highest pitch by the advent of a new cult, was
able to maintain domestic peace undisturbed by political or religious riots. But his personal work, though in some respects brilliant, is never solid. The peace which he established was not
lasting; if Constantinople did, indeed, exist for twelve centuries,
it was but a miserable existence, with the exception of a few
brief periods; and though at sight of the Church triumphant, endowed with wealth and privileges, we might believe that virtue,
justice, and all the minor morals were about to prevail, that the
Emperors would be truly devout persons, that the state would be
strengthened, the Barbarians driven back, and the Heavenly Jerusalem established upon earth, — all this is, unhappily, far from the
truth. Nothing was really changed. The level of public morality
was no higher.[2] The old capital had had sixty-six holidays in the

remained in the hands of the tax-gatherers (Giraud, member of the Inst. of Egypt, *Mémoire
sur l'agriculture*, etc., 1822).

[1] *Concerning Royalty*, sect. 30. The superintendents of the *cursus* levied upon travellers
and provincials by different means, whose result, however, was always the same (*Codex
Theod.* viii. 5, 10, and 2, *annis* 358 *et* 364). The port officers fleeced the ship-masters (*Cassiodorus, apud* Böcking, *Not. Occid., Praef. Urb.* . . .). The army agents pilfered from the
soldiers' pay (Godefroy in the *Codex Theod.* vii. 14, 28, 29); the *navicularii*, from the corn
they brought (*ibid.* xiv. 4, 9); and those who received taxes paid in kind, from the supplies
brought in. The counts and the presidents required the curials to pay to them in money, at
ten times the real value, an equivalent for the supplies which were their due (*ibid.* vii. 4, 32,
anno 412); the receivers (*susceptores*) pilfered with both hands: declaring their own receipts
fictitious, they compelled the tax-payer to pay a second time (*ibid.* xii. 6, 27, *anno* 400; *Nov.
Valent.* iii. tit. i. 3, sect. 3, *anno* 430), and they paid into the treasury counterfeit coin (*solidi
adulterini*) (*ibid.*, law 13, *anno* 367). The recruiting officers made an agreement with the
possessores to accept as soldiers *coloni* no longer useful to their masters . . . *quales domini
habere fastidiunt* (Vegetius, i. 7).

[2] Wietersheim (*Völkerwanderung*, i. 358) is more severe.

year, the new was to have a hundred and seventy-five;[1] the combats of gladiators continued for many years longer; Theodo-

sius sends to Rome Sarmatian captives "to serve for the amusement of the people;"[3] and the festivals of the *Maïuma* continued, with all their scandalous representations.[4] Even in respect to the

[1] Theodosius reduced this number to a hundred and twenty-five (*Codex Theod.* ii. 8, 2).

[2] Divine Providence, and four figures representing Virtue, Power, Military Science, and Felicity (Böcking, i. 115). This design and another resembling it, but entitled The Divine Election, and with its four figures representing the Four Seasons, conclude the *Notitia* of the Eastern Empire. At this time, when insignia and symbols were so much in fashion, these two paintings were doubtless placed in some conspicuous position in the imperial offices.

[3] Symmachus, *Letters*, x. 61. See our Vol. VII. p. 453.

[4] Saint John Chrysostom, vii. 113, 114 (ed. of the Bernardins). His *Homilies*, especially the forty-ninth, give a sad picture of the vices of Constantinople. The *Maïuma*, or May games, were prohibited, after some hesitation, in 399 (*Codex Theod.* xv. 6, 1–2), but these festivals quickly re-appeared. What Procopius relates of Theodora is well known. In the time of Amm. Marcellinus (xiv. 6), during a period of scarcity at Rome, all foreigners were required to leave the city, even those belonging to the liberal professions; but all actors were retained, and three thousand dancing-girls with them. Gregory of Nyssa, who was employed in 381 by

clergy, a too rapid recruiting and hasty ordinations produced disorder which shocked the Fathers of the Church.[1]   Literature and art never regained their lost splendor; and we shall see murders in the palace, sanguinary rivalries in the state, in the provinces civil war, and for the people extreme distress and poverty.

The pagan Empire had lasted three centuries and a half; the Christian was to endure scarcely one century. They who proposed to save the world will not be able to preserve the Empire from the most frightful catastrophes; so that while Christianity in these days did much for the individual, it yet did nothing for the state, and the words of Christ were fulfilled: "My kingdom is not of this world."[2]

Theodosius to reform the Churches of Arabia and Palestine, leaves a sad account of the licentious life of pilgrims on their way to Jerusalem; Saint Jerome confirms this testimony in his letter to Marcella, and Synesius in his correspondence.

[1] The Council of Nice, in its second canon, censures and forbids too hasty ordinations. The most learned French moralist of the thirteenth century, Guil. Perrault, says (*Summa de vitiis*, Book IV. chap. vii. art. 3): "The day when Constantine established the empire of the Church, a voice cried: *Hodie infusum est venenum Ecclesiae Dei.*" Cf. Hauréau, *Mém. de l'Acad. des inscr.* vol. xxviii., 2d part, p. 254.   The author of course speaks only of the political authority of the Church.

[2] Not until the Mediæval period, in the presence of the barbarism brought in by the German invasion, did the Church have an influence upon society.

CHAPTER CV.

I. MURDER OF THE FLAVII; WAR WITH PERSIA; DEATH OF CONSTANTINE II. AND CONSTANS; MAGNENTIUS (337–353).

WE have given a large space to the history of the two Emperors who organized the Later Empire, and to the revolution which changed the religious convictions of the Roman society. After thus narrating these great social facts, we shall have no further occasion to dwell upon administrative details, which belong to the province of archæology, nor upon theological discussions, which make part of ecclesiastical history, except so far as either have direct influence upon events. We shall therefore go on rapidly towards the fatal limit whither all things have for so long evidently tended, — the time when the unity of the Roman world vanished forever, and the final Barbaric invasion began.

Constantine had left behind him three sons, two brothers, a brother-in-law, and several nephews, — the last survivors of this family of Roman Atridae. The sons were all young: the eldest, Constantine II., was twenty-one; Constantius II. was twenty; Constans was seventeen. The first lived so short a time that we know little concerning him; the third was but a boy. Only the second interests us here, because it was he who bore the principal part in the tragedy which followed the funeral.

Constantius was small in stature and in mind; in character, timid and crafty, at once feeble and violent, with extreme vanity, jealous of all forms of merit, and committing murder with perfect indifference when the crime might serve his interests or set at rest his fears; and he suffered from constant fear, because he believed himself surrounded by plots. To conceal his youth from the people, he put on an air of extreme gravity; on public occasions he sat absolutely motionless, — complete immobility seeming to him the necessary characteristic of sovereign majesty, as it is of the gilded idols of the Hindoos.[1] During the illness of

his father, Constantius was in Mesopotamia with the army which had been sent against the Persians. Notwithstanding his diligence in returning, the journey was so long that men's minds in the great palace had time to become extremely unsettled before the arrival of Constantius; courtiers and soldiers around the dead Emperor asked one another with anxiety what masters they should now have to obey.[2] After the funeral, which took place early in June, 337, Constantius main-

CONSTANTINE II.[3]

tained great reserve; and three months passed before he assumed the title of Augustus. Although written proofs are lacking, we have reason to believe that these three months were spent in establishing a perfect understanding among the Caesars; in secret intrigues among the soldiery to bring about a military tumult

[1] Amm. Marcellinus, xvi. 10: . . . *Tanquam figmentum hominis.* See, in this place also, the curious account of his entrance into Rome, and in chap. xxi. 16, the personal appearance of Constantius: . . . *Adusque pubem ab ipsis colli confiniis longior, brevissimis cruribus et incurvis.*

[2] Eusebius, *Life of Constantine,* iv. 70; Socrates, i. 39. Julian says (*Pan.* vol. i. sect. 16) that Constantius arrived before his father's death; but this seems to be a mistake, for the illness was short, and the journey a long one.

[3] The eldest son of Constantine, on horseback, bare-headed, clothed with the paludamentum, and armed with a javelin, about to strike at two prostrate enemies (cameo in the *Cabinet de France,* No. 256). Sardonyx of three layers, 65 millim. by 52.

upon which could be thrown the odium of the catastrophe ; [1] and, lastly, in enticing the victims to Constantinople, where Constantius retained them by a solemn oath, which, Saint Athanasius says, guaranteed to them complete security. The old juristic axiom *is fecit cui prodest* designates the authors of the crime.

The three brothers had certainly observed with displeasure the advantages given to the collateral line of the Flavii. There can be no doubt that they all, and especially the two elder, early interchanged their views as to the means to be taken for recovering the whole of their father's possessions, and for laying the execution of the plan, when completed, upon that one of them who could most readily carry it into effect. This cannot be doubted when we see that, the blow having been struck, no one expressed displeasure, and the three soon after met in peace and cordiality at Sirmium, fraternally to divide the spoils.[2]

Early in September the soldiery rushed into the city and into the palace, crying out that they would have no emperors but the sons of Constantine, and began the massacre. Almost all the male descendants of the peaceful Constantius Chlorus, the issue of his marriage with Theodora, were destroyed. Two half-brothers and six nephews of Constantine, among them Delmatius and Hannibalianus, perished; at the same time were murdered the patrician Optatus, husband of Anastasia, Constantine's sister, the praetorian prefect Ablavius, and a great number of their friends. The assassins spared two boys, Gallus and Julian, sons of Julius Constantius, who with his eldest son was among the victims, although he was the uncle and also the father-in-law of him who directed the massacre.[3]   Gallus was scarcely twelve years

---

[1] Eutropius (x. 9) accepts the legend that Constantius was a mere spectator of an outbreak among the troops which he had in no way instigated: . . . *sinente magis quam jubente.* Socrates (ii. 25) and Julian say the same. But in a eulogium upon Eusebia, Julian could not do otherwise; elsewhere (*Letter to the Athenians*, sect. 3) he formally accuses Constantius. Saint Athanasius, in his treatise addressed to the monks, Saint Jerome in his *Chronicle*, Theodoret (iii. 2), and Zosimus (ii. 40), do the same.

[2] Codinus, the superintendent of the palace, says, in his *Constantinopolitan Antiquities*, that the three brothers were at Constantinople when the massacre was committed.

[3] In his *Letter to the Athenians* (sect. 3) Julian says that at this time were murdered six of his cousins (*ἐξ μὲν ἀνεψιοὺς*), and also his father, his eldest brother, and an uncle of Constantius. A nephew of Constantine, who doubtless was prudent enough not to come to Constantinople, escaped also. We shall soon hear of him again. Gregory Nazianzen says (*Invect.* vol. i. sect. 91) that Julian was saved by Marcus, bishop of Arethusa; but had Con-

of age, and seemed not likely to live; Julian was but six: the
age of the latter, the delicate health of the former, or else some
circumstance of which we know nothing, saved them. They could
at any time be put out of the way if they became troublesome;
and as the three Caesars had no children, it was good policy to
reserve the last scions of the Constantinian stock for some unforeseen necessity which might arise. Eusebius, so often unfortunate in
his eulogies, says that Constantine, after his death, still reigned;
he thus exposes his hero to the suspicion of having, in his last

instructions, recommended this terrible work of blood,
and in the mind of another ecclesiastical historian
this suspicion is changed into certainty.[1] But if
Constantine believed that his brothers wished to
poison him, he was not the man to leave the duty
of punishing them to others. We must also notice
that these assassinations were financially profitable,
the murderers confiscating their victims' property.[2]

GOLD COIN.[2]

The interlude which so tragically inaugurated the bloody scenes
of which the capital of the Greek Emperors and of
the Sultans was to be the theatre, had lasted nearly
four months; it was not until the 9th of September
that the Caesars took the title of Augusti.[4] Immediately were erected in their honor, statues with the
inscription, " To the brothers who love each other." This was
perhaps for the moment true, but it did not so remain for any
long time.

BRONZE.[5]

The year following, in the middle of summer, they met at
Sirmium, in Pannonia, to make a final division of the spoils.[6]
Constantius added to his share Pontus, Thrace, and Constantinople;

stantius wished for his death, no bishop could have prevented the murder. Julian, who was
born on the 6th of November, 331, was only half-brother to Gallus. "My mother," he says in
the *Misopogon*, sect. 14, " whose first and only child I was, died a few months after my birth."

[1] Philostorgius, ii. 17.
[2] The Caesar Delmatius (FL. DELMATIVS NOB. CAES.) on a gold coin.
[3] Julian, *Letter to the Athenians*, sect. 5.
[4] It was at least upon that day, according to the *Chronicle* of Idacius, that the Roman
Senate made a declaration recognizing the three Augusti.
[5] The King Hannibalianus (FL. HANNIBALLIANO REGI), from a small bronze.
[6] The *Chronicle of Alexandria* speaks of a first partition made in 337, which is said to
have given Constantinople and Thrace to the oldest of the three brothers. The question is
obscure and unimportant, since if there was a division made in 337, it was unmade in 338.

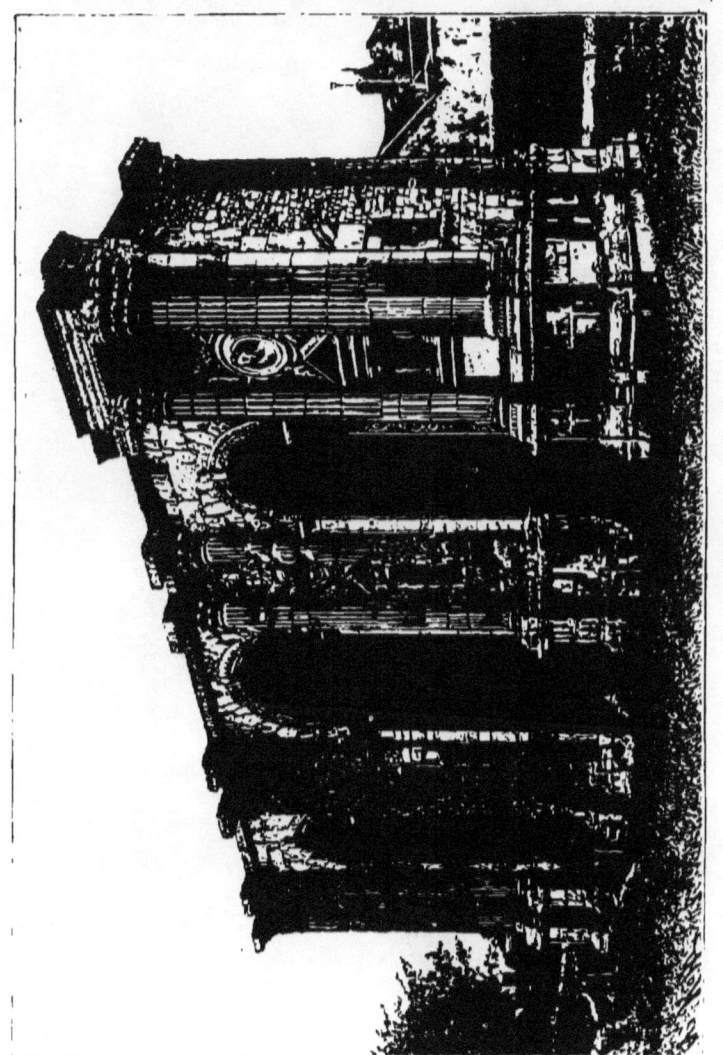

PORTE DE MARS AT RHEIMS.

Constans, Illyricum; Constantine II., the northwest of Africa. The latter, a man of impatient ambition, dreamed of his father's successes, who, beginning at Gaul, had subjugated the whole Roman world. Arianism prevailed in Asia, and the new master of the East was extremely favorable to it. His brother persuaded him to signalize their accession by the recall of the banished bishops. These exiles all belonged within the territory of Constantius, and were so many firebrands of discord sent thither. Athanasius, who had been exiled to Trèves, was intrusted with a letter from Constantine II. to the Alexandrians. When we see this Emperor addressing personally his brother's subjects, and the most turbulent city in the latter's domain, we cannot help believing that some perfidious intention was hidden in this message of the Orthodox faith. The inflexible bishop's return to his episcopal city was in fact destined to re-awaken the religious passions which would throw all the Eastern provinces into disorder; but these disturbances would secure to the Emperor of the Gallic provinces allies in the states of Constantius, as they had earlier given such to Constantine in the provinces belonging to Licinius.[1]

Ecclesiastical writers, who make it a duty to exhibit their gratitude towards the Constantinian family, have explained by religious motives many of the acts both of father and sons. It will probably be much nearer the truth should we substitute for the religious, the political motive, — as policy was at that time understood. To the statesmen of these rival courts it was axiomatic that since Arianism prevailed in the East, and Orthodoxy in the West, the master of the Western provinces should make himself everywhere, and especially outside of his own territory, the protector of all persons hostile to Arianism. We are justified in taking this view of events, first by its probability, and by the not very orthodox selection of high officers, pagans avowed or suspected, such as Anatolius and Magnentius, who were appointed by Constans, himself the fiery defender of Athanasius, — the one, prefect of Illyria,[2] the other, commander of the imperial guards; and further-

---

[1] On the policy of Constantine towards Licinius, see Vol. VII. p. 465. Of this Constantine II. could not be unaware. We shall see his brother Constans acting in the same way towards Constantius.

[2] Eunapius, *Lives of the Philosophers*, s. v. *Prohaer.*, p. 493 (ed. of Didot).

more, by the far from exemplary lives of these Emperors who
with so much facility committed acts of injustice or crime.   This
Constantine II., for example, who writes so pious a letter to Saint
Athanasius, picks a quarrel with his young brother on the subject
of the limits of their African possessions; and taking advantage
of the fact that Constans is far away in Dacia, falls upon Upper
Italy: it is there that the fortune of Constantine the Great had
begun, and thence also his son hopes that his own may arise.   By
a hasty march he subjugates the valley of the Po, and arrives
with his army in disorder near Aquileia, where an able general
awaits him.   More a soldier than a general, he impetuously
attacks the enemy, who, falling back, draw him into an ambush.
There he is killed, and his body, thrown into the Arsia, is
carried by the waves down to the lagoons of the Adriatic.   His
death, following upon the massacre of 337, was a second simplifi-
cation of the problem of the imperial government.   Constantius
permitted the conqueror to appropriate the provinces which had
belonged to the dead Emperor, and claimed no part of them for
himself (March or early April, 340).

This unusual disinterestedness was rendered inevitable by the
embarrassments which the Armenians and Persians were at this
time causing to Constantius.   Christianity had not subdued the
whole of Armenia ; many nobles, indignant at this foreign invasion,
made an attempt, upon the death of the old king Tiridates, to preserve the religion of their fathers ; they drove out the young king
Chosroës and the Christian priests.   The religious revolution was
naturally a political revolution also; the Armenians threw off
their alliance with the Empire and yielded up their strongholds
to the Persians.   This defection, which brought with it that of
the Albanians,[1] increased the danger upon the eastern frontier,
which, even during the life of Constantine, Sapor had threatened.
Constantius had no expectation of conquest; but to allow the
Empire to be encroached upon would have been dangerous: he
was therefore obliged to defend it ; and this defence was for him
a very serious task, since he could not, as his predecessor had
done, call to his aid the brave legions of Illyricum.   Left
with the Eastern troops only, turbulent cohorts and undisciplined

---

[1] A king of the Albanians accompanied Sapor in the great invasion of 359.

RUINS OF THE THERMAE AT TRÈVES.

auxiliaries, this military commander, "who had neither the heart
of a sovereign nor the head of a general,"[1] was not at all
capable, with an army of Goths and "Arab robbers," of striking decisive blows.   On the other hand, Sapor had been very
successful in reviving the warlike ardor of his people; but he
could not give them such a military organization as would secure the conquest of Roman Asia.   His contingents, levied for
each campaign by local chiefs, had not the experience which
standing armies possess; they lacked, moreover, the apparatus
necessary for military engineering.[2]   "They consider infantry useless," says Julian; and their cavalry, excellent for raids, their
cataphracti, whose onset on level ground was formidable,[3] had no
value in sieges; and, as a result of the precautionary measures of
Diocletian on this frontier, only successful sieges could secure to the
Persians durable conquests.   In these circumstances it was difficult
for the two Empires to come into actual collision.   Every spring
Sapor crossed the Tigris, and Constantius the Euphrates.   During
a period of more than twelve years (338–350) many slight engagements took place, nine of which have been called battles; but only
one action, that of Singara, was of real importance.[4]   The two
banks of the Tigris were by turns ravaged, the unwalled cities
sacked, and the fortresses besieged, but not taken.   Nisibis, the
key to Roman Mesopotamia, thrice resisted sieges, which .Con-
stantius suffered to last each two or three months without coming
to interfere with them,[5] — an unprofitable war, which caused great

[1] Julian says (Pan. l. 18) that the provinces of Constantius were destitute of military
resources, and that his brothers refused to aid him.
[2] Amm. Marcellinus speaks of their infantry as Julian does: they are merely servants
(calones); but he values their cavalry highly, which had profited, he says, in the matter
of discipline and tactics, by the lessons which the Romans had given them (xxiii. 6, ad
fin.).   At Singara they protected themselves by a moat; at Nisibis they effected a breach in
the wall of the city (Julian, Pan. i. 25); and we shall see that they employed before Amida,
in 359, the engines which they had captured in several cities of Mesopotamia.
[3] Julian, Pan. i. 32.   From Julian's description of the armor of the cataphracti, they
seem to be the counterpart of Mediæval knights: "A coat of mail covers their shoulders, back,
and breast; the head and face are protected by a metal mask, making them look like glitter
ing statues; the legs, even to the ends of the feet, have their armor, which is attached to the
cuirass by a sort of metallic cloth, completely covering the body, even the hands, without
depriving them of their flexibility."
[4] Amm. Marcellinus, xviii. 5 : . . . Nostrorum copiis ingenti strage confossis.   Julian (Pan.
i. 24) dates this battle six years before the revolt of Magnentius, that is to say, in the year 346.
[5] Julian, Pan. i. 24, 25, and ii. 9.

destruction of life and property. After one more defeat of the
Persians under the walls of Nisibis (350), the two adversaries,
fatigued with this useless struggle, agreed, "without treaty or
oath,"[1] in a tacit truce, which Sapor needed to repulse an invasion of the Northern nomads, and Constantius to be at liberty to
transfer his army to the Western Empire, where important events
had just taken place.

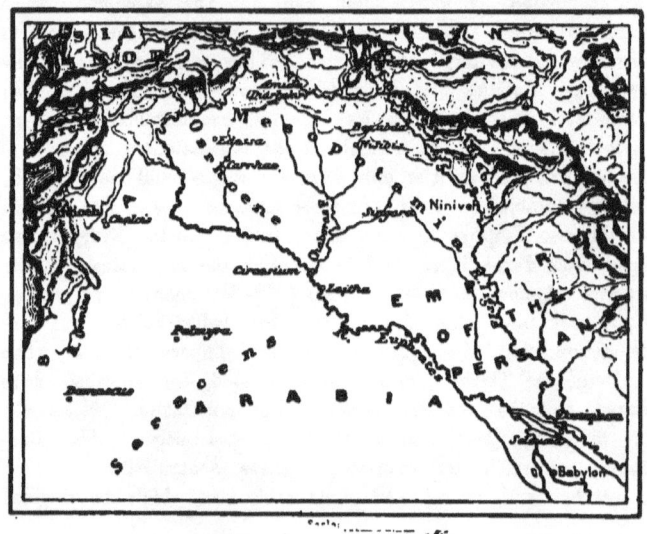

MAP FOR THE WAR BETWEEN PERSIA AND THE ROMAN EMPIRE UNDER CONSTANTIUS.

The Persians had gained more by this war than had the Empire.[2] They had several times defeated its troops, ravaged its
provinces, and threatened its fortresses, and Chosroës, whom Constantius had re-established on the throne of Armenia, had been compelled to return to his alliance with them and pay them tribute.
The Emperor could boast only of Sapor's hasty retreat after the
battle of Singara, and of the capture of that monarch's only son.
But in this latter case Constantius had also to remember an

[1] Julian, Pan. ii. 11.
[2] "Constantius had never the advantage in it," says Socrates (ii. 25).

odious crime. Diocletian had treated with consideration the children of Narses when they became his prisoners, and on their restoration to their father they became for the two Empires pledges of a peace that lasted forty years. Constantius caused the heir of the crown of Ctesiphon to be scourged and put to death, — an impolitic act of cruelty, which must have left an implacable rancor in the heart of Sapor, and was doubtless one of the causes of the sanguinary persecution let loose, or rendered more fierce, against his Christian subjects.[1]

SAPOR II.
(GOLD COIN.)

In the West new tragedies were preparing. Since his brother's death, Constans had remained master of two thirds of the Roman world. What use did he make of so great power? We read of a success over the Franks; but he could not have gained much honor from this equivocal victory, bought rather than won, and it is very little for thirteen years of rule.[2] Athanasius represents him as a saint; Zosimus, as a tyrant; Aurelius Victor and Zonaras, as a profligate of the most degraded tastes. Some blame his ministers, — which is to blame himself, since he selected or retained them; others consider him violent, rapacious, and arrogant with his soldiers. One author relates how he appointed a rhetorician general of the army,[3] — which was not likely to please the professional soldier; another, that his favorites were handsome slave-boys bought from the Germans (*pueros venustiores*). He seems to have been a great hunter, — a quality which history does not admire in a sovereign. In reality, we do not know him. To accept or dispute the accusations and the praises which self-interest in either case lavishes upon him, we need to have information which we do not possess; namely, how he reigned. At the same time, to see how Magnentius flung him down, while not a sword was drawn on his side, we must admit that his grasp upon the helm of state could not have been very resolute. Everything must have been relaxed under a feeble administra-

[1] Tillemont dates this persecution in 343; if this be so, it could not have been an act of revenge for the murder of Sapor's son at Singara.

[2] Idacius and Saint Jerome place in 342 his treaty with the Franks, who at that time occupied Toxandria (Brabant), between the Meuse and the Scheldt.

[3] Eunapius, *Prohaer., ad fin.*

tion; and ambitious designs, at first restrained by the great name which the sovereign bore, reawakened around the incapable ruler, and plots began to be formed.[1]

Magnentius, of Laetic origin, had risen by his own ability and by much audacity to the position of commander of the Jovians and Herculians.[2] He had partisans in the army; the count of the

GOLD COIN.[3]

largesses, Marcellinus, furnished him, from the imperial treasury, the means of increasing their number: civil and military officers were, it appears, agreed in bringing about a revolution. On a day when Constans was hunting in a forest near Autun, Marcellinus gave an entertainment to the principal persons of the court.[4] Wine mounted into men's heads, tongues were loosed, and invectives circulated. When Magnentius saw that the guests had reached a degree of insolence which imperilled their lives unless they passed from speech to action, he left the apartment for a moment, then returned with the purple robe and diadem. They saluted him Augustus and swore fidelity to him; the guards hailed with acclamations this soldier who to many of them was a fellow-countryman, and in a single hour he became master of the palace, the treasury, and the Empire. Constans, being informed, fled with all haste. Some time was wasted in finding his track; the Frankish cavalry sent in pursuit went as far as Helena, at the foot of the Pyrenees, before they overtook him. The Franks are the actors in this tragic drama: one essays to defend the dethroned Emperor; another kills him; a third grasps the imperial authority; and later a fourth, Sylvanus,

[1] Eutropius, x. 9: *intolerabilis;* Aur. Victor, *Caes.* 41: *execrabilis;* Zosimus, ii. 42.

[2] According to Zosimus and Aur. Victor, the family of Magnentius had been transported from Germany into Gaul near the end of the third century; hence Julian calls him (*Pan.* i. 29) "the miserable descendant of a German race reduced to servitude." He was probably neither pagan nor Christian, and we are not justified in saying that the religious question had anything to do with his elevation. His coins are Christian. There has been found in Paris, in a spot corresponding with No. 68, rue de Rivoli, a tomb with the pagan formula *diis manibus* and a coin of Magnentius, of the year 351, bearing the Christian monogram. The dead man was therefore a pagan; but his family had no scruple about placing in his right hand, to pay his passage into the other world, a Christian coin. This tomb also marks the extension of Lutetia upon the right bank of the river (*Bull. épigr. de la Gaule,* 1863, p. 130).

[3] Magnentius (D. N. MAGNENTIVS AVG).

[4] The *Fasti* of Idacius place this event on the 18th of January, 350.

will do the same.   Again we have an Emperor murdered, again
a palace and barrack revolution (350).[1]

The servile populations of the two Gallic prefectures and of
Italy accepted their new master with docility. Vetranio, an old
general commanding in Illyricum, was tempted by
the example of this facility in seizing the imperial
authority; or, rather, his soldiers desired the advantages which were to be obtained by an election; for
he himself, on the first news of the usurpation of
Magnentius, had sent assurances of his fidelity to the
Emperor of the East. Vetranio was a man of sim-

GOLD COIN.[2]

ple manners and amiable character, a native of a wild district of
Moesia, — still another proof that the heart of the Empire, already
growing cold, no longer supplied emperors or generals, who now for
more than a century had been furnished exclusively by the Northern provinces, adjacent to the Barbaric lands. A man of very
low extraction, Vetranio had remained extremely ignorant, and in
skilful hands might be made a very useful tool. Constantina, the
widow of Hannibalianus, resolved to employ him in carrying out
designs whose exact nature is unknown to us. This ambitious
daughter of the great Constantine, who, honored by her father with
the title of Augusta, believed that this distinction gave her the
right to intervene in the government of the Empire, herself bound
the diadem upon the old soldier's head (March, 350). The two
usurpers found it for their advantage to unite. They sent to Constantius a joint embassy, offering him alliance or war. Constantius
would have been disgraced and ruined if he had taken the hand
thus extended to him, red with his brother's blood; a spirit of revolt would at once have invaded his armies and his generals. On
the other hand, the risks of war were formidable, — his legions,
which had not been able to conquer the Persians, were scarcely to
be believed a match for all the forces of the West. He decided,
however, upon war;[3] and we shall not feel obliged to account for
this by the story of a vision which was spread abroad among his
troops, in which, it was said, the great Constantine appeared to him,

[1] Aur. Victor, *Caes.* 41; Eutropius, x. 5; Zosimus, ii. 42; Zonaras, xiii. 6.
[2] Vetranio wearing the diadem (D. N. VETRANIO P. F. AVG.).
[3] See Peter Patricius, pp. 129–131 (ed. of Bonn).

holding in his arms the body of his murdered son and calling for
vengeance. Artful negotiations, which preceded hostilities, were able
to break the alliance of the two usurpers. The treasury of Constantinople was better filled than that of Illyricum; the soldiers and
lieutenants of Vetranio were secretly approached, and were won over
by gifts or promises. The haughty Constantina, disappointed in
Vetranio, regained her brother's confidence, — serving doubtless as
agent of his secret measures. Under pretext of supporting Vetranio
against the Gallic usurper, Constantius sent troops into Macedon,
and proposed an interview, to which the old general agreed. It
took place at Naïssus,[1] in the presence of the two armies ranged
around a tribune, where the two Emperors met each other (Dec. 24,
350). The sight of the son of Constantine, the memory of the
victories of the great Emperor, which Constantius brought to
mind in a skilful address, directed ostensibly against Magnentius
only, but really against him who had enticed the Illyrian legions
into disloyalty, produced its effect upon men already prepared to
be convinced. The cry of "Death to usurpers!" was heard on
every side; instantly comprehending his peril, Vetranio threw off
the imperial insignia and knelt at the feet of Constantius. The
latter, feeling that he had no need to protect himself by a death-
sentence against this incapable old man, sent him away into a
sumptuous exile in Prusa in Bithynia, where the discrowned
Emperor lived six years.[2]

Magnentius was not so easily overpowered. He possessed both
the virtues and the faults necessary for a usurper, — courage, a
certain amount of ability, and an unscrupulousness which made it
easy for him to rid himself of possible enemies by executions, and
to increase his resources by forced contributions, his troops by
levies among the Barbarians, and his party by advances to the
pagans.[3] He made other advances to the orthodox party in the
Eastern Empire, following the habitual policy of the Emperors of

---

[1] This is the place mentioned by Saint Jerome in his *Chronicle*. According to Socrates
(ii. 28), the interview occurred at Sirmium.

[2] Zosimus, ii. 43, 44; Socrates, ii. 28.

[3] He authorized nocturnal sacrifices, which must have gratified the pagans, who were still
numerous in the East (*Codex Theod.* xvi. 10, 5). Julian (*Pan.* i. 20) asserts that he required
from the citizens half their income, under penalty of death. But this assertion occurs in
Julian's panegyric on Constantius, which leads us to suppose it exaggerated in the matter of
the amount required.

the West, sending his ambassadors to Constantius by way of Alexandria, in the hope of gaining Athanasius to his cause. An attempt of Nepotianus, who seized upon Rome (June, 351) and reigned twenty-eight days, was quickly defeated; his mother, Eutropia, the sister of Constantine, and many of his partisans perished with him. Others succeeded in escaping to Constantius,[1] "whose camp became an asylum for Roman senators." For the defence of the provinces which he was about to leave, Magnentius appointed as Caesars his two brothers, Decentius and Desiderius, doubtless assigning to one of them Gaul, and to the other Italy; then he went in search of

MEDIUM BRONZE.[3]

his adversary in the plains of Pannonia, bounded by the Save, the Drave, and the Danube. Constantius, with his army increased by the Illyrian legions of Vetranio, advanced from Sirmium (Mitrowitz) to Mursa (Esseck) and Siscia (Sisseck), three strong positions, which were held by his garrisons; he halted at Cibalis, — a place which seemed to him especially fortunate to his house, since there his father had first defeated Licinius, — and intrenched himself strongly, while his cavalry scoured the adjacent plains.[4] Magnentius employed part of the summer in manœuvres designed to draw the imperial army out of its intrenchments: he defeated one of its detachments; he took Siscia, at the confluence of the Culpa and the Save; and if this be not an error of Zosimus, he attempted to capture Sirmium, in the rear of Constantius' army, the taking of which place would have laid open to him the Eastern provinces. Constantius made war in two ways. An envoy was sent by him to offer peace to Magnentius, on condition that the latter should renounce the prefecture of Italy. This proposition was haughtily rejected; but while negotiating with the usurper, the envoy sought to incite defections among his troops, — at least, a few days before the

GOLD COIN.[2]

---

[1] Julian, Pan. l. 42.

[2] Nepotianus (FL. POP[ilius] NEPOTIANVS P. F. AVG.).

[3] The Caesar Decentius (MAG[nus] DECENTIVS N[obilissimus] C[aesar]).

[4] Cibalis was situated on an eminence near Lake Hiulcas, equidistant from the Drave and the Save, on the road leading from Mursa to Sirmium. It is thought to be in the neighborhood of either Mikanofsi or Vincoucze.

battle of Mursa, the Frank Sylvanus, a distinguished general, went over to Constantius with a large body of cavalry.

Winter was approaching, and Magnentius would soon be obliged to fall back into Italy; he made an attempt first to take the stronghold of Mursa. The garrison held out bravely, giving Constantius time to hasten up with an army more numerous than that of Magnentius. The shock was terrible; as in ancient battles, half the combatants (fifty thousand men) perished: they were

MAP FOR THE WAR BETWEEN CONSTANTIUS AND MAGNENTIUS.

the best troops of the Empire, which for many years remained enfeebled from this tremendous loss. The imperial cavalry, especially the cataphracti and the mounted archers, had the honors of the day. The Frankish and Saxon auxiliaries of Magnentius for a time held back the victors by their desperate resistance (Sept. 28, 351).[1] According to an ecclesiastical writer, Sulpicius Severus, Constantius remained in prayer in a church while thirty thousand men were dying for him; upon the testimony of others we learn that a cross, appearing in the sky, announced his victory to the Eastern populations.[2]

[1] Eutropius, x. 13; Aur. Victor, Caes. 42. Zosimus (ii. 45–53) gives a long and confused narrative of this campaign.

[2] Socrates, ii. 28.

NOTE. — Sarcophagus of Arles. Prometheus, aided by Minerva, forms man. The soul, represented as a winged girl, is brought by Mercury; the Parcae and other divinities approach. (Museum of the Louvre.) See opposite page.

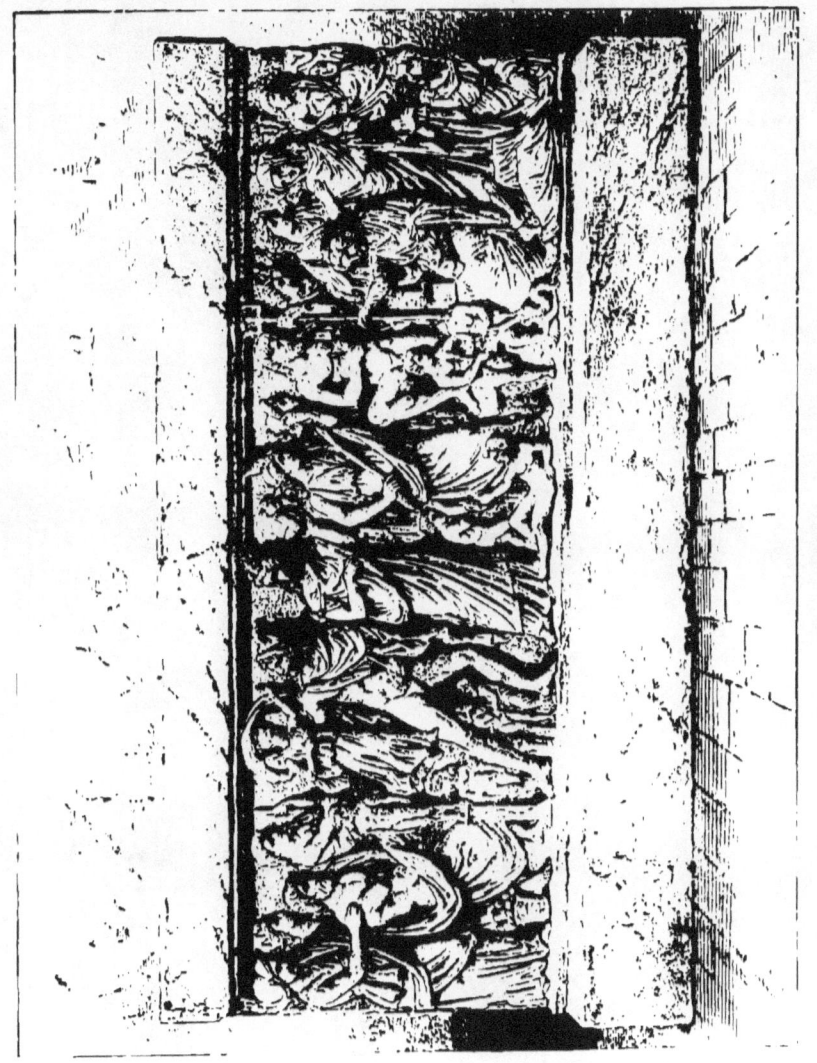

SARCOPHAGUS OF ARLES.

While Magnentius, escaping to Aquileia, was fortifying the mountain passes, an edict of Constantius promised safety to those of his partisans "who had not been guilty of any one of the five crimes which the law punishes with death."[1] The appearance of the imperial fleet on the Italian coast brought about many defections. Rome, which had been the scene of fearful slaughter after the defeat of Nepotianus, threw down the images of the usurper; Africa and Spain saluted those of Constantius as soon as the fleet appeared near their coasts; and gold sent to the Barbarians of the Rhine prevented Magnentius from obtaining soldiers from them.[2] The surprise of one of the forts guarding the defiles of the Julian Alps opened to the Eastern troops the gates of Italy, and at the same time their vessels entering the Po, compelled Magnentius to abandon Aquileia. He gained a slight advantage near Pavia, but was nevertheless driven back into the Cottian Alps, where he again endeavored to make a stand. But this army which had retreated from one lost battle-field to another, all the way from the interior of Pannonia, reduced in numbers and in courage, did not resist in the last encounter. Magnentius fled as far as Lyons. He there learned that the great city of Trèves had risen against Decentius; this was a signal for all the Gallic cities. In danger of being given up to the conqueror, Magnentius fell upon his sword. These events had occupied the year 352 and the first half of 353. It was said that before taking his own life, Magnentius had killed his mother, a kind of German prophetess, and his brother Desiderius; Decentius, the other Caesar, defeated by the Alaman Chnodomar, whom later we shall meet in arms against Julian, took his own life (August, 353). Thus this Barbaric family, which had so audaciously assumed the purple, disappeared entirely. The amnesty, with its vague terms intentionally employed by Constantius, saved no one; judicial executions took place everywhere, even in Britain, whither Constantius sent Paulus, nicknamed Catena, "the Chain," one of his most crafty agents,[3] and seven years later Julian found in Gaul numerous partisans of Magnentius, who lived there as proscribed

---

[1] Codex Theod. ix. 38.

[2] Zosimus, ii. 53.

[3] . . . In complicandis negotiis dirus, unde ei Catenae inditum est cognomentum. (Amm. Marcellinus, xiv. 5, and xv. 3).

persons. Amm. Marcellinus, the only historian of the time who is trustworthy, because he alone is dispassionate, has drawn in the first book which is left of his History a picture of this implacable vengeance. A word was enough, even a vague rumor, to make an innocent man a criminal;[1] and while blood flowed in torrents, Constantius celebrated at Arles, with splendid festivities, the thirtieth year of his *imperium*.[2]

II.—CONSTANTIUS SOLE EMPEROR; GALLUS AND JULIAN; SYLVANUS.

ONCE more the imperial power was held by one man alone. But what a sovereign was this, — suspicious, surrounded by eunuchs whom he obeyed,[3] and by courtiers who took advantage of his timidity, exciting his suspicions[4] that they might obtain the property of his victims! "Whether," says Amm. Marcellinus, "any enemy of the accused man pressed him or not, as if the mere fact that his name had been mentioned was sufficient, every one who was informed against, or in any way called in question, was condemned."[5] During his reign the customary formalities of justice were often omitted. Accused persons were condemned after secret trial; confessions, extorted by torture, led at once to the death-penalty: he who did not confess perished also.

Men are safely led only when the best sentiments of their nature are appealed to; and Constantius had never the gracious frankness which wins fidelity, or the energy of character which compels it. He loved low methods of government, — espionage, the informer's trade, meshes ingeniously woven, even around those

---

[1] The eighteen books of his History which we possess cover the period from 353 to 379, and will be our chief guide.

[2] Appointed Caesar in November, 323, he was invested on that day, not with the imperial dignity, which he did not receive till the year 337, but with the authority represented by the word *imperium*, which belonged to the Caesar.

[3] Amm. Marcellinus (xviii. 4) says ironically of one of these, Eusebius by name, that the Emperor was favorably regarded by him. Julian calls Constantius " a man asleep, who is incessantly duped" (*Disc.* vii. 18).

[4] . . . *Impendio timidus, semper se feriri sperabat* (Amm. Marcellinus, xvi. 8). See in this section the unjust proceedings instituted against innocent persons.

[5] xiv. 5.

who were ready to serve him faithfully, but, wounded by this jealousy, became his enemies. He remained, therefore, crushed under
the weight of a grandeur due to circumstances only, and far too
heavy for him to support.

He was in Pannonia, awaiting the attack of Magnentius,
when the news which came to him from the East decided him
to establish in that portion of the Empire a supreme command,
in order to give unity to the defence of the provinces. This
lieutenant might become formidable, but he was necessary. Constantius believed that the person least to be feared
would be his cousin Gallus, the son of Constantius
the consul, who had been murdered by the Emperor's
command some years earlier. Gallus and his brother
Julian, the last two surviving princes of the imperial
family, had been relegated, one to Ephesus, the other
to Nicomedeia. In 344 they had been placed together, the better to
keep watch upon them, in the castle of Marcellum in Cappadocia,
at the foot of Mount Argaeus; here they lived sequestered from
the world, constantly mindful of the murders of the year 337,
and never without fear of seeing the executioner arrive for them
also.[2] Attempts were made to tranquillize the fiery nature of
Gallus and the precocious austerity of Julian by religious exer-
cises of every kind, — pilgrimages to the tombs of martyrs,
prayers at these holy shrines, sacred chants in the churches, reading aloud the Scriptures to the assembled congregations.[3] Constantius, ordering these procedures, seems like a Merovingian
king preparing for the tonsure those of his race of whom he did
not choose to rid himself by means of the poniard. The usurpation of Magnentius, and the circumstance that Constantius remained childless, caused a change in the condition of the young

GOLD COIN.[1]

[1] Gallus Caesar (D. N. CONSTANTIVS IVN. NOB. C.).

[2] Julian, *Letter to the Athenians*, 3, and Socrates, iii. 1.

[3] Eusebius, bishop of Nicomedeia, had been the director of Julian's earliest studies, and
Saint Cyrillus asserts that the young prince was baptized, — which is, however, very improb-
able, it being at that time the custom, even for others than the imperial family, — *e. g.*, SS. Ambrose and Augustine, Eusebius of Caesarea in Cappadocia, Synesius, etc., — to receive baptism
very late in life. Gregory Nazianzen (*Invect.* i. 30) relates that it was proposed to have a church
built by the two brothers, each constructing half of it, and that the part assigned to Gallus was
completed, while an earthquake threw down Julian's. The earth was not so much in fault; Julian
had been intentionally negligent in his share of the work (Sozomenus, v. 2).

princes. Gallus, at the age of twenty-five or six, was appointed
Caesar, and invested with the government of the Oriental provinces (March 15, 351). The precaution of having him swear
upon the Gospels that he would undertake nothing against the
Emperor did not seem to Constantius a sufficient guarantee; he
gave to Gallus for adviser and guardian an experienced soldier,
Lucillianus by name, and for wife his sister Constantina, widow
of Hannibalianus, hoping that the Augusta, whose pride would
be at last satisfied, would secure her husband's fidelity; and he
reserved to himself the appointment of the officers of the Asiatic
army and of the praetorian prefect and the count of the East,
who should receive his private instructions. No death-penalty
could be ordered by the Caesar without the count's authorization; and on one occasion the latter took the opportunity to
show to all men how much authority he whom they called their
sovereign possessed, by opening the doors of the prison into
which Gallus had thrown the magistrates of one of the cities.[1]
In the very palace, the quaestor, who as government secretary
was present at all councils and gave effect to all decisions, was
much more the Emperor's agent than the Caesar's. The latter
had, therefore, in reality a title only, and no real authority.
Obliged himself to remain in the Western provinces, Constantius
desired to have the chief place in the East filled, so that no man
might be tempted to seize upon it. In the political organization
of Diocletian the Caesar was a lieutenant of the Emperor; Constantius returned to this order of things, but exaggerated it.
His too skilful schemes defeated themselves; they exasperated
a fiery young man whom more confidence might perhaps have
retained in obedience, and who, moreover, up to this time, had
done nothing to deserve such treatment.

[1] Amm. Marcellinus, xiv. 1. See what this historian relates of the proceedings of the
prefect Thalassius, who made it his occupation to exasperate Gallus. The name of Caesar, the
hereditary cognomen of the gens Julia, originally belonged to all related on the father's side
of this house; accordingly, we have designated the Ninth Period of this work as that of the
Caesars (Vol. IV. p. 401). Verus, the adopted son of Hadrian, assumed the name of Caesar,
and henceforth it designated the heir-apparent, but conferred no special authority. The
Caesars of Diocletian (Vol. VII. p. 363), heirs of the Augusti, were invested with extensive
powers: each had his capital city, his army, and his treasury; they exercised executive, judicial, and military functions. Under Constantine the Caesars are boys designated for the imperial station; under Constantius they are lieutenants with very limited authority; and after
Julian the title and position ceased to exist.

Rejoicing at his exchange of a prison for a throne, whose insecurity he did not at first recognize, Gallus threw himself eagerly into all forms of pleasure, going so far even as to scandalize the frivolous inhabitants of Antioch.   For his pleasures, however, he had need of money, and he procured it by exactions and acts of injustice.   Constantina, herself extremely rapacious, seconded him by aid of a system of espionage which she had set on foot to surprise imprudent words and the most secret domestic conversation.[1]   She sold everything, — justice, pardons, and offices, to make for herself what the rulers of that day regarded as the one safeguard of their thrones; namely, a well-filled treasury.   It is our misfortune up to this time to have found in all this royal race no one person, Constantius Chlorus excepted, whom we are able to esteem.

In 354 a period of scarcity caused popular tumults in Antioch. The mob gathered around the palace, demanding bread. "Address yourselves to the governor of the province," Gallus said to them; "provisions are scarce only because he chooses to have it so." This was a confession of his own powerlessness; but it was also a cowardly act: the unfortunate governor thus designated to the popular frenzy was torn in pieces.   The capital of the East was in a state of tumult; Isaurian robber-chiefs ravaged many of the provinces; the Arabs pillaged the lands adjacent to their desert; the Persians resumed their raids in Mesopotamia; and the Caesar put a stop to none of these things.[2]   Constantius, who had given the Caesar no freedom of action, was angry at the latter's supineness, and resolved to destroy his tool, rendered useless as much by the suspicious jealousy of the chief as by the character of the subordinate.   Through Domitianus, the prefect of the East, he sent an invitation to the young prince to come to him in Italy; and when Gallus hesitated, the prefect said roughly: "Do you not understand that it is a command? If you fail to obey, I shall stop the supplies of the palace."   The quaestor used similar language. Gallus incited his guards to murder the two officers, and

---

[1] Amm. Marcellinus (xiv. 1) says of her: *Megaera quaedam mortalis, inflammatrix saevientis assidua.*

[2] In 352 the perpetual quarrel between the Jews and the Samaritans had once more set Palestine in a blaze. The lieutenants of Gallus repressed this outbreak with the cruelty habitual to the Romans in dealing with a Jewish insurrection.

their dead bodies were dragged through the streets of Antioch;
he then pretended that a conspiracy existed against his own life,

THE CREATION OF MAN, ON A GLASS CUP FOUND AT COLOGNE.[1]

and employed this pretext to put to death, after the semblance of
a judicial proceeding, all who appeared to him objects of suspicion.[2]

[1] Prometheus is forming a statue; Epimetheus holds out to him a lump of clay; another
Titan, doubtless Atlas, looks on at the work. Above the bordering is another man, lying on
his back, possibly the fourth son of Iapetus, Menoetius, whom Jupiter smote with a thunder-
bolt. Below, a child is playing near a reclining woman, personifying the Earth. Legend:
ΠΡΟΜΗΘΕΥC ΑΝΘΡΩΠΟΓΟΝΙΑ ΥΠΟΜΗΘΕΥC. Cf. Robert Mowat, Rev. archéol., November,
1882, p. 291.
[2] In respect to the cruelties of Gallus, see Amm. Marcellinus, xiv. 7, and particularly, in
sect. 8, the torture and death of Eusebius, an innocent person.

This was not a revolt, for there had been no order to take up arms; but it was an open insult offered to the Emperor.[1]

Constantius feigned to believe in the existence of a plot against Gallus, and strove the more to bring within his reach the Caesar, — for whom, it was said, a royal robe was secretly weaving in the city of Tyre. He sent friendly messages to the young man; he insisted upon the necessity for both of them to come to a cordial understanding upon the great interests of the Empire; and he reiterated the invitation for Gallus to come into Italy, bringing him his wife, "that beloved sister whom the Emperor ardently desired to see." Meantime he recalled those officers who appeared to be devoted to Gallus; he withdrew from him as many troops as possible, under pretext that unoccupied soldiers soon lose their habits of discipline; and the unfortunate young prince soon found himself completely in the toils of this skilful hunter of his own race. Constantina "knew perfectly of what her brother was capable," and did not deceive herself as to the affection the Augustus had for her; but her personal appeal seemed to be the only possible way to avert the danger: she set out for Italy, and died upon the road. There was nothing left for Gallus to do but to obey. At Hadrianople he was met by the order to dismiss his attendants; at Poetovium he was deprived of his insignia as Caesar; at Pola, in Istria, after a mock trial, he was beheaded, dying at the age of twenty-nine (354). Constantius even took vengeance upon his dead body, refusing to allow it burial in the tomb of the Flavii. Many of his advisers perished with him, and Ursicinus, the ablest general of the Eastern army, was condemned to death by a secret council. But before the execution of the sentence his services were needed, and his life was accordingly spared.[2] Such was the sad condition of the servants of this government, already exposed to secret accusations and mysterious sentences.

GLASS CUP.[3]

---

[1] Amm. Marcellinus represents Constantius as saying that justice had been scorned by Gallus, and that his detestable conduct had drawn upon him the vengeance of the laws.

[2] Julian, *Letter to the Athenians*, 3; Amm. Marcellinus, xv. 2.

[3] Glass cup found at Cologne (Museum of Berlin).

A few months later, another tragedy occurred. Sylvanus, as a reward for his services in the Pannonian campaign, was employed in checking the Barbarian incursions into Gaul. Julian blames him for having done no more than buy their retreat with gold extorted

TRIUMPHAL ARCH OR GATE OF POLA.

from the cities. But Julian, just appointed Caesar at this time, was composing a eulogy on the murderer of all his kindred, in which he is guilty of repeating the calumnies of the eunuchs and the courtiers against the faithful general whose place he was about

to take. In despotic courts the servile troop, in order to maintain
its own credit, is wont to parade a zeal for the monarch's safety,
manifested by craftily awaking suspicions in his mind and by
giving currency to calumnies which grow as they circulate, and
come to the master's ears, who is himself always ready to regard
as guilty every person accused of political offences. Forged letters were attributed to Sylvanus. His friends were immediately
arrested, and an imperial officer, sent into Gaul to bring the general
back to Italy, acted so precipitately that Sylvanus, believing himself ruined, sought safety by assuming the imperial dignity. He
caused himself to be proclaimed Augustus at Cologne just at the
moment when Malaric, the commander of the Franks of the guard,[1]
had succeeded in proving his innocence before the imperial tribunal
at Milan. Ursicinus was sent out to him, bearing complimentary
letters from the Emperor and the assurance that his titles were
to be preserved to him, but with secret orders to send him to
Milan and to take his place at the head of the army. Ursicinus,
however, incited an outbreak among the troops, and the soldiers
murdered him whom twenty-eight days before they had invested
with the purple (August, 355). All who were suspected of being
his partisans perished at the same time, among them the two
counts Lutto and Maudio, whose names indicate their origin.

III. — JULIAN IN GAUL (355–361).

IN studying the career of Julian we find ourselves confronted
with one of the most singular figures in history, — a man who
must be loved and respected, yet whose political course must be
condemned.

Thrown upon himself during eighteen years of a sort of captivity, Julian had pursued, like Marcus Aurelius, his hero, an
ideal of perfection;[2] becoming Emperor, he had so lofty a con-

---

[1] . . . *Gentilium rector* (Amm. Marcellinus, xv. 5).

[2] . . . *Quasi pabula quaedam animo ad sublimiora scandendi conquirens* (Amm. Marcellinus,
xxi. 5). . . . *Rectae perfectaeque rationis imagine congruens Marco (ibid.* 1). In his Seventh
Discourse, sect. 17, *ad fin.,* Julian says: "O Jupiter, or whatever be the name which pleases
thee, show me the road that leads upward to thee!"

ception of his duties that he wrote: "A king should have the nature of a God."[1] But his mind, extremely clear in questions of administration and of war, was often lost in a region of dreams, and the solitude in which, for political reasons, he was long held, developed this natural inclination. He loved, in his nocturnal meditations, to hearken to the inner voices of his mystical imagination, ever dwelling upon Nature and upon the mysterious. He tells us that as a boy he often left his books to follow with devout gaze the triumphal march of the sun, or to contemplate by night the splendors of the starry sky.[2] In the worship of "the divine Star," the noblest of idolatries, he recognized the religion of his fathers,[3] and in Christianity he now hated the religion of his persecutors.[4] However, he drew from the Christians' books, which he carefully studied, those counsels to virtue which harmonized with his own philosophy, — for oneself, purity of soul and body; towards others, benevolence.[5] Even when Emperor he preferred Socrates to Alexander, the life of the mind rather than the career of arms.[6] All of affection that existed in this cold nature — which indeed knew friendship, but never love[7] — was towards humanity, which he would fain render happy; towards the gods, whom he adored with an ardent piety; towards the forces which his dreamy imagination invested with life; and, unfortunately, towards those superstitious practices which philosophy had already long ago condemned.

His brother's changed condition had done no more than lengthen his own "gilded chains." He was permitted to leave his Cappadocian prison and go to Constantinople, where, as a humble student, he attended lectures. His prudent reserve and

---

[1] *Letter to Themistius.* He writes to him again: "O my friends! I could have wished to have no other occupation but to converse with you, as heavily laden travellers sing on the road to lighten the weight of their burdens."

[2] Julian, *Oration on the Worship of the Sun*, sect. 1.

[3] See Vol. VII. p. 485.

[4] In his *Letter to the Christians of Alexandria*, he says that he was himself a Christian up to the age of twenty; that is to say, the year 350. In his oration against Heraclius the reader should observe the history of his childhood, charmingly told by himself.

[5] In his letter to a priest, written shortly before the expedition into Persia, he says that in his childhood, poor though he was, he gave to the poor. Later we shall see how he hoped to found benevolent institutions.

[6] *Letter to Themistius*, 7.

[7] See, in the *Misopogon*, sections 8, 11, and 27. Also Amm. Marcellinus (xxv. sect. 4): *Ita inviolata castitate enituit, ut post amissam conjugem nihil unquam venereum agitaret.*

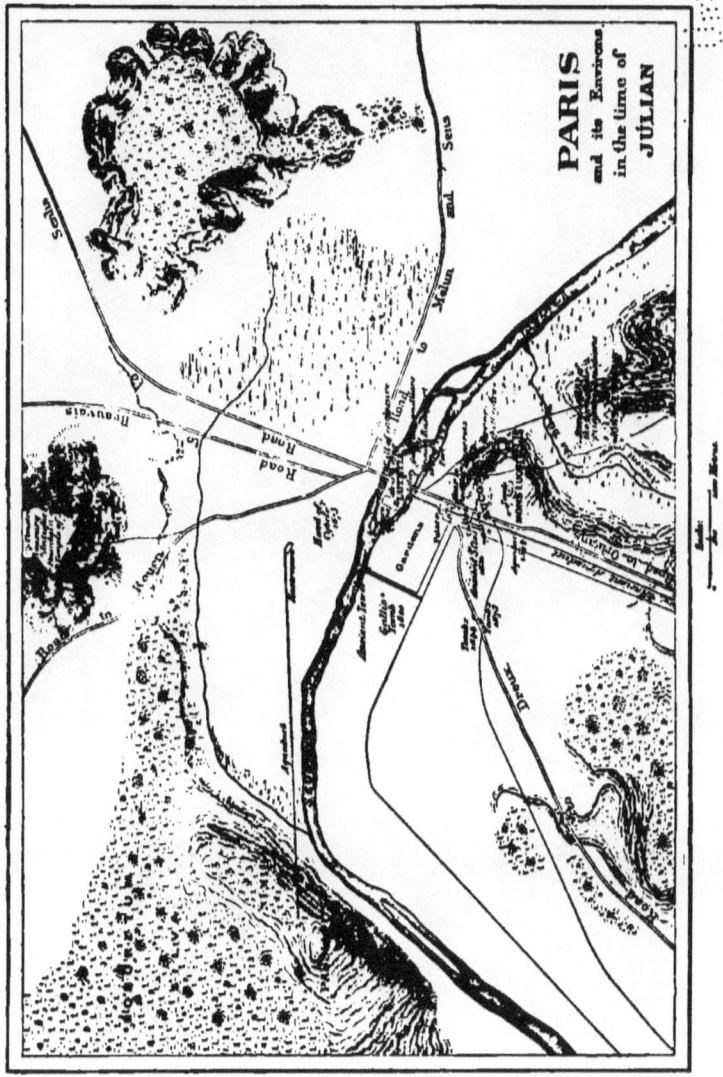

PARIS
and its Environs
in the time of
JULIAN

his industrious and modest life did not prevent men in search of all the chances of the future from seeking the friendship of the young prince. Constantius soon found him a centre of too much observation, and an imperial order relegated him to Nicomedeia, with a recommendation not to attend the lectures of Libanius, the most famous pagan rhetorician of the time, who taught in that city. Constantius already suspected Julian of pagan tendencies, and did not propose to allow him to become a leader for the partisans of the ancient cult. The Emperor's anxiety was not ill founded. Julian read in private the discourses of the eloquent rhetorician to whom he was not allowed to listen; the Iliad was his gospel, Homer and Plato were the enchanters who ruled his mind;[1] and he caused himself to be secretly initiated at Pergamus by a pupil of Iamblichus into the Neo-Platonic doctrines, and at Ephesus by a thaumaturgist into the mysteries of the condemned cult.[2] He had at first addressed himself to the aged Aedisius; but the sage replied: "My body is in ruins; it is a fallen edifice: question my children." The sons of his soul were Maximus

---

[1] Julian, who wrote and spoke in Greek, except in the fulfilment of his official functions, seems not to have been familiar with Latin literature, although Libanius says that he had read a few Latin authors. It would have been a useful counterpoise, of which he had great need; the same is true, however, of the most illustrious theologians of the East, — of Gregory Nazianzen, Saint Basil, and almost all the Nicaean Fathers, for whom it was necessary to translate into Greek Constantine's opening address. I do not say that the knowledge of Latin would have tranquillized the disputatious minds of the Greeks; but I call attention to the fact that the larger number of the heresies, and the greatest of them all, Arianisim, sprang up in the Hellenic East, while the West was never seriously disturbed in that way. If the Greeks of the fourth century had been conversant with the works of Cicero and Sallust, of Caesar, Livy, Tacitus, and the great jurisconsults of Rome, their loquacious subtilty would have given place to a well-balanced eloquence. They would have had an appreciation of realities, and also that sentiment of patriotism in which they are completely lacking, — and which we find at least in a few despairing words of the Pannonian Saint Jerome. Latin literature is a great school of reason and of patriotism; Greek literature of the fourth century is not this. To say that the people of the West were more devoted at that time to public affairs, would not, however, be true. It was that their language and their mental character were not adapted to metaphysical discussions; and while their social virtues were no more active, that which they sought from their religion was not so much controversies as it was consolations and hopes. At the same time it cannot be denied that the great theologian of the Western Church, Saint Augustine, seems, by his subtleties, to have breathed some Oriental atmosphere.

[2] Gregory Nazianzen (*Invect.* 55, 56), who carefully collects all the legends concerning Julian, says that in the midst of the ceremony the neophyte, alarmed by the apparitions which crowded around him, instinctively made the sign of the cross, and that the phantoms at once vanished. We have already come upon (Vol. VII. p. 415) this belief in the power of the sacred sign to drive away demons.

and Priscus, and these two philosophers were Julian's constant companions during the rest of his life.

The young prince divided his life into two portions, — one for the Emperor and his jealous court, the other for himself; carefully concealing his preferences, and under this constraint constantly sinking deeper and deeper into hatred of the religion which drove him to this double-dealing. This was not the heroism of the Christians, willing to die rather than deny the faith. But there are no martyrs to paganism, and Julian felt

PERGAMUS: RESTORATION OF THE ALTAR OF ZEUS AND ATHENE.[1]

no obligation to conform his soul to the external acts which were required of him. A most serious political question was involved also : Were the pagan divinities finally conquered, and was Jesus to be forever triumphant ? In his struggle against the Christians Julian saw a sacred cause, and himself the defender designated by oracles at this time current among the pagan subjects of the Empire.[2] With ideas like these, dissimulation was no longer unworthy. No man has ever censured Solon's feint of madness, nor that of the elder Brutus.

[1] O. Rayet, *Monuments de l'art antique.*   [2] Sozomenus, v. 2; Theodoret, iii. 3.

Plato, while disbelieving in the gods of Athens, spoke of them in such terms that he did not imperil his life; and Libanius praises Julian for having "obeyed the dictates of prudence."[1]

Being summoned to Milan after his brother's death as a suspected person whom the Emperor wished to have in his immediate presence, Julian lived at court for seven months, never secure of his life from one day to the next.[2] When the courtiers perceived this short, thickset man, awkward in manner, with pointed beard, and wearing the philosopher's cloak, his forlorn appearance caused him to be an object of ridicule to them all. A woman, the Empress Eusebia, made herself his protector.[3] Shall we attribute her conduct to pity at sight of this last scion of an illustrious house obliged silently to endure the insolence of eunuchs and of guards, or shall we conjecture that, being herself childless, she wished to secure a friend in the heir-apparent to the throne? Noble natures are so rare in this family that for the sake of finding one we are glad to believe in the sincerity of her whom Julian himself calls "the good and beautiful Eusebia."[4] She induced the Emperor to grant him an audience, and Julian obtained permission to withdraw into Asia and take up his residence on a small estate which he inherited from his mother, and which, when later he gave it to one of his friends, he describes thus: "It is twenty stadia[5] distant from the shore, and therefore undisturbed by trafficking merchants and clamorous or quarrelsome sailors. A hillock near the house commands a view of the sea, the islands, and the city which bears an illustrious name;[6] and the ground-ivy, the thyme, and other aromatic herbs will afford you constant gratification. When with tranquil attention you have pursued your studies and wish to relax your eyes,

---

[1] Libanius, ii. 270 (ed. of 1627).

[2] . . . περὶ τῶν ἐσχάτων . . . κινδυνεύων (Julian, *Letter to Themistius*).

[3] After the death of his first wife, Julian's sister, Constantius had married, near the close of the year 352, Eusebia, a lady of consular family.

[4] A foolish conjecture has been made, ascribing Eusebia's interest in Julian to a tenderer sentiment than sympathy. But the Empress saw him only once, at the beginning of the year 355, and again for a few days at the close of the same year. Eusebia was, it is true, a very beautiful woman (Amm. Marcellinus, xviii. 3); but the cold and austere Julian, whose passions were all intellectual, is not the person for the hero of a romance. Libanius (ii. 325) speaks of him as more chaste than Hippolytus.

[5] [About two miles and a half.]

[6] Constantinople.

the prospect of the ships and the ocean is delightful. In this
retirement I found many charms when I was a boy, for it has
fountains, a beautiful bath, a garden, and an orchard; and when
I grew up, I was still so fond of it that I frequently resorted
thither, and my obtaining it seemed to be a special favor of
fortune. It affords, too, a small memorial of my agriculture, a
sweet and fragrant wine, which is good even when it is new.
The grapes, both when they hang on the vine and are pressed
into the vat, are as fragrant as roses. Why, then, you will say,
did I not plant many more acres with such vines? Because I was
not a very keen husbandman; and besides, as mine is a temperate
cup, there was always enough for myself and my few companions.
Such as it is, my dear friend, you will now accept it. However
trifling the present, it is pleasing both to give and receive 'from
house to house,' according to the wise Pindar." [1]

While Julian occupied himself with these pleasures of rural
life for the sake of escaping from the scrutiny of Constantius, the
latter lived in the midst of suspicions and in perpetual fear.
Some imprudent words let fall by a governor of Pannonia at a
banquet were transformed into a plot, which the Emperor punished
with cruel tortures and executions; at the same time Sylvanus in
Gaul was driven into revolt. The Empire appeared to Constantius
to be full of treasonable schemes; and lest the brother of Gallus
should incite revolt in the Oriental provinces where he had made
his home, the Emperor ordered him to go over into Greece to live,
--- a country in which he owned not an acre of land, and knew not
a person. Julian however at once obeyed, and went to Athens
(July, 355).

This precautionary measure of Constantius was far from being
an act of wisdom. Since Alexandria and the great Asiatic cities
had been occupied with theological disputes, Athens had again
become the most vital centre of Hellenism. "Each land," says
Himerius, "bears its own peculiar fruit: that of Athens is eloquence." Men believed in the old gods, or at least spoke of them
with the art of rhetoricians and the subtilty of sophists; and
Christianity was there subjected to an animated and brilliant
criticism, both as to its history and its dogmas. When in the

[1] *Letter* 46.

midst of this crowd of masters and disciples Julian appeared in
his philosopher's cloak; when his eagerness to learn was manifest,
and his ability to discuss with the wisest, — many pagan hearts
turned eagerly towards him, and many Christians, divining their
secret enemy, said among themselves, "What a monster Rome
keeps here!"[1] But the future Emperor hid his thoughts from
all, unless it were the hierophant of Eleusis, whom he secretly
consulted;[2] and these scholarly enthusiasms, this sincere interest
in all knowledge which made him live in the far-off past, and of
which the courtiers at Milan scoffed, served to protect him against
the jealousy of Constantius.

Since the defeat of Magnentius the Emperor had continued to
reside at Milan. The war with Persia — a war of merely predatory character — could easily be left to the generals in command
in the invaded provinces; upon the lower Danube all, as yet, remained quiet. But serious dangers appeared in the West, and
turned away the Emperor's attention from the eastern capitals
that he might remain near Gaul and Illyricum. The Pannonian
frontier was always harassed by the Quadi and the Sarmatae.
Constantius had been obliged, in 354, to hasten against the Alemanni, who, masters of the Decumatian lands, were seeking to
obtain a footing in the northern part of Helvetia; also from Gaul
came news of disaster. To increase his own army, Magnentius
had withdrawn the garrisons from the Rhenish frontier; and these
posts had not been again fortified, owing to the revolt of Sylvanus:
accordingly, on the death of the latter the Barbarians had combined in a general attack. The Alemanni had fallen upon the
two German provinces, the Franks upon Belgium, and forty-five
cities had been sacked; among them Mayence, Strasburg, and
Trèves, the pride of Northern Gaul. All the left bank of the
Rhine, from the Lake of Constance down to Batavia, was permanently occupied by these Barbarians; and while an immense mass
of booty and a crowd of captives were carried away into the
German forests on the other side, the roads leading into Gaul

---

[1] Words of Saint Gregory Nazianzen, who was at this time at Athens. The saint regrets
that Constantius had not put this young man to death along with the others in 337: . . .
κακῶς σωθέντα. Saint Basil was also in the Greek capital, and Julian had relations with both
of them.

[2] Eunapius, *Maximus*, pp. 475, 476.

were full of wretched fugitives, — the mother dragging her children with her, the son supporting the steps of the aged man, and with them some few heavy carts heaped with whatever fragments had been rescued from pillage. They went their way, cursing the Germans and the Emperor and the Empire; their piteous tales spread terror; and often upon their track, like wolves following the frightened flock, came savage bands, yellow-haired men with eyes of angry blue, who, with wild outcries, destroyed men and things for the mere pleasure of destroying.

While these disasters went on, the single master of the Roman world was assembling councils, discussing the consubstantiality of the Son and the Father, sending into exile bishops whose theological views differed from his own, and risked losing his kingdom in this world by his ambition to regulate the affairs of Heaven. The cry of desolated Gaul, however, pierced through the disputes on ὁμοούσιος and ὁμοιούσιος; Constantius decided to send thither one of his generals. But whom to send? Those whom their services made conspicuous inspired him with endless suspicions. He feared lest an army sufficient to defend the Western Provinces might offer to any commanding officer the same temptation to which Magnentius and Sylvanus had fallen victims. "A kinsman would be better than a stranger," the Empress Eusebia suggested; and Constantius determined to repeat with Julian the experiment he had made in the East, when he had summoned one of his own relatives to occupy the highest position, lest some other man might seize it. That experiment had proved unsuccessful; but Gallus had been struck down, not for revolt, but for maladministration. What, moreover, was there to fear from this student of Athens, whose mind, always in the clouds, was devoid of worldly ambition, who, near or far, could be held in leash, and who, if need were, could be destroyed as readily as his brother had been? Constantius gave to Julian the title of Caesar and the prefecture of the Gallic provinces (Gaul, Spain, and Britain). "It is not a sovereign that I send to Gaul," the Emperor said, "but a figure bearing the imperial image."

Julian wished to refuse. The feeling that he had a duty to perform towards the old gods stood in the way.[1] Immediately

---

[1] Theodoret, iii. 3.

on his arrival in Milan (October, 355) the eunuchs of the Empress seized upon him; he was shaved,[1] deprived of his cloak, and arrayed in a military chlamys having an image of the Emperor attached to it, that none might forget who the real master was. "In this array," he says of himself, "I was a pitiful looking soldier." Constantius presented him to the army, who applauded not so much their new general as the *donativum* promised them on the occasion.

The hero of the day remained anxious and alarmed. When he returned to the palace, seated in the same chariot with the Emperor, Julian, pursued by memories of his brother, replied to the acclamations of the crowd by repeating to himself the lines of Homer, that on its prey "purple Death

JULIAN CAESAR.[2]

lays hold, and mastering Fate."[3] His own purple mantle seemed to him like a blood-stained shroud (Nov. 6, 355).

Constantius caused him to marry Helena, the Emperor's sister, —

COIN REPRESENTING JULIAN AND HELENA.[4]

a sad union, which gave him no sons, and was early broken by death. This daughter of the Empress Fausta, older than Julian, seems to have had no place in his heart or in his memory; his numerous writings mention sometimes the Helen of Homer, but never his own Helen. He was

at this time poor, and on his marriage received many valuable presents, of which the most precious, we may believe, was a collection of the best Greek writers, — a refined expression of regard from the Empress Eusebia. This library of Greek books he kept always with him; even on his expeditions at least some of them were among his luggage. From them he derived instruction and delight; by

---

[1] After his accession he allowed his beard to grow again.

[2] FL. CL. IVLIANVS NOB. CAES., and Julian's head uncovered. On the reverse GLORIA REI PVBLICAE, and two figures supporting a shield on which is the legend VOTIS; and underneath, KONS. XI. (Gold coin.)

[3] *Iliad*, v. 83.

[4] Julian and Helena with the attributes of Serapis (the *modius*) and of Isis (the lotos-flower). On the face, DEO SARAPIDI; on the reverse, the Nile, holding a vessel and a reed, and leaning upon an urn whence water is flowing. (Small bronze.) (Cohen, vol. vi. pl. xii. No. 12.)

means of them, moreover, he found something which he did not seek, namely, that popularity which, notwithstanding Christian hos-

tility, still clings to his name. By his taste for letters Julian belongs to all scholars; and the poets, the orators, and the philosophers whom he loved, plead for him with posterity. His reputation as a writer, however, led him to the committal of an unworthy action. He felt himself obliged, or others persuaded him, to respond to the sudden favor of which he found himself the object by a public expression of gratitude.

BOOKS.[1]

Feigning to accept the official theory that the massacres of 337 were the acts of a mutinous soldiery, and the death of his brother a stern but legitimate punishment, he read, on occasion of some public festivity in honor of his accession to the rank of Caesar, an adulatory discourse upon the virtues and exploits of Constantius, which must have cost heavily to his own sense of honor. It was thus, however, that he paid his ransom; we could wish it might have been paid in any other way.

On the 1st of December, 355, Julian quitted Milan with the Emperor, who accompanied him as far as Pavia, and proposed to share with him the consulship of the following year. Constantius called the young Caesar his brother; Julian wore upon his breast the effigy of Constantius; and the crowd admired this fraternal concord, — "a wolf's friendship," says Julian (*Letter* 70); and the distrust was mutual. Under pretext of organizing the service around the new imperator in a manner worthy of his title and of his birth, Constantius had removed from him his friends and attendants;[2] minute instructions regulated the affairs of his household, even to the food served on his table; and the generals of the Gallic army had orders "to keep a watchful eye upon his conduct," — Marcellus, their chief, having full control of the army. That the soldiers might not look to Julian as a distributor of favors, he was not authorized to make them the gifts habitually

---

[1] Books (*volumina*) found at Herculaneum (Museum of Naples).
[2] Except the physician Oribasus, whom Julian was allowed to retain.

bestowed by a newly appointed Caesar, and was expected, as a
subordinate, to render account of all his acts to the Emperor.[1]
This was the system which had been followed at Antioch. The
distrustful mind of Constantius is rightly recognized in it; also,
however, it is just to see reasonable precautions taken against
the inexperience of a young prince, in whom no one at that time
could foresee the great general.

Julian stopped at Vienne, which with its sumptuous structures
still was worthy of the epithet Martial gives it: " Vienne the beautiful."[2] On the first day of January, 356, he assumed the consular
insignia, and for four months he studied in history the science of
war as practised by the great generals of earlier days, and in the
camp the use of weapons and military drill. " O Plato!" he exclaims, "see what a philosopher has become!" At the end of these
four months the philosopher was a soldier; he knew, at least, all
that books can teach: actual experience of command soon made him
a general at once daring and prudent. Throughout the whole of
Gaul perhaps no man had ever heard his name. But the coming
of a prince of the imperial family appeared to these enthusiastically
loyal populations a promise of real assistance; the soldiers were
gratified when they saw a Caesar ready to learn from them, and
the officers conceived an affection for this studious and sedate
young man, who begged them to tell him the history of their
campaigns, who listened to their counsels, and who did not feel
that he had learned everything on the day when he was made
Caesar.

The condition of Gaul was deplorable. Cologne, one of the
chief bulwarks of the Empire, had recently been sacked; the Rhine
and the Vosges were no longer barriers to the Germans; they
penetrated with impunity into the very heart of the country, and
Autun, which they besieged, was with great difficulty saved by its
garrison and a body of veterans who had thrown themselves into
the place. When summer came Julian visited the gallant city to
congratulate its defenders (June 23); then he advanced, fighting

[1] . . . Tanquam adparitorem, super omnibus gestis ad Augusti scientiam referri (Amm.
Marcellinus, xvii. 11). See, on this point, pp. 76-77 of this volume.

[2] There are frequently found in the neighborhood of this city fragments of valuable
marbles, among them immense pieces of cornice exquisitely carved (Allmer, Revue épigr. du
midi de la France, 1882, p. 318).

as he went, as far as Auxerre, Reims, and the cities of the Moselle.
The Barbarians fell back before a display of courage which since

VIENNE: ANCIENT BUILDING CALLED LE PÉAN DE L'AIGUILLE.

the time of Constantine they had not witnessed in the Roman
troops. In Alsace they suffered a serious defeat, which permitted

Julian to enter Trèves, and also Cologne, whose walls he rebuilt. Then he advanced up the valley of the Rhine for the purpose of

BAS-RELIEF IN THE MUSEUM OF SENS.

supporting the operations of Constantius, who was making a successful expedition into Rhaetia against the same adversaries; after which Julian returned to Sens to pass the winter of 356–357.

BAS-RELIEF IN THE MUSEUM OF SENS.

In order to give his troops more comfortable quarters for the winter, he dispersed them through several cities, keeping but a few with him. This, however, came very near causing a disaster. Scattered through the country for pillage, the Barbarians had been surprised and driven back across the Rhine by an attack resolutely conducted; learning from deserters how small a body of soldiers the Caesar had kept with him, they formed the audacious plan of seizing Julian in his winter-quarters. Making their way stealthily between the Roman outposts, they suddenly appeared under the walls of Sens; but suitable vigilance was observed by the garrison. For a month the Barbarians kept the city besieged, while Marcellus, who chanced to be in the neigh-

MAP FOR THE CAMPAIGNS OF JULIAN IN GAUL, GERMANY, AND PANNONIA.

borhood, made no effort to come to its relief. The Caesar defended himself bravely, and wearied out the besiegers, who finally drew off. Marcellus was evidently to blame; if not treacherous, he was at least incapable. He was recalled, and the Emperor, understanding that his own extreme of prudence was in danger of becoming the extreme of rashness, re-established a unity of command by placing the whole Gallic army under Julian's orders.

The Caesar, at last invested with real authority, acknowledged the favor by a second panegyric on Constantius, which is no more creditable to him than was the preceding one. These panegyrics, characterized by a verbose rhetoric which bristles with classic quotations, were greatly in fashion at that time,[1] and were no more embarrassing to the conscience of the rhetorician, accustomed constantly to maintain the most extravagant theses, than the defence of great criminals embarrasses the

MOSAIC AT GRAND, IN THE VOSGES.[2]

modern advocate. It was a question of art, and one thing only was of importance; namely, that the periods be well cadenced. Julian himself ridicules this lying eloquence which men admire "when it makes small things great."[3] He compensated himself by a sincere eulogy, which he sent to Rome at the same time with the other, upon his benefactress, the Empress Eusebia.

The Gallic army consisted of only thirteen thousand men;[4] but there were brave soldiers in it, like that legionary tribune who afterwards became the Emperor Valentinian. This army advanced, in the summer of 357, into the Vosges to act with the Master

---

[1] A few years earlier, Rome had erected a statue in honor of the rhetorician Anatolius, with this inscription: H ΒΑΣΙΛΕΟΥΣΑ ΡΩΜΗ ΤΟΝ ΒΑΣΙΛΕΥΟΝΤΑ ΤΩΝ ΛΟΓΩΝ (Eunapius, *Lives of the Philosophers and Sophists,* p. 492, edit. Didot [French translation]).

[2] Upon the recent discovery of this mosaic, which represents the stage of a theatre, see the *Comptes rendus de l'Acad. des inscr. et belles-lettres,* xi. 211 (1883).

[3] In the *Second Panegyric,* sect. 23.

[4] This is the number given by a deserter to the Alemanni, and Marcellinus accepts the true as veritable (xvi. 12).

of the Infantry, Barbatio, whom Constantius had sent with a large
force from Italy towards Basle.[1] A body of Alemanni made their
way between the two armies and fell upon Lyons; but the city was
able to repulse them.   When they returned, laden with booty,
Julian had closed the defiles of the Vosges, and not one of the
marauders passed through.   But Barbatio was not able to detain
those who came in his direction; nor was he any more successful in his attempt to throw a bridge across the Rhine, and lost
many men in an encounter with the Barbarians.   These defeats
made the successes of Julian more conspicuous.   Before advancing into Alsace, which was threatened with a formidable invasion,
he had prudently fortified Saverne, one of the gates of Gaul; and
then, secure˙of having, in case of need, this place of refuge behind
him, he went to meet the enemy in the direction of Strasburg.
Almost the whole Alemannic nation was in arms; seven chiefs had
crossed the Rhine with an army of thirty-five thousand picked men.[2]
This was the greatest effort that the Barbaric world had yet
made, on this side, against the Empire.   When the Alemanni in
their engagements with Barbatio had seen flee before them those
soldiers whom by the insignia on their shields they recognized as
the troops who had formerly been their conquerors,[3] their hearts

[1] Barbatio was under the direct orders of Constantius, and not of Julian. His subsequent conduct revealed incapacity, therefore, but not treachery towards the Caesar. He had
25,000 men, — from which we see that the entire army of the West, when gathered for a great
effort against the Germans, was only 38,000 men in all.

[2] Part of these soldiers served in virtue of treaties of mutual assistance made between the
tribes; the others were paid. Thus we see
the Germans in possession of something like a
regular army (Amm. Marcellinus, xvi. 12). A
little later (xvii. 1), the same author shows the
Alemanni building dwellings after the Roman
method (*ritu Romano*), in the midst of well-
cultivated fields, and we have gold coins from
Barbarian mints, in imitation of the coins of
the Empire. (Cf. Eckhel, vii. 316, 330, etc.)

GOLD COIN OF THE EMPEROR GORDIAN FROM A BARBARIC
MINT.

Lastly, certain usages of civilized nations
were established in Germany; for example, the
common frontier between the Alemanni and the Burgundians was marked, says Amm. Marcellinus, by boundary-stones (*terminales lapides*). These were efforts to emerge from barbarism that it would have been wise to encourage, and not the transplanting of German
tribes into Roman provinces.

[3] Amm. Marcellinus, xvi. 12: . . . *Scutorum insignia contuentes norant eos* . . . etc.
Elsewhere (xxxi. 10) he speaks of *arma imperatorii comitatus auro colorumque micantia claritu-
dine*. The usage of placing designations upon the shields was very ancient, existing among the

History of Rome.

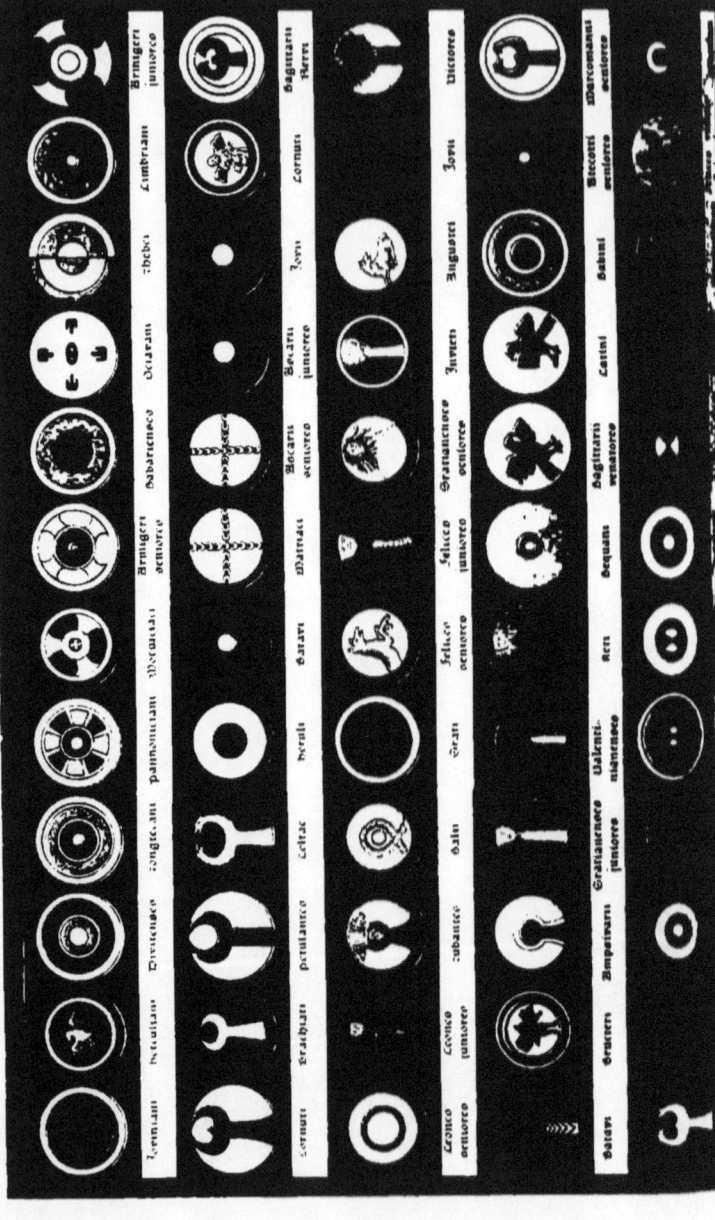

INSIGNIA OF THE MAGISTER MILITUM OF THE WESTERN EMPIRE

were filled with pride and confidence. Accordingly, they assumed towards Julian a very arrogant tone. Before the engagement began, they summoned him to quit a country which they said was theirs, so much had it been infiltrated with German blood,[1] and they showed letters from Constantius which had seemed to relinquish to them this province when he solicited them to enter it for the purpose of making a diversion against Magnentius. The answer made to them was terrible: six thousand men were left dead upon the field. Julian — recognizable by the standard borne behind him, a purple dragon — had shown himself everywhere amid the fight, and at the decisive moment had brought back into the fray his fleeing cataphracti. A great number of fugitives were drowned in the Rhine or killed while attempting to escape by swimming; among the captives were Chnodomar, who had been the terror of Gaul. Instead of having him thrown to the wild beasts, Julian sent him to Constantius (August, 357).[2] The old warrior, kept a prisoner at Rome, lived there six years.

This victory brought joy to the Empire and terror to Germany. Julian took the opportunity to cross the river and ravage in turn the country of these incessant pillagers, and he did not return into Gaul till snow began to cover the hill-tops. Before recrossing the Rhine with twenty thousand Roman captives whom he had set at liberty, he repaired the defences of the fort which Trajan had constructed at the confluence of the Nidda and the Mein.[3] This was giving back to the declining Empire its haughty

Greeks. Cf. Pausanias, *Messina*, 26, sect. 5. Böcking (*Not. Dig.* vol. i., *Einleitung*, pp. 93 *et seq.*) gives many examples of this. Dion Cassius (lxvii. 10) says that during the Dacic war a Roman general caused to be placed on the soldiers' shields each man's name and the name of his centurion. Vegetius (ii. 18) repeats this, adding that to recognize each other in the thick of the fight, the soldiers painted certain figures on their shields. This custom was subjected to regulation later, and each corps had its devices, which remained its own, as in later times the knight had his armorial bearings. The *Notitia dignitatum* gives numerous examples of this.

[1] . . . *Barbari qui domicilia fixere cis Rhenum* (Amm. Marcellinus, xvi. 11).

[2] Amm. Marcellinus relates, at great length and confusedly, the story of this battle, of which Julian speaks modestly, only calling it a fortunate day. Constantius has been accused of foolishly claiming the honor of this victory. He merely followed an old Roman custom in this matter. The real conqueror, though far away from the battlefield, was always he under whose auspices the army had fought, and Christianity had not changed this pagan idea. Constantius, however, exceeded the usual limit by describing the battle as if he had been present at it, and making no mention of Julian.

[3] Vol. V. p. 226.

attitude of the time of Trajan. The alarmed Alemanni begged for peace; Julian granted them only a truce of ten months, and that only on condition that they should supply with provisions the fort built against them.

After this brilliant campaign the soldiers had a right to their well-earned rest; but their young chief could now ask any sacrifice of them. Although in the middle of winter, he led them to the Lower Rhine, where the Franks seemed to entertain the idea of making a permanent settlement. The Alemanni did not like to shut themselves up in cities; and for this reason a battle in the open country, where the advantage was with the tactics and armament of the Romans, sufficed to drive them from Gaul. Endowed perhaps with a more military spirit, the Franks had established themselves within the last twenty years in the delta of the Meuse and the Scheldt, upon partially submerged lands which secured them inaccessible retreats, and for further conquest they recognized the importance of fortified positions. While the Roman army was across the Rhine, they came up the Meuse and rebuilt two old forts, thus rendering themselves masters of the whole river; and from these positions they proposed to advance, on the return of spring, into the interior of the country. Julian resolved not to leave in his rear these bold adventurers. For fifty-four days in the months of December and January he besieged them in these forts, notwithstanding all the inclemency of the weather. Boats constantly in motion upon the river kept the ice broken, so that there should be no chance for the enemy to escape across it. Hunger at last obliged the besieged to surrender. "It was remarkable," says a contemporary, " to see the Franks captives, for their law requires them to conquer or die." Julian sent them to Constantius, and the Emperor enrolled them in his guard.

COIN OF JULIAN.[1]

The next year (358), long before the crops were ripe, the Caesar again took the field, requiring his soldiers to carry with them

[1] Coin of Julian, with the legend, VIRTVS CAESARIS. Julian holding a spear and a globe; on each side, at his feet, a captive (medium bronze). The obverse, which is not given here, bears as its legend *Nobilissimus Caesar*. The coin belongs, therefore, to the time of Julian's government in Gaul.

biscuit for twenty days (*buccellatum*).[1] The Salian Franks, whom the Quadi had formerly driven out of Batavia, surprised by Julian after a rapid march, declared themselves subjects of the Empire, and agreed to furnish a corps of cavalry. In return for this, Julian gave up to them Toxandria, the country around the mouths of the Meuse and the Scheldt.[2] He had like success with the Cha-

ARENAS OF LUTETIA (ENTRANCE FROM THE RUE DE NAVARRE).

mavi, another Frankish tribe, compelling them to return across the Rhine. From them he had taken as hostage the son of their king; but the youth had disappeared during the battle, and the father, believing him dead, deplored the misfortunes which had overwhelmed his race and people. "Your son is alive," Julian said; and showing him the captive, he added: "He is under my care, and shall have all that he needs, so long as he remains

[1] Amm. Marcellinus, xvii. 8. Military operations did not usually begin in Gaul before July.

[2] Northern Brabant, the province of Antwerp, and a part of Limbourg.

faithful to me." These men, accustomed to the murder of hostages, were touched by an act which appeared to them generous, and was certainly politic. Long after, we still find Chamavian auxiliaries in the Roman army.

To remove from the Franks all temptation to go beyond their boundaries, Julian built upon the Meuse three fortresses, provi-

PORTION OF THE ARENAS OF LUTETIA.

sioning them with corn obtained from Britain. A numerous flotilla went to bring this corn, and in so doing exhibited the Roman eagles upon the Gallic rivers which fall into the North Sea, where now for many years Rome had made no manifestation of her power. The prefect Florentius had proposed to buy from the Germans the right of passage at a price of two thousand pounds of gold; but Julian would not agree to this, and such was his ascendency over the Barbarians that they made no attempt to seize upon this rich booty. A reconnoitring expedition into Germany, carried on with energy in the autumn, made the tribes across the

Rhine feel the necessity of prudence, in face of so active a general. Accordingly, in the following year (359) he needed only to make an excursion across the river to secure complete tranquillity on this frontier. The Alemanni themselves brought in the materials necessary for the reconstruction of seven cities; among

OTHER PORTION OF THE ARENAS OF LUTETIA.

them Bonn, Bingen, Andernach, and Nuys, which, with Mayence and Cologne, were to stand sentinel for Rome upon the Rhine.

The winters between these campaigns Julian passed at Lutetia.[1] Situated in the midst of that fertile region so well named the Ile-de-France, almost at the point of meeting of the three valleys of the Oise, the Marne, and the Seine,[2] on the banks of

[1] Julian gives in his *Misopogon* a correct description of this city. He remarks that the river remains usually at about the same level, and that the winters are very mild, owing to the vicinity of the ocean, which moderates the temperature. "The inhabitants have vines," he says, "and even fig-trees, which they wrap in straw during the winter." He speaks of the influence of the sea upon the temperature of countries adjacent to it, or what we call "the marine climate."

[2] "The Plan of Paris and its Environs, here given, is reduced from M. Albert Lenoir's *Plan de Lutèce*, of which a new edition, completed by M. Jacquer, was added in 1882 to the 14th part of *Paris à travers les âges*. Some modifications, however, have been made in it, of which the most important is the distinction between *Lutetia* and *Lucotetia*, which goes back, since it is indicated by Strabo, to the earliest times of the Empire. The name Lutetia desig-

a gently flowing river which falls into the sea opposite the British coast, and rises near the localities where the Rhône and the
Saône descend into the Mediterranean, Lutetia had found in its
geographical position all the conditions of a great commercial
centre; and such it was. From the time of Tiberius the rich
corporation of the boatmen of the Seine, *Nautae Parisienses*, had

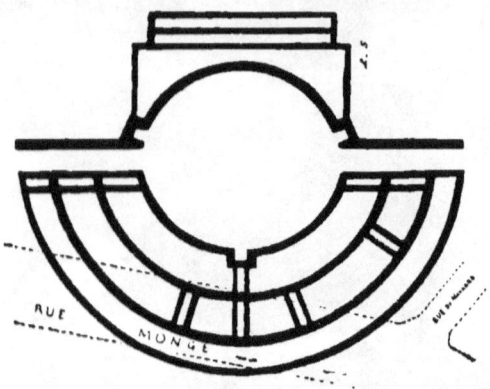

PLAN OF THE ARENAS OF LUTETIA.

been established in the island of *la Cité*, as in a ship at anchor
in the river. Two wooden bridges united this island with the opposite shores, upon which lay, on the northern bank the Gallic city,
on the southern the Roman. Lutetia was therefore an important military position. Caesar had often been there; the later
Emperors had made it an imperial residence, and had formed
military establishments there; for the city was then becoming

nated the island of the city, the old capital of the Parisii, while *Lucotetia* was the name of a
village (*vicus*) situated chiefly on the hill Sainte-Geneviève. Also the indication, made by M.
Lenoir, of antiquities found in the rue Vivienne (upon which discovery the learned academi-
cian rests his theory that the old road to Rouen followed a different course from that of the
rue Montmartre), has not been repeated here, since M. de Longpérier has proved that these
remains were brought from Italy in the seventeenth century. On the other hand, we have
indicated, along the road to Dreux (rue de Vaugirard), the tombs discovered there in 1644 and
in 1873. Lastly, for the modern names of the Bois de Boulogne, Passy, and Chaillot, we give
the Latin names which designated those localities." (Note of M. Longnon, designer of this
map.)

what Paris is to-day,— the centre of resistance against Germany. A bold dash easily brought the Barbarians from the Rhine to the gates of Trèves, the Gallic capital of Maximian Hercules and of Constantine, and they had many times threatened it. But for them Lutetia was too remote. On the slopes of the hill Locoticius, on which now stands the Pantheon, were, at the northeast, a municipal edifice, the arenas, and a theatre which has been lately discovered; on the southwest, the camp of the

THE AQUEDUCT OR SEWER OF THE ARENAS OF LUTETIA.

legions; between the two, the imperial palace, supplied by an aqueduct with pure spring water from Arcueil;[1] on the site of the old Hôtel-Dieu, the remains of some triumphal construction, probably posterior to Julian; lastly, on the hill Locoticius a great pottery. The taste of these early Parisian artists may be judged of by the accompanying representations of vases found in this neighborhood.

Every year in the autumn Julian came to the Palais des Thermes which still bears his name; and men wondered to see this young conqueror lead the life of a philosopher in the impe-

[1] Another aqueduct brought to the Gallic city water from the hills of Passy.

rial residence. In the coldest weather he had no fire; his bed
was a couch of skins; his food, a soldier's rations; and he divided his virtuous and industrious life between public affairs
and books. He secured to the provinces that which they most
needed; namely, an upright administration, conducted in the in-

VASES OF TERRA COTTA FROM THE POTTERY OF LUTETIA.[1]

terests of the persons governed.[2] He prevented the praetorian
prefect Florentius from increasing the taxes; and to show him
that he demanded too much, he examined the latter's accounts.
No informers were allowed in the palace; but if any man sought
for redress, he was sure to obtain it if his cause were good.[3] In

---

[1] Grivaud (*Antiquités gauloises et romaines*, 1807) has represented a great number of fragments found in the excavations made for the substructures of the Pantheon and the Luxem-
bourg. Some of these may now be seen in the Musée Carnavalet. Later (chap. cix. sect. 2)
will be represented the fragments of a triumphal arch (?) recently discovered in clearing the
ground of the last remnants of the Hôtel-Dieu. M. Cousin has collected these bas-reliefs in
the *Musée municipal.*

[2] See his *Letter* 17, addressed to Oribasius.

[3] Amm. Marcellinus relates that when an advocate exclaimed, " What criminal would not
be esteemed innocent if it were sufficient to deny!" Julian replied: " And what innocent man
would not pass for guilty if it were sufficient to accuse!"

NAVE OF THE THILMES (PRESENT CONDITION).

the evening Julian gathered philosophers and learned men about him, if any were in the neighborhood, or else he occupied himself with Eusebia's Greek books.   He did not disdain to listen to the advice of the wise Eutherius, his chamberlain, a faithful servant, who instead of laboring to corrupt his master, as eunuchs were wont to do, placed at his service the results of experience

REMAINS OF JULIAN'S PALACE IN PARIS (PALAIS DES THERMES), EXTERIOR.

and a passion for well-doing.[1] Whether this man was pagan or Christian, we know not. Two of Julian's best friends were, however, followers of the old religion. — Oribasius, his physician, and Sallust, his most valued lieutenant.   He encouraged the former to make an abridgment of the writings of Galen,[2] and with the

[1] . . . Beneficiendi avidus . . . etiam Julianum aliquoties corrigebat (Amm. Marcellinus, xvi. 7). Another eunuch had been Julian's preceptor, from whom he acquired his love of Greek literature.

[2] The Ἰατρικαὶ συναγωγαί, of which nearly half has been preserved.   It is a sort of medical encyclopædia, formed of extracts from the writings of Galen and the most renowned phy-

latter he discussed the campaigns they had made together and, when they were alone, the divinity they both worshipped, the Sun-god. Upon this subject he was with all the rest more silent than Pythagoras, and no man witnessed the secret devotions which he performed every morning to Mercury, "the Supreme Mover of the world and the principle of all intelligence."[1] He wrote much. His History of the Gallic War is lost; but we have many of his books, among others *The Enemy of the Beard*, a satire upon the people of Antioch, composed at a later period, in which he makes mention of his "dear Lutetia" and of the Gauls. "They worship Venus,"—he says, but we cannot take his words as exactly true, — "because they consider this goddess as presiding over marriage ; and in adoring Bacchus and liberally using his gifts, they obtain from the god only an innocent gratification."

Another of his works, *The Caesars*, is a little satiric drama, containing much truth and some malice.[2] We are so soon to take leave of the Empire that it will not be without interest to pass, with Julian, his predecessors in review, and notice his judgments upon them.

The time is the Saturnalia, the great pagan festival. By way of amusement in these days devoted to pleasure, Julian relates to his friend Sallust the story of a celestial banquet. Romulus has invited the gods and the Caesars to a repast. "The gods were entertained on the summit of heaven," says Julian, "and the Caesars below the moon in the highest region of the air. Thither they were wafted and there they were buoyed up by the lightness of the bodies with which they were invested, and by the revolution of the moon. Four couches of exquisite workmanship were spread for the superior deities. That of Saturn was formed of polished ebony, which reflected a divine lustre that was insupportable ; for on viewing this ebony the eye was as much dazzled by the excess of light as it is by gazing steadfastly on the sun.

sicians. At the beginning of his first book Oribasius says: "Emperor Julian, I have finished, according to your desire while we were in Gaul, the abridgment which your Divinity commanded."

[1] . . . *Mundi velociorem sensum, motum mentium* (Amm. Marcellinus, xvi. 5).

[2] [This satire is called by Gibbon one of the most agreeable and instructive productions of ancient wit.]

That of Jupiter was more splendid than silver, and too white to be gold; but whether this should be called electrum,[1] or what other name should be given it, Mercury, although he had inquired of the metallists, could not precisely inform me." When the gods were seated, Silenus places himself near Bacchus, and entertains the god with his sarcastic comments upon the Caesars as they arrive. First comes Julius, strong and handsome, with a lordly air, as of one who has ambition enough to seek to dethrone Jupiter himself. Then Octavius arrives. "He assumed, like a chameleon, various colors; at first appearing pale, then black, dark, and cloudy, and at last exhibiting the charms of Venus and the Graces. In the lustre of his eyes he seemed willing to rival the sun,[2] nor could any one encounter his look." Silenus exclaims at his appearance, and fears he may do some mischief; but Apollo, interposing, consigns Augustus to Zeno for instruction, who in a few moments causes the Emperor to become wise and virtuous.

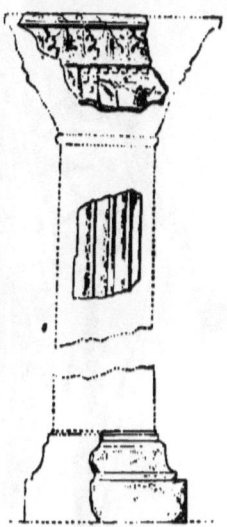

FRAGMENTS.[3]

The third who approaches is Tiberius, with grave but fierce aspect, at once wise and terrible, but showing scars, the traces of his crimes and vices. Silenus calls him an old satyr, although much afraid of him, and wishes him back in his solitary Island of Capri.

Then advances a dreadful monster; this is Caligula. The gods avert their eyes. Nemesis delivers him to the avenging Furies, and he is at once flung into Tartarus.

On the approach of Claudius, Silenus scoffs; he begs Romulus to send for Narcissus and Pallas, and also for Messalina. "Without

<hr />

[1] [This word is used by the ancient writers in two different senses,—either for amber, or for a mixed metal composed of four parts of gold with one of silver.

[2] "His eyes were bright and lively, and he affected to have it thought there was a certain divine vigor in them, and was wonderfully pleased if any one when he looked earnestly upon him, turned down his eyes to the ground, as at the lustre of the sun" (Suet., *Aug. C.* 79).]

[3] Fragments of columns found in the Palais des Thermes.

them," he says, "Claudius appears like guards in a tragedy, mute and inanimate."

Next enters Nero, playing on his harp and crowned with

laurel.   Silenus turns to Apollo and says: "This man makes you his model." "I shall soon uncrown him," replies Apollo; "he did not imitate me in everything, and when he did he was a bad imitator;" upon which Nero is swept away discrowned by the River Cocytus.

After this, seeing many come crowding together, — Vindex, Otho, Galba, Vitellius, — Silenus exclaims: "Where, ye gods, have you found such a multitude of monarchs? We are suffocated with smoke, for beasts of this kind spare not even the temples of the gods."[1] Thereupon, Jupiter calls for Vespasian to come from Egypt and extinguish these flames; but the god sends Titus away con-

JUPITER.[2]

temptuously, and will have Domitian chained with Phalaris, "the Sicilian tiger."

"Then came an old man [Nerva] of a beautiful aspect (for even old age is sometimes beautiful); in his manners most gentle, and in his administration mild. With him Silenus was so

---

[1] The reference is to the burning of the temple of Jupiter Capitolinus under Vitellius and by his partisans.]

[2] Bronze statuette (sixteen and one half centimetres in height), found near Châlon-sur-Saône, in 1763, in a perfect state of preservation (*Cabinet de France*, No. 2,922).

delighted that he remained silent. 'What,' said Mercury, 'have you nothing to say of this man?' 'Yes, by Jupiter,' he replied; 'for I charge you all with partiality in suffering that bloodthirsty monster to reign fifteen years, but this man scarce a year.' 'Do not complain,' answered Jupiter; 'many good princes shall succeed him.'"

Next enters Trajan, bearing Getic and Parthian trophies, — but on his arrival Silenus begs Jupiter to be careful lest his cup-bearer, Ganymede, be stolen away from him, — and then, "a venerable sage [Hadrian] with a long beard, an adept in music, gazing frequently on the heavens and curiously investigating the abstrusest subjects; and then Antoninus, 'important in trifles, one of those who would harangue about a pin's point.'

"At the entrance of the brothers, Marcus Aurelius and Lucius Verus, Silenus contracted his brows, as he could by no means jeer at or deride them: Marcus in particular, although he strictly scrutinized his conduct with regard to Commodus his son, and his wife Fausta, — as to her, his immoderate grief for her death, though she little deserved it; as to him, in hazarding the ruin of the Empire by preferring him to a discreet son-in-law who would have made a better ruler, and studied the advantage of his son more than he did himself. Notwithstanding these failings, Silenus could not but admire his exalted virtue. Thinking his son [Commodus] unworthy of any stroke of wit, he silently dismissed him. And the latter, not being able to support himself or associate with the heroes, fell down to earth."

On the arrival of Pertinax, Nemesis reproaches him with knowledge of the conspiracy by which his predecessor was destroyed. "He was succeeded by Severus, a prince inexorable in punishing. 'Of him,' says Silenus, 'I have nothing to say; for I am terrified by his stern and implacable looks.'" Geta is simply dismissed from the banquet, but Caracalla is sent to be punished for his crimes. Macrinus and "the youth of Emesa" [Elagabalus] are driven from the sacred enclosure, and "Alexander the Syrian" is censured for his avarice and his subjection to his mother.

The seven Emperors next following are omitted, and it is believed the text is here mutilated. Then enters Gallienus with his father Valerian, the latter dragging the chain of his captivity, the former effeminate both in his dress and behavior; and Jupiter orders them both to depart from the banquet.[1]

" They were succeeded by Claudius, on whom all the gods fixed their eyes, admiring his magnanimity, and granted the Empire to his descendants, thinking it just that the posterity of such a lover of his country should enjoy the sovereignty as long as possible." [2] It will be remembered that Julian was the descendant of Claudia, sister to Claudius II.

Then entered Aurelian in haste, as if escaping from those who were accusing him before Minos of many murders which he could not deny or palliate. " But my Lord the Sun," says Julian, "assisted him by informing the gods that the Delphic oracle, ' That he who evil does should evil suffer, is righteous judgment,' had been in this case fulfilled."

While the gods are admiring the energetic Probus, Silenus remonstrates with him upon his harshness, and Bacchus is amazed to hear the old joker speak so gravely for a moment. Carus and his sons Carinus and Numerianus are repulsed by Nemesis, and then Diocletian approaches, and with him the two Maximians and Constantius. " These, though they held each other by the hand, did not walk on a line with Diocletian. Three others also surrounded him in the manner of a chorus; but when, like harbingers, they would have preceded him, he forbade them, not thinking himself entitled to any distinction; and transferring to them a burden which he had borne on his own shoulders, he walked with much greater ease. But Maximian, behaving with imprudence and haughtiness, Silenus, though he did not think him deserving of ridicule, would not admit him into the society of the Emperors. Besides, by his impertinent officiousness and perfidy he often interrupted the harmonious concert. Nemesis

---

[1] ["Gallienus deserved to be excluded. But Julian seems to represent the gods as ungrateful. Ought they thus to treat the unfortunate Valerian, who was so zealous for their worship? Misfortune, after all, is not a crime. But it should be remembered that Valerian was taken by his own fault, and that according to the pagan ideas, being a prisoner, he ought to have shortened his disgrace and not have survived his liberty. When Perseus, king of Macedon, applied to Paulus Aemilius not to lead him in triumph, the Roman considered him a coward, and made answer that the Macedonian king's fate was and had been at all times in his own power." — La Bletterie.]

[2] [In the judgment of Gibbon, this was not adulation, but superstition and vanity.]

therefore soon banished him, and whither he went I know not, as I forgot to ask Mercury.

"To this most melodious tetrachord, a harsh, disagreeable, and discordant sound succeeded. Two of the candidates [1] Nemesis would not suffer to approach even the door of the assembly. Licinius came thus far ; but having been guilty of many crimes, he was repulsed by Minos. Constantine entered and sat some time, and near him sat his sons. As for Magnentius, he was refused admittance because he had never done anything laudable, although many of his actions might appear brilliant ; but the gods, perceiving that they did not flow from a good principle, dismissed him, much afflicted."

Then follows a competition for a seat among the heroes, and Julius Caesar, Augustus, and Trajan, being the greatest of Roman warriors, are recognized as candidates for this honor. But

SILENUS. [2]

Hercules insists that Alexander of Macedon be added to the list. Saturn urges the claims of a philosopher, and Marcus Aurelius is also included. Finally, Constantine completes the number. They urge their respective claims, and when the arguments are ended. "it was expected," says Julian, "that the gods would have immediately determined the pre-eminence by their votes. But they

[1] [Maxentius and Maximin Daza.]
[2] Bronze statuette of Roman workmanship (height, 34 centim.), *Cabinet de France*.

thought it proper first to examine the intentions of the candidates, and not merely to collect them from their actions, in which Fortune had the greatest share; and that goddess, being present, loudly reproached them all, Augustus alone excepted, who, she said, had always been grateful to her." The candidates are then questioned one by one as to what each thought the highest excellence, and at what he had principally aimed in the important actions of his life. Alexander at once replies, "Universal dominion." Caesar declares his chief aim to have been to excel his contemporaries, and neither to be nor to be thought second to any. Augustus announces his great desire, "To reign well." Trajan claims the same view with Alexander, "but with more moderation." Marcus Aurelius, being questioned by Mercury, replies with a low voice and great diffidence : "To imitate the gods." Constantine's answer is that, having amassed great riches, it was his principal aim to expend them liberally for the gratification of his own desires and those of his friends. After each of these answers much debate follows among the gods; the candidates are sharply questioned, and defend themselves as best they can. The answers having all been given, the gods vote, but privately, and Marcus Aurelius receives the coveted honor. To console the defeated, they are allowed to remain and to place themselves under some special guardian and protector. Upon this, Alexander hastens to Hercules, Augustus to Apollo, Marcus Aurelius attaches himself closely to Jupiter and Saturn, Caesar wanders hither and thither till Mars and Venus, moved with compassion, call him to them, Trajan joins Alexander, "but Constantine, not finding among the gods the model of his actions, and perceiving the Goddess of Pleasure, repaired to her; she received him very courteously, embraced him, and then, dressing him in a woman's variegated gown, led him away to Luxury. . . . 'As for you,' said Mercury, addressing himself to me, 'I have introduced you to the knowledge of your father the Sun; obey then his dictates, making him your guide and secure refuge while you live; and when you leave the world, adopt him with good hopes for your tutelar god.'"

To gain victories, to set free twenty thousand captives, to build up cities, to husband the public resources so that instead of extra taxes there were reductions made, bringing down the *caput* from twenty-five to seven *aurei;*[1] finally, to employ in literary pursuits hours stolen from sleep, — such a life as this shows the truly great man. The populations whom he protected against the public treasury and against extortioners, after having set them free from the Barbarians, blessed the young imperator. But the men placed about him to rule over his conduct were full of anger against a prince who gave them no opportunities, who himself watched over everything, examining all questions with such clear-sighted intelligence that he went straight and promptly to the best decisions. The praetorian prefect Florentius, reduced to the position of a subordinate held strictly to account,

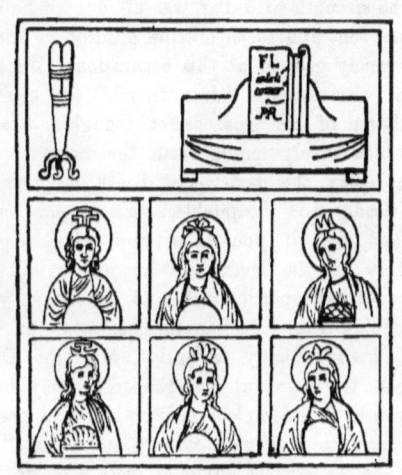

INSIGNIA OF THE VICAR OF THE DIOCESE OF THRACE.[2]

revenged himself by insulting and satirical letters sent to the court. "Of himself," the prefect wrote, "Julian can do nothing; it is Sallust who directs affairs, and with this general the Caesar may become dangerous." At Milan all sorts of scandalous reports were current. The courtiers, disposed to say that Constantius

---

[1] While reducing the amount of the taxation, he was very strict in levying it with punctuality, and would suffer no arrearages, — that scourge of the Roman finances (Amm. Marcell., xvi. 5, and xvii. 2). The tax of twenty-five *aurei* on the thousand (two and a half per cent) was exceptional, and occasioned by circumstances concerning which we are ignorant. When, as a consequence of civil wars or invasions, industry and traffic languished, the indirect taxes and the *chrysargyrum* brought in but little. Then, to make good the deficit, the government bore heavily upon the landed property. This must have been the case in Gaul. The tax of seven *aurei* seems to have been the usual one, for we find it in 445 (*Nov. Valent.* III. tit. v. sect. 4). If the property brought in three per cent, the proprietor retained for income in the first case only one half per cent, and in the second, two and three tenths per cent. This was, therefore, a very considerable diminution of tax in the case of the Gauls, and must have secured their devotion to Julian.

[2] *Notitia dignitatum*, Böcking, p. 65.

in person had gained the battle of Strasburg, turned into derision the bulletins of "the little conqueror," *victorinus*, "the ape clad in purple," "the braggart mole." The Emperor knew how worthless all this gossip was; but it pleased him, nevertheless. He was weary of this increasing fame; and since Florentius declared that the strength of Julian was all due to Sallust, he recalled the latter and sent him to an obscure position in Thrace. The Caesar was extremely grieved at this separation. We have the sad letter which he wrote to his "dear friend," the companion of his labors, the sharer of his most secret thoughts, — a letter ending in words which surely sprang from the heart: "And now, wherever you go, may the benevolent Deity be your guide, and Jupiter, the friendly and hospitable, receive you, conducting you safely by land, and if you take ship, smoothing the waves before you! May you be loved and honored by all men, so that they may rejoice at your arrival, and lament at your departure! Still retaining your affection for me, may you never lack the society of a friend equally faithful! May the Divinity also conciliate to you the favor of the Emperor; may he regulate all concerning you to your complete satisfaction, and grant you a safe and speedy return to your own country and to us!"

More serious anxieties were soon to assail the young Caesar. Constantius was about to call away half of the army of the Gauls.

IV. —THE PERSIAN WAR RENEWED; JULIAN PROCLAIMED AUGUSTUS; DEATH OF CONSTANTIUS (361).

THE Emperor had remained at Milan. This city he rarely quitted, except, as in 357, for a triumphal entry into the old capital of the world, which he greatly admired, but in which the Persian Hormisdas, who accompanied him, remarked that men died, as they did elsewhere;[1] or, as in 358, for a rapid expedition

---

[1] Amm. Marcellinus (xvi. 10) gives curious details concerning this triumphal entry of Constantius into Rome, where for thirty-two years no Emperor had been seen, and Symmachus (x. 54) concerning the Emperor's visits to pagan temples, his respect for the Vestals, his gifts for festivals and public sacrifices, the priesthoods conferred by him upon noble Romans, etc. Lastly, to recompense the city for its welcome, Constantius caused to be

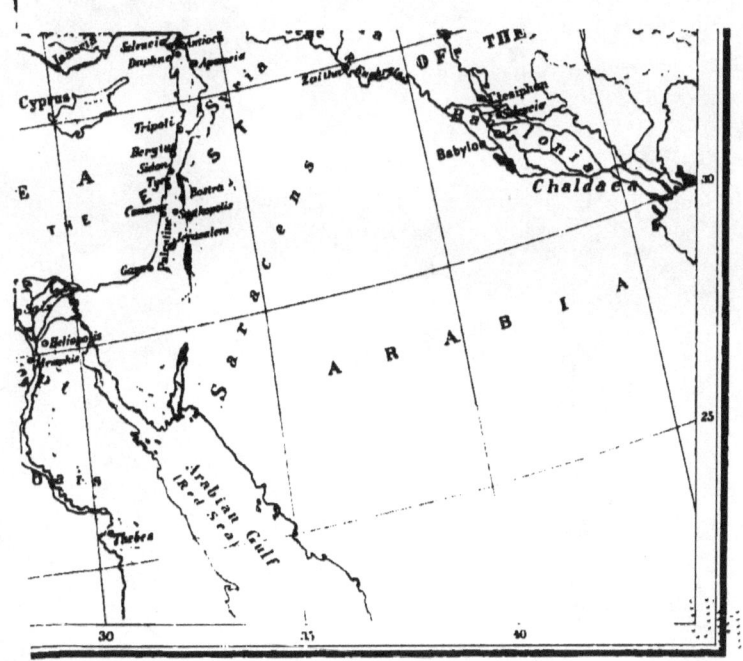

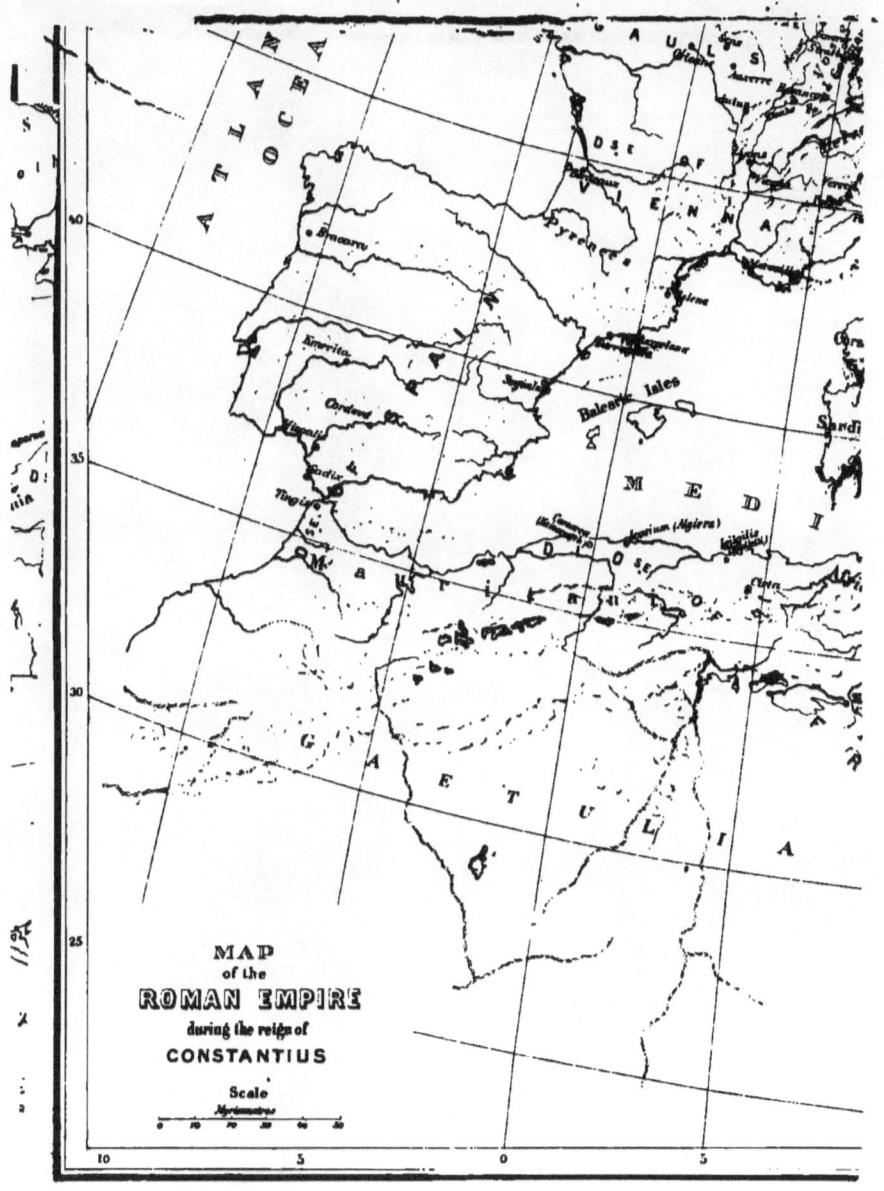

MAP
of the
ROMAN EMPIRE
during the reign of
CONSTANTIUS

Scale
Myriametres

against the Alemanni of Rhaetia and a brief campaign against the Barbarians of the Middle Danube, where an easy victory gave him the surname of Sarmaticus. Religious disputes occupied him much more closely. He wished, like his father, to govern the

THE TRIUMPH OF CONSTANTIUS AT ROME.[1]

Church. To succeed in this, a monarch must be extremely powerful; Constantine himself never obtained anything more than a relative tranquillity. Under Constantius the Empire was perpetually agitated by the disputes of the Arians and the Orthodox; of these we shall speak later: they were quarrels always more

brought from Egypt the obelisk which still stands in the square of St. John Lateran. We may notice that although himself a zealous Arian, Constantius made no attack upon paganism at Rome, except to order the altar of Victory to be removed from the curia while he himself was there. He had made the pagan Themistius senator of Constantinople, and he sent another pagan, the philosopher Eustathius, as ambassador to Sapor.

[1] Collection of Tobias Biehler at Vienna. This cameo, on agate-onyx, published by the Rev. C. W. King, of Trinity College, in vol. iv. of the *Cambridge Antiquarian Society's Communications*, May, 1880, is the eleventh in size among known cameos, but it is among the very poorest as a work of art. Compare it with the cameos of Augustus, Tiberius, and Septimius Severus, represented in the colored plate, Vol. IV., and in the text illustrations, Vol. IV. p. 265, and Vol. VI. p. 504, and its great inferiority will be obvious. In this cameo is the hero of the occasion Constantius, or Constantine? I believe it to be the former, who made a triumphal entry into Rome in 357, while we have no account that Constantine ever did so.

noisy than dangerous.   He also proposed to suppress all indiscreet
search into the future.   The magicians seem to have alarmed him

THE TRIUMPHAL ENTRY OF CONSTANTIUS INTO ROME.[1]

extremely, for he set on foot an actual persecution against all who
questioned the stars or the oracles.   In 359 the *magister peditum*,

[1] Gori, *Diptychon Barberinum*, published in his *Thesaurus diptychorum veterum*, vol. ii.
pl. L p. 168.   Above, two Victories, each holding a shield; between, the Christ blessing

Barbatio, much disturbed by the arrival in his house of a swarm of bees, consulted the diviners as to this omen, and learned from them that it announced an event of great importance. This event which Destiny had in hand could be nothing less, the general thought, than the approaching death of the Emperor, to be followed by his own accession to the imperial dignity; and his wife, Assyria, in her imagination seeing him already invested with the purple, implored him, in a letter written in cipher, not to prefer to herself the Empress Eusebia on account of the latter's beauty. A copy of this letter was brought to Constantius by the treachery of a slave. According to the old beliefs, which when driven out from men's minds had left behind them a multitude of superstitions, an evil thought was a beginning of crime; and these puerile hopes had always been considered as treason.[1] Barbatio and his wife were beheaded; and, as was the custom, the friends of both shared the same fate.

These pretended conspiracies, which disturbed the court, did not agitate the Empire; but an unforeseen peril threatened it in the East.

Sapor, at last making an end of the wars which had long detained him in the eastern provinces of his Empire, claimed anew the whole of Armenia, and Mesopotamia with it.[2] In 359, guided by a deserter who furnished him with plans of the fortresses and details of the condition of the arsenals and of the distribution of the Roman troops in the East, he crossed the Tigris at Nineveh

with the right hand, and holding in the left a sceptre surmounted by a cross. In the centre the Emperor on horseback, and a suppliant Barbarian; the horse has the *phalarae* of which our collections furnish many examples; a woman supports the Emperor's foot, and by what she bears in her robe doubtless symbolizes abundance. Above, at the right, is a Victory holding a palm, its feet are placed upon the globe of the world, representing symbolically the words *toto orbe recepto*, placed by Constantius in one of the four inscriptions of the obelisk transported by him to Rome. At the left is a man holding in his hand a Victory and having a sack of gold at his feet. In the lower section of the diptych is still another Victory, and Barbarians offering gifts. In the effaced compartment at the right are legible the words: *Constantius Dominus noster.*

[1] See in Amm. Marcellinus (xxix. 1) how this passion for penetrating the future had spread, and how many victims it made during the reign of Valens. The methods at that time employed, remind one of the table-tipping of recent times.

[2] Amm. Marcellinus (xvii. 5) has preserved this letter of Sapor (who styles himself "the brother of the Sun"), and the reply of Constantius to his "brother, king Sapor." We observe that the phraseology employed by modern kings towards one another is very ancient. The style of Marcellinus is often diffuse; the account given in the text of the siege of Amida is greatly abridged.

with an army said to be a hundred thousand strong. For this campaign we have the story of an eye-witness, Amm. Marcellinus, who
is able to tell us how in those days a great siege was conducted.

"I was sent," he says, "with a centurion to the satrap of
Corduene, who ordered me to be conducted to the top of some high
rocks, whence with good eyesight a man could see for a distance
of fifty miles. Here we remained waiting for two days, and on
the morning of the third day the whole horizon was filled with
countless hosts of men, the king marching before them, glittering
with the brilliancy of his robes. The king had crossed the river
at Nineveh; and we, calculating that the whole host could hardly
pass over in less than three days, returned with speed to the
satrap and brought word of what we had seen. Upon this, orders
were given to compel the residents of the country to retire with
their families and all their flocks to a safer place, and that all
the standing crops should be burned.

"When these orders had been executed, and the fire was kin-
dled, the violence of the raging element so completely destroyed
all the corn, which was beginning to swell and turn green [April
or May], and all the young herbage, that from the Euphrates to
the Tigris nothing remained. Fearing to be cut off from provisions, Sapor, with his army, advanced through the grassy valleys
at the foot of the mountains; and finding that the Euphrates
could not be crossed, being swollen by the melting of the snow,
determined to direct their march to the right through a region
fertile in everything, and still undestroyed. When our generals
received intelligence of this from their spies, we determined to
march in haste to Samosata to destroy the bridges at Zeugma
and Capersana, and thus check the enemy's invasion if we could
find a favorable chance for attacking them." On the road an
engagement took place, and the Romans, being defeated, fled in
a great panic and threw themselves into the town of Amida, a
fortified position, where the Parthian legion, with a considerable
squadron of native cavalry, were in garrison. They were reinforced
by six legions, two of which were Gallic (who by forced marches
had outstripped the Persian host), and some squadrons of companion
archers, — corps in which all the freeborn Barbarians served, and
conspicuous for the splendor of their arms, and their prowess.

"Marching slowly, on the third day the king came to Amida.[1] And at daybreak everything as far as we could see glittered with shining arms, and an iron cavalry filled the plains and the hills. The king himself, mounted on his charger and taller than the rest, led his whole army, wearing, instead of a crown, a golden figure of a ram's head inlaid with jewels; being also splendid from the retinue of men of high rank and of different nations which followed him. He' rode up to the gates to try the garrison with a parley; and the Deity of Heaven, mercifully limiting the disasters of the Empire, led this king to such an extravagant degree of elation that he seemed to believe that as soon as he appeared, the besieged would be suddenly panic-stricken, and have recourse to supplication and entreaty. Pushing on boldly, so that his very features could be plainly recognized, his ornaments made him such a mark for arrows and other missiles that he would have been slain if the dust had not hindered the sight of those who were shooting at him. His mantle, however, was pierced by a javelin; upon which he withdrew, raging as if against sacrilegious men who had violated a temple, and crying out that the lord of so many monarchs and nations had been insulted, and resolved to use all his efforts to destroy the city. But on the following day he sent Grumbates, king of the Chionitae, to demand first that the garrison should surrender. The garrison, however, replied to this demand by a shower of arrows, one of which struck down the king's son who rode at his side. — a young man in the flower of his age, a prince who in stature and beauty was superior to his comrades. After a whole day's contest the body of the young prince was recovered by the Persians and borne with great lamentations into their camp. Then a cessation of arms was ordered, and for seven days the youth, so noble and beloved, was mourned after the fashion of his nation with a funeral feast, dancing, and singing melancholy dirges; and the women, with pitiable wailing, deplored the hope of their nation cut off in his early youth. . . . Then Sapor determined to propitiate the shade of the dead prince by making the destroyed city of Amida his monument.

"Having given two days to rest, and sent out large bodies of

[1] Saint-Martin, in his *Mémoires historiques*, i. 166–173, places Amida on the site of the ancient Tigranocerta.

troops to ravage the fertile and well-cultivated fields, which were heavy with crops, the enemy then surrounded the city with a line of heavy armed soldiers five deep; and at the beginning of the third day the brilliant squadrons filled every spot as far as the eye could see in every direction, and the ranks, marching slowly, took up their appointed positions. .

"From sunrise to sunset these lines stood immovable, as if rooted to the ground, without changing a step or uttering a word; and then the men, withdrawing in the same order as they had advanced, refreshed themselves with food and sleep, and on the following morning, even before the dawn, led by the clang of brazen trumpets, returned and surrounded the doomed city.

"Then Grumbates, like a Roman herald, gave the signal by hurling at us a blood-stained spear, and the whole army, with clashing arms, rushed up to the walls. The attack was fierce; but soon many of the enemy fell, their heads crushed by great stones hurled from the scorpions. Some were pierced with arrows or transfixed with javelins, and strewed the ground with their bodies; others, wounded, fled back in haste to their companions. Nor was there less grief and slaughter in the city, where the cloud of arrows darkened the air, and the vast engines scattered wounds everywhere. This slaughter lasted till the close of day, and was renewed again the next morning before daybreak, until the losses on both sides caused a longer truce; for when the time intended for rest came to us, continual sleepless toil exhausted our remaining strength, in spite of the dread caused us by the bloodshed and the pallid faces of the dying, whom the scantiness of our room did

NOTE. — The colored plate represents a massive silver cup, which marks the progress of art under the Sassanid kings. This cup (which was presented by the Duc de Luynes to the *Cabinet de France*, where it may be compared with that of Chosroës), of cast and chased silver, with figures gilded and in niello, represents in bas-relief a king of Persia hunting. The monarch, whose horse is going at full speed, is discharging an arrow; before him are fleeing two wild boars and a pig, a buffalo, an *axis*, and an antelope. Many victims of the royal hunter are stretched upon the ground. His costume is very rich; a tiara is upon his head, precious stones adorn his ears, his neck, and his double girdle; the tunic and the *anaxyrides*, or trousers, are embroidered, as also the horse's harness, which, like the bow, is decorated with two floating streamers. These knots, or ends of the *kosti*, are a divine attribute, which from the royal person extend to the objects which are used by him. M. de Longpérier ascribes this cup to King Perosius (fifth century A. D.); but M. Chabouillet is disposed to date this specimen of Oriental silver-work as far back as the reign of Sapor II., the adversary of Constantius. Cf. *Catalogue général*, etc., No. 2,881, pp. 468, 469, and *Annales de l'Institut archéol.* xv. 98.

THE SILVER CUP OF A PERSIAN KING

not permit us even the last solace of burying, since within the circuit of a moderate city there were seven legions, and a vast promiscuous multitude of citizens and strangers of both sexes, and other soldiers, so that at least twenty thousand men were shut up within the walls.

"In the meantime the restless Persians were surrounding the city with a fence of wicker work, and mounds were commenced; lofty towers were also constructed, with iron fronts, in the top of each of which a balista was placed, in order to drive down the garrison from the battlements. But during the whole time the shower of missiles from the archers and slingers never ceased for a moment. . . .

"At the dawn of the next morning we saw from the citadel an innumerable multitude, which, after the capture of the fort called Ziata, was led to the evening's camp; for a promiscuous multitude had taken refuge in Ziata on account of its size and strength, it being a place ten furlongs in circumference. In those days many other fortresses were stormed and burnt, and many thousands of men and women carried off from them into slavery. — among whom were many men and women enfeebled by age, who broke down under the length of the journey, gave up all desire of life, were hamstrung, and left behind. Our Gallic soldiers beholding these wretched crowds. demanded to be led against the enemy, threatening their tribunes and centurions with death if they refused them leave. Permission being at last given them, armed with axes and swords they went forth. taking advantage of a dark and moonless night. And imploring the Deity to be propitious. and repressing even their breath when they got near the enemy. they advanced with quick step and in close order. slew some of the watch at the outposts, and the outer sentinels of the camp who were asleep, fearing no such event, and entertained secret hopes of penetrating even to the king's tent. if fortune assisted them. But some noise, though slight, was made by them in their advance, and the groans of the dying aroused many from sleep, and the bands of the Persians were now to be heard flocking to battle from all quarters. Nevertheless the Gallic troops, with undiminished strength and boldness. continued to hew down their foe with their swords, while some of their own men were also slain, pierced by the arrows which were flying from every side. And they still stood firm when they saw the whole danger collected into one point, and the bands of the enemy coming on with speed, yet no one turned his back; and they withdrew, re- tiring slowly, as if in time to music, and gradually fell behind the pales of the camp, being unable to sustain the weight of the battalions pressing close upon them, and deafened by the clang of the Persian trumpets. And while many trumpets in turn poured out their clang from the city, the gates were opened to receive our men if they should be able to reach them; and the engines for missiles were heard playing, although no javelins were shot from them, so that the Persians might be terrified by the noise into falling back, and so allowing our gallant troops to be admitted in safety.

"Owing to this manœuvre the Gauls about daybreak entered the gate, although with diminished numbers, many of them se- verely and others slightly wounded, and having lost about four hundred men. . . . To their leaders, as champions of valiant ac- tions, the Emperor, after the fall of the city, ordered statues in armor to be set up at Edessa in a frequented spot. And these statues are preserved up to the present time unhurt.

"When the next day showed the slaughter which had been made, nobles and satraps were found lying among the corpses, and all kinds of dissonant cries and wailings indicated the grief of the Persian host. . . . A truce was made for three days by common consent, and we gladly accepted a little respite in which to take breath. . . .

"And now the Persians, rendered more savage than ever, de- termined to proceed with their works, and with extreme warlike eagerness hastened to die gloriously, or else to propitiate the souls of the dead by the destruction of the city. All kinds of structures and iron towers were brought up to the walls, on the lofty summits of which balistae were fitted, which beat down the garrison who were below them, and spread great slaughter in our ranks. At last, when evening came on, both sides retired to rest, and the greater part of the night was spent by us in considering what device could be adopted to resist the formidable engines of the enemy. At length, after we had considered many plans, we

determined on one which appeared the safest, because it could be
the most rapidly effected ; namely, to oppose four scorpions to
the enemy's four balistae, which were carefully moved (a very
difficult operation) from the place in which they were. But before
the work was finished, day arrived, bringing us a mournful sight,
inasmuch as it showed us the formidable battalions of the Persians with their trains of elephants, the noise and size of which
animals are such that nothing more terrible can be presented to
the mind of man.

"And while we were pressed on all sides with the vast masses
of arms and works and beasts, still our scorpions were kept at
work with their iron slings, hurling huge round stones from the
battlements, and baskets of burning pitch and tar, by which the
towers of the enemy were crushed and set on fire, and the balistae
and those that worked them were dashed to the ground, so that
many were fatally injured, being crushed by the falling structures, and the elephants were driven violently back, and also,
surrounded by flames, retreated, and could not be controlled by
their riders. The works were all burnt; but still there was no
cessation of the conflict, for the king of the Persians himself,[1]
who is never expected to mingle in the conflict, sprang forth
like a common soldier among his own dense columns, and as
the number of his guards made him the more conspicuous, he
was assailed by numerous missiles, and forced to retire after he
had lost many of his escort.

"On the following day Sapor, full of rage and indignation,
called forth his people again to attack us ; and as his works had
been all burned, the attack had to be conducted by means of their
lofty mounds raised close to our walls, while we also from mounds
within the walls, as fast as we could raise them, struggled, in spite
of all our difficulties, with all our might, and with equal courage,
against our assailants. The conflict was prolonged until at last,
while the fortune of the two sides was still undetermined, the
structure raised by our men, having been long assailed and shaken,
at last fell, as if by an earthquake ; and the whole space which
was between the wall and the external mound, being made level

---

[1] The personal gallantry of Sapor is well known ; he exposed his life in the same way at
the siege of Bezabde. Constantius was much more prudent.

as if by a causeway or a bridge, opened a free passage to the
enemy.   By the king's command all his troops now hastened
into action, and a hand-to-hand engagement ensued.   The city being filled by the eager crowd which forced its way in, all hope
of defence or escape was cut off, and armed and unarmed, without any distinction of age or sex, were slaughtered like sheep.
. . . After the massacres and plunder of the destroyed city, the
count Aelianus and the tribunes, by whose vigor the walls of
Amida had been defended and the losses of the Persians multiplied, were wickedly crucified; and Jacobus and Caesius, the
treasurers of the commander of the cavalry, and others of the
band of *protectores*, were led as prisoners with their hands bound
behind their backs; and the people of the district beyond the
Tigris, who were diligently sought for, were all slain, without distinction of rank or dignity."   The historian tells us that he succeeded in making his escape (359).   The city fell at the close of
autumn (*autumno praecipiti*).   The invasion by the Persians had
therefore lasted about six months.

Amida had held out seventy-three days, and its capture cost
the Persians thirty thousand men; Sapor was no longer in a

position to undertake anything, and
he returned into his own kingdom.
But encouraged by this success, he
set out again, the winter being over,
with a powerful army, and took
Singara, which he destroyed, and
Bezabde, which he fortified.   Roman

COIN OF SINGARA.[1]

deserters had taught the Persian king that the capture of important
cities was much more useful in extending his empire than victories
in the open field and the richest of booty.   Constantius, alarmed,
proceeded to the East, and ordered Julian to send him most of his
auxiliaries, and with them three hundred picked men from the
other corps.[2]   The demand was not unreasonable; the welfare of

---

[1] ΑΥΤΟΚΡ. Μ. ΑΝΤ. ΓΟΡΔΙΑΝΟC CEB.   Bust of Gordian.   On the reverse: ΑΥΡ[ηλια]
CEΠΤ[ιμια] ΚΟΛ[ωνια] CINΓAΡA; personification of the city, turreted and surmounted by the
sagittarius.   (Bronze coin.)

[2] According to Julian's account, he had already sent to the Emperor four cohorts of
foot, three troops of cavalry, and two legions (*Letter to the Athenians*, sect. 10).   Amm.

the Empire required that the Gallic army, having now no enemies to encounter, should contribute to save the Oriental provinces; but the Emperor's order caused consternation among the troops and throughout the country. The auxiliaries had enlisted with the condition that they should never be called to serve beyond the Alps; and the legionaries, for the most part born in Gaul, were terrified at the idea of being sent into the depths of Asia, whence, even if victorious, they could never hope to return. Soon murmurs are heard; libels upon Constantius are circulated "in the two legions of Celts and Petulantes," where the complaints of "abandoned Gaul" are set forth. Julian, apprehensive of resistance, advises the messengers who have brought the imperial rescript to send the troops away in small detachments, and, above all, not to let them pass through Lutetia, his place of residence.[1] They believe a snare is hidden under this prudence, and insist that the Caesar himself shall give the order for departure. Julian urges the soldiers to obedience; he bids them adieu kindly; he gives them huge wagons, in which, along with the baggage, their wives and children may be carried; and he returns into the palace quite decided to lay down the purple, that he may not be responsible for the woes about to fall upon unprotected Gaul. The remainder of the day passed quietly, without outcries or tumult of any kind, only a growing excitement was discernible in the camp; groups gathered around some speaker, then broke up, to form again. At sunset men seemed to have reached a decision; they gathered in a mass, came down to the palace, surrounded it, and thousands of voices raised the alarming cry: "Julian Augustus!"

When their voices reached the ear of Julian, he was alone in a remote room, extremely irresolute, seeing just before him the throne, or else death, — the latter certain, in case he refused. To end his hesitation, he appealed to the gods. "Through a narrow aperture," he says, "I raised my eyes to heaven, and falling prostrate before Jupiter, I begged the god to give me a sign, which

Marcellinus met near the banks of the Tigris one of the Parisii who had deserted to the Persians.

[1] In 1784 there was found, under the Palais de Justice in Paris, an antique cippus, five feet ten inches in height, without inscription, and bearing on each face a divinity in high relief. These are given on the opposite page. Cf. Dulaure, *Histoire de Paris*, vol. i. p. 75, and pl. 4.

he at once bestowed upon me." The young Caesar felt a new strength descend upon him, before which his reluctance gave way. The resolution towards which he inclined became decided in his mind, and, as often happens, he took the secret impulses of his own heart as a sign of the will of the gods.[1] Going out to the soldiers, he promised each man five pieces of gold and a pound of silver; then, as there was no diadem at hand, a standard-bearer put his own collar upon Julian's head.

The revolution cost not one drop of blood. The new Emperor permitted the adherents of Constantius to go away freely, and he sent to the wife of his most dangerous enemy, the prefect Florentius, the necessary authorization to employ the public post (March or April, 360). It was a usurpation, certainly; one which Julian had neither resisted nor brought about. The demands of Constantius had made rebels; the fame and popularity of the Caesar made an Emperor. After a resistance creditable to his honor and his philosophy, he yielded; but we cannot say, with Gregory Nazianzen, that he seized upon the crown to make himself master everywhere.[2] If we search to the bottom of this man's mind, it becomes clear that he never desired the imperial station. All his letters attest this. "Three or four philosophers," he says, "can do the human race more service than a multitude of kings."[3] His supreme ambition was philosophy; but with it there was now mingled a desire to bring about the triumph of this philosophy and of the religion which he had deduced from it.

Julian hoped that Constantius would ratify the wish of the army, and that civil war might thus be avoided. He wrote to the Emperor a truthful account of all that had taken place. His letter was firm, and worthy of himself. He promised to remain faith-

---

[1] The extreme anxiety in which he was at the moment increasing the tendency of his mind to enthusiasm and mysticism, he regarded as a sign from heaven — as an old Roman augur would have done — whatever object happened to appear before his eyes. Later, the unknown sign of which he speaks in his *Letter to the Athenians*, sect. 14, became an apparition of the Genius of the Empire, which predicted to him obscurely his approaching end. This prediction gives date to the account of Amm. Marcellinus (xx. 5). This story was made up after the death of Julian, so that the pagan Emperor might have his celestial vision, as the Christian Emperor had his. Amm. Marcellinus (xxv. 2) represents the Genius of the Empire appearing to Julian a second time on the eve of his death. See close of the following chapter.

[2] *Invect.* i. 46.

[3] *Letter to Themistius*, sect. 8.

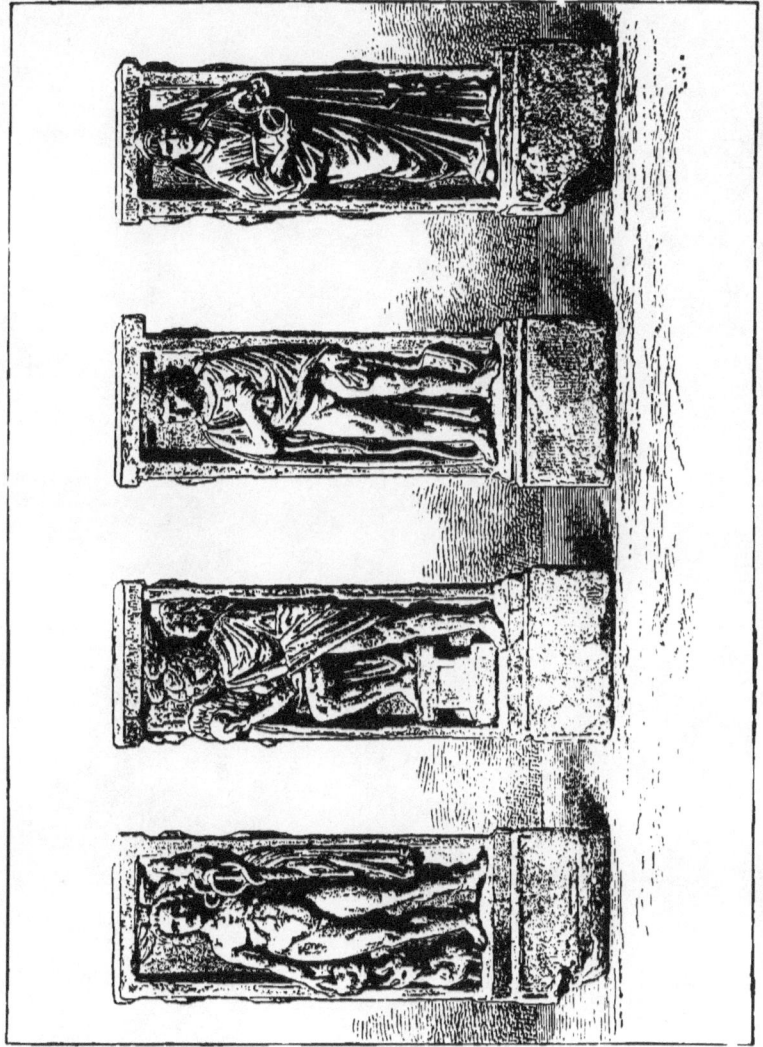

DIVINITIES CARVED ON THE FOUR FACES OF AN ANTIQUE CIPPUS FOUND IN 1781 IN PARIS UNDER THE PALAIS DE JUSTICE

ful to Constantius, to accept from him a praetorian prefect, and
to send to him some military aid, though not as much as the
Emperor had called for.[1]   The legions, on their part, wrote sup-
plicating the Emperor to permit the Caesar to retain the title of
Augustus.   As had occurred a century earlier, Gaul, speaking by
soldiers who were, for the most part, her own children, asked for
a national government.   The Emperor received these communications, in the middle of the year 360,
at Caesarea in Cappadocia, where he
was preparing to march against Sapor.   In order to gain time, he replied with moderation, advised Julian
to content himself with the title of
Caesar, and to receive those whom

JULIAN AUGUSTUS.[2]

he had sent to fill various offices in the army and administration of
the West.   When the messenger of Constantius, the quaestor Leonas,
arrived at Lutetia, Julian, without entering into any discussion
with him, called together the army and had the imperial letter
read aloud in their presence.   The soldiers interrupted the reading
by unanimous cries of "Julian Augustus!"   "You see this," said
the new Emperor to the envoy; "it is the army which refuses to
obey, not I."   In answer to the charge of ingratitude made in the
letter of Constantius, Julian replied only: "It is true that I was
an orphan when the Emperor ascended the throne; and he knows
how I became so."

However, to indicate his respect and his desire for peace, he
accepted the praetorian prefect who was sent him; but the other
officers he dismissed, saying that he had need to choose for himself
those who should serve under him.   A rupture was inevitable.   The
Empress Eusebia had just died; we may hope, and it is possible,
that she never knew of the breaking of those ties which she had
formed.[3]

---

[1] Amm. Marcellinus (xx. 8) speaks of a second letter, stern and threatening, which
was to be given to Constantius privately.

[2] FL. CL. IVLIANVS P. F. AVG. Bust of Julian, bearded and wearing the diadem. On the reverse, VIRTVS EXERCITVS ROMANORVM. Soldier seizing a prisoner
by the hair. (Gold coin.)

[3] Amm. Marcellinus (xxi. 6), speaking of the marriage of Constantius with Faustina at
the close of the year 360, says: *Amissa jampridem Eusebia.*

After an unsuccessful campaign in Mesopotamia, where he had vainly endeavored to retake Bezabde, Constantius returned to pass the winter at Antioch. He occupied his leisure in completing public works for the embellishment of this capital of the Syrian provinces, and for the improvement of the basins of Seleucia, which served it as a harbor; and also in festivals on occasion of a third marriage, and in quarrels with his bishops, — deposing this one, exiling that, and not discerning that it was for his interest, on the approach of civil war, to secure peace in men's souls.[1] Meanwhile he had decided to begin in the spring his campaign against the new Magnentius: he collected troops, ordered great quantities of provisions to be gathered in the fortresses of the Western Alps, and by secret emissaries strove to hurl the Alemanni upon Gaul;[2] he also hoped to shut Julian up in his provinces. A final imperial letter promised "to the Caesar" his life on condition of absolute submission. This haughty language did not intimidate the Gallic Augustus. Julian made ready for the struggle calmly and prudently. He granted a general amnesty to the partisans of Magnentius, who for seven years had been living in concealment in Gaul or among the Germans, dreading the hatred of Constantius; and he thus gave himself ardent supporters of his own cause. That his provinces might not be exposed to alarm during his absence, he employed three months in visiting the banks of the Rhine, fortifying cities and castles, supplying them with provisions and men, and bringing the Roman standards so near to the Barbarians that he had reason to believe that the latter would retain a respectful fear of them.[3] He returned through the valley of the Doubs, visiting the strongholds of Mandeure and Besançon, which protected the valley of the Rhône[4] against the Barbarians; and he halted at Vienne, whence he watched during the winter the passes of the Alps. The Gauls gave him everything he needed, — money, provisions, and soldiers.

---

[1] Socrates, iv. 7; Sozomenus, vi. 26 and 28.

[2] See, in Amm. Marcellinus, xxi. 3, the story of the Aleman king Vadomar, who made an agreement with Constantius to betray Julian, and whose letter was intercepted. Julian, in his *Letter to the Athenians*, and Sozomenus (v. 2) attest the solicitations addressed by Constantius to the Alemanni to induce them to attack Gaul.

[3] Amm. Marcellinus, xx. 10; Julian, *Letter* 38, and *Misop.*, sect. 22.

[4] He has given us, in his *Letter* 38, a very exact description of Besançon.

THE CASCADE OF THE DOUBS.

He proposed to leave to them as their defender his friend Sallust, who at news of the events that had taken place in Lutetia had hastened to join him.   Determining to take the offensive, Julian sent out a manifesto designed to rally to his cause all the

BESANÇON: ROMAN RUINS IN THE SQUARE OF ST. JEAN.

pagans in Greece and Asia.[1] We have his letter addressed to the senate and people of Athens. In this he related his life, his campaign, his elevation, and the murders of Constantius; and he very distinctly stated his belief in the old gods.

At that time an oracle was current among the pagans.

---

[1] At Vienne, where he passed the winter of 360, he was present in the church of that city at the Christian festival of the Epiphany (Amm. Marcellinus, xxi. 2). A few weeks later he offered a sacrifice to Bellona, *placata ritu secretiora Bellona* (*Ibid.* 5).

announcing that the magical arts which Peter had employed to
cause the Christ to be worshipped, would lose their power at the
end of three hundred and sixty-five years.[1] This period was close
at hand; and the oracle was doubtless well known to Julian, who
may easily have believed himself the person designated by the
Sibyl as the avenger promised to the ancient divinities.

The soldiers had revolted that they might not be torn away
from Gaul; but they now joyfully consented to cross the Alps and
the Rhine under their chosen leader. Julian divided his small army
into three corps, — one to advance through the Alps and Upper
Italy; the second, through Rhaetia and Noricum; with the third
— three thousand picked men — he made his way through the
Black Forest to the banks of the Danube. Sirmium was the place
appointed for the rendezvous. Each corps was ordered to advance
by forced marches, that the enemy might not have time to organ-
ize a defence. The flotilla of the Danube, captured by a sudden
advance, in eleven days carried the army, without fighting, into
Pannonia.[2] The population of the river-banks, gathering to see
these soldiers from Gaul pass by, welcomed with clamorous enthusiasm the young general whose victories had already made him
famous. Even Sirmium offered no resistance; his advanced guard
captured the imperial *magister equitum*, and when Julian himself
arrived, both people and soldiers came out to meet him with
torches and garlands of flowers. With a rapidity like that of
the first Caesar, Julian arrived before it was known that he had
set out.

He hastened to occupy Naïssus, where he established his head-
quarters, and the pass of Succi, a defile separating the Rhodope
from the Haemus, and Illyricum from Thrace.[3] Strangely enough,
Constantius had done nothing to protect this important position,
nor had he closed the passes of the Alps in Italy and Noricum.[4]

---

[1] Saint Augustine, *Civ. Dei*, xviii. 53.

[2] Zosimus, iii. 10, and Mamertinus, *Pan. vet.* xi. 8. See, in Sozomenus (v. 2) what
puerilities the Christians at this time accepted with confidence, — the dew which falls on the
garments of the soldiers makes the figure of a cross, and in the entrails of a sacrifice a
crowned cross appears to Julian. Credulity, placed at the service of enthusiasm, was the
malady of the time.

[3] Between Sophia and Philippopolis.

[4] Two legions, faithful to Constantius, had taken refuge in Aquileia, but opened the gates
on hearing of the Emperor's death.

Trusting in his usual good fortune in civil wars, where he had always been victorious, he had concerned himself but little about this new rival, considering the Gallic war as of no more importance than a hunting-party;[1] and he had fulfilled his imperial duties by employing the summer of 361 in a last expedition into Mesopotamia against the Persian king. He was at Edessa when he learned that Julian had taken possession of Illyria. He returned in haste to Antioch, and although in feeble health set out for Europe. At Tarsus he was seized with a fever, and died at Mopsucrene (Nov. 3, 361) in his forty-fifth year, a few days after he had received baptism.[2] Gregory Nazianzen accuses Julian of having poisoned Constantius, — a calumny pleasing to the irritable bishop, but so manifestly false that the Church historians have not ventured to repeat it.

Amm. Marcellinus points out certain good qualities in Constantius, virtues belonging to him as a man rather than as an Emperor, — good morals, sobriety, and a taste for letters: but also the superstitiousness of an old woman,[3] and wordy subtleties with the priests; a rapacity which the cry of the oppressed provinces never abated; a suspicious policy which was ready to put to death even the innocent; lastly, a cruelty which surpassed that of the worst tyrants, taking pleasure in the most ingenious refinements of torture, that punishment might be carried to the utmost extreme without taking life.[4] Such is the portrait of Constantius, drawn by a contemporary friendly to Julian, it is true, but even more a lover of the truth.

It is said that on his death-bed Constantius designated Julian as his successor. A conqueror without having fought, and the last scion of the Flavian family, Julian had no need of this declaration. No man hesitated in recognizing the rebel of yesterday as the legitimate Emperor. The Counts Theolaif and Aligilde[5]

---

[1] . . . Tanquam venaticam praedam caperet (Amm. Marcellinus, xxi. 7).

[2] As early as the year 359 his death had been regarded as near at hand (Ibid. xviii. 3). His posthumous daughter Constantia married the Emperor Gratian.

[3] Anilis superstitio (Ibid. xxi. 16).

[4] . . . Caligulae et Domitiani et Commodi immanitatem facile superabat . . . mortemque longius in puniendis quibusdam, si natura permitteret, conabatur extendi (Ibid.).

[5] Amm. Marcellinus, xx. 2. Observe the German names of these deputies of the imperial court and council.

brought to him the oath of fidelity of the ministers, the generals, and the court. All Constantinople went out to meet him (Dec. 11, 361), and the Roman Senate, which had lately received with disfavor an accusing document from Julian on the subject of Constantius, hastened to repair this fault by sending to Julian a *senatus-consultum* decreeing to him the imperial honors.

[1] D. N. CONSTANTIVS P. V. AVG. Diademed bust of Constantius II. wearing the *paludamentum* and the cuirass. On the reverse, SABINAE and the rape of the Sabine women: in the foreground, two men, one of whom is dragging away a kneeling woman, and the other grasps a woman with outstretched hands, who is apparently calling for help; in the background, six women and three obelisks. (Bronze medallion.)

COIN OF CONSTANTIUS.[1]

CHAPTER CVI.

THE RELIGIOUS QUESTION DURING THE REIGN OF CONSTANTIUS.

I. — PAGANISM AND THE DIVINERS.

THE pagan reaction which Julian sought to make victorious is the most important fact of his reign. To understand this error we must remember the life to which he had been condemned before his accession, and we must take into account the religious state of the Empire during the reign of Constantius. We have shown that the perils which threatened Julian's youth, his hatred for the religion of those who persecuted him, and his love for Greek letters and philosophy, had early won him over to Hellenism. We have now to see how, in view of the fierce discords in the Church itself and of the presumption of certain of the bishops, this man, who was by conviction a pagan, might easily believe, on becoming master of the Roman world, that the tranquillity of the Empire required him to strive against the Christian revolution and the independent attitude of the clergy, by restoring the old system of religion and the old authority of the Emperors.

The religious history of the reign of Constantius has a twofold aspect, for there were two religions in the Empire, or, we might say, three, — Paganism, Nicaean Orthodoxy, and Arianism in all its shades. Of these religions Constantius persecuted two. This was not because the pagans made any disturbance. They had legal and historic possession; a prefect of Rome called their cult the religion of the Empire; and they nowhere formed communities for purposes of resistance or for the observance of religious rites. But the government was hostile to them, and the mind of Constantius was not firm enough to keep to the tolerant policy of his father. From the imperial palace came forth, now and then, menacing words, which authorized, if not persecution against individuals,

at least, here and there, the pillage and destruction of edifices
consecrated to the old cult. Libanius asserts that Constantius prohibited sacrifices and overthrew temples.[1] This man is a rhetorician, and the rule of his special kind of writing is to generalize
even from a single fact. As there had been for two centuries
local acts of violence against the Christians, so now, under Constantius, such acts were committed against pagans, and probably
in considerable number. What, however, shall we think of many
laws, preserved in the *Theodosian Code*, formally proscribing paganism? This subject has been much discussed. The law of 341 is
open to much doubt; the genuineness of the edicts of 346 (?) and
356 (?) have been regarded as equally questionable.[2] I admit them
myself because so many witnesses attest them and because Amm.
Marcellinus refers to them in speaking of contrary decrees made
by Julian.[3] These were made in order to gratify those Christians
who, like Firmicus Maternus, clamored for the despoiling, the overthrow, and the complete annihilation of idolatrous impiety. "Destroy the temples," he said to Constantius, "and in their place rear
trophies of Victory." But the execution did not follow the threat,
except in certain places, and in spite of their formidable language,
these laws remained without efficacy. The armies of Magnentius
and Eugenius were in the main composed of pagans, and the
troops of Julian showed their joy when he publicly professed himself a believer in the old faith. In 333 Constantius put an end
to the nocturnal sacrifices which Magnentius had authorized;[4] but
he did not speak of the public sacrifices which Constantine had

---

[1] Ὁ μὲν γὰρ [Constantine] ἐγύμνωσε τοῦ πλούτου τοὺς θεούς· ὁ δὲ [Constantius] καὶ
κατέσκαψε τοὺς ναοὺς καὶ πάντα ἱερὸν ἐξαλείψας νόμον ἔδωκεν αὐτὸν οἷς ἴσμεν (vol. ii. p. 591,
edit. of Venice. Cf. *Id.*, *Letter* 1080, and the *Discourse for Aristophanes*).

[2] *Codex Theod.* xvi. 10, 4, and 6. Lasaulx (*Untergang des Hellenismus*) and Hänel
(*Corpus jur. antejustin.*) regard as authentic the laws of 346 and 356, closing the temples
and prohibiting sacrifices under penalty of death. Beugnot and the Duc de Broglie (iii.
364) adopt the conclusions of La Bastie, who thinks that if these laws were issued, they
were certainly not executed.

[3] xxii. 5. When he says of Julian: *Sui pectoris patefecit arcana et planis absolutis-
que decretis aperiri templa, arisque hostias admoveri ad deorum statuit cultum.* In chap.
ii. of the same book he says that the temple of Serapis was threatened with destruction,
"like so many others" (*ne illud quoque tentaret evertere*); and, in his treatise *Against Heraclius*, sect. 17, that the sons of Constantine overthrew the national temples which their
father had despoiled; finally, we read in Sozomenus (iii. 17): ναοὺς ἁπανταχοῦ κειμένους
ἐν πόλεσιν, ἐν ἀγροῖς κεκλεῖσθαι προσέταξαν.

[4] *Codex Theod.* xvi. 10, 5.

allowed to continue, which the usurper certainly had not prohibited, and which scan-
dalized the Christians
much more. When,
a few months after
the publication of the
law of 356, the Em-
peror went to Rome,
he ordered the altar
to be removed from
the curia, so that the
customary libations
should not be made
in his presence ;[1] but
he did not interfere
with the privileges of
the Vestals, he dis-
tributed priesthoods,
granted money for the
ceremonies. and, ac-
companied by the Sen-
ate, visited the sanc-
tuaries of the gods,
read with composure
the inscriptions en-
graved to them, and
listening to the his-
tory of each temple,
expressed his approv-
al of the men who
had founded them.
"Notwithstanding
his attachment to
another faith, he

GOLD MEDALLION OF CONSTANTIUS II.[2]

[1] Julian annulled this order.
[2] FL. IVL. CONSTAN-
TIVS NOB. CAES. Lau-
relled bust of Constantius, with the *paludamentum* and the cuirass, holding a spear and a
shield, upon which is represented the Emperor galloping to the right, preceded by a Vic-

respected that of the Empire." [1]   Symmachus was in the right in saying this; paganism was still so powerful in Rome that a sophist of
great renown, the intimate friend of nobles, lost his popularity on
the day when he inscribed his name among the catechumens. [2]   Constantius always regarded the college of pontiffs as religious magistrates in charge of the national cult, [3] and a law of 358 regulates the
election of the pontifex maximus for the province of Africa. [4]
Constans, so full of zeal for orthodoxy,—in the provinces belonging

to his brother, — gave the prefecture of Illyria to a pagan
very devout towards the old
gods, and the same Emperor
prohibited the destruction of
temples in the neighborhood
of Rome. [5]   In the city itself
these edifices all remained

COIN OF JULIAN. [5]

undisturbed, and Memphis, Alexandria, and Antioch, like the old
capital of the world, still kept theirs.   Memphis had its sacred
bull, Apis, always an object of public worship; Alexandria, its
great temple of Serapis, still full of all the beautiful objects
which Marcellinus mentions as belonging to it; and the statue of
the Apollo of Daphne, which rivalled in splendor the best works
of pagan art, still stood just outside the gates of the great Syrian
city in which "the disciples were first called Christians."   When
Julian entered Antioch, shortly after his accession to the throne,
he saw the smoke of sacrifices arise from many altars, and the
inhabitants celebrating with great display the death of Adonis,

tory, followed by a soldier, and putting to flight a crowd of enemies. On the reverse:
GAVDIVM ROMANORVM. Constantine in the centre with two of his sons, all three
standing, in military costume, and leaning on their sceptres; a celestial hand holds a crown
over the head of Constantine; his son at the left is crowned by a soldier; the one at the
right, by a Victory. Underneath, M. CONS. Weight, 9 oz. (Museum of Vienna.)

[1] Symmachus (*Letters*, x. 54), Amm. Marcellinus (xvi. 10), and the anonymous author
of a Description of the World who visited Rome at this time, all say the same: . . . *Colent
et deos, ex parte Jovem et Solem* (Hudson, *Geogr. minor.* iii. 15).

[2] Saint Augustine. *Confessions*, viii. 2: *Superbi irascebantur, dentibus suis stridebant et
tabescebant.* Under Julian, he was obliged to close his school.

[3] *Codex Theod.* ix. 17, 2 (law of 349). He calls the tombs *aedificia manium.*

[4] *Ibid.* xii. 1, 46.

[5] Coin of Julian, with Apis on the reverse. Great bronze in the Museum of Lyons
(Comarmond, *Descript. des Antiques*, pl. 216, No. 13).

[6] *Codex Theod.* xvi. 10, 3.

symbol of the harvest falling before the sickle, to spring up again a few months later in a new harvest.[1] "At Alexandria," says a contemporary, "the gods are worshipped fervently; the temples are richly adorned; the priests and augurs, numerous. . . . Heliopolis, Olympia, Athens, Eleusis, all preserve their sanctuaries," etc.,[2] and men continue to interrogate the future on the banks of the sacred lake of Aphaca. The Jupiter of Pheidias is still at Olympia, the Poliac Minerva in the Parthenon, and the Greeks still celebrate their four great games,[3] and even their mysteries. The official orator in the reign of Constantius, Themistius, — a pagan whom the Emperor made senator, as he made another pagan his ambassador to Persia,[4] — represents Egypt as all lighted up with illuminations at the festival of the Minerva of Saïs; and as late as 362 the pagans in Alexandria were numerous enough to make a sanguinary riot on occasion of a word of contempt uttered against the temple of Serapis by the bishop of the city.[5] At Bostra the number of idolaters equalled that of the Christians,[6] and the most famous pagan of the time, Libanius, had a school successively at Constantinople, Nicomedcia, and Antioch, without being anywhere molested. This persistence of the old cult should not surprise us; the contrary would be remarkable; for in history we find no abrupt changes : revolutions, even those which have been compared to thunderclaps, have had their long antecedents, and their results are of long duration. The philosopher Chytras in Alexandria, accused in 359 of consulting diviners, was set at liberty when he explained that from his childhood he had been a worshipper of the gods, and that he had now consulted the oracle, not through ambition or sacrilegious curiosity, but to render the divinity favorable to himself.[7]

The last of these facts confirms those which precede it, and shows us the true nature of the persecutions of Constantius, and

[1] Amm. Marcellinus, xxii. 11, 13, 14, and 16. Julian (*Misop.* 8) says that at Antioch he sacrificed in the temples of Jupiter Philius [the patron of friendship, identical with Jupiter Hospitalis], Ceres, and Fortune.

[2] *Vetus orbis descriptio,* pp. 15, 17, etc.

[3] Julian, *Letters* 8 and 35.

[4] Amm. Marcellinus, xxii. 5. Eunapius speaks also (p. 466) of the embassy of the sophist Eustathius in 358.

[5] By the bishop's own avowal (Julian, *Letter* 52).

[6] Amm. Marcellinus, xxii. 11.   [7] *Ibid.* xix. 12.

his hostility towards all foolish persons who were attracted by
astrology or magic. In these men who sought to penetrate the destinies of the Empire, he saw, as his father and all his predecessors
had seen, fabricators of conspiracies, and he designates them, as
three centuries earlier Nero had styled the Christians, "enemies of
the human race." He decreed death, with all forms of torture,
against persons, however elevated their station might be, who should
inquire of soothsayers and diviners concerning the future, — *sileat
. . . perpetua divinandi curiositas* (358).[1] In the rapacious and
wicked hands of informers these laws were a valuable means of
finding criminals and confiscations. Amm. Marcellinus says of Constantius : " This feeble mind, incapable of application to serious
things, was singularly in fear of the oracles. . . . Free rein being
once given to calumny, a crowd of men, noble and obscure, accused
of having consulted the Apollo of Claros, the oaks of Dodona, or
the Delphic tripod, to know when the Emperor should die, were
dragged from all parts of the Empire to be examined before a
commission which sat at Scythopolis in Palestine. As the crime
charged was treason, the usual exemption from torture in case of

---

[1] *Codex Theod.* ix. 16, 45 : . . . *Sit equuleo deditus ungulisque sulcantibus latera*, and 6,
annis 357 *et* 358. The elder Pliny (xxx. 1 *et seq.*) did not believe in magic, and ridicules
the men who thought that by swallowing the heart of a mole — "that animal so ill-used by
Nature" — one could obtain revelations of the future. Lucian (*The False Prophet*) thinks
the same. But both are sceptics, and they were never popular leaders. All the world —
pagans, Christians, even philosophers — believed in magic. See the *Apologia* of Apuleius,
who had to defend himself from a formidable accusation of this kind ; Maury, *La Magie et
l'astrologie ;* De Voguë, *Inscr. araméenes,* p. 81 ; and Vol. VI. p. 397 of this work. " Astrology," says M. de Voguë, "which had its beginning in Chaldaea, attributed to the planets a
special agency in human affairs. These stars of periodical revolution (*errantes*) were considered divinities of the first rank, — some benevolent, others the reverse ; they served as visible
intermediaries between the earth and the Supreme Power, invisible, incomprehensible, and
fatal, whose soul filled all Nature, and whose special abode was the inaccessible region of
the upper air, above the zone of the fixed stars. The planets, agents of this power, had to
do with all the phenomena of the visible world, — some as demiurgi, others as sources of life
or death, of good or evil ; they presided over the succession of seasons and events, and the
least details of terrestrial existences. The zodiac was their sidereal abode ; each had its nor-
mal residence in one of the signs. There its power was greatest, and reciprocally was modified as it passed into other signs and constellations. The movement of the planets among
the heavenly bodies determined therefore a multitude of actions and reactions, — some favorable, others unfavorable ; and the study of them, and application to the facts of existence, were
the sum and substance of astrology. Certain conjunctions of stars were regarded as very fortunate, and these were represented on amulets, to apply their virtues to the persons wearing
them. Moreover, vows and prayers were addressed to these sidereal divinities ; notwithstanding the inevitable character of their movements, they were believed to have a will of their
own, which could be conciliated by homage and sacrifices."

AMPHITHEATRE OF APHACA (AFKA), SOURCE OF THE RIVER ADONIS (AFTER A PHOTOGRAPH BY DR. LORTET).

the *honorati* was not granted; many died upon the road from the weight of the chains with which they were loaded, while others perished under torture in the prisons." Such, then, was the condition of paganism under Constantius: "The pagan cult was officially maintained and often honored, and it was at the same time insulted with impunity. Everything depended on the disposition of the people and of the magistrates, on the strength of one party or the other, — often on a mere accident of place." [1]

This inquiry into practices which in a certain measure made part of the national cult, and these threats hanging over those who still remained believers in the old religion, disturbed pagan society. The other, the Christian part of the community, was even more agitated; but its disturbances came from within. Never had moral disorder like this been seen before in the Empire, and Constantius seemed to take pleasure in making it worse. "By his foolish superstitions," says Amm. Marcellinus, "he disfigured the Christian religion, which is in itself simple and clear, and he excited controversies rather than appeased them. The high-roads of the Empire were full of troops of priests going to their interminable discussions in the synods." [2]

II. — STRUGGLE BETWEEN THE ARIANS AND THE ORTHODOX; COUNCIL OF SARDICA.

THE truths of mathematics are not discussed, because they are absolute certainties; but the demonstration of religious doctrines being impossible, men quarrel and kill each other about them. Accordingly, at all periods the civil power seeks to prevent these disputes. In order to introduce into the Church the same peace which he had caused to prevail in the State, Constantine had ordered the Nicene Fathers to draw up a confession of faith, which he then undertook to impose upon all the bishops; for he proposed to govern the new clergy as he had the old, — with absolute authority. The Orthodox, especially their leader, Athanasius, had quickly made the Emperor see that they intended to be themselves

---

[1] This judicious language is that of the Duc de Broglie, iii. 133.   [2] xxi. 16.

sole masters of the Christian conscience of the world; on the other hand, the Arians had shown towards him a docility which pleased his imperious spirit, and he had died a believer in the Arian doctrines, after having sent into exile the chiefs of the Orthodox party.

The situation was not the same for his sons. Constantine II. and Constans reigned in countries where the Nicene creed had been

CONSTANS I.[1]

willingly accepted; nothing disturbed the peace in religious matters, and the Emperors naturally shared the faith of their subjects, — for them it was a question of policy, and not of conscience. Accordingly, they had decided at Sirmium, in 338, to recall the banished bishops. Arianism, on the contrary, in its different forms,[2] prevailed in the East because the bishops in that part of the Empire were anxious to preserve their religious independence and the authority of their Councils. Rome had long disturbed them by her discreet but persistent claims to be made the centre of Catholic unity. To strive against her they needed the assistance of their Emperor, which they had secured by their submission, and he was favorable to a clergy who seemed to remain national in refusing to recognize a foreign authority. Constantius in the East was the partisan of the Arians, from the same motives that retained the Emperors of the West in the Orthodox faith. Thus Valentinian and Valens at a later period separated from each other in their religious faith when the one reigned at Milan and the other at Constantinople.[3]

Constantius must have been strengthened in these inclinations by his monarchical instincts when he learned that Athanasius, on returning to Alexandria, had called together eighty bishops of Egypt and Libya; that he had caused them to prepare an encyclical letter condemning in violent terms the council assembled by

---

[1] Constans I., third son of Constantine (FL. IVL. CONSTANS P. F. AVG.). Gold coin.

[2] The strict Arians, rejecting the word ὁμοούσιος, which for the Orthodox expressed identity of substance, maintained a difference in substance between the Father and the Son; the semi-Arians admitted resemblance of substance, ὁμοιούσιος; the Acacians (so-called from their leader, Acacius of Caesarea) admitted neither unity nor equality, nor even resemblance between the Father and the Son. The semi-Arian bishop of Constantinople, Macedonius, deposed in 360, taught a new heresy, — that of the Pneumatomachi, who deny the deity of the Holy Spirit.

[3] Magnentius sought also to gain over the Orthodox of the East; see above, p. 70.

Constantine at Tyre;[1] that, finally, the Alexandrian bishop had addressed himself for justice to the Bishop of Rome, — a subject of the Emperor's brother, — whose approbation, secured in advance, would determine that of all the Western prelates.

Constantine's latest counsellor, Eusebius of Nicomedeia, continued to direct the policy of that Emperor's son. When Pope Julius convoked the synod demanded by "the Egyptians," Constantius authorized their adversaries to hold another in his presence at Antioch. Ninety-seven bishops were present. They prepared twenty-five canons, which the Church has received, and a very orthodox confession of faith, with the single exception that the word which at Nicaea had been employed to express the consubstantiality of the Father and the Son was not employed in it. One of the canons, the twenty-fourth, declared that as the possessions of the Church were the patrimony of the poor, the bishop should take of them for his personal needs only so far as was absolutely necessary for his subsistence. Two other canons, the fourth and the twelfth, were directed against Athanasius. who while under sentence of deposition from a council, still held the see of Alexandria. The Fathers appealed for the execution of sentences passed by the council to the external authority. or. as was said later, to the secular arm.[2] The Cappadocian Gregory. ordained bishop of Alexandria. went into Egypt with a military escort commanded by the dux Balac. A soldier, the prefect Philagrius, went before them to prepare the way. If we may believe the ecclesiastical writers, who derive their authority chiefly from the person most interested. namely Athanasius himself,[3] Philagrius

---

[1] See, Vol. VII. p. 553, an extract from this letter.

[2] At the same time they recognized the disadvantages of rashly calling in the imperial authority; and while they solicited it in the Alexandrian question, they condemned by their eleventh canon the bishop (or priest) who should appeal directly to the Emperor without the consent of his metropolitan and his fellow-bishops of the same province.

[3] The maxim of law, *unus testis, nullus testis*, is applicable in history in cases where it is legitimate to expect either prejudice or self-interest. Compare, for example, in the *Monumenta* placed at the end of the works of Saint Optatus (Migne, *Patrologie*, xi. 1179), what the Bishop of Carthage says of "the very religious Constans" and of his two envoys, Paulus and Macarius, who came into Africa "as ministers of a holy work," and how the Donatist author of the *Marculi Passio* speaks *de Constantia regis tyrannica* .... , and "the two wild beasts" whom he sent to declare "an accursed war upon the Church." The same thing is true in respect to the Alexandrian troubles. In their circular letter to the bishops, the Fathers of Philippopolis lay them all at the door of Athanasius and his partisans, — which by no means proves that he ought to be personally accused of causing them.

let loose Jews and pagans against the Christian community, the church was sacked, believers were insulted and beaten, and a sort of persecution extended throughout the whole of Egypt. It is not easy to see what interest the government and the bishop could have in stirring up tumults which no man can be sure of arresting at the desired point. Athanasius was beloved in Alexandria, and the turbulent population of that city, consisting of pagans, Jews, and Christians always in a state of hostility, was fond of riots. Street-brawls there doubtless were, in which blows were given and received; and of these the partisans of Athanasius got the larger and heavier share, because the soldier, who was ordered to take part in the affair, brought to it his customary brutality. A strange spectacle was this episcopal entry assuming the aspect of civil war, and old pagans well might say that their gods had been more pacific.

Athanasius had escaped to Rome, uttering an eloquent war-cry, his *Letter to the Orthodox*, in which he compares himself to the Levite who cut into twelve pieces the body of his murdered wife and sent it to the twelve tribes of Israel.[1] At this time fifty bishops were assembled in Rome, but not one of the Fathers of Antioch was among them (547). These latter had replied to the Pope's letter of convocation that Julius was wrong in receiving into his communion Athanasius, whom two councils had condemned; that all the bishops having equal authority, their jurisdiction was not dependent on the size of the cities; and that it would be fitting to remember that the preaching of the gospel had begun in the East, — by which they wished it understood that the true tradition was to be found there.[2] In his reply, Julius reproaches the Eusebians for not agreeing with him and the bishops of the West on the subject of Athanasius, so that "sentence could be given unanimously; this is the custom," he says.[3] And, in fact, when a bishop had been cut off from the communion of the other bishops, it was necessary that the sentence be communicated to the absent:

---

[1] *Works* of Athanasius, i. 110 (edit. of 1698). [See *Judges* xix. 29.]

[2] This sentiment was so general in the East that we find it expressed in the Council of Constantinople (381) at the very time when Theodosius was seeking to reunite the two churches. See, in Gregory Nazianzen, the poem Περὶ τὸν ἑαυτοῦ Βίον, line 1560.

[3] . . . πᾶσιν ἡμῖν ἵνα οὕτως παρὰ πάντων ὁρισθῇ τὸ δίκαιον. This long letter occurs in the *Apology* of Athanasius against the Arians, in his *Works*, i. 123 *et seq.* The passage quoted is in sect. 34.

if they accepted it, it became the decision of the Church; if not, another council was called to decide the matter. Forty years later, Ambrose, writing to Theodosius, maintained the same doctrine,[1] and two Emperors had put it in practice, — Aurelian in the case of the Bishop of Antioch, and Constantine of him of Carthage.[2] Pagans and Christians alike recognized in the Roman see a dignity superior to the other episcopates; but they also thought that, in the exercise of jurisdiction, the bishops of Italy and the West should be associated with the Bishop of Rome. At this epoch the pontifical monarchy had not yet come into existence; the Christian republic was governed by synods and councils, — that is to say, by the representative system.

Graver disturbances than those of Egypt took place in the capital of the Empire. In 340 Eusebius of Nicomedeia and Paul of Thessalonica disputed the see of Constantinople. Eusebius had against him the canons,[3] and Paul, the Emperor. The former gained the victory, and the latter was driven out. But Eusebius did not long survive the Council of Antioch; Paul reappeared in the city to take possession of his episcopate, and a party in the Church promised to obey him. The Eusebians did not propose to abandon so lucrative a position; they caused Macedonius, a deacon, to be consecrated bishop, and the master of the cavalry, Hermogenes, confirmed the election in the name of the absent Emperor. Open hostilities at once began. The partisans of Paul, gaining the advantage, burned the palace of Hermogenes, seized his person, and dragged him through the streets till he was torn in pieces. The murder of a lieutenant of the Emperor implies many other murders, of which we have no report, for the victorious party allowed nothing to remain of whatever may have been written on this riot in Constantinople. It was a repetition of the scenes which had occurred in Alexandria, made in this case by the Orthodox; and it was an aggravated case, for the murder of Hermogenes was nothing less than treason. At news of what had occurred, Constantius with his guards hastened to the city. The inhabi-

---

[1] *Letter* 14, edit. of the Benedictines.

[2] See Vol. VII. p. 301.

[3] The 15th Nicaean and the 21st of Antioch forbade the transference of a bishop from one see to another. In the election of Paul, the Emperor had not been consulted.

tants received him with every demonstration of penitence. Contrary to his habit of extreme severity, the Emperor forgave; the criminals were persons of very little importance, from whom nothing was to be feared. The city, however, lost half its customary distributions, and the bishop, Paul, seized unawares, was carried on board a vessel and sent a second time into exile. But when the praetorian prefect, escorted by a mass of soldiers, attempted to conduct Macedonius to the church and place him in the episcopal chair, it was necessary to make a pathway of blood through the midst of the exasperated crowd, and more than three thousand persons perished.[1]

The enthroning of the two bishops, Gregory and Macedonius, *manu militari*, shows the importance of the struggle which was going on in Constantinople and in Alexandria. It was reproduced in other cities; Athanasius, who neither knew all nor tells all that he knew, makes mention of riots in many cities of Thrace. The disputatious Greeks had found in Christian theology inexhaustible subjects of discussion. As in earlier times the crowd had gathered to literary entertainments, public recitations, and the carefully prepared improvisations of the rhetoricians, so now men frequented the assemblies where the new teachers discussed the essence of the Father and the Son; and these assemblies were of every day occurrence. Amm. Marcellinus shows us the roads thronged with priests on their way to these discussions, and each man, he says, sought to bring the others to his way of thinking.[2]

The West, where men's heads were not made hot by so ardent a sun, had a faith more tranquil, more exactly defined; and the Roman clergy, who already manifested a spirit of government akin to that of the old Senate of republican Rome, by degrees took

---

[1] Socrates (ii. 16) says three thousand one hundred and fifty.

[2] *Constantius . . . excitavit discidia plurima, quae progressa fusius aluit concertationes verborum: ut cateris antistitum jumentis publicis ultro citroque discurrentibus per synodos . . . dum ritum omnem ad suum trahere conantur arbitrium, rei vehiculariae succideret nervos* (Amm. Marcellinus, xxi. 16 *ad fin.*). The twentieth canon of Antioch had decided that in each ecclesiastical province there should be two synods annually, and the Benedictines of St.-Maur enumerate more than forty of them in the reign of Constantius, of which one, that of Milan, in 355 brought together over three hundred bishops. We have seen (Vol. VII. p. 530, and note 1) that Constantine had placed the *cursus publicus*, with all its accompanying advantages, at the disposal of bishops or priests whom he summoned to court or convoked for a council. The Bishop of Centumcellae also makes allusion, in 355, to the great expense this involved (Theodoret, ii. 16).

control of the religious movement. Its head had never allowed himself to be present at a council held outside his own diocese, where it would be necessary to settle questions of precedence or doctrinal authority, preferring to leave this in a vague distance, whence, under favorable circumstances, uncontested rights might, at some future time, emerge. At this moment he was making good use of the distractions of the Eastern Church to represent Rome as the centre of the Orthodox faith, and the refuge of those who suffered in its name. With a boldness which was politic, and also noble, the Pope took part with Paul of Constantinople, Athanasius of Alexandria, Marcellus of Ancyra, Asclepas of Gaza, and Lucius of Hadrianople, who were all persecuted by the Eusebians.[1] But to defend in the great Oriental cities the new rights to which the Church laid claim, was to raise the hand against Constantius. The Pope needed therefore to have a sword at his command. The Emperor of the West was adroitly approached. This young man,[2] of feeble intellect and coarse manners, was incapable of comprehending that the question to be decided was this, — should the bishops be simply religious functionaries of the Empire, or should they be in their respective dioceses each a supreme authority freely elected, and independent of the laic power. Constans was at this time in the north of Gaul, occupied in fighting or in negotiating with the Franks. The Pope wrote to him at great length; he sent to him Hosius of Cordova, the confidential adviser of Constantine the Great, and he charged the Bishop of Trèves, who had kindly received Athanasius during his exile, to see to it that Constans remained firm in the Orthodox faith. The Emperor seeing his bishops in harmony among themselves and his subjects submissive to their bishops, remained with them. At the request of the Pope he proposed to his brother to hold a general council at Sardica (Sofia), on the confines of the two Empires; to this

---

[1] The Eusebians, who had assembled at Antioch, replied to the Pope by a very animated letter, in which they asserted that it did not concern him to make inquiry into their conduct in expelling certain bishops from their churches, since they had not interfered with his jurisdiction within its proper limits (Socrates, ii. 15). In this passage and in chap. xvii. Socrates makes reference, in defence of the Pope's intervention, to canons which did not exist. See, on this subject, President Cousin's discussion prefixed to his translation of Socrates.

[2] He was born in 320.

Constantius agreed, and issued the necessary letters (344).[1]   One hundred and seventy bishops presented themselves in the city designated; Pope Julius did not attend, sending two priests to represent him, and Hosius, in whom he had entire confidence, presided over the debates, as at Nicaea.

The matter to be settled by this council was decided in advance. One party intended to annul the decisions of the councils

CONSTANTIUS II.[2]

of Tyre and of Antioch; the other, to maintain them. The question in reality had a political aspect : Should the Churches of the Eastern Empire be subordinated to those of the Western? This is why Constantius remained so firmly attached to his Arian clergy. When the Oriental bishops saw Athanasius admitted to the council, they refused to sit with "the excommunicate," and to the number of eighty withdrew to Philippopolis. Then the conflict began, and thunderbolts were interchanged. The two councils fulminated against each other: the Fathers at Sardica deposed eleven bishops of the Eastern Church; the Fathers at Philippopolis excommunicated Athanasius anew, and with him eight of his adherents, — Hosius and Pope Julius himself included. The separation was final; the limits of the two Empires marked the limits of the two Churches.

This council, which began the schism from which Christendom suffers to this day, was a misfortune for religion, but it was a benefit to the Papacy. The Western bishops, threatened by the Eastern in their faith and in their desire to preserve the unity of

---

[1] The chronology of this period is very confused in respect to religious events. Socrates (ii. 20), Sozomenus (iii. 12), and, following them, Tillemont, Fleury, and the *Art de vérifier les dates*, place in 347 the Council of Sardica, which Hefele and the Duc de Broglie place four years earlier. In my judgment 344 is the true date, drawing this inference from the motive assigned by the Eusebians for their departure from Sardica. They were recalled, they said, by Constantius to attend the celebration of his triumph over the Persians; now this solemnity, which the Emperor wished to render brilliant, must have been in honor of the victory at Singara (see p. 65, note 4). The date 344 agrees, moreover, with the *Chronicle* of Saint Jerome, who places the return of Athanasius to Alexandria in 346, and it is well known that this return took place two years after the council. The learned Archbishop Mansi of Lucca, in his *Supplem. ad collect. concil.* 1748, also adopts this date.

[2] Constantius II. (FL. IVL. CONSTANTIVS PIVS FELIX AVG.). Silver medallion.

CONSTANTIUS IN IMPERIAL COSTUME, AND HOLDING A VICTORY.

(Copy of a miniature by Kondakoff, in a Russian "History of Byzantine Miniature-painting.")

the Church, felt more intensely than their predecessors had done, the need of a head, and they gathered more closely around him who, occupying the most eminent see, appeared most authorized to support the principle of unity. In every age peril from without has increased in the bosom of the Church the spirit of discipline and the concentration of strength. In a letter addressed to the Pope, the Fathers of Sardica communicated to him what they had done, "because," they said, "it is fitting that the bishops make report to the chair of Saint Peter:" namely, that since the Emperors have permitted new examination to be made, they have gone over the case of Athanasius, justifying him, and of the partisans of Arius, condemning them; and in conclusion, they beg the Pope to make written communication of what they have done to the Churches of Italy, Sicily, and Sardinia. Another letter was, according to usage, sent directly to the absent bishops, to the end that all who should give in their adhesion to the decisions of the council should be "in fellowship" with the Fathers of Sardica. Thus was constituted that great body, the Orthodox Church.

Three points are to be considered in the letter to the Pope, — the right still recognized of the civil power to authorize, and consequently to limit, the deliberations of the council; the special jurisdiction of the Pope over the suburban Churches contained in the Roman vicariat; thirdly, the deference of the Fathers towards the Roman see, where appeals of bishops condemned in their own provinces might, "in honor of Peter's memory," be brought and examined by new judges, if the Pope so directed.[1] In recommending to bishops dissatisfied with the decision of their co-provincial colleagues this recourse to the Roman see, the council did no more than attribute to the Pope the voluntary jurisdiction granted by Constantine to bishops in their dioceses;[2] but this canon was the corner-stone of that vast edifice whence in all coming time the Pope was to rule with supreme authority over Roman Catholic Christendom.

The Eastern bishops had also prepared a circular letter, in which they related and explained their proceedings. We shall refer only to their doctrine in the matter of councils, and their

---

[1] Letter to the Pope, and Canons 3, 4, 5, and 10 of the Council of Sardica; Latin text.
[2] See Vol. VII. pp. 510-11.

opposition to the part which the Papacy was striving to assume. In the excommunication of Pope Julius they had struck at the head of this Western Church, which appeared to them so ready to accept a master ; and in rejecting the decision of the Fathers of Sardica they proposed to maintain the authority of their own councils, the only spiritual rule to which they were willing to submit.   The Western Churches accepted indeed the same principle ; but among the councils they held that some were legitimate, and others were not so, — the councils of their adversaries being naturally of the latter character.   "They have judged our judges," said the Oriental bishops, "and reconsidered the decisions of those who are now with the Lord.   That which legally assembled councils have decreed must remain fixed ; the Church cannot alter it. She has received from God no such power."   To refuse to the Church the right of reconsidering her own decrees was equivalent to denying that revelation was continued in her by the Holy Spirit, and it was to deprive her of that principle which was her strength against the civil power.

It is said that Constantius, after the Council of Philippopolis, continued the persecution of the Orthodox.[1]   Many bishops were deposed and banished; and it could hardly have been otherwise. The eighty bishops who had separated from the Council of Sardica could not in their provinces do otherwise than break with those who sympathized with the Western Churches; and the Emperor expelled from their sees all to whom his bishops refused the kiss of peace.   If we judge from what occurred in Hadrianople, we may suppose that here and there riots broke out, inevitable in the midst of passions over-stimulated by the religious crisis of the time.   When the Eusebians, returning from their synod, arrived in the capital of Thrace, the bishop of that city refused them fellowship, and the people, taking sides with their clergy, made a riot, wherein ten money-changers were the victims; and their death in this way has entered them on the Church's list of martyrs.   As for the bishop, he was sent into exile with chains upon his wrists. A contemporary, Saint Cyrillus of Jerusalem, exclaims sadly : " Bishops rise up against bishops, priests against priests, communi-

---

[1] Socrates makes no mention of any such persecution, but Sozomenus and Athanasius speak of it at great length.

ties against each other; and bloodshed follows."[1] But he reminds himself that among the disciples one was a traitor, and is consoled in thinking that the discords in the Church were prophesied in Holy Scripture.[2]

Constantius had taken great precautions to prevent Athanasius from returning to Alexandria; but urgent letters, followed by threats, from his brother shook the resolution of a man in whom courage was not the dominant quality. "Receive Paul and Athanasius," Constans wrote, "and punish those who without cause have molested them; otherwise I shall go myself to reinstate them."[3] Lest he should have on his hands two wars at once, — that with the Persians, which was just now breaking out anew, and that which his brother threatened, — the Emperor of the East, taking advantage of the opportune death of Gregorius, gave permission for Athanasius to return to Alexandria (346).

III. — THE ORTHODOX PERSECUTED; ATHANASIUS; LUCIFER; HILARY.

RENDERED pacific by the fear which the protector of the Orthodox caused them, the Eusebians dropped the religious question for a time, and the Empire had five years of tranquillity. But on the death of Constans the war broke out again. During the winter which preceded the battle of Mursa (350–351) twenty-four bishops who had followed the court, meeting in council at

---

[1] . . . μέχρις αἱμάτων (*Instructions upon Religion*, xv. 7).

[2] Socrates (ii. 23) says that all the Eastern bishops justified by the Council of Sardica were restored to their sees, that Lucius returned to Hadrianople, and that in Constantinople Paul and Macedonius divided the city between them, each having his own church and his own assemblies. The Arian clergy of Alexandria also preserved their immunities.

[3] Socrates, ii. 22. Cf. Tillemont, *Mém. ecclés.* viii. 693. Constantius and his courtiers accused Athanasius of having instigated Constans against his brother, and after the death of the Emperor of the West the Bishop of Alexandria was accused of coming to an understanding with Magnentius Athanasius in his *Apology* stigmatizes these rumors as calumnies. But the fact that they were current at the court of Constantius shows that at Antioch it was feared lest the Orthodox of the East should enter into relations with the subjects of the Western Emperor. In his letter, Constans urges his brother to make investigation into the crimes of Stephen, bishop of Antioch, and his partisans. This interference must have been extremely displeasing to Constantius, and revealed to him dangerous adversaries in those who directed his brother's policy.

Sirmium, accused the bishop of that city of denying all distinction among the persons of the Trinity, and condemned him as guilty of the Sabellian heresy. This was a blow skilfully aimed at the Orthodox, who, with their doctrine of the consubstantiality of the Father and the Son, seemed to incline towards Sabellianism and to cast doubt upon the true humanity of Jesus. Magnentius being defeated, and the Emperor of their choice having become master of the West, the Eastern bishops, with singular persistence in their animosity, again took up the endless quarrel against their great enemy. Besides the former accusations, of which they averred that Athanasius was in no degree acquitted, they accused him of throwing all Egypt into disorder and of performing ordinations outside of his own diocese.[2] Con-

A COUNCIL.[1]

stantius, at this time in the city of Arles, assembled a council there, and Athanasius was again condemned (353). Saint Paulinus of Trèves, refusing to subscribe to this sentence, was banished to Asia Minor. But there remained refractory persons. The Emperor, resolved to put an end to the religious war, as he had ended the civil war, summoned to Milan more than three hundred bishops, almost all from the Western provinces, with the determination to oblige them to sign the act of deposition (355). He succeeded in doing this, but only after very sharp controversies. The gospels recommend submission to the temporal power; but the Old Testament often counsels revolt, and its books were read in all the Christian assemblies. Orators ani-

---

[1] Martigny, *Dict. les Antiquités chrétiennes*, from a very ancient painting.
[2] Socrates, ii. 24 and 26.

mated with the spirit of the old prophets of Israel gave utter-
ance to very independent language. When they were bidden to
remember the right of the sovereign whom Heaven had consecrated by sheltering him with its constant protection, they made
mention of kings whose wickedness Jehovah had for a time endured,
that they might be hurled down to a more conspicuous destruction. One of the assembly, Lucifer of Cagliari, scoffing at the
pretended theological knowledge of Constantius, went so far as to
say aloud the word which the Orthodox were all whispering to
themselves: "He is as was his father, one of those Arians who
are the precursors of Antichrist."[1] The Gaul, Hilary of Poitiers,
repeated the same language, with an Oriental eloquence full[2] of
vivacity, but also of anger; he calls Constantius a dog, a ravening wolf, an unclean beast. But his words are sometimes beautiful. Reproaching the Emperor for the many creeds prepared by the
Eastern bishops, he says: "You are like ignorant architects who
are never content with their own work; you are continually building and pulling down. But the Catholic Church, when first it assembled, made an immortal structure, and gave in the Nicene
Creed so clear an expression of the truth that we have only to
repeat it, and Arianism is eternally condemned."[3]

The bishops of Milan and Vercelli had been almost as harsh
as Lucifer, and the imperious requirements of the Bishop of Tripoli
in the case of the Empress Eugenia show how haughtily these
priests spoke to the successors of the men who had been accustomed to regard themselves as the undisputed masters of the world.[4]
Here we have the tribunes of the people, forgotten for nearly five
centuries, reappearing, and threatening the oppressor not with any
powerless human anger, but with the wrath of God. — a new
method of inciting revolutions; and in fact a riot came near break-

---

[1] See Lucifer Calaritanus, *Duo Libri pro Athan. ad Const. imper.*, his *Moriendum esse
pro Filio Dei*, and the *De non parcendo delinquentibus in Deum* (edit. of Venice, 1778), in
which he says to Constantius: "We know what obedience we owe to you and to all who
are in authority, but we owe it in good works only." But what are good works? The
bishops set themselves up as judges of the civil law and of measures adopted by the temporal power. Tertullian had already used similar language, and later we shall see how
Athanasius and Gregory will speak.

[2] Hilary, *Contra Constant. imper.* 5 and 11, and *passim;* Benedictine edit., 1693.

[3] Bossuet, in his preface to the *History of Variations*.

[4] Fleury, *Hist. ecclés.* iii. 445, 451, 531; Tillemont, iv. 381.

ing out in Milan. Constantius had listened to the debates of the
Council, sheltering his imperial majesty behind a curtain; and when
he heard the language used by Lucifer, he appeared in person upon
the scene, and replied to the haughty words of the Christian priest:
"You are to regard my will as your rule.[1] My bishops in Syria
accept it, and God is with me; for he has put the whole Roman
world under my authority. Those who do not obey me shall be
sent into exile." And accordingly, Hosius of Cordova, Paulinus of
Trèves, Dionysius of Milan, Eusebius of Vercelli, Lucifer of Cagliari,
and a number of priests were exiled, and with them Liberius, the
successor of Pope Julius, who, brought forcibly to Milan, did not
bend before the sovereign will. When the Emperor reproached
him with standing alone in the defence of a great criminal, and
refusing to restore peace to the Empire, he replied: "Three Israel-
itish youths resisted the most powerful monarch of the East, and
against them the fiery furnace had no power."[2] The Church loved
this symbol of faith triumphant over kings and their cruelties,
and it is found among the paintings in the catacombs.[3]

Constantius, so ready to strike an isolated individual, regained
his prudence when he had reason to fear that the execution of a
sentence might occasion a popular outbreak. He wished that Athanasius would depart voluntarily into exile; but the bishop did not
do this, being determined to yield to force only. Saint Anthony
and his monks came down from their mountains to attest the

---

[1] ὅπερ ἐγὼ βούλομαι τοῦτο κανὼν, ἔλεγε, νομιζίσθω (Athanasius, *History of the Arians
written for the Monks,* i. 33).

[2] Theodoret, ii. 16; Sozomenus, iv. 11. Amm. Marcellinus, who served in the body-
guards (*protectores*), and was then at Milan, speaks of this conference between the Pope
and the Emperor, and the ardent desire of the latter to have the Pope accept the deposition of Athanasius: . . . *auctoritate qua potiores aeternae urbis episcopi* (xv. 2). These
words in his mouth should not surprise us. When the pagans understood the episcopal
organization of the Church, they always regarded, reasoning from their own history, the
Bishop of Rome as superior to the others in dignity.

[3] The sentence, "We ought to obey God rather than men," has been the everlasting
cry of all religious minorities, as political minorities have often made insurrection "the
most sacred of duties." Origen (*Contra Cels.* v. 37) endeavored to give Saint Peter's
language (*Acts* v. 29), which so many bishops have repeated, a rational basis, contrasting
the law of Nature, which comes from God, with the written law, which comes from men.
Doubtless human law is not always in accordance with reason and conscience; but unless
it be admitted that this law must be obeyed until we have succeeded by peaceful en-
deavors in having it changed, society is at an end; and society is divinely ordered, for
it springs from the law of Nature.

purity of the doctrines of Athanasius, and the bishop went on tranquilly fulfilling his episcopal functions at Alexandria, while those who had fought for him at Milan, being taken unawares, far from their churches and their friends, were scattered in different places of exile.

After crafty attempts to induce Athanasius to leave the city,

THE THREE YOUNG MEN IN THE FURNACE.[1]

the duke Syrianus had recourse to military violence; and again men were wounded and killed in the quarrel. Athanasius, "fleeing like David before the ministers of Saul," escaped to the monasteries of the Thebaïd, where the monks of Antony and Pachomius were a safer guard for him than the imperial *protectores* were for their master. George of Cappadocia was installed in the Alexandrian see. The Orthodox, expelled from the churches which the Arians now filled, sought to hold meetings in the suburbs and outside the walls; and the soldiery dispersed them, killing and wounding as usual. Sixteen bishops were deposed, and thirty took

[1] Montfaucon, *Antiquité expliquée; supplément,* vol. iii. pl. xviii.

flight, hiding themselves in caverns and in ancient tombs.[1] According to the ecclesiastical authors, Diocletian's persecution was less cruel.   Athanasius, whose letters were current everywhere, called Constantius the murderer of his family, the tyrant of the State, and for the Church the image of Antichrist.[2] Lucifer of Cagliari,

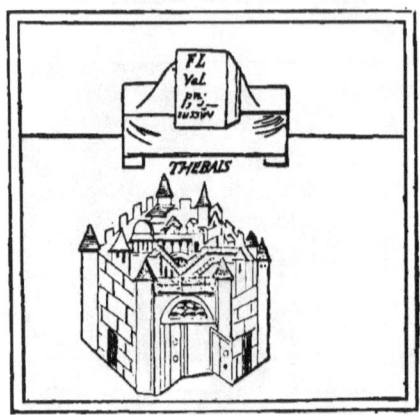

INSIGNIA OF THE PRESIDENT OF THE THEBAID.[3]

detained in Palestine, addressed a letter of the bitterest reproach to the Emperor, wherein Constantius read these words : " If thou hadst fallen into the hands of Mattathias or of Phineas, thou hadst perished by the sword; and thou sayest that I do thee wrong because I wound with my words thy soul dipped in the blood of Christians. Emperor, why takest thou not vengeance on me? Why dost thou not smite this mendicant who dares insult thee? . . . Thou wouldst gladly do so, but hast not received power from Him who permits me to reproach thee for thy crimes.   Thinkest thou that we shall respect thy diadem, thy earrings, thy bracelets, and thy costly garments in contempt of the Creator?   Like the fool, thou saidst : I am shamefully insulted by a wretch — I who am Emperor; and didst not say rather, — by a bishop who sees that I am a ravening wolf!"   And Constantius, intimidated by "Christ's beggar," dared not strike.[4] At Constantinople a riot broke out; at

---

[1] Cf. Athanasius, *Apology*, and *Concerning his Flight*; Theodoret, ii. 14; Tillemont, *Mém. ecclés.* vol. vii. *passim*.

[2] In his *Letter to those who lead a Solitary Life*.

[3] *Notitia dignitatum*, Böcking, p. 112.

[4] The works of Lucifer of Cagliari contain the richest vocabulary of insult that was ever addressed to a sovereign. (See in the *Index* to the Venetian edition, 1778, under the word "Constantius.") Athanasius, Hilary of Poitiers, and Gregory Nazianzen show no greater respect for Emperors.   Naturally, heretics are handled even more roughly.   A famous book of Athanasius, the *History of the Arians*, is, says the learned biographer of the saint, only

Rome and at Naples the bishops who held the sees of the exiles were abandoned by a part of their clergy; in Gaul, Hilary of Poitiers rejected from the Church the accusers of Athanasius, and the latter obtained against him a sentence of exile. " Hell was unchained." [1] Men murdered each other in the name of religion at that time, and for many subsequent centuries; later, the motive became political, but the result was the same. If man, as is asserted, is an improved animal, he has yet much to gain before becoming a humane animal.

When Constantius visited Rome after the Council of Milan (357), certain matrons begged from him the recall of Liberius. He replied that he would consent to it if the exile would agree to share his functions with Felix, who had been appointed his successor, in such manner that each of the two bishops should govern his congregation in peace.[2] Thus Macedonius and Paul had done at Constantinople; at Alexandria, even in the presence of Athanasius, an Arian clergy had held its ground. At the death of Constantius, Antioch had no fewer than three bishops, each surrounded by his own followers, who were respectively heretics in each other's eyes. It is probable that in many of the cities rival Christian communities existed. The Orthodox at Rome, better disciplined, refused the proposed partition. But Liberius gave way, worn out by the fatigues of exile ; he wrote a submissive letter to the Emperor, and gave his adherence to a formula of belief which did

---

"an oratorical lampoon " [*pamphlet oratoire*] (Fialon, *Saint Athanase*, p. 207). But the bishops and doctors do not even spare each other. Jerome utters biting words against Ambrose (see Canon Hermant, *Vie de Saint Ambroise*, pp. 128, 129), Athanasius against all his adversaries, Gregory Nazianzen against the Fathers of the Council of Constantinople, whom he calls a flock of jays and a swarm of buzzing wasps. Elsewhere Gregory reproaches Basil, who had appointed him to the bishopric of the small town of Sasima, with giving him this very undesirable residence so that he might keep guard, in the interests of Basil, over the mountain roads by which dues were brought in to the episcopal residence of Caesarea. (See his *Carmen de Vit. sua*, lines 400 *et seq.*) In his *Letter* 49 he says : " To interchange insults is to act as a bishop " (*ἐπισκοπικῶς κινούμεθα*). That we refer to these facts is not due to any desire to degrade great men. or for the sad pleasure of finding vile dross in the gold, but because this tone in polemics became habitual, and this violence of language in theological discussions led the way to violence of action in repressing heresy and in the religious wars.

[1] Bossuet, *Discours sur l'Hist. univ.* 2d part, chap. xx.

[2] Theodoret, ii. 17. It appears from this singular proposition how far the Emperor was from the idea which the Western bishops had adopted, of the importance of the Roman see, and its work in making the Church a unit. Sozomenus (*Hist. eccl.* iv. 15) says that Liberius and Felix did in fact govern conjointly the Roman Church.

not contain the crucial word "consubstantiality." The great Hosius
did the same. The Councils of Rimini and Seleucia, held in 359,
by order of the Emperor, under the supervision of his counts, appeared to insure the success of the religious policy of Constantius.
"The world," says Saint Jerome, "with amazement found itself
Arian;"[1] and a contemporary exclaims: "While the released

CONSULAR PALESTINE PERSONIFIED.[2]

Barabbas triumphs, Jesus is crucified afresh." But the union and
peace infused by the civil power were only superficial; and although
the faith, Orthodox or Arian, continued to extend, — since in this
very year, 359, Junius Bassus, the prefect of Rome, received baptism on his death-bed, — confusion was greater than ever in men's
minds, and disorder in the churches.[3] Meletius, consecrated bishop
of Antioch, was, a month after his election, deprived of his see
by a council which promulgated a new confession of faith, — the
sixteenth since that of Nicaea. Still another became necessary;
for after the heretics in respect to the Son, came those in respect
to the Holy Spirit,[4] who were not finally subdued till at the

---

[1] *Ingemuit totus orbis et Arianum se esse miratus est* (Saint Jerome, *Adv. Luciferianos*).
[2] *Notitia dignitatum*, Böcking, p. 110.
[3] Socrates, ii. 37 *ad fin.*
[4] Tillemont (*Mém. ecclés.* vi. 477) enumerates eighteen creeds.

Œcumenical Council of 381. And now bloodshed began. Paul, the Orthodox bishop of Constantinople, four times dispossessed of his see, had been dragged in chains to the foot of the Taurus, shut up in prison, and put to death. His rival, the semi-Arian Macedonius, had savagely attacked the Orthodox and the Novatians (a rigid sect, who made the way to heaven very narrow);[1] he had destroyed their churches and deposed their bishops. Socrates relates of him acts of atrocious cruelty which it would be difficult to believe, did we not know that of all social hatreds, religious animosities have long been the most violent. Macedonius was in turn deposed, after a sharp encounter had deluged with blood the courts of the church of the Holy Apostles (360).[2]

When, on the second day of August, 358, Liberius re-entered Rome, a popular outbreak drove Felix from the city. Shortly, his partisans, clerical and lay, recalled him; another riot again obliged him to escape from the city, leaving many dead behind him.[3] In Alexandria like scenes of violence took place; against the bishop who now occupied his see, Athanasius casts the accusations of rapine, theft, and simony, with which the Arians had loaded him.[4] Thus, while the truly Christian believers, those who had received into their souls the Master's great lesson, *beati pacifici*, lived in retirement, in silence and prayer, seeking God and finding Him in charity and self-sacrifice, the disputatious and quarrelsome carried their angry arguments everywhere, and for a word, whose obscure depths only a few could fathom, men took each other's lives. But this word was, in the opinion of the Orthodox theologians, the capital point of doctrine; in the eyes of the Arian theologians it was of no importance at all; to the philosopher it appeared an impertinence towards the Creator, whose essential nature these men presumed to understand; and the crowd, led by the crafty or the violent, added to the theological arguments sedition and murder. It was because the word served as a rallying cry to the different parties, which in this new society disputed with each

---

[1] At Nicaea, Constantine, after hearing one of their leaders, Acesius, is reported to have said to him: "Take a ladder and go up into heaven by yourself alone" (Sozomenus, i. 22).

[2] Socrates, ii. 38, 42.

[3] Socrates, ii. 42.

[4] Athanasius, *History of Arianism*, etc., p. 75; Epiphanius, *Haer.* lxxvi. 1 (edit. of 1622, vol. i. p. 915).

other for the honors and emoluments of the Church and for the
right of leading the laity to heaven by roads definitely marked
out.   This right to rule — the supreme ambition of so many men
— which, for the benefit of the State, had been hitherto reserved
to the civil power, was now seized by the Church in the name of
Heaven and given by her to her ministers. A determined or an
unconscious ambition was united, in the case of some, with the
most selfish designs, in the case of others, with the sincerest faith;
so that Earth and Heaven united to stimulate the passions which
strove for this new power over the souls of men, this second
empire established within the first.[1]

At Constantinople, at Rome, and at Alexandria there was a
strongly organized police system, and yet murders went on with
impunity; what must it then have been in cities where no armed
force protected the public peace ?   " Under Constantius," writes
Julian, "citizens were imprisoned, persecuted, and banished. At
Cyzicus, at Samosata, crowds of men said to be heretics were
murdered; in Paphlagonia, in Bithynia, and in the country of the
Galatae, whole cities were ravaged and destroyed." An ecclesiastical writer speaks of a battle in some religious war, where
four thousand soldiers were killed, — which would lead us to
suppose that the slaughter on the other side was also great.
Amm. Marcellinus, laying aside his habitual moderation, exclaims:
" Wild beasts are not more fierce towards man than most Christians are to each other; " and Gregory Nazianzen laments that
the kingdom of heaven should be a chaos in which all the passions of the lower regions strive with each other.[2] The virtues
hidden in many Christian homes were not conspicuous to the
eyes of all. All men, on the other hand, witnessed the interested
conversions of public officials, and the distractions produced by

---

[1] It was inevitable that in this ecclesiastical body, now become so numerous and already
so rich, quarrels of ambition should be mingled with quarrels of doctrine, and that there
should be great rivalry for the possession of lucrative positions. Gregory Nazianzen (vol. i.
pp. 5 and 335, edit. of the Abbé de Billy) complains of "men without virtue, who throw themselves upon the altar to obtain their support from the table of the Lord;" and Saint Basil
(*Letter* 54) speaks of those who become priests to avoid a military life. These discreditable
acts belong to all periods.

[2] Julian, *Letter* 52; Socrates, ii. 38; Amm. Marcellinus, xxii. 5: . . . *Nullas infestas
hominibus bestias, ut sunt sibi ferales plerique christianorum.* To these disturbances in the
provinces of the East we must add those in Africa, where the fanaticism and crimes of the
circumcelliones continued. See Vol. VII. p. 556.

SARCOPHAGUS OF THE ROMAN PREFECT BASSUS JUNIUS (CRYPT OF THE VATICAN).

the sharp disputes of theologians, and riots caused by heretics or by Orthodox believers. We are justified therefore in believing that Julian's pagan fervor was increased at the sight of this wide-spread disorder and at the vast claims of the Church, which, already placing the bishop above the emperor, threatened to overthrow both the religion of the Empire and its political institutions.

At the same time, if this episcopal ambition was an evil thing, the contrary theory of the subordination of the Church to the State was no better. When Constantine and his son made their bishops obedient functionaries, they developed that Eastern Church, subservient to the civil power, whose share in the general work of civilization has been so small. And though it is true that the Roman Church, becoming sovereign over nations and kings, caused the shedding of much blood, and for centuries restrained the free action of the human mind, she at least made amends for that tyranny by magnificent achievements in art and literature, by use-ful institutions and acts of heroic self-sacrifice. In the middle of the fourth century what she claimed was liberty, and she did not as yet aspire to the authority that circumstances should one day place in her hands.[1] Accordingly, we are the partisans of Athanasius and his free Church against the Eusebians and their clergy, the docile instrument of autocratic power, as later we shall be against those who seek to make the Church only the arm of the State. Anti-quity lived — without suffering from it except in times of persecu-tions — by that adulterous union of politics and religion which made the strength of the ancient states. The Middle Ages lived by it also, and in their turn were persecutors. Modern societies desire to give liberty to each of the two adversaries. When this is done, we reach the end of one great stage of human progress. To be just, we should add that in the fourth century neither prince nor priest could foresee the possibility of the independence of these two mighty social forces; but they strove so violently with each other that "this age of theologic splendor was the pre-lude to the Dark Ages."[2]

In the preceding narratives we have read of angry words and

---

[1] In his *History of the Arians*, which is solely an attack on Constantius, all that Atha-nasius claims is liberty; Ambrose went much farther.

[2] Villemain, *L'Éloquence chrétienne au quatrième siècle*, p. 513.

deeds of violence; it is the story of the Church militant: the religious convictions of some find satisfaction therein; the political convictions of others are wounded by it. If we have shown what usually is concealed, and if we pass silently over private virtues which it is usual to extol and which we also honor, it is because our task is the study of the public life of the Roman people, and an investigation of the causes which ruined the state. Let the hagiographers set forth as a compensation for the woes of the Empire the pure and charitable lives of pious bishops, of holy men, and of noble matrons; for ourselves, who have so long lived with this nation and now are witnessing its death-scenes, we must pass sadly through this fourth century, in which the noise of religious altercations prevents men from hearing the approaching footsteps of the Barbarians, — an age in which many men, from self-interested motives, worshipped God, but no man worshipped his country.

[1] On the base are these unintelligible words : ΙΔΙΗΧΩΥΟΙΗ ΙΤΘΣ ΑΙ ΧΧΧΘΕΘΘ4. Gnostic stone on saphirine chalcedony, 20 millim. by 16 (*Cabinet de France*, No. 2,183).

MYSTIC SPARROWHAWK ON THE HEAD OF A GENIUS HOLDING A SERPENT.[1]

CHAPTER CVII.

JULIAN (NOV. 3, 361, TO JUNE 26, 363).[1]

I. — The Pagan Reaction.

JULIAN was not the philosopher who, master of himself, keeps his mind free from superstitious fears and dangerous or idle curiosity; he was a devotee, and all the more sincere as such, in that he had reasoned out his faith, and that his religion was a system. In constructing it he began by putting aside the contradictions of the masters of human thought[2] and the fables of a too charming mythology; then, from the confused mass of instruction given in books, in schools, and in the mysteries, he derived, for his own use, a sort of revelation, which may be called Hellenism, and was regarded by him as contrary to the

JULIAN AUGUSTUS.[3]

revelation of the Jewish Scriptures. Did not pagan wisdom also come from the gods and from men who were their interpreters? Later we shall examine his theology; here, we need mention only his firm faith that the gods, intervening in human affairs, sent to men divine inspirations to direct them in life, for this faith determined his political conduct. "What motive," he wrote, "brought me from Gaul after the death of Constantius? A command from the gods, who

---

[1] A list of ancient and modern works relative to the Emperor Julian will be found in G. H. Rendall's work, *The Emperor Julian, Paganism, and Christianity*, pp. 291 *et seq*, Cambridge, 1879. Two interesting articles on the same subject are those of MM. Boissier and Martha, in the *Revue des Deux Mondes*. M. Talbot has made a good [French] translation of Julian's works.

[2] He did not grant to the materialists and the sceptics, to Epicurus and Pyrrho, the honor of including them among philosophers. He calls the sceptical Oenomaos, the author of *The Charlatans unveiled*, "a bestial soul" (*Discourses* v. and vii.).

[3] D. N. FL. CL. IVLIANVS, P. F. AVG. Diademed bust; on the reverse, Isis suckling Horus, with the legend, VOTA PVBLICA. (Medium bronze.)

promised me safety if I obeyed." [1] Accordingly, the religious question was the chief concern of his reign; the rest is by way of episode, and will be related in a few words, after which we shall be more at liberty to examine the pagan reaction which he attempted.

In politics, as well as in religion, Julian is a man of the past. He does well to renounce the servile ceremonial of the court, to refuse the titles of Master and Lord, and to believe that in the transmission of the imperial authority the principle of adoption is better than that of hereditary succession; but it is a mistake for him to copy and exaggerate the conduct of the Antonines towards the Senate, for this is to misconceive both the men and the times in which he lives. We have explained what were the motives of the respect shown by those Emperors for this last relic of the old Republic, which, though no longer formidable, might still be useful. In the fourth century these motives had ceased to exist, and an affected deference towards the humble assembly now gathered at Constantinople was in contradiction with the new phase of the government, of the court, and of public manners. When Julian takes his seat in the curia as a mere senator with the others, or conducts the consuls thither, walking on foot beside their state-chariot; [2] when in the circus he holds his imperial majesty in the shade, that he may let the consular dignity have its due splendor; when, lastly, having through inadvertence himself enfranchised the slaves whom the consuls on their day of taking office were about to set free, he condemns himself to a fine of ten pounds of gold for thus taking what he chose to regard as undue precedence of those magistrates, — all this is trivial and unworthy, a policy of outward shows; we should indeed say a hypocritical policy, if Julian, the literary man, the scholar, who had more memory than imagination, did not show himself manifestly sincere in his attempts to call back the past. On one occasion, when a vindication of Christianity had been offered him, he wrote underneath it: "I read, I understood, I condemned." The words of Caesar which he imitated had expressed an heroic fact;

---

[1] *Letter* 13. The gods had already forbidden him, when he was at Milan, to send to Eusebia his refusal to accept the title of Caesar (*Letter to the Athenians*, sect. 7). "A god suggested the idea to me," he wrote to Themistius. Amm. Marcellinus (xxx. 4) says of him: *Superstitiosus magis quam sacrorum legitimus observator.*

[2] . . . *Quod quidam ut adfectatum et vile carpebant* (Amm. Marcellinus, xxii. 7).

JULIAN. STATUE OF GREEK MARBLE (PARIS, PALAIS DES THERMES, FORMERLY IN THE LOUVRE).

Julian's were but a pedantic reminiscence. His last utterances were of the same nature. On the banks of the Tigris he died, as did Socrates in Athens, repeating a page of the *Phaedo.*

The first man whom he appointed consul was a rhetorician, Mamertinus; and the new functionary thanked the Emperor in a sonorous and empty harangue, wherein he said: "Philosophy, of late suspected and judged guilty, but to-day clad in purple and crowned with gold and pearls, is now seated upon the imperial throne."[1]   She was not always thus sumptuously apparelled. While certain sophists, whom the Emperor had gathered around him, displayed, thanks to his liberality, an insolent ostentation,[2] he himself went poorly clad, and his frugality would have made a Cynic discontented. This affectation of simplicity, good in ancient Sparta, but ridiculous upon the Byzantine throne, reveals in this amiable and lofty mind and this honest heart the weakness of a child. The Emperor's contempt for official display at least saved an innocent man, who under Constantius would have been a criminal punished with death. A person was accused of entertaining ambitious designs because he had a purple robe. Julian's reply to this information was to charge the informer to carry to the supposed offender, to complete his costume, a pair of shoes of the same imperial hue.

These eccentricities, however, did not prevent him from keeping intact the plenitude of imperial power, and in Gaul he had learned how to use it. Notwithstanding his philosophy, or perhaps by reason of it, he held the highest ideas of the duty of the sovereign, "who should expel from his mind whatever is unworthy, must rise above other men, and become a sort of divine being. . . . That the ruler may be better than the ruled, it must needs be that the law, the emanation of pure reason, reign alone, and not the arbitrary will of man, who may be but a wild beast

---

[1] *Pan. vet. in Jul., ad fin.*

[2] Eunapius, *Maximus,* and Amm. Marcellinus, xx. 12, 13. Julian wrote two treatises against the false Cynics who sought to derive profit from his philosophy and austerity. Saint John Chrysostom, in his *Babylas against the Gentiles,* represents this Emperor as surrounded by magicians, enchanters, and men and women of the most degraded character. Saint Gregory Nazianzen confirms this. It is strange to see to what depth of hate and injustice zeal for a good cause will sink even very noble minds. Julian doubtless had about him far too many pagan priests, diviners, augurs, and thaumaturgi (see Amm. Marcellinus, xxii. 12); but his palace was forever closed to men of evil life and to shameless women.

in a palace." [1]   These ideas are noble, but difficult to put in practice. Julian, however, sought to approach to this ideal. A page of Marcellinus on this Emperor's spirit of justice does him great

JULIAN.[2]

honor, coming from a writer who was an honest man, a patriot, a soldier, and never a courtier; who loved Julian, yet censures certain of his acts; who, though a pagan, had no unwise zeal for paganism, shows himself just towards the Christians, and in religious matters would have every man left to follow the dictates of his own conscience. "Instead of yielding to temptations," he says, "Julian applied all the powers of his mind to doing justice, to repressing dishonesty, and to protecting the right. In no case did the religion of the person concerned have any influence upon his decisions. A judge should take into account only the right and wrong; and Julian no more forgot to observe this rule than the sailor forgets to be mindful of the shoals in the seas." [3]

He began by bestowing favors upon Constantinople, where he was born, and whose inhabitants delighted to call him "the child of the city." [4] He increased the privileges of its senate and improved its harbor; also he built a portico and a library, and made to the latter a gift of books. For the Empire he remitted the arrearages of contributions, reduced the taxes, and announced that

---

[1] *Letter to Themistius.* Julian says: "Train three or four philosophers, and you will have done more service to humanity than many kings would do." There was an interchange of flatteries between the Emperor and the orator which we must not take too literally.

[2] Intaglio, No. 161 of the De Luynes Collection, in the *Cabinet de France.* Cornelian, 16 millim. by 14.

[3] Amm. Marcellinus, xxii. 10.

[4] Zosimus, iii. 11 : . . . τρόφιμον ἑαυτῶν. Julian himself called Constantinople his home.

the heavy tax of coronary gold should henceforth be voluntary.
This was his "gift of happy accession." [1]

Amm. Marcellinus calls the court of the late Emperor a sink
of all vices; and we have seen what exactions, rapines, and cruelties were there committed. From the time of his arrival in Constantinople Julian was assailed with complaints and accusations
against those "savage beasts." [2] He refused to inaugurate his
reign by summary executions, but he established at Chalcedon a
tribunal composed of the highest personages in the Empire to
make pillagers disgorge, and to judge those ministers of Constantius who had sent so many innocent men to punishment for im-
aginary crimes. It was one of those political tribunals which are
always bad, because, under the cover of justice, hatred, cupidity,
and all evil passions combine against the vanquished, who are
already punished by their defeat. Many persons really guilty were
exiled or put to death, but also many who had done no more than
obey Constantius. [3] These condemnations have been regarded as a
persecution of the Christians; they were, however, nothing more
than a reaction against the last reign; but Julian should have
arrested its excesses sooner than he did. The praetorian prefect
had already condemned to be burned the commander of the legions
at Aquileia, and had caused two curiales of that city to be decap-
itated, guilty of having remained faithful to their Emperor until

[1] Themistius wrote, in 367, in his eighth discourse (edit. Hardouin, p. 113) that within
the last forty years — that is to say, under Constantine and his sons — the taxes had been
doubled. The government, however, was none the richer for that. Julian shows the treasury empty, and the cities and provinces impoverished; and he holds responsible for this destitution those who had bought with gold peace from the Barbarians. — *principes auro quiete
a barbaris redempta* (Amm. Marcellinus, xxiv. 3). This system of subsidies had been carried
so far that the meanest enemies, like the Saracens, received them (*Ibid.* xxv. 6).

[2] Julian, *Letter* 23.

[3] Most of the condemned were sent into exile; but there were also death-penalties.
Amm. Marcellinus says that Justice wept at the death of Ursulus. This person had insulted the army by reproaching it with having exhausted the Empire by its demands,
while it did nothing for the public protection. His remarks, says Amm. Marcellinus
(xx. 2), occasioned his death at Chalcedon. He adds (xxii. 7) that Julian refused to
listen to two informers who knew where Florentinus, his personal enemy above all others
who were condemned at this time, was hid. Julian, announcing to Hermogenes (*Letter* 23)
the formation of this tribunal, which he would not have held its sessions at Constantinople, lest he should be accused of dictating its sentences, writes: "I will not have these
savage beasts, who made Constantius cruel, suffer the least injustice, by Jupiter I will not!
But as they have many accusers, we have given them judges." Rendall (*op. cit.* p. 154)
says in this connection: "Julian may be acquitted without reserve from the odium of
wilful persecution."

they heard of his death. Such was the harshness of the times that
the honest Marcellinus regards the sentence as legitimate.

We have seen what a crowd of useless servitors and hungry
courtiers infested the palace, which had become a gulf in which
the larger part of the imperial revenues were swallowed up; Julian
dismissed all this gilded train, and sold the eunuchs, "who were '
more numerous than flies on a summer day."[1]

The exactions and venality of officials of every grade were
harmful at once to the tax-payers and to the treasury; immunities made the city burdens very heavy, and the prodigality of
permits granted for free travel ruined the imperial post.[2] Julian
strove to render the administration honest, and reduced the class
of privileged persons who lived as parasites at the country's expense. All governors were required to pay into the treasury within
thirty days the sums received for taxes, on penalty of a fine of
ten pounds of gold in their own case, and twenty pounds from
their employers, who, thus rendered responsible together with their
chief, found it for their interest not to lend themselves to cul-
pable indulgences in making out their accounts. Any false record
involved the penalty of torture, and, that the evidence against such
offender could be given without danger to him who testified, all
officials were to be suspended from their office for twelve months
out of every five years, — a precaution no less singular than the
preceding, and, like it, a sure index of the intensity of the evil.[3]
He reduced the number of those who enjoyed municipal immunities. For this, Amm. Marcellinus blames him, and that historian
finds his reform of the palace too severe; we, on the contrary,
praise him for it, and also applaud the decree which limited to
public functionaries travelling for the service of the State the use
of the *cursus publicus*.[4] He relieved, as he had done in Gaul, the
provinces that were too heavily taxed,[5] and restored to the cities
the revenues of which they had been deprived, at the same time

---

[1] *Misopogon*, 14.
[2] See above, p. 144, n. 2.
[3] *Codex Theod.* xi. 30, 31, and viii. 1, 6–8.
[4] *Ibid.* xii. 1, 48, 50–54; viii. 5, 12–15.
[5] . . . φορῶν ἄνεσις (Gregory Nazianzen, *Disc.* iv. sect. 75). Gregory recognized also
that Julian was prompt in the pursuit of robbers (λῃστῶν ἐπιτίμησις). Eutropius (x. 16)
bears him witness that he was *in provinciales justissimus et tributorum, quatenus possel,
repressor, civilis in cunctos, mediocrem habens aerarii curam.*

maintaining the severity of the laws against the curiales who deserted their office. We have seen for what reason the prosperity of the town was the condition of the Empire's prosperity. The *curiosi* were like the police in so many countries, regarded with aversion by a part of the population; he reduced their number, — which might well be necessary after the enormous system of espionage organized by Constantius.[1] Libanius asserts that he abolished the office completely.[2] This would have been a foolish attempt to gain popularity, a simple-minded and quite too philosophical confidence in the respect of the subjects for their Emperor and for the law.

But to heal the maladies from which the Empire suffered, time was needed, and this Julian had not. He believed, moreover, in the efficacy of quite a different remedy; namely, the regeneration of the Empire by the return of the Roman world to the worship of the old gods.

On his return from Gaul, Julian had opened the temples which he found closed all along his road, and he made amends for the long indifference which he had been obliged to manifest towards the gods, by sacrificing victims to them daily. His letter to the Athenians, of which a copy was addressed to other cities of the Empire,[3] announced to the world that a pagan Emperor had succeeded to two generations of Christian Emperors.

SMALL BRONZE.[4]

The long-suspected change did not appear to be a revolution. Amm. Marcellinus attaches no importance to it; and many like himself. men of calm reason, much more preoccupied with the too-certain perils of the Empire than with disputes upon the unknown, aspired to that domestic peace which was disturbed by so many vain words,

---

[1] Constantius himself was obliged to moderate their zeal (*Codex Theod.* vi. 29; cf. *Codex Just.* title 23).

[2] This author was mistaken; for at Caesarea in Cappadocia the clergy, as a punishment for a riot, were enrolled as police (Sozomenus, v. 4; Saint Basil, *Letter* 20).

[3] Zosimus says (iii. 1) that he wrote to the Athenians, the Lacedaemonians, the Corinthians, and through them to all the Greeks, τὰς αἰτίας τῆς σφετέρας ἐμφαίνων ἀποστάσεως.

[4] Coin of Julian, bearing the effigy of the Pharian Isis. ISIS FARIA holding the *sistrum*, with a lotus-flower on the head. On the reverse is Harpocrates, his right hand raised to his mouth and holding a cornucopia. The legend is VOTA PVBLICA. Many coins have these Egyptian types, especially the head of Serapis, personification of the Sun and the supreme divinity. Julian sometimes is represented as Serapis, and Helena as Isis. See above, p. 89.

noisy councils, and episcopal seditions. As Julian appeared desirous of allowing to others the religious liberty which he took for himself, the Orthodox saw in his accession only the close of the Arian persecution, and Saint Jerome wrote: "At last the Lord awakes; the beast is dead, and tranquillity returns." If the adversaries of Orthodoxy regretted Constantius, they believed themselves strong enough in the East, of which they had held possession for thirty years, to do without the support of the government, from whose interference they themselves had more than once suffered. As to the world of functionaries, they, with their usual servility, bent the knee to the new master; and the crowd, wherein the lukewarm and indifferent always compose the majority, passes so easily from one faith to another that Julian could write, even before the death of Constantius: "We adore the gods publicly, and all the army that is with me is devoted to their worship."[2] The ancient symbols replaced the Christian monogram upon the standards, and pagan types reappeared upon the coins, which were refused by no one. "Authority," says Themistius, "has great powers of persuasion; in changing religion we are more mobile than the waves of the Euripus."[3]

BRONZE.[1]

In these first moments of liberty and of power, Julian, by words and conduct, personally endeavored to spread his own views; but he never did this in any violent way. It is even to a Christian that he proposes the work of writing a history of the recent events. "If you intend to set forth," he says, "the causes of my return, and write its history, I will acquaint you with everything, and transmit to you the original letters and other authentic evidence."[4] Another instance of moderation is related of him in regard to the funeral rites of Constantius. When the body arrived from Asia in the harbor of Constantinople, Julian went to receive it with uncrowned head, in sign of mourning, and accompanied it to the Church of the Holy Apostles,

---

[1] Julian as Serapis. Small bronze.

[2] Julian, *Letter* 38, *to the philosopher Maximus*. The day of the distribution of the *donativum* a few soldiers, impelled, after carousing, by their companions' raillery, who reproached them for accepting pagan coins, made a little disturbance; but Julian contented himself with sending them away into other corps.

[3] In *Discourse V.*, p. 67 of the Hardouin edition.

[4] *Letter* 2, *To the rhetorician Proaeresius.*

where the Christian ceremony took place. The pagans, on their
part, offered funeral sacrifices in the temples, in which the Emperor
participated, pouring the usual libations.[1] "He congratulated those
who had followed him," says Libanius, "and advised others to imitate them, but exercised constraint towards none." Putting this
toleration into practice, he recalled all who had been exiled by Constantius, — Orthodox, Arians, Novatians, Donatists; but he did not,
however, dispossess those who had been installed in the episcopal
sees vacated by banishment of the former holders.[2] He restored
confiscated property,[3] and forbade that any injury should be done
to the Christians. "These persons," he says, "are religious after
their own manner; for the God whom they worship is the same
good and powerful Being to whom we address our prayers under
other names."[4] "He ordered the priests of the different Christian
sects, with the adherents of each sect, to be admitted into the
palace, and expressed his wish that, their dissensions being appeased, each, without any hindrance, might fearlessly follow the
religion he preferred. . . . And he often used to say: 'Listen to
me, to whom the Franks and the Alemanni have listened.'"[5]
With extreme good sense, he sought for a cessation of these
interminable feuds; for, he says, "we should rather pity than
hate those who in the most important concerns act ill; and as
piety is the greatest of blessings, impiety is certainly the greatest
of evils." In the same letter,[6] which was written nine months
after his accession, he thus expresses his policy towards the
Christians: "They who had been banished are allowed to return;
and to those whose goods had been confiscated, all have been re-

---

[1] In respect to this ceremony we have two accounts, — one from Gregory Nazianzen
(*Disc.* v. 16–17, edit. of 1840), who does not say that Julian entered the church; the other
from Libanius (*Disc.* x. 289, edit. of 1627), who represents the Emperor as "inaugurating at
Constantinople the worship of the gods."

[2] Julian, *Letter* 31.

[3] Id., *Letter* 52.

[4] Id., *Letters* 7 and 63.

[5] Amm. Marcellinus, xxii. 5: . . . *Monebat civilius ut discordiis consopitis quisque, nullo
vetante, religioni suae serviret, intrepidus.* Ammianus adds that in reality Julian desired by
indulgence to increase the mutual hostility of the theologians, for the purpose of augmenting
the confusion in the Churches. But this interpretation is contrary to the Emperor's words
quoted by the historian, of which the sincerity is attested by many of Julian's letters. We
have seen, moreover, that in that religious caldron, the Christian East, there was no need of
crafty incitement to occasion the bursting forth of quarrels.

[6] *Letter* 52, to the people of Bostra.

stored. . . . We suffer none to be dragged to the altars against their will. We also publicly declare that if any are desirous to partake of our lustrations and libations, they must first offer sacrifices of expiation, and supplicate the gods, the averters of evil. So far are we from wishing to admit any of the irreligious to our sacred rites before they have purified their souls by prayers to the gods, and their bodies by legal ablutions. . . . It is my pleasure to declare to all the people that . . . they may assemble together if they please, and offer up such prayers as they have established for themselves; but if the clergy endeavor to persuade them to foment disturbances, let them by no means concur, on pain of punishment. . . . For the future, let the people agree among themselves; let no one be at variance, or do an injury to another, — neither you who are in error to those who worship the gods rightly and justly in the mode transmitted to us from the most ancient times, nor let the worshippers of the gods destroy or plunder the houses of those who, rather by ignorance than choice, are led astray. Men should be taught and persuaded by reason, not by blows, invectives, and corporal punishment."

While making no attack, he still proposed to defend himself, and he did this by reactionary measures. Constantine and the Christians had been the radicals of their time; Julian was a conservative. Although he put a somewhat free interpretation upon past events, it was his desire that the words *mos majorum*, which had been so forceful to the old Romans, should remain the rule of conduct for both Emperor and people. "The nation," he said, "ought to keep the same gods which have been handed down to it from the remotest antiquity, and the citizen ought not to abandon his country's religion." [1] In his mind paganism was a principle of conservation. What, however, should this paganism be? That of Rome or of Greece, of Egypt or of Syria? On this point the conservative became, in his turn, an innovator. He accepted freely from Plato and the Alexandrians, — kindred thinkers, [2] — from the solar myths of Asia Minor, and even from Christianity, whose discipline was agreeable to his moral ideas and his instincts

---

[1] Naville, *Julien l'Apostat*, p. 77.

[2] Saint Augustine, who is a pupil of Plato as much as he is a disciple of Christ, who rises towards God by philosophy as well as by faith and love, and finds in the Platonic school many ideas in conformity with his own, regards Plotinus as a second Plato (*Works*, i. 294).

of government. His *Discourse in Honor of the Sun-King* was the
gospel of the new official cult; and as a religion requires the mysterious, he gave to his the dark marvels
of theurgy. Aedesius, the successor of Iamblichus in the school of Neo-Platonism,
was believed to have intercourse with the
gods. Julian had besought this philosopher to reveal to him the divine science;
but Aedesius replied that he himself was
an old man and very near to death, and
that the Emperor must question his sons.[1]
These sons of the philosopher's soul were
Maximus and Priscus, and both became
the trusted friends and counsellors of Julian, continuing with the Emperor until
his death.

THE SUN.[2]

In Julian's theology[3] three worlds are recognized: the Cosmic,
wherein matter appears with all its imperfections; the Intelligible (τὸ νοητόν), which is filled with pure immaterial being, or,
in other words, the Intelligible Gods, who possess in the highest degree all the attributes of beauty, eternity, absoluteness, and
spirituality; and between absolute immateriality and matter, between
that which is immutable and that which changes incessantly, —
in brief, between these two worlds, so remote that one could not
have issued from the other, there exists the Intellectual World
(τὸ νοερόν), the faint copy of the one, the model of the other.
The visible world, therefore, is only the image of an image, —
that of the absolute world, — as its visible gods correspond, but
reduced in power and dignity to the Intelligible Gods of the
highest world. Each of these worlds has its Sun: the Sun of
the highest world frequently entitled King of the Universe, chief
among the Intelligible Gods; the Sun of the lowest, that heavenly
body which we see; the Sun of the Intellectual World, a divinity

---

[1] Eunapius, *Life of Aedesius.*

[2] The Sun, wearing the radiate crown, and holding a whip in his hand. Intaglio, agate of
three layers, 10 millim. high and 5 wide (*Cabinet de France*, No. 1,478).

[3] On Julian's theology, see Naville, *Julien l'Apostat et sa philosophie du polythéisme:*
Boissier, *L'Empereur Julien;* and G. H. Rendall, *The Emperor Julian, Paganism, and
Philosophy.*

whom we do not see, but whose power in this secondary sphere
is universal and beneficent. This is the King-Sun of Julian's
system; he is considered the source of being, the central principle,
ruling all by his wisdom. This is the Logos of Plato, possibly
the Word of God of the Nicene Council,[1] and certainly the dream
of a dream.

It matters little whether Julian in his theogony has done
nothing more than follow the Alexandrians, or whether, well informed as he was in Christian doctrines, he proposed to establish
a relation between the Second Person of the Trinity and the most
popular of pagan divinities. What he actually did was to take
up the Platonic thesis of a mediator; and Porphyry, Iamblichus,
all the thaumaturgists, who had destroyed philosophy by mingling
superstition with it,[2] taught the worshipper of King Sun to put
himself in communication with the gods by fasting, which prepared for visions, and by ecstasy, which caused them to appear.
It was a so-called science, having its rules and a name, — theurgy.
By these mysteries the pagan priests supplied the place of the inspiration, the divine afflatus, that they no longer found among men;
and they believed that in this way the divine will was made known to
them also, and with it, the conditions of salvation. The two faiths,
therefore, claimed to possess the same weapons. But Julian's heaven
is very dark, notwithstanding its three suns. And his cloudy
theology, which substitutes for Homer's gods, dazzling with life
and beauty, these subtle abstractions which we can with difficulty
comprehend, these strange sounds heard in the depths of sanctuaries, these statues which are seen to move in the darkness,[3] these
apparitions which men in a condition of ecstasy thought they
beheld, — all these things had effect upon only a small number of
adepts and illuminati. Only a narrow sect could believe in things
like these, and not a multitude; for in theurgy all was personal and
secret. How different from the Church, which recognized divine

---

[1] Lamé (*Julien l'Apostat*, p. 235) and Naville (*Julien l'Apostat*, etc., p. 104) entertain
this idea; but Rendall (*The Emperor Julian*, etc., p. 93) rejects it, and rightly, as I think.
See, Vol. VI. pp. 401 *et seq.*, how familiar to philosophers was the theory of the λόγος θείος.

[2] See, in Eunapius, *The Life of Iamblichus, and the Miracles done by him.* J. Simon
(*Hist. de l'École d'Alexandrie*, ii. 266) says: "Maximus, Cleanthes, and Julian are, through
Aedesius, the descendants of Iamblichus."

[3] Eunapius, in his *Life of Maximus*, asserts that this thaumaturgist could give life to
statues by his spells.

inspiration only in the decisions of its bishops assembled in council, where all was done openly and with free discussions!

Julian seems to have been no more successful with his clergy than with his system of dogmas. This adventurous theologian was a man of lofty morality. Plato had bidden men strive to resemble God, — ἐξομοίωσις τῷ θεῷ. Jesus had said : " Be ye therefore perfect, even as your Father which is in heaven is perfect." And the Church repeated the sentiment of Saint Basil : " The rich man is God's steward sent to relieve the poor." Many in the pagan world sought to approach this ideal, and Julian was of the number.[1] He used his authority as pontifex maximus to require from his priests virtues which cannot be assumed by order. In time he might have been able to introduce more discipline into his Church, more morality into the lives of his priests, more institutions of benevolence into the community : these things are useful to the state. He has at least the honor of having attempted them. " The office of a priest," he writes, in a kind of encyclical letter of which a fragment has been preserved, " being necessarily more worthy of respect than that of any other citizen, may be proper for me now to consider that, and to teach you its obligations. . . . In the first place, above all things cultivate philanthropy, as this is attended by many other blessings, and particularly by that which is the greatest and most excellent of all, — the favor of the gods. . . . Of philanthropy there are various kinds : one is the punishing offenders sparingly, and that for the good of the punished, as masters correct their scholars ; another is the relieving the wants of the poor, . . . especially when any of them are in morals irreproachable. . . . Who was ever impoverished by what he gave to others? I for my part, as often as I have been liberal to the poor, have been abundantly rewarded by the gods. . . . I will add, though it may seem paradoxical, that it is a duty to give clothing and food to our enemies, for we give it to

---

Note. — The diptych of Anastasius, consul in 571, represents in its lower portion scenes of the amphitheatre. The richness of the costumes shows the Oriental luxury of the Byzantine court. This diptych, long preserved in the Cathedral of Bourges, is now in the National Library (Paris).

[1] Another pagan, Macrobius, who was praefectus cubiculi to the younger Theodosius, wrote in the fifth century : " We ought to speak to men as if the gods heard us, and to the gods as if all men could hear " (Saturn. i. 7).

their nature, and not to their conduct. And therefore I think
that those who are imprisoned in dungeons are also worthy of
this attention, since this humanity by no means interferes with
justice. . . . Above all, it is indispensable that the priests be active
in works of piety, that they may approach the gods with religious
awe, and that they may not say or hear or read anything that
is shameful. Far, therefore, from us be all licentious jests and all
scurrilous discourse. . . . I am of opinion that a priest should in
every respect be immaculate. . . . The hymns of the gods should be
learned, which are many and beautiful, composed both by ancients
and moderns; and chiefly those which are sung in the temples. . . .
These deserve to be studied; and the gods should frequently be addressed in private as well as in public,—generally, three times a day,
or at least in the dawn and the evening; . . . for as the dawn is
the beginning of the day, so is the evening of the night, and therefore it is reasonable to offer the first-fruits, as it were, of both
these intervals to the gods. . . . Let no admittance be given to
the doctrine of Epicurus, nor to that of Pyrrho. The gods indeed
have wisely abolished them, many of their writings being lost; but
it cannot be improper to mention them, for the sake of example,
to show what kind of books the priests ought chiefly to shun. . . .
Be assured that the gods have given us great hopes after death,
and on them we may with confidence rely, as they are incapable
of deceiving not only in such matters, but in any of the concerns
of human life. If by their excellent power they can correct all
the disturbances and monstrous abuses that happen in this life,
how much more in the other — where the contending parts are dis-
united, the soul being separated and the body dead — will they be
able to perform all the promises they have made to mankind! . . .
It becomes us, therefore, to minister to them, as supposing them
present, and seeing us — though we see not them — with a sight
superior to every kind of splendor, penetrating our most secret
thoughts. . . .

"Let me add that I think it becoming for the priests to wear
in the temple, during their ministration, a most magnificent habit,
but out of it a common plain dress. . . . But for us to wear the
habit and not lead the lives of priests, is in itself a summary of
every transgression, and the greatest contempt of the gods. . . .

COURT COSTUMES OF BYZANTIUM, AND SCENES OF THE AMPHITHEATRE.

"Let the priests be chosen from among persons of the best character in every city. . . . And let no distinction be made between the noble and the man of low condition. . . . Though a man be poor, or a plebeian, if he have these two endowments, love towards the gods, and love towards men, let him be elected into the priesthood."

Julian proposes to have these precepts followed by his priests. One of them has beaten a colleague; the Emperor suspends him from his priestly functions for three months, counsels him to repent, and ends the reproof in these words: "And knowing that the priests are the ministers of our prayers, I join my hopes and prayers to yours, that by many and earnest entreaties you may obtain the pardon of the gods."

Maximin, the colleague of Galerius and Licinius, had established in each province a pontifex who was to exercise superintendence over the doctrine and life of the inferior priests, as the metropolitan of the Christian Church was the spiritual guardian of the bishops in his province. This institution Julian strengthened still further. "The commission which I now give you," he writes to Theodore, appointing him pontifex of the province of Asia, "is the superintendence of all the priests in Asia, both in the cities and in the country, with full powers to treat every one according to his deserts."[1] In a letter addressed to Arsacius, pontifex in Galatia, he writes: —

"That Hellenism does not yet succeed as we wish, is owing to its professors. The gifts of the gods are indeed great and splendid, superior to all our hopes, to all our wishes. . . . But why should we be satisfied with this, and not rather attend to the means by which this impiety [the Christian Church] has increased; namely, humanity to strangers, care in burying the dead, and pretended sanctity of life? All these I think should be really practised by us. It is not sufficient for you only to be blameless; entreat or compel all the priests that are in Galatia to be also virtuous. If they do not, with their wives, children, and servants, attend the worship of the gods, expel them from the priestly function. . . . Admonish also every priest not to frequent the theatre, nor to drink in taverns, nor to exercise any trade or employment that is

[1] *Letter* 63.

mean or disgraceful. Those who obey you, honor; and those who disobey you, expel. Erect also hospitals in every city, that strangers may partake our benevolence; and not only those of our own religion, but, if they are indigent, others also.

"How these expenses are to be defrayed, must now be considered. I have ordered Galatia to supply you with thirty thousand bushels of wheat every year, of which the fifth part is to be given to the poor who attend on the priests, and the remainder to be distributed among strangers and our own beggars. For when none of the Jews beg, and the impious Galileans relieve both their own poor and ours, it is shameful that ours should be destitute of our assistance.[1] . . . Let us not suffer others to emulate our good actions, while we ourselves are disgraced by sloth; lest by negligence we lose our reverence for the gods. If I hear that you practise this, I shall overflow with joy."[2]

Pagan priests there were who practised all these virtuous lessons. Read the noble letters written, fifty years later, to the Bishop of Hippo by the philosopher Maximus of Madaura, the pontiff Longinianus, and the honest pagan Nectarius, and you will find in them many worthy thoughts, — those which philosophy, aside from any creed, has made the patrimony of the whole human race.

Preaching is a powerful agent in spreading a religion; we have seen that it was employed with ardor by the philosophers of the second century, and Saint Augustine recognizes their success in it. In the centuries that followed, the Christians had taken the place of the philosophers. To dispute it with them, Julian proposed to establish in the temples that moral and religious instruction which paganism had always lacked; we know from Libanius that this enterprise was begun, and from the Bishop of Hippo that it continued up to his time.[3]

---

[1] In referring to these attempts made by Julian, Gregory Nazianzen (vol. i. p. 101) calls him "the ape of Christianity." But an ape like this is a very worthy person. Does not all social progress arise out of imitation of what is good? Are we able to say that Christianity has borrowed nothing?

[2] *Letter* 63.

[3] In one of his letters Libanius congratulates the rhetorician Acacius — concerning whom Eunapius writes (*Acac.* p. 497) that had he not died young, he would have surpassed Libanius himself — upon a "sermon" on Aesculapius, delivered in a recently reopened temple. "We now have," says Saint Augustine, "for the public who gather in the

II. — THE GREAT BISHOPS AND THE MONKS OF THE FOURTH CENTURY.

THE rapid progress thus far made by Christianity had been due to its love for the poor, and to the definiteness of its promises concerning the future life. Julian, who had certainly read and pondered the two treatises of Plutarch *Concerning Superstition* and *On the Delays of Divine Justice*,[1] did not leave to " the Galileans " alone this sanction of religious and moral duties, at once a blessing and a terror to the mortal life. Plato's imperial pupil had not his master's hesitation in respect to the nature of the soul, or at least the permanent character of human personality. At the beginning of his reign he celebrated King-Sun in a hymn of

temples, very useful interpretations of the history of the gods; yesterday, or the day before, we heard some of them " (*Works*, ii. 278). "Julian intended," says Gregory Nazianzen. " to establish schools and professorships in all the cities, lectures on Greek doctrines, explanations of Nature, in order to form habits of virtue, . . . and reprimands appropriate to different classes of sinners. He also wished to found asylums, hospitals, monasteries, houses for virgins, and places of devotion " (*Invective I.* p. 138, edit. 1842. Cf. Naville, *Julien l'Apostat*, p. 163). Christianity was a law of inner improvement, and this law made men saints; it was not a cause of social renovation, — hence it neither saved the state nor improved the public morals. But the basis of this religion being love, while theologians carried on long and subtle discussions on doctrines, pious hearts employed the time in establishing these charitable institutions which do honor to the Christian spirit. Justinian (*Codex Just.* i. 2, 19) speaks of donations made . . . *in sanctam ecclesiam, vel in zenodochium, vel in nosocomium, vel in orphanotrophium, vel in ptochotrophium, vel in gerontocomium, vel in brephotrophium, vel in ipsos pauperes;* and he recalls the fact that these gifts were regulated by ancient laws, *ex veteris legibus* (cf. *Ibid.* law 22, and title 3). I do not, however, believe that any one of these words occurs in the Theodosian Code, which was compiled in 438. But it is certain that the Church very early favored institutions of benevolence. Saint Basil, who died in 379, had constructed at Caesarea, for sick travellers, a hospital to which were attached physicians and nurses, where there were work-rooms, beasts of burden, and guides for the service of the house (*Letter* 94). It will be remembered, however, that the pagan cities had long possessed ξενῶνα, or caravansaries, to receive travellers, that they had furnished medicine gratuitously to the poor, that the philosophers had taught benevolence, and mighty monarchs had practised it when they founded alimentary institutions Pliny had already said : " To do good to men is to be as God." Charity was not unknown in the ancient world, for it is a sentiment which is found in the human heart; but it had its chief development only under Christianity, which greatly enhances its force by making of this natural sentiment one of the conditions of salvation.

[1] Vol. VI. p. 413.

ardent devotion,[1] which he ends with these words: "I implore the Sun, king of all beings, to

HANASTASIVS·PAV·PRO
MOSCHIAN·PROB·MAGNVS

CHARITY BESTOWED ON THE POOR.[2]

[1] Addressed to his friend Sallust, whom he had appointed prefect of the Gallic provinces. He says, in closing, that it had been his wish in composing this hymn to manifest his gratitude towards the god. To Plato, the immortality of the soul was a hope to be cherished as the delight of a man's life; but he did not attempt to prove the point of chief importance, — namely, that in the future life the individual would preserve his personal existence.

[2] *Cabinet de France*, No. 3,265. Half of a consular diptych of the consul H. (probably for Fl., by an error of the engraver) ANASTASIVS PAVL[us] PROB[us] MOSCHIAN[us] PROB[us] MAG-N[us] (size, 38 centim. by 13). The gifts are represented, in the lower part of the diptych, by the two slaves who are pouring out pieces of money from sacks. Magnus is represented as a beardless youth. Rome and Constantinople personified stand one on each side of his curule chair, which is supported by lions and has its arms ornamented with statuettes of Victory. It will be observed, as in the diptych represented on an earlier page, that the consul's robe is loaded with embroideries. Asterius, bishop of Amasia about the close of the fourth century, has left us in one of his homilies (Photius, *Cod.* 271) a sarcastic description of these costumes, some of which contain as many as six hundred figures: "When men thus attired appear in the streets," he says, "the passers-by look at them as at painted walls. Their garments are pictures which children call each other to behold. There are lions, panthers, and bears. There are rocks, woods, and hunters. The more devout have pictures of the Christ, his disciples and his miracles: here is the marriage of Cana, and the vessels full of wine; the man sick with the palsy taking up his bed, or the woman who was a sinner, at the feet of Jesus, or Lazarus restored to life. . . ." Herr Grauf, of Vienna, has a very curious collection of these materials, broché, embroidered, or woven after the manner of tapestry, which have recently been collected in Egypt. One of the most

respond to my devotion by his favor, to grant me a pure life, the
knowledge of divine things, and, when the fatal hour shall come,
a tranquil end and a swift flight to him, and, if it be possible,
an eternal abode in him."[1] This nearly resembles the idea of
Malebranche : "God is the place of spirits, as space is the place
of bodies." But this dogma of an immortal Existence in an arid
sky, whose gods are formless and lifeless, had no attractions in
comparison with the hope of the heavenly blessedness which the
Christians believed themselves called to enjoy amid celestial splendors and the music of golden harps and sacred songs intoned by
choirs of angels, of virgins, and of triumphant martyrs at the
foot of the throne of the Almighty, whose Divine Wisdom would
make all things known to the elect.

Julian had attempted to seize upon the two great forces of
Christianity, — charity, and the hope of a future life. His ambition was a worthy one, and we cannot censure the acts by which
he strove to fulfil it, so long as he carried on the struggle by
word only, and by meritorious acts. It was a return to the wise
policy of the edict of Milan. But was he to be able to hold to
this policy more consistently than its original author had done?
This was to become difficult for him, for he had a sectary's
enthusiasm ; and when he recognized the vanity of his efforts in
opposing to Christianity a religion which he had based on moul-
dering foundations, he became irritated at his own powerlessness.
His honest nature counselled him to toleration ; his pagan fervor

interesting is the angusticlave of a Roman knight of the fourth century.   It represents an
Emperor seated on his throne, with two Persian prisoners kneeling before him.
    [1] In his second treatise against the Cynics, he again speaks of "hidden retreats where
dwells the Supreme God, the absolute Good, with whom our souls desire to be united ;"
and he represents the Sun and Minerva as saying : " Remember that thou hast an immortal soul, and that if thou followest our counsels thou shalt be a god as we are, and
shalt enjoy the sight of our Father." He repeats nearly these words in the form of a
prayer at the close of his treatise on Cybele: "Mother of gods and men, . . . grant unto
the Roman people first of all to wipe off the stain of atheism, . . . and to mine own self
vouchsafe, as the fruit of my services towards thee, truth in all my views concerning the
gods, perfectness in theurgic art, and in all things, to whatsoever tasks of peace and war
I lay my hand, virtue and success, and to the end of this life peace within and a fair
name without, with a good hope for the journey that shall bring me to the gods" (Disc.
V.). This faith was a Vedic doctrine. The Vedas assign to souls as their final dwelling
the sky or the sun (Bergaigne, La Religion védique, i. 74, iii. 111-120). The old doctrine
naturally reappeared with Jesus, and in the time of Julian all men, whether pagan or
Christian, believed in this ascent of souls.

at last drove him to anger against those whom he could not overcome,[1] and who anathematize him, and in whom he barely avoids seeing rebellious subjects. Then he resorted to measures of hostility against the Christians, and believed these measures legitimate, since he gave only orders which he believed to be just, but which were not so, by reason of their inevitable consequences.

Already some of the measures mentioned above appeared to be the beginning of what has been called Julian's persecution, although they were only acts of justice and wise administration. The persons whom he had expelled from the palace or sent to the tribunal at Chalcedon had called themselves Christians without deserving to be so considered. Those whom he had deprived of lucrative privileges, too liberally granted by preceding Emperors, were also Christians, but they had no right to complain of being subjected to the general law; and when he recognized the claims of those who had suffered spoliations from the Christians, it is equally true that religion had not allowed the robbery.

His policy showed itself more clearly when he deprived the bishops of voluntary jurisdiction, and the Church of the right of receiving legacies. These rescripts were not included in the Theodosian Code, and could not be; but we have proof that they were promulgated in the following words of Julian in his letter to the Bostrenians. "The clergy . . . are no longer permitted to act as judges, or make wills, or embezzle the estates of others and appropriate everything to themselves." He seemed to restore the former order and justice in annulling recent privileges. But in giving back criminals to the jurisdiction of the ordinary magistrates, and their patrimony to families, it was in reality the whole work of the first Christian Emperor that he sought to destroy.

Constantine had very early returned to the old Roman doctrine of a state religion. Julian did the same with a contrary result: in his eyes polytheism was the national cult, and throughout his reign the indulgence of the government was towards the pagans, and its severity towards the Christians. The decree concerning restitu-

[1] See, in the *Misopogon*, in what a sad condition he found the pagan cult at Daphne, whose pitiful celebrant perhaps suggested to Bouilhet the idea of his fine lines upon the old priest bringing the last sacrifice to the last altar. Repeatedly Julian complains of the lukewarmness of pagan zeal (*Letters* 4, 27, and 63). In *Letter* 49, however, he congratulates himself on a success which has surpassed his hopes.

tions presented this double character of being in appearance an act
of justice, and in reality one of those reactionary measures which
exasperate the present, and do not bring the past to life. Temples were, like the banks of modern times, places of deposit for
private property, and in the passage of centuries the devout had
accumulated rich offerings there.[1] To obtain, by a change of religion, the right to lay hands upon these treasures, with the aid of
a pious sedition followed by pillage, had been an irresistible temptation; and we know too well the character of revolutions not to
be certain that, in the confused state of religious affairs, guilty
excesses were committed. We have ample testimony that among
the sincere iconoclasts of the time there were not a few marauders who pillaged systematically.[2] When the government changed,
claims came in; cities complained that the treasures had been stolen
from their temples, that the temples themselves had been destroyed,
the land on which they stood confiscated, and that the jewels and
rich stuffs with which Christian churches were ornamented were
thefts from the shrines of the ancient gods. Julian, while prohibiting acts of violence against persons, directed that the possessions
of which the cities had been deprived by the late Emperors should
be restored. To despoil the churches, the Christians clamored,
was nothing less than to authorize sacrilege. But who had begun
it? In the eyes of the pagan populations, was it not also a sacrilegious iniquity to despoil the temples, and also a wrong towards
those who had enriched the temples with their gifts? Spoliations
of this kind had taken place in cities whose inhabitants were
largely pagan. At Heliopolis, for instance, there were still but a
small number of Christians half a century after the sanctuary
of Venus had been destroyed there. Unfortunately, to authorize
these claims for redress and direct recapture of the spoils taken

---

[1] See, in Vol. VI. p. 556, a law of Septimius Severus on this subject, and on the same
question many papers of the French School at Athens. Lucian, in his *Syrian Goddess*,
10, mentions rich offerings which were continually arriving at the temple of Heliopolis
from all the countries situated between the Tigris and the Mediterranean.

[2] Amm. Marcellinus shows the palace of Constantius full of persons who had enriched
themselves with the spoils of the temples: . . . *pasti templorum spoliis* (xxii. 4): according
to Libanius, this Emperor gave away a temple as he would have given a dog, a horse,
or a slave; and Eunapius, in his *Life of Aedesius, ad fin.*, relates the sack of the Sera-
peum, where the assailants divided the offerings according to the order established in the
case of spoils taken from the enemy. In certain places lands belonging to the temples
had been sold and honestly paid for by the purchasers. Cf. Libanius, *Letter* 636.

from paganism, instead of empowering the state to proceed itself in the matter, with compensations acceptable to both parties,[1] was to prepare the way for local or individual acts of violence. The decree of Julian might have set the whole Empire in a blaze; for it was a weapon of war striking full at the Church, and she would have sought to break it, had she not already become so strong that in very many places the order established by her had been accepted by the populations. The edict did not cause a complete overthrow, but it produced tumults which we shall now see, — a condition of disorder which should never have been brought on by those who had the charge of the public peace.

This measure — in appearance, at least — was one of reparation; another was manifestly an iniquity. Julian forbade Christian instructors to deliver lectures on the Greek authors in the public schools, on the ground that since these authors constantly refer to the gods, it is not suitable that men who are hostile to these divinities should speak falsely concerning them, or should belie their own consciences by giving true accounts of the same.[2] When the Emperor said: "Men ought not to turn our own arrows against ourselves, and arm themselves with our books in order to fight with us," he denied the chief rights of religious criticism; and when he added: "Let them expound Matthew and Luke; . . . and though it might be proper to cure them by force, as if they were afflicted with madness, yet let all be indulged with that disease,"[3] he insulted while he smote them, — an unprincely act; but in this letter he many times forgets the empe-

---

[1] Under like circumstances Constantine had made a more equitable decision. See Vol. VII. p. 521.

[2] We have not this document in the form of an edict inserted in the Code, for the Christian Emperors naturally did not place it there; it is a long letter (No. 42), and seems to concern only the official professors in the public schools, those receiving salaries from the state, or from the cities after passing an examination before the municipal council, — a class of instructors not very numerous, for Antoninus allowed but ten of them in the largest cities. (See Vol. V. pp. 442.) Julian concerned himself with them for the purpose of conferring the privileges granted them by his predecessors (*Codex Theod.* xiii. 3, 3–5). The Empire had not an academic organization, by means of which it could control what went on in the independent schools, and render everywhere effective the prohibition which could easily be enforced in the public schools. In ancient times such a question would never have arisen, when public affairs and religion were the same; but now there were two religions in the Empire, and Julian wished to put the instruction of youth at the service of the religion which he preferred. This ambition has been shared by nearly all governments since his time.

[3] *Letter* 42. To heal them he would, if he could, have burned their books (*Letter to Ecdicius*).

ror. A pagan author who respects him refers to this decree as an act of intolerance which it would be well to bury in eternal oblivion.[1] The measure was without effect, being continued in force only for a few months. Moreover, like the Hebrews spoil-

THE EVANGELISTS.[2]

ing the Egyptians, the Christians had already stolen the gold of Greece, and were to adorn with it a new world.

Julian, who expelled Christian instructors from the public schools, also closed to "the Galilaeans" the public offices. "It

[1] Amm. Marcellinus, xxii. 10, *ad fin.* Victorinus at Rome, and Prohaeresius at Athens, closed their schools, and Musonius was obliged to leave his . . . *ἐδόκει γὰρ εἶναι χριστιανός* (Saint Jerome, *Chron.*; Eunapius, *Prohaer.*). Orosius (vii. 30) speaks of numerous dismissals. It has been said — but this is an error — that he prohibited Christian children from attending the public schools. On the contrary, he would have persuaded them to it, if he had been able, since in these schools instruction was now given by pagan professors. It was, however, only instruction in the higher grades. The private and elementary schools were numerous.

[2] Bas-relief of the fourth century; fragment of a great sarcophagus in the Museum of the Louvre, which, in its principal carvings, represents Jesus near a great city and surrounded by his twelve disciples. Here the evangelists are represented clad in Roman costume, except the third, perhaps Saint Luke, who was a Syrian by birth.

is better," he wrote, "to prefer the pious." In revolutionary
epochs all governments have followed the same course. But ancient though the practice is, it is not the less unjust, nor the less
impolitic; for it makes malecontents or else hypocrites, and in either

CONTORNIATE MEDALLION.[1]

case the community suffers. These men,
whether sincerely or officially "pious,"
whom Julian seeks for and promotes, will
manifest a compromising zeal for paganism.
They will make the Emperor appear a per-
secutor when his firm resolve is to perse-
cute no man. Fortunately, from words to
acts the distance is great. Christians are
seen to fill the highest offices, even those

which imply the Emperor's full confidence, — like the positions
held by Valentinian and Valens,
two future Emperors, and by Jovian, who succeeded Julian after
serving him as principal lieutenant in the Persian expedition.
We therefore have the right to
suppose that many other Christians had remained in the administration and in the army, their
departure from which would have
caused a complete disorganization.[2]

GROOM OF THE CIRCUS.[3]

These edicts of Julian had been called forth by a violent attack from Athanasius. When the Alexandrian bishop saw paganism upon the throne, he resolved to abandon the concessions made

---

[1] Champions in the circus drawing their places by lot. Cf. Charles Robert, *Étude sur
les Médaillons contorniates*, 1882, p. 51. See, page 7, the same scene, on the second part
of the bas-relief found at Constantinople.

[2] The ecclesiastical writers mention a disgrace of Valentinian on account of religion; but
the candid Tillemont doubts this. Socrates (iv. 1) says in effect the contrary; and his testimony is confirmed by Zosimus (iii. 35, and iv. 2), who tells us that Valentinian was sent by
Jovian to announce Julian's death to the legions in Pannonia and Gaul, — whence it is to be
inferred that the former was still with the army, and not in exile in Egypt or at Melitene, on
the frontiers of Armenia. The first care of a new Emperor was always to make this an-
nouncement in all haste to the provinces; and there can be no doubt that Jovian took a messenger who was close at hand. When emperor, Valentinian manifested no very ardent zeal,
and his wife, Justina, an Arian, lived on friendly terms with the pagans.

[3] Groom of the circus driving four horses. From Agostini, *Gemmae*, pl. 193.

by the councils of El-
vira and Arles,[1] and to
enforce again the old
disciplinary laws of the
Church which for a
half century had fall-
en into neglect.   In
362 he called together
an Egyptian council,
which reasserted the
Nicene creed as the
one rule of faith; and
to raise an impassable
barrier between Chris-
tians and pagans, pro-
hibited the former from
being present at games
in the circus, hunts in
the amphitheatre, and
scenic representations
of any kind, also from
taking part in Gentile
feasts or even entering
public inns, and from
taking the oath re-
quired by Roman law
in courts of justice.
As if he sought to
make all Christians one
great community of
monks, Athanasius de-
clared excommunicate
ipso facto those who
served in the army or
in the administration,

GAMES OF THE CIRCUS.[2]

[1] See Vol. VII. p. 530.
[2] Games of the circus upon
the dyptich of Brescia. Gori,
Thesaur. Vet. diptychorum.

those who should communicate with a soldier, a governor, a trader,
or a publican. It was a challenge, and Julian accepted it.[1]

This Emperor fights with both hands : as monarch he decrees,
as philosopher he argues. His great work against Christianity is
placed by Libanius above that of Porphyry, and certain of his
arguments have been used again by modern criticism or sarcasm.
But while the Emperor was writing this book, say the Church
historians, he whom Julian called the carpenter's son was putting
together the coffin in which this unbeliever and his gods were to
be interred together.[2]

The measures, the words and writings of Julian naturally had
the effect of uniting against him all the Christian sects lately so
hostile towards each other, and of making the pagans — who since
the reign of Constantine had not dared to defend themselves —
feel that the time for reprisals had come. Had he lived longer,
there can be no doubt that great tumults would have occurred,
although he himself taught toleration to those about him, as on
the occasion when, at the altar of his gods and in the midst of a
sacrifice, he suffered himself to be insulted with impunity by an
aged bishop. His officers sought to gratify him by using the influence of the government in reawakening paganism, which was fast
falling into decline. There were stately festivals, sacred hymns,[3]
processions of young girls marching to the temples flower-laden;
but also there were legal proceedings, not always justified by equity
or prudence,[4] and on the part of certain governors a guilty toleration of popular seditions.[5] In Syria fermented countless germs
of trouble. There lived side by side all races, all religions, all
sects, with their mortal hatreds; and between the cities existed
animosities centuries old. The inhabitants of Gaza, for example,

---

[1] See, in the *Archives des missions*, 1877, pp. 468 *et seqq.*, the report of M. Revillout in
respect to a mission for the study of Coptish manuscripts concerning the Council of
Alexandria.

[2] Sozomenus, vi. 2; Theodoret, iii. 23.

[3] See, in the *Misopogon*, sect. 23, the description of one of these pagan displays. In Egypt
Julian organized what we should call a great school for sacred music. See his *Letter* 56.

[4] See Libanius, *Letters* 622, 624, 680, 1,057, and that which he relates (*ibid.* 636) of
Theodule, who had built a house on the site of a temple in Antioch, of Orion (*ibid.* 673 and
7:10), and of Basiliscus (*ibid.*, 669), who had taken part in the pillage of temples.

[5] Socrates (iii. 14) says: "The governors, wishing to profit by the Emperor's superstition, did more harm to the Christians than had been ordered; they demanded from them
greater sums of money than they ought, and used violence towards certain."

never forgave Majuma for the favors which she had received from
Constantine.[1] They destroyed her chapels, killed three of her citizens in a riot, and received no punishment for these crimes.   In
Palestine the Jews made common cause with the pagans in burning churches and destroying the tombs of martyrs ; many of the
Christians perished in these riots.   Those who relate these things
had an interest and satisfaction in exaggerating the importance of
them ; but Amm. Marcellinus says nothing on the subject which
authorizes us in the belief that they were less serious than has
been asserted, or that they were readily arrested.   In the city of
Edessa, Arians and Valentinians had come to blows, and the former had pillaged the church of the latter.   Julian reconciled them
by distributing to the soldiers the stolen treasure, and confiscating
the property of the Arian church.   "As they are taught," says
the Emperor, "in their wonderful law that poverty is the easiest
method of entering into the kingdom of heaven, we, for this purpose
co-operating with them, have ordered all the wealth of the church
of the Edessenes to be confiscated and given to our soldiers, and the
lands to be annexed to our domains.   Thus being poor, they may
become wise, and not fail of that heavenly kingdom to which they
aspire." [2]   This irony was out of place on the part of a sovereign
and in a rescript which ended with a menace of death for the chief
magistrate of the city in case these seditions should occur again.
At Damascus, Berytus, Epiphania, and Emesa, churches were burned
or transformed into temples.   The Bishop of Arethusa, refusing to
rebuild a pagan sanctuary destroyed by the Christians, or to furnish the sum necessary for its reconstruction, was shamefully ill-
treated ; at Heliopolis many Christians perished, at Bostra there
were riots,[3] at Cappadocian Caesarea executions.   The Christians
in this latter city had destroyed, as a direct insult to the Emperor, the last temple in which their pagan fellow-citizens could worship ; [4] others, in Phrygia, had broken, in a consecrated place, the
statues of the gods.   In all three cases the offenders were pun-

[1] See Vol. VII. p. 502.

[2] *Letter* 43.

[3] In his letter on this subject, Julian advises the populace to expel the bishop from the
city as an accuser of the people to the Emperor. The bishop had said that the Christians
were restrained only by his exhortations from becoming tumultuous.

[4] Sozomenus, v. 4.

ished with death.[1] The Christians represented these rioters as martyrs, and such they were; but the pagans could see in them only criminals justly punished.[2] The Christian sects which had suffered under Constantius — the Donatists in Africa, the Novatians in Asia Minor — attempted to regain possession of their churches as the pagans again obtained their temples.[3] These rival competitions augmented the general disorder, and we can only wonder that it was not greater, amidst the violent excitements produced by so many contending creeds.

Springing up suddenly, as popular emotions are so apt to do, these outbreaks could not be prevented, owing to the inefficiency of the local authorities. Julian, who in all his writings attests his desire for peace,[4] was their involuntary author. He wished gently to restore that past which never can be restored; but scenes took place which remind one of the sad occurrences of which certain of the provinces of France were the theatre less than seventy years ago. The government, by the very fact that it had again become pagan, appeared to authorize corresponding acts of violence with those which Christian Emperors had permitted or ordered; and the pagans, in those cities where they were conscious of being the stronger party, avenged themselves for their long humiliations: it is the inevitable law of historic reactions. It was not, therefore, a persecution, but a series of imprudent measures and angry words, in which too-zealous subordinates saw an encouragement to let go on what it suited them to regard as a legitimate expiation.[5]

---

[1] Socrates, iii. 15.

[2] See Vol. IV. p. 465, the explanation of the *crimen majestatis.*

[3] See in Socrates (iii. 11) and in Sozomenus (v. 5) the disturbances in Cyzicus, where the Orthodox had destroyed the church of the Novatians.

[4] In the *Misopogon*, sect. 22, he says that the anger let loose against the impious (the Christians) raged much more fiercely than he had himself wished; and in sect. 27, enumerating the favors he had granted the city of Antioch, he says: "In that which concerns one Christ, I have made you all the concessions which you could expect from a ruler who desires only the good of all men." Sozomenus, however, accuses him of blaming the governor for wishing to punish the ringleaders in a riot; and we shall see later that he himself did not punish the murder of Bishop George at Alexandria.

[5] G. H. Rendall, who has examined one by one the facts called by ecclesiastical writers acts of persecution, concludes this investigation with the following words: "On judicial survey of the whole evidence in array, it is just to conclude: 1, That no organized or wide-spread persecution prevailed during Julian's reign; 2, that the sporadic instances which occurred were in almost every case provoked, and in part excused, by aggressive acts of Christians;

The Western provinces seem to have been forgotten in this religious strife; at least we hear of no agitation in that quarter, except it be the disturbance made in Gaul by Hilary of Poitiers to secure the acceptance of the Nicene Creed rather than that of Rimini. The East, where the question of Arianism had been so hotly contested, appeared to Julian the great Christian fortress, and he believed that when that had fallen, all the rest would go with it.

The opponents whom Julian attacked were his superiors in strength, for already the mighty theologians were at work, or were preparing for their task, who overthrew the ancient world and began to build a new social edifice, — Athanasius, Basil, Gregory Nazianzen, Gregory Nyssen, Chrysostom, Ambrose, Hilary of Poitiers, Jerome, and Augustine. The great men of this period were inevitably drawn to the side of Christianity; the pupils of Plato and Porphyry found in the Gospels a living God, who explained for them the Alexandrian abstractions, and permitted them to pass beyond the hypostases of philosophy into the contemplations of faith. The history of the great theologians of the fourth century shows the influence that the Church exercised, even amid high social conditions, by its doctrine of detachment from the world. Saint Ambrose lays down a great civil office to accept the episcopate; Paulinus, a man of consular rank, allows himself to be consecrated bishop of Nola; Chrysostom, son of a general in the army, flees to the desert to escape the worldly distinction which his birth promised him; Basil, who also was in a position to aspire to the highest honors, sells his possessions and distributes the money among the poor and embraces a monastic life, draw-

---

3, that, while culpably condoning some pagan excesses, the Emperor steadily set his face against persecution; 4, that he never authorized any execution on the ground of religion; that, where his conduct amounted to persecution, he did not abjure, but set a strained interpretation on the laws of toleration which he professed " (*The Emperor Julian, Paganism, and Christianity*, p. 202). A. Naville (*Julien l'Apostat et sa philosophie du polythéisme*) shares this opinion: " We ought to recognize the fact that this reign is one of those in which religious liberty was most respected." Saint Jerome says, in his *Chronicle : Blanda persecutio illiciens magis quam impellens ad sacrificandum.* Another ecclesiastical writer, Socrates, says distinctly (*Hist. eccl.* iii. 12) that Julian forbore to impose tortures and punishments upon the Christians, and Gregory Nazianzen, that this persecution was a short and feeble attack of the devil; Saint Chrysostom speaks only of teachers of schools prohibited from the exercise of their profession, and physicians and soldiers discharged; and Bossuet esteems Julian's government equitable (*Disc. sur l'Hist. univ.,* 1st part, chap. xi.).

ing up for it a code of regulations still in force in the monasteries of the East. Gregory, son of a bishop and the successor to the paternal dignity, persuades his brother, Julian's physician and much trusted by the Emperor, to refuse the senatorial rank and fortune rather than abandon his faith. What mattered to these noble minds, inheritors of all the grace of the Greek genius, the edict withdrawing from Christians the right to teach? The Emperor may close the schools; the letters, the discourses, and the poems of these men are a new literature, read everywhere, full of life and splendor, which has quite another charm than the endless commentaries of the rhetoricians upon the ancient Homer, — faded flowers now, without perfume or color. The Church begins to assume the moral government of the world, and Julian, with his superannuated philosophy and his gods icy with the chill of the tomb, cannot dispute it with her.

"We have the eloquence and the arts of Greece," he said; "you have ignorance and rusticity." And Gregory Nazianzen replies to him: "Wealth, honor, authority, — all these earthly advantages, which vanish like a dream, we abandon to you; but we keep the gift of eloquence." And they did keep it. Listen to Saint Basil describing the retreat where his poetic genius lived with Nature and with God: "My dwelling is upon a hill-top which is covered with a thick forest where many streamlets rise, and, falling over the rocks in cascades, unite to form a considerable brook, of which the fish furnish me with abundant food at all times. I look down over the valley which lies beneath me, more beautiful than ever was Calypso's island, and full of flowers and the singing of birds. Here I enjoy tranquillity, that greatest of all blessings. I am not disturbed by the noise of cities, and I hear only the sounds made by the hunters who come into the forest; for we have also wild animals, not bears and wolves as upon your mountains, but deer, hares, and wild goats. Here I would gladly remain, as Alcmaeon tarried when at last he had found the Echinades." [1] From this cheerful landscape his eyes are lifted to Him who made it. He loves to contemplate the stars, — "the flowers which God's hand has scattered through infinite space;" and he exclaims: "If the things that are seen are

---

[1] In 360 Gregory visited his friend in this delightful retreat.

so beautiful, what must the unseen be! If the perishable sun brightens all with its light, what must be the Sun of Divine Righteousness!" In his *Hexameron* — an explanation of the six days of Genesis — and in his *Homilies* upon the Psalms, the Greek inspiration mingles with that which descends from the hills of Galilee, and some of his letters have a truly Attic grace. "Everything comes in its season," he writes to a friend, — "the flowers in spring, the ripe corn in summer, fruit in autumn; the winter fruits are conversations with one's friends."[1]

Basil, the first in date of the great Christian orators, was poetical in his eloquence; in many of the innumerable verses[2] of his friend Gregory Nazianzen we find a pensive sadness not at all native to that violent and passionate age. "My soul," Gregory exclaims, "whence comest thou? Who has bidden thee to carry about a corpse? To-day a man, to-morrow I shall be but dust. If thou art indeed a celestial being, O my soul! teach it to me. One man weeps for his country desolated by war; another, for his house burned by fire from heaven; the maid in her bridal attire laments over the dead body of him who should have been her husband; the mother, who has lost her son now grown to manhood, suffers keener pangs than those of childbirth. And thou, my soul, what lamentation shall be fitting for thy loss! I shall lose the fame of eloquence, the pride of station, pleasures, wealth; I shall leave behind the light of the sun and the stars, — brilliant crown of the earth! — and, an icy corpse, with fillets wrapped about my head, I shall be stretched upon a bed; and after that, under the stone of the tomb, awaiting destruction. But it is not for this that my soul is filled with anxiety; I tremble only before the justice of God." And he goes on in this strain. Finally, he cannot endure his uncertainties; he turns away from them, and hope springs up again in his heart. "Now there is darkness; soon there will be the truth; then, contemplating God, thou shalt

[1] *Letter* 13.

[2] More than thirty thousand lines, — which indicates that there is much more prose in them than poetry. The Greek Fathers of the fourth century, sometimes so eloquent, have the endless fluency of their race. Usually pupils of Libanius or Himerius, they retained from the teaching of the rhetoricians the excessive use of comparisons and figures, together with something of Oriental emphasis. But being sustained, as they were, by a mighty reality, their rhetoric, although too highly colored, was often the brilliant decoration of lofty and severe ideas.

know all things."[1] Like brave soldiers who have gained possession of their adversaries' weapons, and use them to better advantage, Gregory and Basil captivated by the charm of their language
even the most famous pagan rhetorician of the time, Libanius,
who had been one of their masters,[2] and now remained their friend.

Basil, when he became archbishop of Caesarea in Cappadocia in 369, was still
accustomed to send pupils
from that province to Libanius, and he wrote thus to
him: "I have read your oration, O most learned of men!
and I admire it. O muses!
O eloquence! O Athens!
what gifts ye bestow on
those who love you!"[3]
These Christian disciples of
Plato and Homer took pos

DOUBLE-HEADED EAGLE.[4]

session of half of the domain of art, and their writings, which probably contributed to save from destruction a portion of the classic
literature, continue to defend that which remains to us of it
against those who would be blinded by excess of light.

These fragments present but one side of their genius, the
side to which we call attention to show that a new source of
poetry had been opened, and to demonstrate that Julian's decree
as to the schools was doubly a mistake, — first, as being unjust;
secondly, as being ineffectual.

---

[1] Villemain, *L'Éloquence chrétienne au quatrième siècle* : De Broglie, *op. laud.* (book v.),
of which an entire chapter (the second) is devoted to Saint Basil; Fialon, *Étude sur Saint
Basile.*

[2] Socrates, iv. 26.   [3] Basil, *Letter* 353.

[4] Bas-relief found in Cappadocia. Texier, *Voy. en Asie Mineure*, pl. 78. The Mohammedan legends seem to have made the double-headed eagle, the Ilanca, the emblem of
omnipotence, "for he carries off the elephant and the buffalo as the kite carries off a
mouse." The Turks placed this ancient Persian symbol on their standards; the Turcomans
of Palestine, on their coins; and later the German Emperors, in their armorial bearings.
By a singular freak of fortune the Turkish race saw itself, at Belgrade, at Lepanto, and
at Peterwaradin, debarred entrance into the West by that very eagle which had led it to
victory on the banks of the Euphrates and the shores of the Bosphorus (De Longpérier,
Œuvres, i. 102).

We have no occasion to speak of the works which have given
to Gregory the surname of the Theologian (Θεόλογος); but we
ought to add that this bishop — a restless and dissatisfied mind,
a poetic nature delicate and nervous — suffered more than others
from the armed resurrection of the enemy whom the Christians
had believed destroyed, and that his passionate *Invectives* against
Julian, and his poem against the Fathers of the Council of Constantinople, have a character of irascibility which religious polemics
early assumed and have retained to this day.

Saint Ephraem was a friend of Basil; but there is nothing
Greek either in his language or his ideas, he is entirely Biblical
and Oriental. He wrote and spoke in the Syrian language, like one
of the old prophets, except that in him mercy and charity take
the place of wrath and denunciation. He has the fruitful, inexhaustible imagination of the Oriental story-tellers, and the subtle
forms of Arab poetry. His verses were repeated all the way from
the Mediterranean seashore to the mountains of Persia; long after
his time they continued to be sung, and it is possible are at this
day recited in the valleys of the Lebanon on occasion of funeral
rites.[1] Saint Ephraem represents the popular poetry, completing
with dramatic or tender imagination the severe work of the theologian, and employing the two great Christian forces, love and
charity, in uniting souls which disputes of doctors and of synods
tend to separate.[2] This Syrian enthusiast, this poet who knew
not Athens, extols, however, like Basil and Gregory, profane learning. "O man!" he says, "read carefully books, that thou mayst
obtain wisdom from them. Knowledge weaves a crown for those
who love her, and makes them sit upon a kingly throne."

Synesius, that eccentric bishop, the devoted friend of Hypatia,

---

[1] A long and very beautiful *Lamentation* by this author is translated by M. Dabas in
his *Mémoire sur quelques poésies de S. Ephrem*. The account that Ephraem gives of his
first meeting with Saint Basil shows him as the clairvoyant, in modern parlance, whose recol-
lections take the form of voices that he has heard, and apparitions that he has seen. "When
I was in Cappadocia a voice said to me: 'Rise, Ephraem; go and eat thoughts!' I said,
'Where shall I find them, Lord?' And the voice replied: 'Go to my house; thou wilt there
see a royal vase (βασίλειον, a play upon the word Basil) full of the food that thou requirest.'"
Ephraem obeyed, and went to the church; from the porch he perceived a priest addressing
the people; on the shoulder of the priest a dove whispered in his ear the words that he
should speak, etc. (De Broglie, *op. laud.* v. 182).

[2] Gregory Nazianzen was not in favor of too-frequent synods; he believed that discussions give birth to heresies.

and so ardent a lover of pagan culture, also composed much poetry; but he belongs to the subsequent generation.

He who was to take the first rank, the greatest of all the Greek Fathers of the fourth century, by his melodious speech and his often angry eloquence, Saint John Chrysostom, was at this time a boy,[1] who had as yet written nothing. He would, however, already have devoted himself to a monastic life had he not been dissuaded by his mother, Anthusa, who, left a widow at the age of twenty, had been unwilling to remarry, devoting her life exclusively to her son. " My son," she says, " my only consolation has been to see in your face the likeness of him whom I have lost. I ask this favor of you: do not make me a second time a widow; wait until I shall be dead. When you have buried me, laying my remains beside those of your father, then do what pleases you, travel in remote lands and upon any sea; but while I live, endure my presence."[2] Gentle and tender words are these of a mother who, like many Christian women of the time, exercised a religious influence over her son; but this woman believed that salvation was not irreconcilable with the fulfilment of the duties of family life.

A religion whose Christ was born of a virgin, and among whose earliest believers were holy women who hung upon the Lord's words, who followed him to Calvary, who announced his resurrection, — was sure to appeal to those whom Nature has made to love. In times of persecution they furnished martyrs to the faith, and now they were its apostles. Macrina, sister of Saint Basil, herself an ardent believer, snatched their brother, Gregory Nyssen, from Plato and led him to Christ. The mother of Gregory Nazianzen, Nonna, to convert her husband, by day related to him the Gospel narratives, and at night lulled his sleep with sacred sing-

---

[1] His birth is said to have occurred on Jan. 14, 347. He was, like Basil and Gregory, the pupil of Libanius, who on his death-bed is reported to have said : " I should have left my school to John had not the Christians stolen him from us " (Sozomenus, viii. 2). Later it was said of him : " It were better the sun should lose his rays than Chrysostom his words." The surname applied to him signifies the Golden-mouthed.

[2] In his treatise περὶ Ἱερωσύνης, i. 2, in vol. i. of the edition of Montfaucon. Chrysostom, like Gregory Nazianzen and Gregory Nyssen, had a disturbed episcopate (398–403). His violent language caused him to be deposed from the see of Constantinople and exiled into a severe climate, where he met his death. He suffered, however, in a just cause; he had refused to condemn the writings of Origen, and was full of gentleness towards heretics, asserting that we should strive against doctrines, and not against persons.

ing, that she might lead his mind to pious visions. And how remarkable was the zeal of Monica, the mother of Saint Augustine; of Fabiola, who employed her wealth in founding a hospital; of Marcella and Felicitas, the correspondents of Saint Jerome; of Demetrias, the richest heiress in Rome, who entered a convent in Carthage; of the devout Eustochia and her mother Paula, "that daughter of the Scipios and the Gracchi, who, preferring Bethlehem to Rome, exchanged the gold of her adornments for a cabin in Judaea!"[1]

Other laborers wrought for the spread of the Christian faith. The new religion, which called the flesh accursed, condemned life to be but a preparation for death. This doctrine made men monks.[2] While the leaders were organizing Christendom into a body, powerful through unity of dogma and discipline, many of those to whom it was taught that the flesh is the soul's prison, and the contemplative life the ideal of perfection, had fled into solitude, there to hasten by macerations, both of body and spirit, their reunion with God. Daily the devout listened to maledictions of the flesh and praise of the ascetic life. All the Fathers of the fourth century urged men into this path: Basil, Ephraem, and Jerome by their instructions and example; Gregory Nazianzen by his poems and sermons; Ambrose and Saint Jerome by their books and their letters on the merits of virginity; Athanasius by the important part he assigned to the monks in his struggle with three Emperors.[3] To him the anchorites of the Thebaïd were the

---

[1] It is Saint Jerome who gives Paula this illustrious ancestry; but as he also calls her *Agamemnonis inclyta proles*, we may regard the other statement with doubt. Convents at this time were becoming numerous. Saint Ambrose wrote in 377 his three books on *Virginity*; his sister, like the daughter of Paula, consecrated herself to the Lord.

[2] In respect to pagan and Jewish monks and hermits, see the monograph of M. Brunet de Presles on the *Sérapéon de Memphis*. Ancient Egypt had also its holy virgins. Plutarch dedicates his treatise on *Isis and Osiris* to a consecrated virgin. A hieroglyphic inscription in the Louvre mentions an abbess of the recluses of Ammon, and a fortunate accident has preserved to us the anathemas pronounced by a pious Egyptian woman against her son who had become a Christian (Revillout, *Cours de langue démotique*, p. 31). Paganism had also its literary women, who honored philosophy and followed its precepts. Of these the most famous are Hypatia of Alexandria, Asclepigenia of Athens, her rival, Aedesia (Suidas, s. v. *Damascius*), Sosipatra, of whom Eunapius says that she was learned, rich, and beautiful (edit. Didot, p. 461), etc. In respect to the monks of Egypt and their miracles, see Socrates, *Hist. eccl.* iv. 23.

[3] At the same time this ardent friend of the monks is not unaware of the peculiar egotism which is sometimes at the bottom of this solitary devotion. "What answer will you

true people of God. When he contemplates their monasteries scattered along the mountain side, he is seized with Balaam's enthusiasm, and exclaims: "How goodly are thy tents, O Jacob, and thy tabernacles, O Israel!"[1]

Hilary of Poitiers goes even further; he sacrifices his own daughter to the new faith. In order to deter her from a marriage which unites all worldly advantages, he writes her a letter in which paternal affection conceals under a flowery garb the bishop's severity. He would have for Abra only the Divine Spouse, "that Youth of marvellous beauty, richer than all the rich of this world, who promises his bride a wonderful robe which renders sickness and old age and death unknown." Saint Jerome cannot allow a mother's heart to his penitents. Paula abandons her children for seclusion from the world; on news that one of them is dead, she weeps because she had deserted the girl, and Saint Jerome says to her with severity: "This grief saddens the heart of Jesus." And he gives her as an example Saint Melanie, who, losing her husband and two children on the same day, sheds not a tear, but says, smiling: "Henceforth I shall be more free to serve the Lord." It is a fierce and ardent faith, which, while it merits heaven, loses earth.

As early as the reign of Aurelian, Anthony had withdrawn into the desert; he was merely a hermit; Hilario, Pachomius, Macarius, Saint Basil, and others organized the cenobitic life, and Martin, a legionary in the time of Constantius, founded in Gaul the first monastery.[2] Other religions had known this spirit

make," he writes to one of them who refused the duties of the episcopate, "if you leave the people without the bread of life upon which you yourself are feeding? When the Lord cometh, what can you say to him in your own justification?" (*Letter to Dracontius.*) His *Life of Saint Anthony* has made the legendary reputation of this singular personage, who was extremely ignorant, but had the second sight which accompanies hallucination. Athanasius dares not in his own person relate the marvellous and terrible things which took place in the cell of the anchorite, but he makes Saint Anthony himself recite to the assembled monks the story of his conflicts with Satan, or of his too fascinating visions.

[1] [*Numbers*, xxiv. 24.] Athanasius, *Life of Saint Anthony*, 44. Upon the religious condition of Egypt at this time, see the curious biography of Senuti the Prophet, analyzed from a Coptic manuscript by M. Revillout in the *Revue de l'Histoire des religions*, vol. viii. No. 4, pp. 401 *et seqq.*

[2] Saint Basil greatly preferred for the monks a life in common rather than that of the hermits. His rule divides the time among prayer, manual labor, and study. His monks aided the secular clergy in preaching, and in their houses the traveller and the poor could always find help.

of self-renunciation, but Christianity alone made it an element of
power. In the monasteries her most useful soldiers were trained,
— that body of men who so often did her vast service, and also
at certain epochs were pioneers of civilization and of scholar-
ship, and in every age offered asylums where noble hearts felt
themselves nearer God, and where others found a living grave
wherein to hide their griefs and their despair. Before the close
of the fourth century Egypt alone had seven or eight hundred
monks. How many others there were in Palestine, in Syria, in
Asia Minor, Armenia, and Africa! "The cities were depopulated
to fill the deserts." [1] These monks had austere virtues, sometimes vices, with which Saint Ephraem reproaches them, and eccentricities of costume, language, and conduct which offended Saint
Jerome,[2] but were held by the people as marks of sanctity. Voluntary poverty, like that of the Buddhists or of the Franciscan
friars, has often won the hearts of the multitude, who love this
ostentatious contempt for the good things they themselves can
never hope to possess; and the self-denial of the monks seemed a

---

[1] Saint Augustine, who by his preaching propagated the monastic order in Africa,
shows in his treatise on the *Morals of the Church* the great number of religious communities which had been formed throughout the Roman world. The Emperors early took
the alarm at this desertion from the social life: *Quidam ignaviae sectatores, desertis civitatum muneribus, captant solitudines ac secreta, et specie religionis, cum coetibus monazonton
congregantur. Hos . . . erui e latebris . . . mandavimus . . . (Codex Theod.* xii. 1, 63,
anno 365). See also the very curious canons of the Council of Gangres in 376, several of
which are a condemnation of the excesses of the ascetic life and of the abandonment of
family obligations.

[2] His *Letters* to Eustochius, to the monk Rusticus, and others, are severe upon the
vices of the monks, — gluttony and lewdness; but in many other letters he extols the merits
of the solitary life. The African Church was disturbed by discussions whether the monastic life should be one of idleness or of industry, and also in respect to the idleness of
the wandering monks. Saint Augustine in his *De Opere monachorum*, and in his *Enarra-
tiones in Psalmum CXXXII.*, blames this pious inactivity; at the request of the Bishop of
Carthage, he writes against "those hypocrites who, in the dress of monks, wander about
the provinces, carrying pretended relics, amulets, preservatives, and expecting alms to feed
their lucrative poverty and recompense their pretended virtue." One of his correspondents, the tribune Marcellinus, makes the objection that Christianity, teaching that men
should not resist the evil-doer, and, to him that taketh away the coat, should give the
cloak also, were advancing a doctrine of morals contrary to the civil law. This was in
advance the argument of Bayle, that sincere Christian believers could not found a state
capable of enduring. It is true that an anchorite is not a citizen, and that he withdraws
himself from the aims of society. But the human mind is, happily, illogical. Christians
have been as good citizens and as brave soldiers as a state could wish to have; and
counsels of abnegation are always useful, although the precept to turn the left cheek to
him who smites the right, has no more put an end to war than the prohibition against
usury has brought business to a stand.

testimony to the power within them of the Divine Spirit, and also an expiation of the crimes of the age which they could not prevent. Accordingly, they were extremely popular : for their superior officers, the bishops, they were discreet and valuable messengers; for the laity in stormy times they were ardent auxiliaries against pagans and heretics. "Without the monks," says Sozomenus,[1] "the East would have remained Arian. On one occasion five hundred of them, summoned to Egypt[2] by the archbishop, came very near killing the prefect." Fasting, ecstasy, visions taken for realities, gave them a robust credulity; and in their cells the Church again recovered that power of miracle-working which no longer was manifested among the secular clergy, now that they lived in the open light of day.

But of all these adversaries the most formidable were the new ideal — the hope of heaven, and love to one's fellow-men, which Christianity had substituted for the old ideal of absolute devotion to the earthly country — and that discipline of the Church which by means of the Christian sacraments held the believer at the most important moments of his life. When the cities had lost even the shadow of their old privileges, another liberty, the right of choosing their religious leaders and of discussing the points of their faith, sprang up in the Christian communities and the councils; religion restored a part of what political events had taken away, and the episcopal office gave back to certain of the great families the influence of which for a long time they had been entirely deprived.[3] This further explains the power of the Church, democratic at its base, aristocratic at its summit, and thus gathering into its own hands all the strongest social forces.

Observe also that it was not at all distracted from its religious

[1] vi. 27. Eunapius (Aedes.) attributes the fall of paganism to the monks. Concerning their alleged miracles, see Socrates, iv. 24.

[2] Socrates, vii. 14.

[3] Before being bishop, Ambrose had been a governor, Paulinus of Nola a consul, Nectarius a praetor, Synesius the richest citizen of the Cyrenaïca, etc. The participation of the people in episcopal elections is constantly noticeable during the fourth century. Also, however, we observe the tendency of the great bishops to reduce as much as possible the popular franchise. Basil and Gregory Nazianzen seek to have the election made exclusively by the clergy, — which would place it under the direction and influence of the metropolitan. " These are our affairs," said the elder Gregory to the governor of Caesarea; and Basil wrote : " It is God's right to designate those who shall represent him upon earth" (Gregory, i. 309, 310 (Billy); Basil, Letters 28 and 230).

work by the patriotic duties which had been the very life of the old Roman society. Saint Basil wrote: "The monks have shown me how a man can be a stranger to the concerns of this world, and live only in heaven;" and elsewhere: "Man must leave in his soul no earthly affection."[1] When the Empire seemed about to fall in ruins; when the Roman army had been destroyed, an Emperor burned alive, the provinces covered with slaughter and desolation, — this great bishop was absolutely unmindful of the public misfortunes; in his innumerable works there is not one word of patriotism. This conception of life was diametrically opposed to the ideas and sentiments which had made the greatness of Greece and Rome; but it left the mind free for religious propaganda and strifes concerning dogmas. Julian was not thus at liberty. He thought far too much about King-Sun, it is true; but he was compelled also to think about the Franks, the Goths, the Persians, and the administration of a vast empire. Hence he was unable to contend against a faith so ardent, with this paganism which he strove to reconstruct, while giving to it a character which, since it did not spring from the pagan principle, was incapable either of permanency or of growth.

III. Julian at Antioch (July, 362, to March, 363).

Julian remained at Constantinople[2] till June, 362, at which time he went into Asia to prepare for a great expedition against the Persians. He passed slowly through Asia Minor, bringing help to Nicomedeia, which had just suffered from an earthquake, visiting Pessinus (where he worshipped the Bona Dea, and wrote a treatise explaining the singular amours of Cybele and Atys), Ancyra, Cappadocian Caesarea[3] (at the foot of Mount

---

[1] *Letter* 223.

[2] Zosimus (iii. 11) says he remained there ten months; but Amm. Marcellinus (xxii. 9) represents him as arriving in Antioch at the time of the festival of Adonis, which occurred in July.

[3] At Caesarea had just taken place a tumultuous episcopal election, which displeased him, because the person selected was one of the most important citizens, who was thus withdrawn from the senate. Julian wished to annul the election. The old Bishop of Nazianzen,

Argaeus, the highest peak of Asia Minor), and the city of Tarsus, the last stage of the journey before reaching Antioch. On the way he filled, as occasion required, the *rôle* of judge, and did it well. In Ancyra he caused a Christian, Basil by name, to undergo

CYBELE AND ATYS.[1]

the punishment of the rod; but this man had insulted the imperial majesty with invocations of evil, which, according to law and to old religious ideas, was nothing less than treason. "Jesus Christ will quickly punish thee; thou shalt die in torments, and thy body, left without burial, shall be trodden under foot." [2]   A

father of Gregory, remonstrated, and Julian let the matter drop (Gregory Nazianzen, i. 309, edit. of Billy).

[1] The Mother of the Gods and Atys, the divine shepherd, receiving the prayers of the devout. We have already remarked that to indicate divine personages it was usual to represent them of height superior to that of their worshippers. This was a Greek usage. Cf. *Bull. de corresp. hellén.* No. VII. p. 562. (Museum of Venice.)

[2] xxii. 10; Sozomenus, v. 12. These excesses of language were not unusual; the most saintly men authorized them by their example. Saint Jerome calls Julian "a mad dog;" and the two *Invectives* of Gregory Nazianzen are extremely violent. In the case of the *Acts* of Saint Basil of Ancyra, Tillemont (iv. 698) does not affirm their authenticity.

count, hoping to gain the Emperor's favor, put the zealot to
death. Sozomenus declares that the act was not authorized; and
we shall see later that Julian was resolved to have no martyrs,

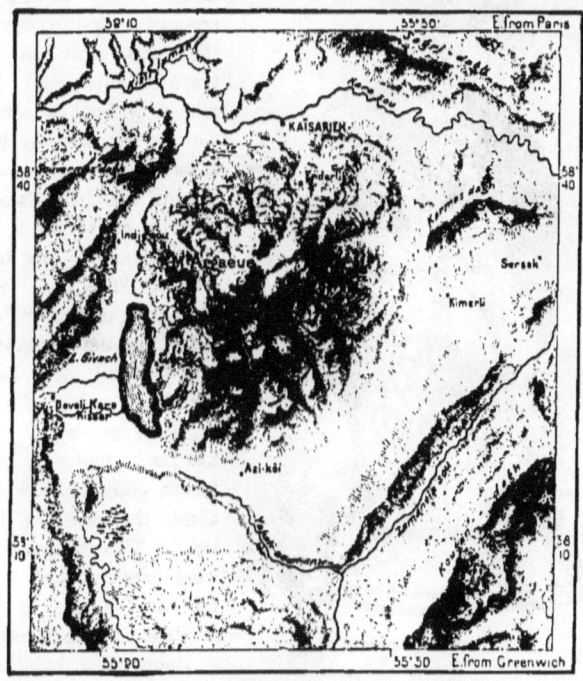

MOUNT ARGAEUS.[1]

considering such dead enemies much more dangerous than living
ones. Formerly there had been but one master of the Empire
whom it was necessary to respect in word and act; now there
were two, and the Christians gave obedience to the second only,
whenever the first displeased them.

[1] This mountain, over thirteen thousand feet high, is an extinct volcano; the scoriae
which cover its sides show that it was once formidable. In the time of Strabo, and even in
the fifth century of the Christian era, it was occasionally active. Caesarea (Kaisarieh), on
the Kara-Soo, an affluent of the Kisil-Irmak, was at a height of 3,280 feet above the sea.

Julian entered Antioch on the day when the city was celebrating with great pomp the festival of Adonis.

ADONIS AND APHRODITE.[2]

He showed himself unmindful of personal insults, refused to hear an accusation against one of the spies who had betrayed Gallus, and dismissed without a severe word a decurion who had asked of Constantius the head of the Gallic Caesar, that he might set it on the walls of his city as a trophy. The man was filled with terror. "Fear not!" the new Augustus said to him; "if I have enemies, I seek to diminish their number."[1] He had not, however, that foolish good-nature which blunts the sword of justice. Two conspirators were executed, and several hated agents of the cruelties of Constantius, — among these the notary Gaudentius, the vicar Julianus, and the duke of Egypt, Artemius, who had been guilty of extortion, pillage, and murder. This duke appears to have had as an accomplice in some of his crimes, George the semi-Arian bishop of Alexandria.[3] On learning that

---

[1] Amm. Marcellinus, xxii. 14.   See Julian's *Letter* 59.

[2] From a vase found at Corinth (Museum of Berlin).   O. Rayet, *Mon. de l'art antique.*

[3] Amm. Marcellinus, xxii. 11 : *Alexandrini . . . vipereis, ut ita dixerim, morsibus ab eo saepius appetiti.* The Catholics accused George of having required fees for baptisms, burials, and the like, and of having secured the monopoly of salt, papyrus, and saltpetre. The Arians had brought like complaints against Athanasius. These abuses perhaps had arisen out of certain innocent usages of the Alexandrian Church which were represented as monopolies unfavorable to the merchants of the city. There remains, however, the testimony of Amm. Marcellinus against Bishop George.

Artemius had been beheaded in Antioch, the pagan populace rushed
upon the bishop, perhaps aided by some of the Catholic party, and
tore him in pieces.[1] This sedition deserved punishment; but the
victim was a bishop, and Julian contented himself with addressing
a homily to the Alexandrians, in which were, however, threats
against those who in future should violate the law. This indulgence was neither just nor wise.

George being dead, Athanasius returned to Alexandria and
took possession of his see.[2] His presence was at once marked by
new discussions, another council, and a twentieth creed, prepared
this time in a manner to satisfy some of the Arian party, but
offensive to the extremists like Lucifer of Cagliari. The pagans
of the city were displeased, and complained to the Emperor, com-
municating to him the violent commentary that Athanasius had
added to some of the acts of the council.[3] Julian replied to them
by the following edict : " One who had been banished by so
many imperial decrees should have waited at least for one edict
before he returned home, instead of contumeliously insulting the
laws, as if there were none in being. For we have not allowed
the Galilaeans who were banished by the divine Constantius to
return to their churches, but only to their countries. Yet I hear
that the most audacious Athanasius, with his usual insolence,
has again usurped what they call the episcopal throne, and that
this has not a little displeased the people of Alexandria. We
therefore command him to depart from the city on the very
day that he shall receive the letter of our clemency ; and if
he remain there, he may expect a much severer punishment." [4]
The Alexandrian Christians cried out against this fourth banishment of their bishop, and Julian addressed them a letter, in
which he says: "If you will listen to my admonitions, my joy
will be very great ; but if you still persevere in that superstitious

---

[1] Amm. Marcellinus (*ibid.*) speaks only of pagans. Gregory Nazianzen (*Discourses*, xxi.
36) seems to say that the Catholics had a share in the tragedy. At this we cannot wonder ;
the hatred of the Orthodox against George, as the successor of Athanasius, was equal to that
felt by the pagans for him as a Christian bishop.

[2] It is believed that he was the first to take the title of archbishop (*Art de vérifier les
dates*, iii. 468).

[3] See above, pp. 185, 186.

[4] *Letter* 28.

institution of designing men, agree at least among yourselves, and do not desire Athanasius. There are many of his disciples who are abundantly able to please your itching ears, desirous as they are of such impious discourses. Any one whom you may select from the people, in what relates to expounding the Scriptures, will be by no means inferior to him. But if you are pleased with the shrewdness of Athanasius (for I hear the man is crafty), and therefore have petitioned, know that for this very reason he was banished. That such an intriguer should preside over the people is highly dangerous. I ordered him formerly to leave the city, but I now banish him from all Egypt;"[1] and Julian wrote to the prefect: "If that enemy of the gods does not leave Alexandria, or rather Egypt, before the kalends of December, the cohort that you command shall be fined a hundred pounds of gold."[2]

If the distinction made by Julian between the return of exiles into their cities and their restoration to their former positions, was contained in the letters of recall, — and we cannot doubt that it was, since the Emperor affirms it, and its reason is comprehensible, — Athanasius was in the wrong, and Julian might justly reproach him with a violation of the law.[3]

At Antioch the Emperor restored the temple of Apollo, which stood in the beautiful grove of Daphne, just outside the city.[4] A fire—set by a flash of lightning, the Christians asserted; by an imprudent worshipper, says Amm. Marcellinus — destroyed it. Julian

---

[1] *Letter* 51.

[2] *Letter* 6. I have already mentioned (page 10, note 2) this strange administrative method, the fine, which is the sole punishment of Barbaric times, and was so in the Middle Ages. Cf. the law of the Franks, and for the Middle Ages, Seignobos, *Le Régime féodal en Bourgogne*.

[3] Another proof exists in the fact that Athanasius did not take advantage of the recall of the exiles to return to Alexandria so long as George lived; that is, while the episcopal chair was occupied. If Julian had designed to restore it to him in ending his time of exile, he would have begun by expelling George, — a measure quite after the manner of Constantius, but not characteristic of Julian. Moreover, Athanasius was a most unruly subject to any authority which did not please him. Being banished from Alexandria by Julian, he openly left his place of exile, say the historians (Socrates, iii. 14; Theodoret, iii. 8; Sozomenus, v. 15; Rufinus, i. 3, 4), returned by night to Alexandria, and concealed himself in the city. The Roman Church, which has profited by his perseverance, is justified in making him a hero and a saint; but may no state ever again know so turbulent a prelate!

[4] Amm. Marcellinus, xxii. 13; Libanius, *Upon the Temple of Apollo;* and Theodoret, iii. 11, 12. Daphne is supposed to have been the modern Beit-el-Ma.

had no doubt that this destruction was, like that of the palace in
Nicomedeia in Diocletian's reign, the work of "the Galilaeans,"
and certain devout authors maintain that he took his revenge by
a cruel persecution. These writers depict the Orontes as filled with
the dead bodies of the martyrs; in wells and cellars and in un-
frequented recesses of
the palace there are
the remains of mur-
dered Christians,
skulls of children and
maidens who had
been offered in sacri-
fice. The pagans had
long accused their ad-
versaries of sacrific-
ing children in noc-
turnal orgies ; they
were now in turn pur-
sued by the same fool-
ish accusation : it is
the ordinary justice of
partisans. But against
these lying accusa-
tions the life of Julian

MAP OF ANTIOCH AND DAPHNE.

and his whole moral nature protest, — an historic document also,
and most precious in judging an emperor. By way of reprisals upon the destruction of the Daphnean temple, he closed
the great Arian church of Antioch and confiscated its possessions, — in execution, perhaps, of the decree in respect to res-
titutions ; and to discover the incendiaries he ordered a number
of Christians to be put to torture. One of them, Theodoret,
was executed; four soldiers had already undergone the same fate
for insults offered to the gods, and probably also to the Emperor.
Theodoret had called him a tyrant and the most contemptible of
men.[1] Some refusal of military obedience from conscientious
scruples, as we have seen in the time of Diocletian, had caused
the death of the soldiers, and the words of Theodoret were

[1] Dom Ruinart, *Actes de Théodoret.*

treason ; the ancient laws therefore authorized these unjust
sentences.   Julian had repeatedly declared that he would use no
violence against the Christians, and yet one of the Christian clergy
had just fallen by the sword.   The Emperor was angry with
the judge, who was his uncle. "What have you done?" he said.
"Do you not know that I am displeased by these executions?
What will they not say against me now that you have made a
martyr?"[1] His friends regarded the matter in the same light
that he did. Libanius deplores that by the tortures inflicted on Mark
of Arethusa the latter had been raised to the rank of a demigod;
and he wrote to the governor of Phoenicia: "Set Orion at liberty; do not make a saint of him."[2] This was the new policy;
it was not destined to succeed any better than that of Diocletian,
but it was milder.   We find it at work in transferring the
remains of the martyr Babylas, whose tomb was in the grove
of Daphne.   "Apollo," says Libanius, "not being able to endure
the vicinity of this dead body, had quitted his temple, and the
Castalian spring gave no more oracles."[3] When Julian brought back
into the sacred valley the old pomp of pagan worship, he purified
the enclosure according to the rites employed by the Athenians at
Delos,[4] and ordered the removal of any dead bodies that had been
interred there. Babylas in his turn quitted the grove; the Christians
took up his body and carried it in solemn procession to a church
in Antioch.   The Emperor saw this funeral train and the angry
eyes of the Christians; he heard the chanting of psalms, chosen
designedly for their malediction of the impious man, but he did
nothing to disturb this pious and hostile ceremony.   As he
found it advantageous not to increase the number of the martyrs,
he did not interfere with those who did them honor; and this
gives us the right to conclude that the relics of the Christian dead
were profaned only in public outbreaks, without orders from the
Emperor and contrary to his wishes.   But he became anxious
lest these funeral ceremonies might become to both parties an

---

[1] Some months after the death of this magistrate the Emperor again says of him, in
the *Misopogon*, sect. 25, that "he did not manage the affairs of the city with the utmost
prudence."

[2] *Letter* 1,057.

[3] Libanius, *On the Temple of the Daphnean Apollo*.

[4] . . . *Eo ritu quo Athenienses insulam purgaverant Delon* (Amm. Marcellinus, xxii. 12).

opportunity to display their numerical strength and an occasion of conflicts; accordingly, a decree prohibited funerals by day.[1] His policy was much better than his philosophy; the latter had led him to say with Iamblichus: "It is not fitting to deal with those who deny the gods as one deals with men: we should strike them down like wild beasts." The experience of the ruler had mitigated the violence of the sectary; changes for the better, of a nature like these, are not without parallel in all ages.

Meantime he loaded Antioch with favors, — a remission of all arrearages of taxation: a diminution of one fifth in the assessment; a distribution among the poor citizens of three thousand lots of land (doubtless the common lands, by which the rich alone had hitherto profited); an increase of the senate by the addition of two hundred new curiales, so that municipal burdens, divided among a larger number, would be less heavy to each individual.[2] To remove the danger of a threatened famine, he obtained great quantities of corn from Egypt; and to restore order in the city's finances, he placed honest and capable men in charge of them. But in the hope of keeping down the ever-increasing prices of commodities, and what he calls the insatiable cupidity of proprietors, he fixed a *maximum*, — a bad measure, which interfered with the customary provisioning of the city, rendered food scarce, and raised the popular displeasure to the greatest height.[3] In this sensual and frivolous city, whose real religion was pleasure, all, pagans and Christians, were about upon a level; all blamed the Emperor for the severity of the seasons.   He had already offended them by his contempt for their favorite amusements, the circus and the theatre, by his affectation of coarse attire, his scrupulous piety, and, most of all, the austerity of his life.   Soon he became an object of ridicule; he was called a bear, a hairy ape, and, in

---

[1] . . . *Per confertam populi frequentiam et per maximam insistentium densitatem* (*Codex Theod.* ix. 17, 5). The pretext given is not the same which we suggest; but the date of the decree (Feb. 12, 363) shows that the idea was connected with the public demonstration in the case of Babylas. The prohibition of funerals by day was a return to the custom of early days (Servius, *Ad Aen. XI.* 103), which had always prevailed in the case of the poor (Festus, s. v. *Vespae;* Suetonius, *Dom.* 17).

[2] *Codex Theod.* xii. i. 53. He had done this same thing at Constantinople (*Letter* 11), and in the case of arrearages in Thrace and Africa (*Misopogon* and *Letter* 47).

[3] Julian, *Misop.* 13, 25, 28, 39.   Antioch had distributions of "perpetual bread." Malalas, xii. 289.

allusion to his numerous sacrifices, a victim-killer.[1] For insults
less than these, Licinius, it is said, caused two thousand inhabitants of Antioch to be put to death; Julian avenged himself by

BRONZE LAMP.[2]

a satire. But an Emperor should never take revenge, even in a
way like this.

The *Misopogon*, or "The Enemy of the Beard,"[3] of which the
idea is ingenious, would be a charming production had it not a
tiresome length, showing that Julian did not take time to be brief.

---

[1] He merited this appellation by the number of victims which he sacrificed. See Amm.
Marcellinus, xxii. 12 and 14. He shared in the processions, surrounded by devotees, *stipatus
mulierculis* (*id. ib.*), — words which Gregory Nazianzen (*Disc. upon Saint Babylas*, 14), as
might have been expected, translates as meaning women of immoral lives.

[2] Bronze lamp found at Paris in 1863 in a sort of columbarium. This lamp (which
perhaps is not really an antique) is now in the British Museum; but a reproduction of it
may be seen in the Musée Carnavalet.

[3] Written in January or February 363.

He wrote rapidly, and boasts of this, — a twofold conceit, which
hindered him from writing well. " Archilochus and Alcaeus," he
says, "alleviated the weight of their cares by railing at their
enemies. The law, however, forbids me, as well as every one else,
to reproach any one by name, even
among those who, since I have in
no respect injured them, are unjustly the aggressors. . . . But no
law forbids my writing a panegyric
or a satire upon myself, — though
if I were desirous of praising myself I could not; but blame I can,
in many cases. And first I will
begin with my face. To this, formed
by Nature not over beautiful, grace-
ful, or becoming, my own perver-
sity has added this long beard, —
to punish it, as it were, for not
being handsome. . . . Furthermore,
my hair is rough and seldom
combed, my nails are unpared, and
my fingers are usually black with
ink. . . . Not satisfied with such
an uncomely person, I lead a very
rigid life. I absent myself from
the theatre through mere stupidity, nor do I allow a play at court,
such a dolt am I, except on the
kalends of the year, — when I re-

STATUE FOUND AT PARIS.[1]

semble a poor farmer bringing his rent or taxes to a rapacious
landlord; and when I am there, I seem as solemn as at a sacrifice. . . . To add something further. I have always hated horse-
races as much as a debtor hates the forum. . . . As to domestic
affairs, sleepless nights on straw, and food less than enough
give a severity to my manners totally repugnant to a luxurious
city, . . . — a city in which there are many dancers, many

[1] Statue found at Paris (Lutetia) in 1863, in the Rue des Fossés-Saint-Jacques (Museum
of Cluny).

pipers, more players than citizens, and no respect for rulers. . . .
All these are handsome, smooth, and beardless; all, both young
and old, imitate the pleasures of the Phaeacians, and prefer luxury and revelry to what is just and right. ' Do you think,
Julian,' you say to me, ' that your rusticity, savageness, and
moroseness are agreeable to us? Is your soul so foolish that
you think it requires the ornaments and trappings of wisdom?
First tell us, for we know not, what wisdom is. With the name
only we are acquainted, but of its meaning we are ignorant. If
it be that which you now practise, it consists in enforcing subordination to the gods and the laws, in teaching equals to bear with
equals, in observing moderation, in preventing the poor from being
oppressed by the rich, and for these purposes stifling resentment,
encountering enmity, anger, and reproaches,— in short, supporting all these with firmness, without being provoked or giving
way to passion, but keeping it as much as possible under due
subjection. . . . If this be wisdom, you ruin yourself and would
also. ruin us. The very name of servitude, either to the gods or
the laws, disgusts us. Liberty is sweet in all things. . . . You
say that you are not Lord (*dominus*), and you cannot endure
the name. You resent it so much that you have induced many
to banish it from the empire as invidious; yet you oblige us to
obey the magistrates and the laws. How much better would it
be for us to call you Lord, and be allowed freedom in fact! O
mild in appearance, but in deeds most cruel! how unmerciful
it is to require moderation from the rich in the courts of justice,
and to restrain the poor from slander! By abolishing the stage,
the players, and the dancers, you have ruined our city, . . . but
we have succeeded by our scurrility, transfixing you with sarcasms
as with arrows. If you are thus intimidated by our taunts, how
will you be able to sustain the darts of the Persians?' "

Julian then refers to the story that Seleucus, the founder of
their city, resigned his wife, the beautiful Stratonice, to his son
Antiochus, who was dying of a guilty passion for his young step-
mother. "That his posterity should resemble their founder," the
Emperor says, "is not blamable; for among men the manners of
the descendants are likely to be similar to those of their ancestors.
. . . I myself am descended from the Mysians, who are abso-

lutely inelegant, boorish, austere, uncivilized, and obstinately tenaci-
ous of their opinions, — all which are people of lamentable rusticity.
. . . Let me turn your resentment against my governor, who when
I was a boy inculcated those moral lessons. He is the cause of
all your dislike to me, having fixed, or, as it were, carved upon
my mind what I ought to shun. He exerted himself with the
utmost earnestness, calling rusticity gravity, and stupidity temperance, saying that to resist the passions is fortitude, and
that the gratification of them does not constitute happiness. He
used to say to me: 'Do not suffer yourself to be attracted to
the theatre by the crowd of your companions, nor be enamoured
of such entertainments. Do you wish to see a chariot-race?
It is elegantly described in Homer; open the book and read.
Do you hear of pantomime-dances? Away with them! The
Phaeacian youths [whose dances are described in the Odyssey] are
less effeminate. You have there the harper Phemius, and the
singer Demodocus. His trees too are more delightful to the ear
than ours to the eye; and the woody island of Calypso, and the
groves of Circe, and the garden of Alcinoüs, be assured you will
see nothing more enchanting.'

"Would you know the name and race of this governor? He
was a Barbarian, a Scythian. . . . At seven years of age I was
intrusted to his care. From that time he persuaded me that this
was the only right way; and as he himself would not know nor
would suffer me to pursue any other, he has exposed me to your
resentment. . . . Whatever manners I have formed, whether gentle
or boorish, it is impossible for me to alter or unlearn. Habit
is said to be second nature; to oppose it is wearisome: but to
counteract the study of more than thirty years is extremely difficult, especially when it has been imbibed so carefully." And he
goes on at great length, turning into ridicule the effeminate and
scandalous lives of the people of Antioch.

Possessed with a mania for arguing and writing, Julian at times
forgot that he was the ruler. At Lutetia he did well to relieve the
tedium of the inactivity forced upon him by Constantius by giving part of his time to study; but an Emperor should not have his
fingers always ink-stained. We are not pleased to find him, at Constantinople, writing treatises upon King-Sun and upon the Cynics;

at Pessinus, an oration upon Cybele; at Antioch, the *Misopogon*
and a work against the Christians which was employed by the
infidels of the eighteenth century against the Bible and the dogmas

IVORY TABLETS.[1]

of the Church; and lastly, we know not where, the *Caesars* and
quite a number of books now lost, which the Christians perhaps
destroyed, as we know that they erased passages from those which
remain to us.   He says indeed that in this literary labor he

---

[1] Triumphal march of King-Sun and of the Moon giving light to the world. Ivory tablets of the fourth century used as a book-cover from the Library of Sens (Jules Labarte,
Hist. des Arts industriels, vol. i. pl. xv.).

employed his nights only. But if these works, always moral, but often confused, — with the exception of the last-named, which is the best, — were written by night, they must have been meditated by day; and they give us reason to fear that in the idleness of the palace his mind — at once alert, satirical, and mystical — took pleasure in pointing sarcasms rather than in preparing decrees, and that public affairs were less attractive to him than were scrupulously performed devotions, Alexandrian reveries, or the investigation of the future in the entrails of sacrificed animals. He loves Plato, — a charming guide, though not always a safe one, — and Aristotle is to him the second column of the temple built by Hellenism to philosophy and pure religion;[1] but the firm intellect of the Stagyrite at times displeases the imperial dreamer. "Aristotle," he says, "has made only feeble attempts to inquire as to what is beyond;"[2] and this search is the sum of Julian's philosophy. His faith in oracles and omens is strong. After speaking of the miracle which signalized the entrance of Cybele into Rome, he adds: "Unbelievers may say that these are old women's stories; but as for me, I confide more willingly in the popular testimony than in these subtle minds which see nothing as it really is."[3] This credulity, good for a devotee, is to be regretted in a ruler; for it makes it impossible for him to take a clear view of subjects. Matters of that time, so singularly confused, needed the keen inspection of a statesman, and not the subtle meditations of an Emperor whom his friends called "the great philosopher" (φιλοσοφώτατος).[4]

Among the lost works of Julian, the most important is his Κατὰ Χριστιανῶν, a refutation of the Gospels. All the copies of it that could be found were destroyed by order of the Emperor Theodosius II., and we have only a few extracts from the first three books which Saint Cyril preserves in his Reply. The principal historic interest attached to this work is that it doubtless suggested a design which made great stir in the world. The men of the Old Dispensation felt the bitterest hatred towards those of the New. This animosity of the Jews against the Christians gave the former importance in the eyes of Julian; and to do them a favor which would at the same time prove the inanity of the Gospels, he pro-

[1] Julian, Letter 55.   [2] Cybele, 5.   [3] Cybele, 1.   [4] Theodoret, iii. 15.

posed to rebuild the temple at Jerusalem which had been condemned
by Jesus.[1]   The work began, but a miracle brought it to a stop.
Balls of fire coming out of the ground dispersed the workmen.
Amm. Marcellinus relates this; but the old soldier, whom we must
believe when he tells us what he himself has seen, is naïvely credu-
lous on the subject of omens and portents.   Asia Minor and Syria
were about that time, as often happened, shaken by earthquakes,
which twice within a few years destroyed Nicomedeia.   Many cities
in Palestine, Libya, Sicily, and Greece suffered severely.[2]   Alexandria narrowly escaped destruction by a tidal wave, and for many
years preserved the memory of it in an "earthquake festival."
Did Mount Moriah also feel the shock of these subterranean forces?
It is possible.   Shall we suppose that gases, formed by the decom-
position of organic matter in recesses of the earth closed for centuries, took fire on contact with the oxygen of the air when the
pickaxe of the laborer broke through the soil?   This is at least
probable.   The Christians, eager to assert a fulfilment of the Gospels' prophecy against the temple, were likely to have added to
the natural phenomena circumstances of marvel, whose story,
spreading rapidly, reached the historian.   The expedition against
the Persians and Julian's death preventing the resumption of the
work, the malediction which Christ pronounced against the temple
of Jehovah seemed to have been fulfilled.

IV. THE PERSIAN WAR; DEATH OF JULIAN.[3]

MEANWHILE Julian had not forgotten that the conqueror of
the Franks and the Alemanni had the long-continued insults of
the Persians to avenge, and to prevent their repetition by over-

[1] The collections of Julian's works contain a letter to the Jews (No. 27) which has
caused legitimate doubts to commentators.   The idea of making Jerusalem his capital and
of adoring the God of the Mosaic revelation, whom elsewhere he treats with such disdain,
and who is the absolute negation of his polytheism, could never have entered Julian's mind.
[2] Cf. Libanius, who speaks of many earthquakes in Palestine in the time of Julian, and
Amm. Marcellinus, xxii. 13, xxiii. 1.   Constantinople was also shaken, and Nicaea nearly
destroyed, on the fourth of the nones of December.   It is noteworthy that Saint Jerome
makes no mention of a miracle.
[3] Libanius, Letter 1,186, and Amm. Marcellinus, books xxiii., xxiv., and xxv. 1–4.

throwing that warlike king who for a quarter of a century had
made life so hard for the dwellers on the eastern frontier of the
Empire. The West was now tranquil; Sallust kept watch over
the Gallic provinces, and upon the Rhine and the Danube the
Barbarians, who were audacious only when the
Emperor was effeminate, dared not stir. Fame
had carried far the name of the young conqueror
who had become the dreaded chief of the Roman
world. All the nations bordering on the frontiers had sent him embassies and presents. These
had even come from India; and the tribes of

JULIAN.[1]

independent Mauretania had sought to be received into the Empire.
As soon as the Emperor arrived in Constantinople, his courtiers
proposed to him an expedition against the Goths. "I shall go,"
he said, "against more formidable enemies. Let the slave-traders
deal with those men." Along the Danube Julian renewed the
defensive policy of Diocletian; in Thrace and on the river-banks
he repaired all the fortresses, provisioned them amply, and supplied them with an abundance of weapons and clothing, and also
secured to the soldiers their regular pay. "While this great
monarch reigned," says Amm. Marcellinus, "not a Barbarian
crossed the frontier."[2]

During the winter of 362 the preparations for the Persian
expedition were completed. Sixty thousand men were collected
under the standards; more than a thousand transport vessels,
fifty fighting galleys, and many barges for constructing bridges,
had been assembled upon the Euphrates. On the 4th of March
Julian left Antioch; but he did not leave behind him displeasure against the city, for he gave it for governor "a man
of turbulent and fierce disposition, saying that he had indeed
not deserved such a post, but that the Antiochans, being covetous and insolent, required such a governor." He set out on his
journey accompanied by his habitual travelling companions, —
certain books of Plato, which fed his mind with lofty thoughts
and refreshing poetry. "The spring has returned," he writes to

---

[1] Julian in military costume and crowned by a Victory. Reverse of a silver coin (Cohen,
vol. vi. pl. xi. No. 4).

[2] xxii. 7 and 9.

a friend; "the trees are again covered with leaves, the swallows appear, and they invite the soldier out of his winter-quarters, and send us over the frontiers." And to another: "I have taken a well-shaded road, where there are many brooks and springs of water. At noon we halt, and repose under the tall plane-trees and cypresses, and I read the *Phaedrus*, or some other of Plato's dialogues." [1]

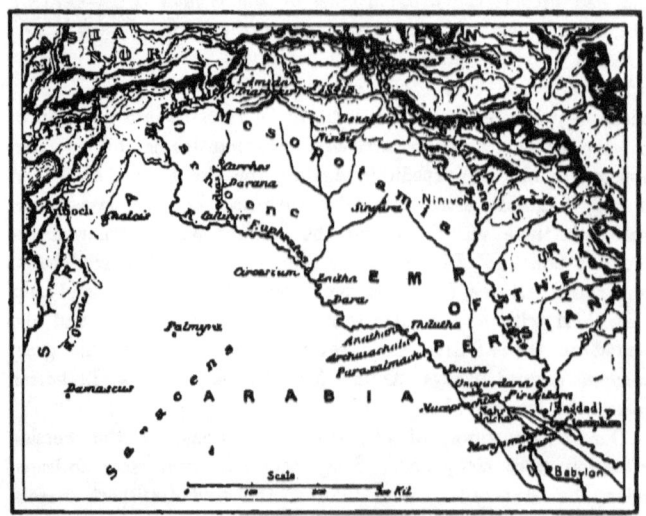

MAP FOR JULIAN'S EXPEDITION AGAINST THE PERSIANS.

He had appointed a rendezvous at the city of Carrhae, situated on the farther side of the Euphrates, upon the road to Nisibis, thus leaving the enemy uncertain as to the direction which the Romans might intend to take; and here he divided his troops into two armies. Eighteen thousand [2] men under Procopius, his kinsman, marched due east into Upper Mesopotamia, there to act upon the

---

[1] *Letters* 69 and 74.

[2] Amm. Marcellinus (xxiii. 3) says 30,000; Libanius (*Letter* 108), 20,000; Zosimus (iii. 12), 18,000; Magnus (*Fragm. Hist. Graecor.* iv. 4), 16,000, — a more probable number, since this corps accomplished nothing. Zosimus (iv. 4) says expressly that Procopius was to rejoin Julian.

left bank of the Tigris, and thence march southward towards Ctesiphon; and Arsaces, king of Armenia, received orders to join Procopius with his contingent. Julian, however, rejected the proposition of the Saracens, offering troops on condition that the former subsidies should be again paid them. "I have no gold," he said to them, "I have only iron;" and he sent them away.[1] With his main army and the fleet, he himself sailed down the Euphrates.[2] By way of the river he would come into a region not indeed the centre of the hostile kingdom, but through its agriculture the most fertile, and by its memories the most sacred, portion of Persia.

In this expedition Julian displayed all his military virtues, — the vigilance of an old general, the courage of a soldier (even to killing enemies with his own hand), bravery kept in check by prudence until the last day, and a temperance which allowed no man to murmur when provisions became scarce. Every encounter turned to the advantage of the Romans; the strongholds, battered down by powerful engines, were carried by assault or undermined. Great engineering works cleared and brought back water to the Naharmalcha, — a canal connecting the Euphrates with the Tigris, which the enemy had drained and filled with stones; and thus the fleet, which carried the army's supplies, its engines, and its sick and wounded, enabled it to traverse a country otherwise impassable. The Tigris near Ctesiphon[3] is a broad and rapid river, and its eastern shore was defended by the troops of the Surena.

---

[1] Amm. Marcellinus, xxv. 6 : . . . *Ad similitudinem praeteriti temporis.*

[2] Amm. Marcellinus indicates his route by the fortress of Davana upon the Belias, Callinicus on the Euphrates, and Circesium at the confluence of the Chaboras and the Euphrates. Beyond this city began the Persian frontier, defended by strong posts, — Ziatha, Dura, Anatha (on an island in the river), Thilutha (also an island), Achaicala, Paraxmalcha, Diacira, Ozogardana (which still preserved a tribunal of the Emperor Trajan), Macepracta, Pirisabora (an island), and Maogamalcha, where the Emperor himself narrowly escaped falling into an ambush. At this point the Roman army was ninety stadia distant from Ctesiphon. I have followed Amm. Marcellinus in this list of names, of which Sievers (*Studien zur Geschichte der röm. Kaiser,* pp. 239-262) has made a particular study.

[3] . . . *Civitas situ ipso inexpugnabilis defendebatur* (Amm. Marcellinus, xxiv. 7). — The engraving facing page 218 represents the Arch of Ctesiphon, which still stands. "This enormous structure, made of large baked bricks, has a façade 298 feet in length, 115 feet high, in the centre of which opens an arch of the same height with the structure, and 85 feet wide. This arch, which dates from the earliest centuries of the Christian era, reproduces one of the characteristic types of the most ancient Persian architecture." (Note by M. Dieulafoy, Engineer-in-Chief of Bridges and Highways.)

Against the judgment of all his officers, Julian ordered the army
to cross the river.   The passage was made with great gallantry;
the Persian army, put to flight, took shelter behind the walls of
Ctesiphon.   The city was extremely strong, and the arrival of
Sapor for its relief was expected at any hour.   The council of war
was averse to a siege; and "this opinion," says Amm. Marcellinus,
"was the dictate of reason."   Sieges in ancient times were often
very much prolonged; and this one, even if successful, would not
have ended the war, and would certainly have cost much precious

LEGIONARY ON A BOAT LADEN WITH BARRELS (COLUMN OF TRAJAN).

time.   What advantage had Trajan or Severus obtained by entering Ctesiphon?   And was it by sieges or by battles that Alexander
made himself master of Asia?   The most fruitful of all the Persian provinces had just been ravaged with impunity; the humiliation to Sapor was great, but his army remained intact and his
courage unimpaired.   Only a battle could crush him, and permit the
Emperor to terminate the expedition, not by a conquest, — of which
he had never dreamed, — but by re-establishing upon the Persian
throne Hormisdas, who had accompanied the Roman Emperor on
this expedition.   This success Julian resolved to seek in the very
heart of the hostile empire.   Such had evidently been his plan from
the first, for he had burned all the strongholds captured along the

ARCH OF CTESIPHON, CALLED ARCH OF CHOSROËS. (FROM A PHOTOGRAPH BY MADAME DIEULAFOY.)

Euphrates. Had he intended to take the same road on his return, and thence enter Assyria, he would have retained these fortresses, and would have left garrisons in them to make himself secure. Envoys from Sapor having come with overtures of peace, Julian was confirmed in his idea that his adversary could not resist him in the open country, and he refused to enter upon a negotiation which, under the circumstances, could have had for him no important results. He resolved to return northward, in the hope of finding on this route a second victory of Arbela; in this way also he would be approaching Procopius, who had orders to enter the valley of the Tigris, and so rejoin the Emperor. Greece and its history, always present to Julian's mind, showed him Xenophon, with his ten thousand Greeks, accomplishing after a defeat what he himself now, with a powerful army, undertook after a victory.[1] His march northward was not, therefore, a retreat; he was still acting on the offensive, but with different means. The fleet became useless for a campaign in the open country, and his galleys and heavy transport-vessels could not have ascended the Tigris, whose current, even when swollen by the melting of the snows of Armenia, has many shallows which render its navigation upward impossible.[2] Julian burned his vessels, after landing from them twenty thousand men, soldiers or marines, which by so much increased his army; he kept for the crossing of the streamlets only twenty-two light skiffs, and these were carried on wagons after the army. Amm. Marcellinus blames this course; Eutropius, who made the campaign, does not seem to regret it; Zosimus evidently approves it; and the circumstances of time and place appear to justify Julian's decision.[3]

As soon as the march towards the north became apparent to the enemy, parties of Persian horsemen appeared on the wings and in the rear, without coming to any serious engagement. It

---

[1] The younger Cyrus had, like Julian, descended the valley of the Euphrates until within two or three days' march of Babylon. Not to return along a route where all supplies had been exhausted, the Ten Thousand had retreated by way of the valley of the Tigris.

[2] An accomplished engineer who has lately passed fourteen months in Persia, M. Dieulafoy, tells me that it is usual to descend the river on rafts, but that it is impossible to ascend it any farther than Bagdad, on account of the shoals that fill its channel.

[3] Zosimus, iii. 26. This author says, however (sect. 29), that later the army regretted the destruction of the vessels. But the soldiers forgot, as all historians appear to have forgotten, that the fleet could not have ascended the Tigris.

being now the middle of summer, the sun had dried up the fields, and the Persians set fire here and there to the withered herbage, so that the army had to guard against two enemies, — the flames devouring the necessary forage, and the scouting parties of the Persian king. None of the attacks made by the latter succeeded,[1] but one of them was fatal. Julian had just repulsed, near Tummara, a party of cataphracti, when word came to him of an attack at another point. Without stopping to put on his breast-plate, he snatched his shield and ran to the scene of danger. Two other attacks almost simultaneously threw the army into confusion, and Julian was seen wherever the danger was hottest. Suddenly a spear, flung at random, pierced his side. He sought to pull it out, but cut his hand severely with the double-edged point of the weapon; and falling to the ground, was borne with speed to his tent. After a few minutes, being somewhat relieved, he called for his horse, desiring to encourage his troops once more by his presence. But he was weakened by loss of blood, and soon became aware that death was near; upon which he called for his friends and distributed among them his private property, at the same time addressing to them words of heroic resignation. Anatolius, the *magister officiorum*, had been killed only a few moments after the Emperor had received his fatal wound. Julian asked for him; and receiving from Sallust[2] the reply that Anatolius was now happy, he understood that his friend was slain, and bitterly bewailed the other's death, though he had so proudly disregarded his own approaching fate. All who stood around the dying Emperor wept, seeing him thus torn from them in his youth; but Julian reproved them, saying that they should not mourn for an Emperor about to be united to heaven and the stars. Then calling for his two philosophers,[3] Maximus and Priscus, he talked with them concerning the immortal destinies of the soul. He had no need of their counsels, for he felt the most absolute certainty that he was about to ascend into heaven, to dwell forever

---

[1] The most serious encounter took place on the 22d of June near Maranx; the Persians held their ground but a moment, notwithstanding their archers, their elephants, and their cataphracti.

[2] This Sallust, praetorian prefect, is not Julian's old friend of the same name, for we learn from Amm. Marcellinus (xxiii. 5) that the Emperor received despatches from Sallust, the prefect of Gaul, as he was descending the Euphrates.

[3] Concerning these spiritual advisers, see Vol. VI. p. 369.

among the stars.[1] During the conversation his breath became
labored ; he called for water, drank it, and expired quietly about
midnight. It was a philosopher's death.

He had not completed the thirty-second year of his age, nor
the twentieth month of his reign (June 26, 363) ; and before he
had suffered the humiliation of a single reverse, he fell a victim
to his own imprudent courage. If he had lived, there can be no
doubt he would have brought his army home victorious,[2] and
certainly he never would have signed the treaty made by Jovian.

Christian authors have called him " the Apostate," — an unde-
served reproach, for those about him had taken shameful advantage of his youth and his misfortunes to enroll him by force in
the Christian ranks ; and they reckon him among the persecutors, — another great injustice, for he recommended and he always
practised toleration towards all men.[3] The indirect war which he
made upon Christianity is not unlike that which Constantine made
upon paganism. If Christians perished, they perished as victims of
popular tumults or condemned for acts which the law pronounced
criminal, such as the destruction of temples, the breaking of consecrated statues, refusal of obedience, or military mutiny. These acts
were the inevitable consequence of the accession of a pagan Emperor,
and the circumstances are to be blamed much more than Julian
himself. But he must be held responsible for the moral persecution
that he practised, and for his guilty toleration of pagan riots. This
makes us severe towards the statesman who was a sectary, bending
his fine intellect to an impossible, and consequently a dangerous,
task, — one which would have been especially fatal to himself had he
lived to pursue it many years. He went counter to the movement
of the world, and so he failed ; nor could it be otherwise. But history will love the man for his virtues, the general for his military qualities, this scholar by accident an Emperor, who had his

---

[1] . . . *Caelo sideribusque conciliatum.* These are the Emperor's own words a few
moments before his death (Amm. Marcellinus, xxv. 3).

[2] An eye-witness, Eutropius, who was one of his officers in this campaign, says :
Remeans victor, quum se inconsultius praeliis inserit (x. 8) ; and Zosinus (iii. 29) : οὐ πόρρω τὴν
Περσῶν ἡγεμονίαν ἀπωλείας καταστήσας ἐσχάτης.

[3] Eutropius : *Religionis Christianae insectator, perinde tamen ut cruore abstineret ;* and Saint
Jerome, in his *Chronicle : Blanda persecutio fuit, illiciens, magis quum impellens, ad sacrificandum.*

ideal of perfection.   Dreamers of this kind are rare among monarchs; therefore we do honor to this one![1]

This early death appealed to the imagination of contemporaries.
The pagans related how, the night before his death, as Julian lay
sleepless in his tent, he saw pass silently before him, in an attitude
of mourning, his head covered with a funeral veil, the Genius of the
Empire, who had promised royalty at Lutetia, and now deserted
him.   It was a classic reminiscence of the apparition which announced to the younger Brutus his approaching death.

The Christians gave currency to another legend.   Struck with
the mortal blow, Julian looked angrily up into the sky, crying:
"Thou hast conquered, Galilean!"   These words were never said,
but there is truth in the idea: paganism had fought its last battle,
had lost it, and was destined to die of its defeat.

[1] See the portrait of Julian drawn by Amm. Marcellinus (xxv. 4): *Vir profecto
heroicis connumerandus ingeniis;* Saint Augustine (*De Civ. Dei,* v. 21) says of him: . . .
egregia indoles.

[2] Divinities of paganism on an engraved stone, furnished by M. de Witte. In the centre,
the three divinities of the Capitol, Jupiter, Juno, and Minerva; at the right and left, the
Dioscuri; around the edge, the seven divinities which preside over the days of the week.
(See Vol. VII. p. 488.)

DIVINITIES OF PAGANISM.[2]

CHAPTER CVIII.

JOVIAN, VALENTINIAN I., AND VALENS (363-378).

I. — JOVIAN (363-364).

THE news of Julian's death spread rejoicing among the Christians. The pagan Libanius accuses them of suborning the assassin, which is absurd; and a historian of the Church comes very near claiming for one of them the honor of being himself the murderer, which is disgraceful.[1] Saint Gregory, more Scriptural, represents Julian as falling by the hand of an angel. His invectives against "the Apostate" begin and end with a sort of hymn which throbs with a fierce joy: "Ye people, hearken to my words, all ye who are to-day, and ye who shall be to-morrow; and may my voice reach the angelic choir who have made an end to the tyrant's life. . . . He whom their hands have just now slain . . . was the crooked serpent, the apostate, the scourge of Israel and of the world. . . . Awake, ashes of the great Constantine! If there be any consciousness in the grave, hear my voice! Come also, ye noble athletes, defenders of the truth, who have been unjustly banished from your earthly country, I bid you to share in our rejoicing. . . . O thou who didst forbid us to speak, how art thou fallen into eternal silence!"

How much more worthy are the simple words of a Christian poet, who says: "He was a very brave leader in battle, and a great law-maker. By his arms and his judgment he served the state well, but he did not serve religion. The worshipper of a thousand divinities, he had no faith in the true God; yet he did honor to the state."[2]

This death, which caused so much joy in the Church, was a disaster for the Empire; discouragement seized upon the hearts

---

[1] Sozomenus, vi. 1. It was a revival of the old doctrine of tyrannicide.
[2] Prudentius, *Apotheosis*, 450-454.

of the soldiers, and insubordination broke out in the army, — a twofold presage of disaster.

On the morning of the 27th of June a great council was held in the imperial tent. The officers who had served under Constantius desired a man of their own party; the Gallic nobles, Nevitta and Dagalaiphus, sought for a man from their ranks. The purple was offered to Sallust, the praetorian prefect, who excused himself as too old a man; and the proposal was rejected — made perhaps by Amm. Marcellinus — to wait before proceeding to an election until the two armies of Julian and Procopius were united. While the chiefs deliberated, a few persons clamorously proclaimed Jovian,

OOIN OF JOVIAN.[2]

the chief officer of the guards.[1] He was a native of Pannonia, as all the Emperors had been for a century, and was not yet thirty-three years of age. His father, count of the domestics, had made the son's way clear; and though the latter had only the amiable virtues, and was a man without brilliancy or talent, timid, gluttonous, addicted to wine and to women, he had rapidly risen to the higher grades. As he made public profession of the Christian faith, it was doubtless the Christians who had precipitated his election; and the crowd, eager for a leader, applauded. The Gauls, deceived by the similarity of the names Julian and Jovian, at first believed that the acclamations saluted their Emperor restored to life. "But," says Amm. Marcellinus, "when the new Emperor, who was both taller and less upright, was seen, they perceived what had happened, and gave vent to tears and lamentations."

With an able emperor the situation of the army would not have been dangerous. The Persians had lost heavily in the late engagement. Their two best generals had fallen, fifty satraps, or men of note, a vast number of soldiers, and nearly all their elephants.[3] But Julian's death had prevented the Romans from

---

[1] Amm. Marcellinus calls him *domesticorum ordinis primus*, — a rank which made him very conspicuous. Diocletian was *comes domesticorum* at the time when he was elected emperor.

[2] D. N. IOVIANVS. P. F. PERP. AVG. Diademed head. On the reverse, SECVRITAS REI PVBLICAE. Rome and Constantinople supporting a buckler. (Gold coin.)

[3] . . . *Foedas suorum strages et elephantos, quot nunquam rex ante meminerat interfectos.*

making the most of their victory, the enemy was near, provisions were scarce, and Procopius was a hundred miles distant.[1] There was needed a resolute will to command, and a firm hand to secure obedience; Jovian had neither. The soldiers clamored that the army must cross the Tigris as quickly as possible; the gods became the accomplices of the soldiers' fears, or rather, they gave wise counsel : in the entrails of the sacrificed animals their priest found the presage that Jovian would be victorious if the army continued its march, but would ruin everything if he remained in the camp as he proposed.[2] Did the new Emperor retain a certain respect for revelations obtained from sacrifices, or did he merely yield to the wishes of the army and the advice of experienced leaders ? This we know not; but he gave the order to cross the river. Unfortunately the movement was badly performed ; two days were lost in constructing a bridge of boats which was immediately swept away by the current.

Sapor, meanwhile, having been informed by a deserter, a personal enemy of Jovian, of the great disorder prevailing in the Roman army, and of the incapacity of the new leader, resolved to prevent the junction of the two Roman armies — which would have greatly increased the dangers of his situation — by an attempt to gain from negotiating, that which he dared not await as the result of a battle. He proposed peace, with the condition that the two Empires should resume the limits which each had had before the famous treaty of 297. This was for the Romans the loss of the five provinces on the other side of the Tigris and of the brave cities of Nisibis and Singara, the two outposts of Mesopotamia, and the abandonment of Armenia, whose useful alliance Rome had secured by four centuries of effort. Jovian was anxious in respect to the intentions of Procopius, for whom, it was believed, Julian had destined the Empire.[3]

---

[1] Less than forty leagues. Amm. Marcellinus, who since the burning of the fleet has taken gloomy views, exaggerates the difficult situation of the army. As soon as they move away from Ctesiphon, he speaks of a scarcity of provisions; but it does not appear that the army lacked food, for in the treaty with Sapor there was no stipulation that the Persians should furnish provisions. His text has been altered, moreover, in this place. Zosimus, on the contrary, who seems to write from a journal kept on the march, speaks (iii. 27, 28) of cities, numerous in this fertile region, where the Romans found τροφὴν ἄφθονον, and in such quantities that after taking all they needed, they destroyed the rest. The generals of Carus, after that Emperor's death, had led the army back by this same route, and without suffering from famine.

[2] Amm. Marcell., xxv. 6 : . . . *Hostiis pro Joviano extisque inspectis, pronuntiatum est eum omnia perditurum, si intra vallum remansisset ut cogitabat, superiorem vero fore profectum.*

[3] Jovian well understood his own incapacity, and the treaty with Sapor increased his

Personal interest rendered him regardless of the public welfare, and he accepted the shameful conditions of Sapor. The attempt has been made to excuse him by recalling Hadrian's relinquishment of the ephemeral conquests of Trajan, Aurelian's abandonment of Dacia, and Diocletian's withdrawal of Roman troops from the desert of the Blemmyes; but those Emperors took, at their own instance and with entire freedom of action, these important measures to give the Empire more solid frontiers. The treaty of Jovian was nothing less than a capitulation, and Sapor so understood it: "It is your

FRAGMENTS OF TERRA-COTTA FROM TARSUS (MUSEUM OF THE LOUVRE).

ransom" (*pro redemptione*), he said to this army which he had never once defeated. Vainly did the inhabitants of Nisibis offer alone to defend their city, which had so checked the advance of the Persians; they received the order to abandon it, under pain of death. Armenia, also sacrificed, was soon to lose several provinces; her king, Arsaces, was to be carried into captivity; and the great fortress which had protected Roman Asia remained in the power or under the influence of Rome's hereditary enemy.

At Nisibis, Jovian put to death his namesake Jovian, the chief of the *notarii*, who had received some votes for the Empire. Procopius was more dangerous; Jovian dared not strike him at the head of his army, but he took the command from him, giving him the duty of transporting to Tarsus, at the foot of the Taurus, the body of Julian, who had wished to be buried — far away from Constantine and Constantius — in a city where paganism still flourished, and where the Emperor Maximin,[1] a violent enemy of Christianity,

fears of seeing a competitor arise: *Quod magis metuebatur, si casus novi quidam exsurgerent opponendum . . . extimescit aemulum potestatis* (Amm. Marcellinus, xxv. 8 and 9).

[1] The tomb was placed outside the city, on the road leading to the defiles of Mount

THE LAKE OF EYERDIR, IN THE TAURUS.

had been interred. If we may believe the Bishop of Nazianzen,
the earth shuddered at the contact of the Apostate's body, and
cast out the sacrilegious dust.   To the pagans Julian's tomb was
a temple. They engraved upon it this epitaph: "Here lies Julian,
killed beyond the Tigris, a good emperor, a brave soldier." [1] The
funeral being over, Procopius disappeared, and concealed himself
from all eyes; he reappeared in 365, clothed with the purple.

Early in October Jovian arrived in Antioch, whose incorrigible
population received him with sarcasms.   Thence he went to Tarsus, where he ordered some deco-
rations for the tomb of Julian; [2]
then crossed the Taurus; and
returning into Tyana in Cappadocia, received there the deputies from Gaul.   The soldiers
had refused to believe that Julian was dead, and an outbreak
had cost the lives of two of the
envoys of the Emperor, one of

FRAGMENTS OF TERRA-COTTA FROM TARSUS
(MUSEUM OF THE LOUVRE).

whom was his father-in-law, Lucilianus. [3] But the general, Jovinus,
had restored peace, and the deputation brought to the Emperor
the oath of fidelity of the Gallic army.   At Ancyra he assumed
the consulship, taking as his colleague his infant son; and a few
days later he ended in Dadastana, a village of Bithynia, his feeble
and melancholy reign of seven months.   He was found dead in
his bed.   After an abundant supper the preceding night, he had
retired to rest in a room recently plastered, where, as a protection against the dampness, a fire of charcoal had been lighted, the
gases of which had asphyxiated him (Feb. 16, 364).

We should mention to this Emperor's credit his moderation in
religious matters.   Although a Christian, he instigated no reaction
against paganism, which, no longer held up by the Emperor's hand,

Taurus, and near the River Cydnus, — *gratissimus amnis et liquidus* (Amm. Marcellinus,
xxiv. 10).

[1] Zosimus, iii 34.

[2] Amm. Marcellinus, xxv. 10.

[3] The third envoy, Valentinian, escaped death only by prompt flight. Jovian had
appointed Malaric, the Frank, commander of the forces in Gaul, but the latter had refused
the office (Amm. Marcellinus, xxv. 8 and 10).

sank never more to rise. Jovian restored to the Church the privileges which Constantine had granted it, reducing, however, by two thirds the annona granted to the clergy; and he recalled Athanasius, the great champion of Orthodoxy, who, with his habitual independence, had returned to Alexandria without  waiting to receive the imperial letter. But the Emperor took no interest in the theological disputes which had seemed so important to Constantine, Constantius, and Julian. Themistius, who had the courage to remain the

SMALL BRONZE.[1]

official orator of the new Emperor, after having served his two predecessors in that capacity, said to him these just and noble words: "God, who has put the religious sentiment in the hearts of men, is willing to be worshipped in the way which each man prefers. The right of going to him as a man pleases cannot be destroyed by confiscations, tortures, or death. From the lacerated body the soul escapes, and carries with it a free conscience." Jovian promulgated a general law of toleration; that is to say, of liberty to all forms of worship.[2] The spirit of the edict of Milan, lost for half a century, reappeared; an Emperor of very ordinary intellect had found, in the simplicity of his heart, a truth which greater men had failed to recognize.

II. — VALENTINIAN (367–375).

WHILE the body of Jovian was on its way to Constantinople, to be buried near the two Emperors whose vicinity Julian had shunned, the army marched towards Nicaea, where the civil and military leaders were endeavoring to give the Empire a new master. Sallust again refused the purple for himself and for his

---

[1] Coin of Jovian, with the figure of Isis Faria, and the legend VOTA PVBLICA. Among the coins of Jovian there are some which, with the legend VOTA PVBLICA, have the same types with those of some of Julian's coins, — Isis suckling Horus, Isis and Anubis, or Anubis alone, Harpocrates, etc. It is evident that Jovian's Christianity was not of an uncompromising type. We have already mentioned the pagan sacrifices offered on his election (p. 225).

[2] This law is not in the *Code*, and could not have been inserted there by the jurisconsults of Justinian; but Themistius, in his *Fifth Discourse*, from which we have quoted the words given in the text, attests its existence in a manner which admits of no doubt.

son; "I am too old," he said, "and he is too young." After
long but peaceable discussion, the choice fell upon Valentinian,
tribune of the second company of the *scutarii*, or imperial guards.[1]
On the 26th of February, 364, the army was collected in a great
plain, and Valentinian, ascending a tribune which had been built
in the middle, was unanimously proclaimed Emperor, was invested
with the imperial robe, and crowned. He then began to harangue
the multitude in a premeditated speech, but was interrupted by
a great clamor of the troops. Having probably been persuaded
in advance by those for whose interest it was to have two courts,
two sets of officers, and two *donativa*, the soldiery demanded a
second Emperor; and the welfare of the Empire justified their demand. This division of power was indeed so necessary that, with
one exception, for eighty years every Emperor had been forced
to adopt it. Julian only, by reason of his military fame, which
held the Barbarians in check, had been able during his reign —
which was, moreover, so short — to dispense with a colleague at
Milan or at Trèves. His friend the prefect Sallust watched over
Gaul, and Gaul being well guarded, there was no disturbance in
the West. His death, however, had shown the peril of leaving the
succession uncertain, and the government exposed to an accident
of war.

Valentinian accepted very unwillingly the injunction, at once
selfish and patriotic, of the army; he promised to proceed to the
decision as soon as he had maturely reflected. "O excellent Emperor," said Dagalaiphus, the master of the cavalry, to him, "if
you love your own kindred, you have a brother; if you love the
state, then seek the fittest man." Valentinian did not seek; his
choice was made, but he did not declare it until the 28th of
March at Constantinople, when he presented to the army his
brother Valens, six or seven years his junior, and likely to prove
a docile colleague. He had ended his first address to the troops
with a promise of the customary gifts,[2] and the appointment of

---

[1] He was born in 321 at Cibalis, in Pannonia. The *scutarii* and the *protectores* had, like
the body-guard of the early kings of France, the rank of officers. At the time of the disturbances in Africa caused by the negligence of the governor, Romanus, Valentinian sent a
notarius for civil affairs, and a *scutarius* and a *protector* for military affairs, to re-estab-
lish order. The tribuneship of the *scutarii* was therefore a high rank.

[2] . . . *Ob nuncupationem augustam debita protinus accepturi* (Amm. Marcellinus, xxvi. 2).

Valens doubtless caused a second *donativum*. The Roman citizens took part in the elections of Emperors only by furnishing the gold which these elections cost.

The Emperors spent the spring and summer in establishing the two Empires; they divided the provinces, the army, and the civil and military administration. Valentinian took the West, — that is to say, the provinces where the Latin language was used; Valens the Eastern, or Greek-speaking provinces. Milan was to be the residence of the one, Constantinople of the other. The two Empires communicated through the defiles of the Haemus (Balkans), which led from Dacia Aureliana into Thrace by the pass of Succi on the road to Naïssus, and of Sardica at Philippopolis, and by that of Acontisma on the Egnatian Road through Macedon.[2] The common frontier therefore followed a part of the Haemus and the watershed of the Adriatic and the Aegaean. The Eastern Empire had only one praetorian prefect and three *magistri mili-tum*; the West had two prefects, one for Gaul, the other for Illyria, Italy, and Africa, and three generals-in-chief. Valens accompanied his brother as far as Sirmium, where they parted in July, 364, never to meet again.

BRONZE COIN.[1]

The Empire was irrevocably divided; for the unity established by Theodosius lasted but three months. We shall accordingly divide its history from this time forward.

Valentinian was a civilized Pannonian; he knew very little Greek, but he could write Latin verses, and model figurines in clay, — harmless tastes, which made him neither a poet nor an artist. He had virtues more suited to his new position, and vices which make the historian hesitate how to rank him in the imperial series. A brave soldier, without barrack-faults, and a vigilant officer, he loved discipline in the army and order in the state, and he had the good sense sometimes to listen to the honest statements

---

[1] Coin of Sardica or Serdica. Triptolemus, on a chariot drawn by dragons, the gift of Demeter, traverses the earth, diffusing everywhere a knowledge of agriculture. Legend: ΟΥΛΠΙΑC CEPΔΙΚΗC.

[2] The ruins of Sardica are to be seen near the great city Sophia, and Naïssus is now Nissa, or Nisch, on an affluent of the Morava. The *Succorum angustiae* correspond to the Ssulu-Derbend, or the Demir-Kapi, and the Acontisma to the defile of Kavala.

of courageous subordinates. But he was irascible, violent, harsh even to cruelty; and the public misfortunes increased these natural tendencies, for he had to encounter three evils let loose upon the Empire, — insurrections in the provinces, attacks upon the frontiers, and robbery everywhere, from the magistrates in their offices to the brigands upon the highways.[1] He expended little for himself; but the expenses of the state were heavy, and as he justly subordinated private interests to the general security, he paid no attention to the extreme impoverishment of the provinces, and required the taxes to be rigorously levied.[2] Whoever did not succeed in bringing in his full share, ran great risks; decurions and duumvirs suffered death for negligences or delays in this service. On one occasion, having for some slight offence ordered the execution of three of the magistrates in each of

VALENTINIAN.[3]

---

[1] Amm. Marcellinus relates (xxviii. 2) that a brother-in-law of the Emperor was killed by bandits; and in the *Codex Theod.* ix. 30, 1–3, xv. 13, and *Codex Just.* xi. 46, *anno* 364, we find laws forbidding subjects to keep weapons and horses without permission from the Emperor: *Nulli, nobis insciis, quorumlibet armorum morendorum copia tribuatur.* Laws such as these reveal a very sad condition of society, and they also explain why the provincials offered no resistance to the Barbarians. The evil was deep rooted, for this legislation was ancient, a *Lex Julia* prohibiting the possession of weapons (*Dig.* xlviii. 6, 1). As to dishonest magistrates, we have often mentioned them before. It may be added that in the one year 380 Theodosius issued nine laws against them (cf. Godefroy, in the *Codex Theod.* vol. i. p. cviii), and that in his *Letter* 190, Saint Basil congratulates himself that he has obtained what he had occasion to ask of the magistrates, sometimes for nothing, more frequently at a reduced price; but he regards these miracles of unselfishness as expressly due to "the intervention of the Lord." Even in the Church, elections were bought; says Saint Athanasius: "The Church becomes a place of traffic and a market." Gregory Nazianzen speaks of bishops lovers of gold rather than of Christ, μᾶλλον φιλόχρυσοι, ἢ φιλόχριστοι, and quoting Isidore of Pelusium: "formerly the flock stood in awe of the shepherd; now the shepherd must reverence the flock" (Fialon, *S. Athanase*, p. 117). It was inevitable that prelates should be intriguers and worldly-minded, since the Church had become rich, and bishops were always at court.

[2] His legislative activity exhausted itself in the preparation of fiscal laws; a great number of his constitutions concern, either directly or indirectly, the levying of taxes in kind, services due by corporations, the responsibility of *curiales*, and the like. On his fiscal severities, see Zosimus, iv. 16.

[3] Valentinian, with laurel-wreath and *paludamentum*. Cameo No. 257 of the *Cabinet de*

several cities, the prefect Florentinus asked him what should be done
in case any one of the cities had not as many as three magistrates;
the Emperor replied: "Let the execution of the sentence be delayed
till the number is complete." [1] His very virtues became, by his un-
governable character, formidable faults, and through love of the
public good he became a tyrant.   To the soldier who brings civil
society to the strict standard of the military law, all difference between a fault, a misdemeanor, and a crime disappears.[2] A page holding a large hound which had been brought out for hunting, let the
animal loose before the appointed moment because it leaped up
and bit him; upon which the boy perished under the rod.   The
master of a workshop brought the Emperor an offering, a breast-
plate most exquisitely polished; but because there was less weight
of steel than was usual, the man was ordered to execution.   The
master of the imperial stables having ventured to exchange a few
horses, was stoned to death.   A charioteer of the circus suffered
some imprudent words to escape him, and perished at the stake.
The governor of one province wished to change it for another.
His request being brought to the Emperor, Valentinian replied
roughly: "Let his head be changed instead."   "And by this
sentence," says Amm. Marcellinus, "a man of great eloquence
perished only because, like many others, he wished for higher
preferment.   I fear," continues the historian, "lest I should appear
to make a business of pointing out the vices of an Emperor
who in other respects had many good qualities.[3] But this one
circumstance may not be passed over in silence, — that he kept
two ferocious she-bears, who were used to eat men; and they
had names, Golden Camel, and Innocence; and these beasts he
took such care of that he had their dens close to his bed-chamber,
and appointed over them trusty keepers who were bound to take

France; sardonyx of three layers, 35 millim. in height, 27 in width. It is not certain that
this cameo represents Valentinian.

[1] Amm. Marcellinus xxix. 3.

[2] *Delictis supplicia grandiora* (Amm. Marcellinus, xxviii. 1). He does not say all;
the Code — an unexceptionable witness — gives other proofs of this severity. By the constitution of 371 (*Codex Theod.* ix. 3, 5) he who has a prisoner in charge and allows him to
escape, incurs the penalty the prisoner would have suffered.

[3] Amm. Marcellinus, who seems to have retired from the service after the death of
Julian, might indeed be suspected of exaggeration, did not other testimony coincide with
his.

especial care that the odious fury of these monsters should never be checked.   At last he had Innocence set free, after he had seen the burial of many corpses which she had torn to pieces, giving her the range of the forests as a reward for her services." A sultan in our own time used often to be present at the dinner of his lions, and has been known to require a courtier to enter the cage.   Doubtless Valentinian allowed himself this Oriental diversion.

The servants imitated their master, — like that Leo, " by occupation originally a brigand, as savage as a wild beast, and insatiable of human blood; " or that Maximin, deputy-prefect of Rome, " like a serpent that glides underground," and on his tribunal " vociferating, in a tone like the roar of a wild beast, that no one could ever be acquitted unless he chose," who, under pretext of magic and adultery, filled Rome with blood, caused senators to be put to death, and — a thing which seemed still more dreadful — put them first to the torture, in violation of their ancient rights in this respect.   This executioner was called to court and made praetorian prefect, " where he was as cruel as ever, having, indeed, greater power of inflicting injury."   Maximin had rivals,[1] who, like himself and the Emperor, were Christians, — whence we may conclude that conversion had changed the faith but not the characters of these men.   But should we multiply these tales of murder, we should finally believe that there was nothing good in the reign of Valentinian.

This formidable man was in certain phases of his government wiser than Constantine or Julian.   He did two great things, — he created a new office of much utility, that of the *defensor civitatis ;* and he respected the religious liberty of his subjects.   From the very earliest days of his reign he recognized full liberty to all cults,[2] and the acts attesting his own Christian convictions had no irritating results towards the pagans.   He replaced the cross upon the *labarum,*

---

[1] Read what Amm. Marcellinus says of Count Romanus, of Remigius, of Ursacius, of Palladius, and others, and what Synesius relates of the evil deeds of Andronicus, governor of the Cyrenaïca forty years later.

[2] *Testes sunt leges a me in exordio imperii mei datae, quibus unicuique, quod animo imbibisset colendi libera facultas tributa est (Codez Theod.* ix. 16. 9. *anno* 371).   Only the Manichaeans and the Donatists were excluded from this general toleration.   The former were suspected of disloyalty, and the latter created disturbances in Africa.   Amm. Marcellinus says of Valentinian : *Inter religionum diversitates medius stetit, nec quemquam inquietavit, neque, ut hoc coleretur, imperavit aut illud* (xxx. 9).   Socrates (iv. 29) says the same.

prohibited the bringing of suits on Sunday against the Christians, authorized those who were imprisoned to come out on Easter Day in order to attend church,[1] and formally recognized the spiritual jurisdiction of the diocesan synods.[2] But he respected the old religion of Rome (*concessam a majoribus religionem*); he forbade confusing rites of the ancient cult, even divination, with magic, which remained a crime; and he condemned nocturnal sacrifices. He even allowed the Greeks to celebrate their mysteries,[3] and refused to interfere in the theological disputes of the Christian sects. "This should be settled by the bishops," he said; "I am not their judge."[4]

VALENTINIAN I. HOLDING THE LABARUM.[5]

By this wise reserve he kept the priests at a distance, and allowed them to have no hold upon the government. He restrained the too forward zeal of Saint Martin in destroying pagan sanctuaries; he repudiated his first wife, Severa, in order to marry the Arian Justina; and he had a priest beheaded who had concealed a proscribed person, — things not pleasing to the austere Christians, and the last of them an act of iniquity. In again depriving the pagan temples of the lands which the Christians — or rather the hangers-on of the palace — had seized in the time of Constantius, and Julian had restored to their former possessors, the Emperor gave these estates to the public treasury, and not to the churches; so that it was the state that finally profited by this twofold spoliation. He renewed the laws of Constantine which prohibited admission to the clerical office of persons possessed of property, and adjudged to the public treasury donations and legacies made to ecclesiastics, considering, as was later said by Valentinian III., that it was enough for

---

[1] *Codex Theod.* viii. 8, 1; ix. 38, 3–4. This permission was granted only to persons imprisoned for trivial offences.

[2] *Codex Theod.* xvi. 2, 23; cf. *ibid.* xvi. 11, 1. The clergy (*presbyterium*) of the bishopric formed the diocesan synod, over which the bishop presided. The chapter of the cathedral later took the place of the diocesan synod as the usual council of the bishop.

[3] *Codex Theod.* ix. 16, 7, and 9; Zosimus, iv. 3.

[4] Sozomenus, vi. 7; Ambrose, *Epist.* 13.

[5] D. N. VALENTINIANVS. P. F. AVG., and the Emperor with a diadem. On the reverse, Valentinian laurelled, holding the *labarum.* (Silver medallion.)

them to be rich in piety.[1] The pagan pontiffs of the provinces,
on the contrary, received important privileges, and even the rank
of count.[2] In restoring the right of giving instruction to those
who united talent with integrity of life, this annulling of the decree of Julian was useful to all, and did injury to none. The prohibition of intrusting to Christians the guardianship of a temple,
and of condemning them to fight as gladiators, was in their case a
measure of domestic discipline; and it was no more an insult to
the worshippers of the gods than, on the other hand, was it such
to their adversaries that the pagan Symmachus should be appointed
prefect of Rome, and the counts Rumoredus and Bauto, both pagans,
commanders of the army. Certain soldiers take possession of a
synagogue; the Emperor drives them out because it is not proper
that they should make their quarters in a house of prayer.[3] And,
lastly, we have explained that prosecutions against magic, which
reappeared in this Emperor's reign, were the execution of old
republican laws.[4]

[1] Constitution of the three Emperors, addressed in 370 to Pope Damasus (*Codex Theod.*
xvi. 2, 20, and Vol. VII. of this work, p. 509). By these laws Saint Ambrose, when he was
raised to the episcopate, was obliged to relinquish his great wealth, of which he gave the life
interest to his brother and sister, and the property itself to his church. But his brother died
shortly after, and his sister embraced a religious life; he therefore remained very rich while
yet having obeyed the law, since as bishop he had at his disposal the wealth which personally
he no longer possessed. It had been the intention of Constantine to impose poverty upon all
the clergy; but in authorizing the Church to receive legacies, he prepared the way for her
immense ownership of land in the Middle Ages; and we see by the case of Milan that
this was beginning at the period of which we speak (Saint Ambrose, *Homily* 21, *in I. Epist.
ad Cor.*, and *Hom.* 35 and 37, *In Matth.*). Saint John Chrysostom already speaks of the vast
wealth of the Church. In respect to the clergy, Saint Ambrose says, in his *Letter* 18, *anno* 384:
" The legacy a Christian widow makes to the priests of the idols is valid; that which she makes
to the ministers of God is not so." The difference is easily explained. The Christian clergy
could attract to themselves legacies and donations by means which the pagan clergy had never
possessed. The Emperors of the fourth and fifth centuries, seeing how rapidly the collective
wealth of the churches increased, applied themselves with extreme tenacity to the task of
preventing the clergy from the acquisition of personal fortunes. It would have been detrimental
to the cities, from whose burdens the priests were completely exempted (see Vol. VII. p. 508);
and we have seen what solicitude the Emperors manifested for that muncipal prosperity upon
which depended the prompt and full payment of the taxes. But the law which decreed that
the clergy should receive nothing, could be easily evaded, and Saint Jerome tells us that it
was evaded by fraudulent trusts (*Hieron. Opera*, iv. 260).

[2] A law of the year 371 grants under certain conditions to those who possess the *sacer
dotium provinciae* the privileges of the *honorati*, the dispensation from *munera civilia*, and the
right to obtain *honorem ex comitibus; quem hi consequi solent qui fidem diligentiamque suam in
administrandis rebus publicis approbarent* (*Codex Theod.* xii. 1, 75, and Godefroy's commentary
ad leg. iv. 451).

[3] *Codex Just.* i. 9, 4.   [4] *Codex Theod.* ix. 16, 7.

Valentinian carried so far his firm resolve to remain outside
of all clerical disputes that he did not interpose, either in the
noisy debate between the Arian bishop of Milan, Auxentius, "the
minister of Satan,"[1] and Saint Hilary of Poitiers, the Athanasius
of the West, nor in the fierce rivalry of two bishops for the
Roman see.

The popular intervention in episcopal elections still continued.[2]
Most frequently it was useful, as in the election of Ambrose, Synesius, and many others. Sometimes, however, it was violent, capri-
cious, or brought forward unworthy candidates, ready to sign any
confession of faith that might be required of them, "the ink
making no spot upon the soul."[3] Gregory Nazianzen complains,
in his Funeral Oration upon Saint Basil, that "grace is held to
be conferred by the votes of an unreasoning crowd and a vile
populace." Each community — Orthodox, Arian, or semi-Arian
— appointing its leader, multiplied elections gave many bishops
to a single city. Antioch had three at once, and Rome, in the
presence of its popes, had a succession of Donatist and Luci-
ferian bishops; hence arose quarrels. "Damasus and Ursinus,"
says Amm. Marcellinus,[4] "being both immoderately eager to obtain
the bishopric, formed parties and carried on the conflict with
great asperity, the partisans of each carrying their violence to
actual battle, in which many men were wounded and killed; and
as the prefect of the city was unable to put an end to it, or even
to mitigate these disorders, he was at last by their violence compelled to withdraw to the suburbs. Ultimately, Damasus got the
best of the strife by the strenuous efforts of his partisans. It is
certain that on one day a hundred and thirty-seven dead bodies
were found in the basilica of Sicininus,[5] which is a Christian

---

[1] *Satanae angelus, vestator perditus, etc.* (Hilary, *Contra Auxentius, passim*).
[2] See Synesius, *Letter* 123.
[3] Gregory Nazianzen. *Funeral Oration upon his Father.*
[4] xxvii. 3; also, Socrates, *Hist. eccl.* iv. 29.
[5] This basilica is perhaps that of Santa Maria Maggiore. Pope Damasus is almost
like one of the literary popes of the fifteenth century. He employed Saint Jerome to
make from the Hebrew text a Latin translation of the Scriptures to replace the faulty versions that were in circulation, of which Saint Jerome says (*Praefatio in Evangelia ad
Damasum papam*): "If any say that the Latin versions give authority, let him tell me which,
for there are almost as many of them as there are copies." The work of Jerome is known
to us as the Vulgate. Damasus built churches and decorated them with paintings; he

church; and the populace, having been thus roused to a state of ferocity, were with great difficulty restored to order." And although the worthy chronicler was not perhaps familiar with this sentence of the Gospel, "The Son of Man came not to be ministered unto, but to minister,"[1] he adds: "I do not deny, when I consider the ostentation that prevails at Rome, that those who desire such rank and power may be justified in laboring with all possible exertion and vehemence to obtain their wishes, since, after they have succeeded, they will be secure for the future, being enriched by offerings from matrons, riding in carriages, dressing splendidly, and feasting luxuriously, so that their entertainments surpass even royal banquets.[2] And they might be really happy if, despising the multitude of the city, which they excite against themselves by their vices, they were to live in imitation of some of the priests in the provinces, whom the most rigid abstinence in eating and drinking, and plainness of apparel, and eyes always downcast, recommend to the eternal Deity and his true worshippers as pure and sober-minded men." To put an end to this

repaired the Christian cemeteries (catacombs), and put metrical inscriptions on the tombs of the martyrs, some of which the Chevalier Rossi has collected or restored.

[1] *Matt.* xx. 25.

[2] These words of Amm. Marcellinus, who resided for several years at Rome, are confirmed by the saying of the pagan Praetextatus to Pope Damasus, reported by Saint Jerome (*Letter* 6, edit of Migne, i. 415, or *Letter* 24 of the edition of Erasmus): "Make me bishop of Rome, and I will make myself a Christian." Elsewhere, in speaking of the Roman clergy, he writes: "I am ashamed to say it, but there are men who seek the priesthood and the diaconate in order to see women more freely (*ut licentius mulieres videant*), and rival in luxury the consuls, the governors, and generals of armies. They care only for their adornment; their hair is curled, their fingers glitter with the sparkle of diamonds. . . . They are like young bridegrooms rather than priests." Cf. Saint Jerome, *In Michaeum*, 20, and *Letter* 84, to Eustochia; Gregory Nazianzen, *Disc.* xxxii.; Sulpicius Severus, *Dial.* i.: . . . *Qui ante pedibus aut asello ire consueverat, spumante equo invehitur;* Salvianus, *Adversus Avaritiam*, book i., wherein he shows the Church "enfeebled by her fecundity, diminished by her increase, and *quasi viribus minus valida.*" Saint Augustine (*Letter* 148) acknowledges *Nihil esse in hoc tempore* . . . *laetius, hominibus acceptabilius, episcopi, aut presbyteri, aut diaconi officio, si perfunctorie atque adulatorie res agatur;* and Fleury (*Mœurs des Chrétiens*, chap. 48) adds: "Nothing is more common in the fourth and fifth centuries than superscriptions like these: To the Lord, the very holy, very pious, and venerable N., bishop." It was a matter of common custom to kneel before the prelate and kiss his feet. It was to God's representative, certainly, that these acts of homage were addressed; but can it be doubted that the man thus honored conceived a pride which reacted upon his public conduct, and inspired him with a spirit of domination? *Recidisse jam sacerdotii dignitatem ad regnandi cupiditatem apparet, ab humilitate ad superbiam,* says again a disciple of Saint John Chrysostom, Saint Isidore of Pelusium (*Letters*, v. 21). By their social and political consequences these extravagances fall under the judgment of history.

domestic strife in the Church there were needed guards, the executioner, and death-penalties. Ursinus, who had been expelled from

MOSAIC OF SANTA MARIA MAGGIORE AT ROME.[1]

the city, returned thither, was again driven out, and the excitement
continued for several years. It might have been promptly ended

[1] This mosaic, which is of the fifth century (pontificate of Sixtus III.), represents Joshua
imploring the God of Israel while his soldiers, clad as Roman legionaries, are fighting before
a fortified city. If the encounter of which Amm. Marcellinus speaks really took place in
Santa Maria Maggiore, it was unwise to recall the memory of the sad occurrence by a work
of art like this.

had the Emperor taken energetic measures. But Valentinian, who often found the laws not severe enough, in this case would not bring the imperial authority to bear.

He was, however, extremely solicitous to maintain peace in the cities by introducing justice everywhere. He strove to suppress certain strange abuses which must have facilitated dishonest transactions, — for example, that a man should be at once advocate and judge in a given case; or that a magistrate should render decision in private session in his own house; and the Emperor ordained that decisions should be given in the open court-room, after a public hearing which any person might attend. The disasters of the times had interrupted at many points the old institution of provincial assemblies, or had caused it to fall into disuse. Valentinian re-established them, defined their powers, and authorized their deputies to employ the public post when they came to bring to the court the complaints of their constituents.[1] His successors endeavored also to revive public life in the provinces; Theodosius alone published five constitutions on this subject. The famous edict of Honorius, in 418, was, so to speak, a last appeal of the Emperor to subjects whom a bad government could defend neither from foreign foes nor domestic disasters.

Valentinian still further manifested his solicitude for municipal interests by creating in each city a new office, whose incumbent — *defensor civitatis*, also called *patronus plebis*[2] — had the duty of protecting the weak and of putting a stop to abuses by calling upon the praetorian prefect. He was to be, say the edicts, a father to the plebs, the defender of the innocent, the patron of the humble population of the city and the country. He was to protect them against the insolence of officials, the insults of the judges, overcharges in the matter of taxes, and exactions of every kind. The poor are his children (*liberorum loco tueri debet*); to secure his independence the Emperor decided that the *defensor*, whose office was of five years' duration,[3] should be chosen outside of the

---

[1] *Codex Theod.* i. 61, 9, *anno* 364; ii. 10, 5; xii. 12, 3-6.

[2] *Ibid.* xii. 12, laws 7, 9, 10, 13, and title i. law 148.

[3] *In defensoribus* . . . *erit administrationis haec forma et tempus quinquennii spatii metiendum* (*Codex Just.* i. 55, 4). A constitution of Honorius requires the *principales* to serve fifteen years (*Codex Theod.* xii. 1, 171, *anno* 409. Cf. Savigny, vol. i. sects. 20-21). The early rule was the annual election of municipal magistrates. The tendency to make each permanent

curia and the administration, among persons no longer in office,
so that he should have neither colleagues to satisfy, nor superior
officers to obey, with the exception only of the praetorian prefect,
who could annul his election.[1]

The new office was perhaps a reminiscence of very ancient
functions. The protection of the weak reappears under various
forms throughout the history of this people in other respects so
severe. It was at first clientship which fed the poor of Rome;
later, under the Republic and the Early Empire, the patronage of
the great which provided the poor with defenders of their cause in
the Senate or in the presence of the Emperor; in the Antonine
epoch it was the *syndicus* (σύνδικος, ἔκδικος), whose existence is
proved in many cities of Italy, Asia, and Africa. "If any man,"
says Hadrian, in a decree addressed to the Athenians, "has complaints to make to me or to the proconsul, let the people appoint
a syndicus."[2] This municipal advocate was neither the *patronus*
of the early days nor the *defensor* of the later period; but he
represented the idea which had given the provincial assemblies
the right to carry their complaints to the Emperor, and had lasted
across the centuries with singular and honorable tenacity.

The institution of the *defensor civitatis* was not to the credit
of the imperial functionaries, whose misdeeds Amm. Marcellinus
reports on every page; and it must have been extremely displeasing
to them, for this was an inspector whom Valentinian placed over
the agent of the treasury, the assessor, and the judge "who loves

in his employ is manifested in this duration of five and of fifteen years given by Valentinian I.
and Honorius to the offices of *defensor* and *principalis*.

[1] *Non ex decurionum seu ex cohortalium corpore, sed ex aliis idoneis personis huic officio
deputentur* (*Codex Just.* i. 55, 1–4). Their duties were to watch *ut plebs omnis officiis patro-
norum contra potentiam defendatur injuriis* (*Codex Theod.* i. 11, 1, anno 364). It has been
said that the two offices of *defensor* and *duumvir* could not have existed contemporaneously.
Valentinian, who created the former in 364, mentions the latter in 372 (*ibid.* xii. 1, 77).
The three great offices of the cities and colonies were those of the *sacerdotales*, *flamines per-
petui*, and *duumviri* (*ibid.* xii. 5, 2, anno 337). The rôle of the *defensores* became very
important; it was so especially after Justinian, who extended their jurisdiction — at first
limited to suits not involving over fifty *aurei* — to cases where the amount in dispute was as
much as three hundred *solidi* (*Nov. Just.* xv. 3, sect. 2. See, in the *Codex Theod.* i. 29, in
Hänel's edition, more complete than Godefroy's, the caption *Defens. civit.*, and Godefroy's
commentary, i. 67 *et seq.*).

[2] *ἐὰν δὲ ἐκκαλέσηταί τις ἢ ἐμὲ ἢ τὸν ἀνθύπατον, χειροτονείτω συνδίχους ὁ δῆμος* (*C. I. G.*,
No. 355). Cf. Pliny, *Letters*, x, *passim*. Alexander Severus also gave a *defensor* to the corporations which he formed. See Vol. VII. p. 126.

to judge in darkness," but to whom the *defensor* would always have free access.[1]   In investing a layman with this patronage of the poor, the Emperor perhaps proposed to withdraw from the Church's influence that plebs which had been her earliest conquest. If this was his policy, his successors did not follow it.   When Honorius, in 409, called all the clergy of the city to make the

VALENTINIAN AND ROME.[2]

election, with the concurrence of the nobles, he placed the new magistracy in dependence upon the bishops.

All public officers were not extortioners or murderers, many of these as there are in the pages of Amm. Marcellinus.   Praetextatus and Olybrius, both prefects of Rome, doubtless suggested the regulations which we read in two constitutions addressed to themselves. The first of these organized a medical service for the poor in the fourteen *regiones* of Rome;[3] the second concerned the regulation of the schools in that city.   It was required that students should be furnished with a permission from the magistrates of their province ; on their arrival they were obliged to register, in the office of the census, the name of their country and of their family, the studies they wished to pursue, and the address of their lodging in the city, so that it could be ascertained if they were doing well the work for which they professed to have come, and were leading a moral life, avoiding dangerous societies, and not too much occupied with festivals and games.   Those guilty of misconduct were to be publicly beaten with rods, expelled from the city, and sent home to their province.   Industrious students might remain in Rome twenty years; but the idle should be at once sent away.   Every month the urban prefect was to send the provincial magistrates a report

[1] . . . *Ingrediendi, cum voles, ad judicem liberam habeas facultatem* (*Codex Just.* i. 55, 4).

[2] D. N. VALENTINIANVS P. F. AVG., and the bust of the Emperor with diadem and *paludamentum.* Rome, helmeted, seated, looking to the right, holding in the right hand a globe surmounted by a Victory, and in the left a spear, point downwards. (Large bronze.)

[3] *Codex Theod.* xiii. 3, 8.   The custom of securing to the poor of the cities (*tenuioribus*) the assistance of a physician ἄνευ μισθοῦ ἐπὶ συγγραφῇς was ancient. (See Vol. VI. p. 112.) When one of the fourteen places became vacant, it was filled by a person whom the remaining thirteen designated.

concerning the students from their provinces, and each year to
the Emperor a special account of the most distinguished scholars,
that the latter might be able to select those of his subjects who
were suited to the various public employments.[1] Regulations like
these in respect to students would — with exception of the rods —
be useful at the present day.

We must now speak of Valentinian's great anxiety, — the defence
of the Empire. On the death of Julian the Barbarians at once shook

off the fear with which that Emperor
had inspired them. "At this time"
(the year 365), says Amm. Marcellinus, "the trumpet, as it were, gave
signal for war throughout the whole
Roman world, and the Barbarian tribes
on our frontier began to make incursions on those territories which lay
nearest to them. The Alemanni laid
waste Gaul and Rhaetia at the same
time. The Sarmatians and Quadi ravaged Pannonia. The Picts, Scots, Saxons, and Atacotti harassed the Britons
with incessant invasions ; the Austori-
ani and other Moorish tribes attacked

VALENTINIAN I.[1]

Africa with more than usual violence. Predatory bands of Goths
plundered Thrace; the king of Persia poured troops into Armenia ;" and, finally, in the East, Procopius attempted to make a
revolution.

Valentinian left Valens to extricate himself as he best could.
The lieutenant of the Western Empire in Illyricum did no more than
prevent the revolt from extending into the West; and the Emperor

himself in October, 365, left Milan to visit Lutetia, Reims, and Trèves, the three great cities of Northern Gaul, where he passed ten years in defending and fortifying the frontiers.   The great effort of Germany against the Empire was at that time made in the southwest, whither were attracted all those who sought adventure or booty.   The Decumatian Lands (Baden and Wittenberg)[1] had formerly been as a

HALL IN THE IMPERIAL PALACE OF LUTETIA (PRESENT CONDITION).[2]

wedge driven by Rome into the centre of Germany; the Black Forest was now a fortress whence the Barbarians made incessant sorties against Gaul.   The Alemanni, dissatisfied because the presents sent them this year were less splendid than usual, had rejected them with scorn, and sought compensation in the pillage of the Rhenish provinces.   They were at first easily repulsed; but during the winter of 366 they crossed the Rhine upon the ice and surprised the troops posted in the two German provinces, who in an engage-

[1] See also pp. 103-105 of this volume.
[2] See, Vol. VII. p. 185, map of the defensive lines of the Decumatian Lands.

ment which took place not far from Besançon lost a standard and their leader, the Frank Charietto.[1]   Valentinian deprived the

Roman fugitives of their weapons, and threatened to sell them as slaves. They implored the Emperor to give them another trial; and in the second campaign, which was ably conducted by the commander of the cavalry, Jovinus, the Alemanni, who had come as far as Châlons-sur-Marne, were defeated.   The battle lasted a whole summer's day; six thousand dead and four thousand wounded

MOGUNTIACUM, CASTELLUM, AND THE BRIDGE OVER THE RHINE.[2]

on the side of the Barbarians, and twelve hundred dead and two hundred wounded of the Romans, covered the Catalaunic fields, where, later, a very different hecatomb was to be offered up. These numbers and the heat of the encounter show that the day of the definitive invasion was drawing near.   The news of this victory reached Lutetia just as the messengers arrived who brought to Valentinian the head of Procopius, — a frightful tribute sent by the Emperor of the East to his brother (367).

At the battle of Châlons a king had been taken prisoner,[3] and the

---

[1] . . . *Charietto tunc per utramque Germaniam comes* (Amm. Marcellinus, xxvii. 1). Another Gaul, Dagalief, or Dagalaiphus, was consul in 366.   Balcobaudus had an important command at the battle of Châlons-sur-Marne.

[2] Large lead medallion of the time of Valentinian I., found in the Saône ; this medallion shows the fortifications which covered the two banks of the Rhine at Mayence and Cassel (*Cabinet de France*).

[3] Vithicabius, son of that Vadomar who had a secret understanding with Constantius to betray Julian (see p. 126, note 2).

soldiers hanged him; Valentinian blamed them, but probably without much sincerity, for, shortly after, a traitor won over by Roman gold assassinated in Germany the principal instigator of these incursions. But the Barbarians kept no account of their dead. They began almost immediately again to make raids into the provinces. Taking advantage of a Christian festival which had drawn the population away from the gates and the walls, they surprised Mayence and carried off a great number of captives. Valentinian resolved to retaliate upon these incessant pillagers the sufferings

LARGE BRONZE.[1]

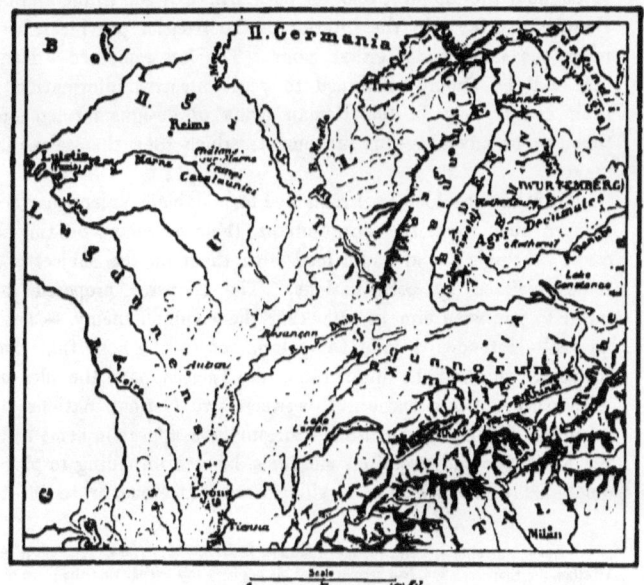

MAP FOR VALENTINIAN'S WAR AGAINST THE FRANKS AND THE ALEMANNI.

that they had inflicted upon the Roman provinces. He crossed the Rhine and went fifty miles beyond it, burning houses and villages;

[1] Valentinian, restorer of the Empire. The Emperor, standing, holds a standard, and a Victory upon a globe (Cohen, vol. vi. pl. xiii. No. 58).

the bravest of the Alemanni, who had posted themselves upon an elevated plateau, were reached and destroyed (368).[1] After this blow struck in the heart of the enemy's country, Valentinian returned to Trèves, where he made every endeavor to consolidate the lines of defence of the river and establish some outposts upon the right bank. A strong castle, built near the place where Mannheim now stands, commanded the entrance to the valley of the Neckar, one of the great roads by which the Romans went into the interior of Alemannia, and the Barbarians came down into Gaul (369). The Emperor took a further precaution: he prohibited marriage between Romans and Barbarians.[2] But these had taken place everywhere throughout the Empire; and on both banks of the Rhine and of the Danube, and far into the interior of the frontier provinces, life was much the same, under either name. The law remained a dead letter, and the enemy continued to receive secret information from their countrymen in the Roman army of designs formed against them, or of advantageous movements which they themselves might make.[3]

Meantime the Alemanni remained formidable. Valentinian sought to turn upon them the Burgundians, their neighbors on the northeast (Thuringia), who had a feud with them on the subject of salt-mines claimed by both nations. The Emperor proposed to the latter to join with him in attacking the common enemy, — not that he really intended a joint campaign, but in the hope that, having instigated this war, he might then, like Tacitus, have the pleasure of witnessing a fierce encounter between two German nations. But when he saw eighty thousand Burgundians appear in arms to claim his assistance and promised subsidies, he was unwilling to place his small army at the side of auxiliaries so numerous, or to substitute

---

[1] Amm. Marcellinus, xxvii. 10, and Ausonius, *Mosella*, v. 421 *et seq.* The poet, tutor of Gratian, the Emperor's son, had accompanied his pupil on this expedition: the place of action is thought to have been between Rothwell and Rothenburg. The *Gentiles* made the attack, and Amm. Marcellinus mentions the gallantry of the *scutarius* Natuspardo, whose name tells his origin. A little later Valentinian appointed an Aleman king, Fraomar, tribune of a corps of his fellow-countrymen who served in the Roman army. He also gave military commands to Bitharid and Hortar, two other Alemanni; but the latter having had treasonable correspondence with the Barbarians, was burned to death (Amm. Marcellinus, xxix. 4).

[2] *Codex Theod.* iii. 14, 1.

[3] . . . *Quae apud nos agebantur, aliquotiens barbaris prodidisse* (Amm. Marcellinus, xxviii. 5).

for the divided Alemanni a people so united that they could bring into the field an army like this. Under various pretexts he retarded the concentration of his troops, and the angry Burgundians returned into their own country. The Alemanni, warned by the danger, which had been imminent, remained comparatively quiet until the close of Valentinian's reign. In 374 their king, Macrianus, made with the Emperor a treaty which held the Barbarian the ally of Rome until the last day of his life.

In 370, Saxons, in their frail canoes of wicker, came up by the Belgian rivers into the interior of the province and destroyed the military corps which guarded it. A device, which the upright Amm. Marcellinus considered treacherous, caused their destruction. Those who did not fall under the sword or lance of the cataphracti were reserved for the amphitheatre; and at Rome twenty-nine strangled themselves rather than serve for the amusement of the populace.

In Britain the Picts, who cultivated the plains of Scotland, and the Scots, whose flocks ranged the hills, had always been troublesome neighbors to the Roman provinces. So long as a bold and vigilant commander kept watch from Eboracum upon their movements, men lived tranquilly on the south of Hadrian's Wall, the cities flourished, and the fields were fruitful, — we have seen that Julian obtained from Britain corn for his army. But if, remote from the master's eye, the governors yielded to the temptation of the times, rapacity, and the legions did not receive their pay duly; if deserters from the army lived by pillage upon the highways, while Saxon or Frankish pirates ravaged the sea-coast, — it naturally resulted that the inhabitants lost their love for a government which required much and gave nothing. In the midst of this disorganization the audacity of the Barbarians increased. They scoured the whole country as far south as Kent, and did not fear to match themselves against the regular troops. This condition of things had lasted, with intervals of repose, since the great insurrection of Carausius, which laid open the island to the Franks and Saxons. Constantius Chlorus and Constantine had restored order for a time; but Constantine II. had been obliged to go over into Britain, and Julian had found it necessary to send troops thither. In 368 Valentinian received news at Trèves, where he was residing in order to keep close watch upon the outposts of the Rhine, that the two Roman commanders in Britain had been killed, and that the province was almost lost. He took energetic measures to recover it.[1] A skilful and faithful general, Theodosius, crossed the Straits with a force that enabled him to drive the Saxons

MOSAIC FOUND AT WITHINGTON, GLOUCESTERSHIRE, ENGLAND.[2]

into the sea, and the Scots into their mountains, and the Roman standards reappeared on the wall of the Picts (369).

Theodosius, rewarded with the rank of commander of the cavalry, became the useful lieutenant of Valentinian, who employed him in repressing a dangerous insurrection.

---

[1] On this war, see Amm. Marcellinus, xxvii. 8; I do not speak of the hyperboles of Claudian, *In III* et IV* consulatu Honorii*, nor of the panegyric of Pacatus.

[2] Lysons, *Reliquiae Britanniae Romanae*, vol. ii. pl. xix.

The Barbarians of the South, like those of the North, had become aware that the great Roman Empire was sinking, slowly but continuously, under the weight of its constitutional defects and the blows delivered at so many points along its immense frontier. The Getuli ravaged and plundered as far as the very suburbs of the cities of Tripolitana; Leptis had been besieged for a week; and the ancient assembly in which the common interests of the province were discussed, sent deputies to the Emperor to complain of the indifference of Romanus, the governor. The latter bribed the commissioners, who were appointed to examine into his conduct, and five of the chief notables were put to death as calumniators (370). While the Getuli thus spread terror in the eastern part of the province of Africa, Firmus, the son of a powerful Mauretanian chief, being condemned to death by Romanus, incited an insurrection among his people in order to escape from the threatened fate.[1] Imperial functionaries, military chiefs, prefects, and tribunes, and soldiers recruited in the province, went over to his side; a tribune of the Constantinian infantry placed his gold collar around the Mauretanian's head by way of diadem, and he was proclaimed king. Julian had been crowned in the same way, but fortunately Firmus was not Julian. He took Icosium, the great city of Caesarea (Algiers), and burned it; and for a moment believed himself master of Roman Africa when he saw the native population and the Donatists rally around a chief of their own nation. But, unused to war, badly armed, without discipline or drill, the provincials could not stand against regular troops well directed by an able soldier (372). Theodosius, sailing from Arles with a small force, landed at Igilgilis (Djidjelli) before his approach was reported. Employing the tactics of Marius against Jugurtha, he pursued Firmus under the blazing sun of Africa into regions where it seemed impossible that troops drawn from the North of Gaul could endure the heat. With his little army of thirty-five hundred picked men, agile and well equipped, obtaining provi-

---

[1] Africa very early had *latifundia*. Pliny mentions enormous ones in the time of Nero. This system of ownership, combining with the tribal system, covered Africa with imperial or private domains as vast as the territory of cities; those, for example, of the Lollii, the Arrii, of Lusius Quietus, of Firmus and, later, of Gildo. There were always great chiefs in Africa, but under the Romans, flourishing cities balanced these principalities, so to speak. Cf. *Bull. de corr. Afric.* 1882, pp. 60–67 and 154.

sions from the *silos* of the natives or from depots judiciously prepared, he went everywhere, burning the villages and destroying
the harvests of which he had no need. He knew how to outwit
his unscrupulous enemy, and he made it his duty to learn the interior affairs of the tribes, so that he could reorganize under faithful chiefs those that were submissive. But, a fit lieutenant to the
most severe of Roman Emperors, he waged war without mercy, and
ruled without indulgence; deserters, traitors, cowards who had fled
during battle, employees who had been accomplices in the frauds
of Romanus, perished under the axe or at the stake, after having
been subjected to torture. Firmus, hunted down on every side,
was about to suffer a fate like that of Jugurtha when given up by
Bocchus; but one night, his guards being asleep, the Mauretanian
hanged himself. This suicide at least spared him the torture which
the executioners of the time were very skilful in prolonging.
Igmazen, king of the Isaflenses, with whom Firmus had sought
shelter, placed his body on a camel and carried it to Theodosius;
and thus the war ended.

While this general was restoring one province to the Empire,
his son, who was later the Emperor Theodosius, saved another.
Valentinian was fortifying the line of the Danube as far as Dacia
Aureliana,[1] in the same way that he had made the left bank of
the Rhine secure. He wished also to have an outpost in the
country of the Quadi, as he had established one on the Neckar in
Alemannia. Gabinius, the king of the Quadi, came to make humble remonstrances on this subject to the duke of the province
Valeria, who invited him and his attendants to a banquet, and
murdered them. To avenge this treachery the Quadi and neighboring tribes crossed the Danube and invaded Roman territory,
where they almost succeeded in capturing the daughter of the
Emperor Constantius, Flavia Constantia, whom the Church has
canonized,[2] and who, at that time betrothed to Gratian, son of
Valentinian, was on her way to be married. Two legions were
defeated by the Barbarians, and it became necessary to rebuild in
all haste the walls of Sirmium. But the younger Theodosius, duke

---

[1] *Codex Theod.* xv. i. 13.

[2] For reasons which it is needless to detail here, I believe this Constantia, wife of
the very pious Emperor Gratian (Amm. Marcellinus, xxi. 15; xxv. 7, 9 ; xxix. 6), who died
before her husband, leaving him no children, to be the Saint Constantia of the Church.

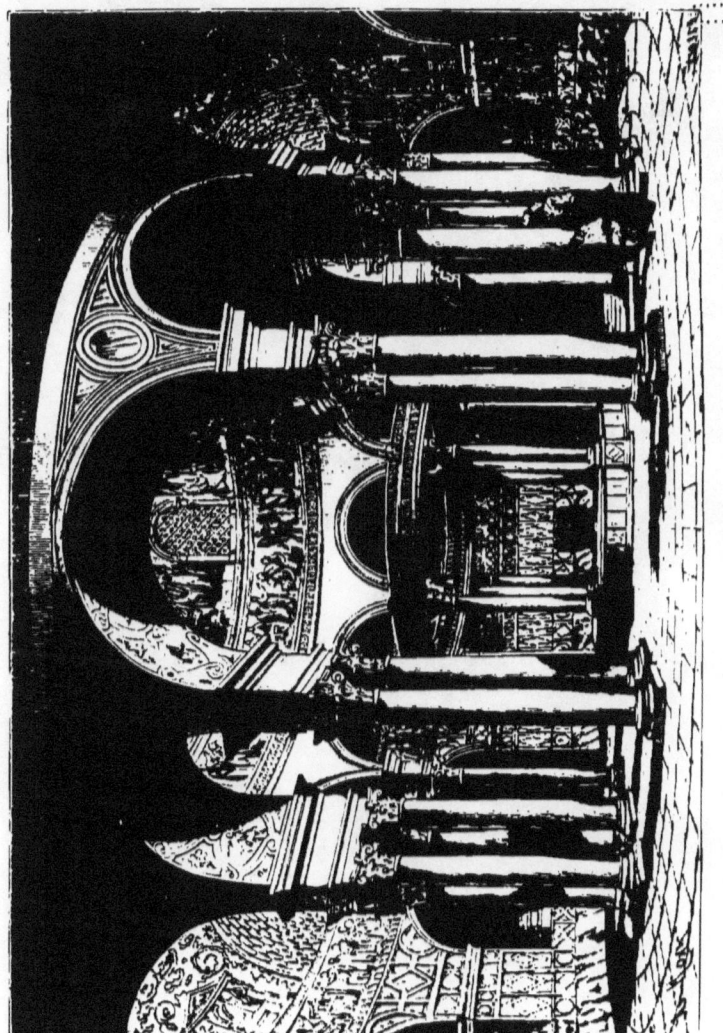

CHURCH AND TOMB OF SAINT CONSTANTIA (ISABELLE, LES ÉDIFICES CIRCULAIRES, PL. 35).

of Moesia, defeated in several engagements the Sarmatae who had invaded his provinces, and obliged them to sue for peace.

Valentinian sent into Pannonia a division of Gallic troops, whom he followed closely in person. Such was the life of a Roman Emperor at this time, — always upon the frontiers, sword in hand, to keep out the Barbarians who from contact with Rome had acquired some arts of peace and war, who had now better weapons and a more formidable system of tactics than the Empire possessed, and who could never be forgotten for a moment. Not long since, the stern and haughty ruler of the West had not disdained to cross the Rhine and treat almost on equal terms with a king of the Alemanni. Along the Danube he found once flourishing cities almost destroyed, and ancient fortresses little more than ruins. He crossed the river near Aquincum. All the Quadi who fell into his power, warriors and old men, women and children, were murdered; the rest, from the mountains where they had taken refuge, looked down upon their villages in flames. Struck with fear, they sent envoys to beg for peace and oblivion of the past. The Emperor received them at Bregitio [1] with great displeasure; he broke out against them in violent language, while speaking burst a blood-vessel in his lungs, and died the following night. This end, so characteristic of his life, should not, however, cause us to forget that, at least so far as the protection of the Empire and religious peace were concerned, he had filled his office well (Nov. 17, 375).

He left two sons, Gratian, whose mother, Valeria Severa, he had repudiated, and Valentinian II., the son of his second wife, the Empress Justina. In 367, while very ill, he had conferred on Gratian, then eight years of age, the title of Augustus, without making the lad pass through the preliminary grade of Caesar.[2] After negotiations and intrigues which lasted six days, of which the details are unknown, but may be conjectured, the principal officers of the camp at Bregitio gave the title of Augustus to Valentinian II. also, and assigned to him Illyria, Italy, and Africa.

[1] A fortress on the Danube in Lower Pannonia; the fifth cohort of the First Adjutrix had its quarters there. The ruins of Bregitio are to be seen near Szony, east of Comorn.

[2] According to Idacius, Gratian was born April 18, 359; according to the *Chron. Paschale*, May 28.

Gratian would doubtless recall his mother, who, returning to court, her heart embittered by seven years of insult, would reign as empress, while Justina would be reduced to the condition of a subject. The latter could only escape from the humiliation and dangers which threatened her, by having her own son raised to the same rank with the son of Valeria; and she was sure to find friends who would willingly be masters of a new court and a boy emperor. The most important of these persons, and the man who had most to do in the matter, Mellobaudes, commander-in-chief of the army of the Danube, was her kinsman.[1] By this election the risk of civil war was incurred, but the best troops of the army had accompanied Valentinian into Illyria; the elder Augustus accepted the younger fraternally, without jealousy of any kind, and there was rivalry neither between the two Empresses nor the two brothers. History sees at this period in the West only these two colorless figures of ephemeral Emperors, destined to vanish from the stage, one at the age of twenty, the other at twenty-four.

III. — VALENS (364–378).[2]

VALENS was no more consulted than Gratian had been in the matter of the division of the Empire; but the Eastern Emperor was too much occupied to dispute a title or a province with his nephews. His reign had begun with a revolt imperilling his throne. That Procopius of whom it was asserted that Julian had regarded him as a successor to the Empire, had remained concealed during Jovian's lifetime. A few months after the accession of the new Emperor he had emerged from his retreat, and with the aid of a few mutinous soldiers caused himself to be proclaimed emperor in Constantinople while Valens was absent in Asia (Sept. 28, 365). The latter was

---

[1] Zosimus, iv. 17. Justina had accompanied her husband into Illyria, and was only a hundred miles distant from the camp with her son Valentinian and her brother Cerealis (Amm. Marcellinus xxx. 10). Besides her son, she had three daughters, one of whom married Theodosius.

[2] He was born about 328, and was therefore thirty-six years of age at his accession.

not a person made to gain the popular favor. Small in stature, swarthy in complexion, having a cast in one eye, he had none of those exterior advantages of grace or dignity which charm or impress the multitude; and it very soon became apparent that he was cruel in disposition, and rude through lack of education,[1] — he was even ignorant of the language spoken by his subjects. Hence Procopius not unnaturally believed that he was a sovereign easily to be over-

GOLD MEDALLION (1).[2]   GOLD MEDALLION (2).[2]

thrown. The friends of Julian had been deprived of their offices, even the praetorian prefect, Sallust, who had refused the Empire. They were malcontents ready to encourage a revolt, and doubtless some of them aided Procopius in gathering an army. The sedition spread rapidly in Thrace and among the chief towns of Bithynia. But this chance Emperor was even more worthless than his rival. His enterprise met its ruin in Phrygia, almost without a battle, from the defection of one of his generals, an Aleman by birth, whom Valens had bought over. Procopius fled, accompanied by two of

---

[1] Amm. Marcellinus, xxxi. 14.

[2] Cabinet of Vienna. Arneth, *Gold- und Silbermon. des antiken Cabinet in Wien*, pl. cxiv. 12, p. 52; and Cohen, vol. vi. *Valens*, No. 10. First medallion: Valens, with diadem and *paludamentum*, the right hand raised. Second medallion: Valentinian I., with nimbus, between Valens and Valentinian II., all three standing, each holding a sceptre and leaning upon a buckler. Legend: PIETAS DDD. NNN. AVGVSTORVM. Weight of the medallion about 2 oz., without the rim. On medallions of great size given as rewards instead of money, see Vol. VII. p. 211, note 5.

his officers, who, to save their own lives, fell upon him and dragged him, bound with ropes, to the Emperor. Valens caused him to be beheaded (May 27, 366); and, doubly traitors, the two officers shared his fate. A kinsman of Procopius, Marcellus, an officer of the guard, attempted to continue the revolt for his own profit, but

COIN OF PROCOPIUS.[1]

gained by it only a cruel death. Valens had been alarmed, and he was pitiless. "The executioner and the rack and most cruel modes of torture now attacked men of every rank, class, or fortune, without distinction. . . . For the Emperor was quick to inflict injury, always ready to listen to informers, admitting the most deadly accusations, and exulting unrestrainedly in the diversity of the punishments devised. . . . Nor was any limit put to the cruelties which were inflicted, till both the Emperor and those about him were satiated with plunder and bloodshed."[2]

In 374 magic and the stars gave Valens another competitor, Theodorus, one of the imperial secretaries,[3] who was made to believe himself the designated Emperor. Amm. Marcellinus relates, from the deposition of the conspirators, how the god had been constrained to reveal the future. The method was simple, within the reach of any man, and for that very reason specially dangerous to those who for the moment were the masters. "We did construct, most noble judges," Hilarius said, "under most unhappy auspices, this unfortunate little tripod which you see, in the likeness of that of Delphi, making it of laurel-twigs; and having consecrated it with imprecations of mysterious verses, and with many decorations and repeated ceremonies in all proper order, we at last used it in the following manner: it was placed in the middle of a building carefully purified on all sides by Arabian perfumes; and a plain round dish

[1] D. N. PROCOPIVS P. F. AVG., and the diademed head of the Emperor. On the reverse, REPARATIO FEL. TEMP. The Emperor, standing, holding a spear and leaning upon a buckler. (Gold coin.)

[2] . . . *Quamdiu principem et proximos opum satietas cepit et caedis* (Amm. Marcellinus, xxvi. 10).

[3] . . . *Secundum inter notarios adeptus jam gradum* (Amm. Marcellinus, xxix. 1).

was set upon it, made of different metals. On the rim of this dish the four and twenty letters of the alphabet were engraved with great skill, and at equal distances one from another.

"Then a person clothed in linen garments and shod with slippers of linen, with a small linen cap upon his head, bearing in his hand sprigs of vervain, as a plant of good omen, propitiated the deity who presides over foreknowledge, and thus took his station by this dish, according to all the rules of the ceremony. Then over the tripod he balanced a ring which he held suspended by a flaxen thread of extreme fineness, which had also been consecrated with mystic ceremonies. And as this ring touched and bounded off from the different letters, which still preserved their distances distinct, he made with these letters, in the order in which he touched them, verses in the heroic metre, corresponding to the questions which he had asked, the verses being also perfect in metre and rhythm, like the answers of the Pythia which are so renowned, or those given by the oracles of the Branchidae.

VALENS ON HORSEBACK.[1]

"Then, when we asked who should succeed the present Emperor, after it was said that it would be a person of universal accomplishments, the ring sprang up and touched the letters ΘΕΟ; it then added another letter, and one of the bystanders cried out that Theodorus was the person thus pointed out by the inevitable decrees of Fate. We asked no further questions concerning the

---

[1] Reverse of the gold medallion represented, p. 259.

matter, for it seemed quite plain to us that he was the man who was intended."

In all ages, whether those of the diviner's circle or of table-tipping, the broad space between wisdom and folly is quickly bridged by human stupidity. To-day we laugh at this idle credulity; in the Roman Empire it cost men their lives. Denounced before he had done anything to aid Destiny in keeping her promise, Theodorus was beheaded, and, as usual, a great number of distinguished persons (*honorati*) perished with him. The war against magicians began again; and as the philosophy of those times was only theurgy, the philosophers became victims of persecution. Maximus, the friend and spiritual director of Julian, was beheaded. Valens ordered a severe search to be made for books of magic, and even the army was employed in this service. The books discovered were burned, and their owners with them. Saint Chrysostom describes the alarm which he felt when, having picked up one day, on the banks of the Orontes, a book which had been prudently thrown into the river, he discovered that he had in his hand a treatise on magic. A soldier was near by, and the saint dared not in the man's presence either tear up the book or throw it away; he finally succeeded in hiding it under his mantle without attracting observation, and he considered himself saved from a great peril.[1]

In the religious question, Valens followed the policy of Constantius. Orthodoxy made progress in the East; Alexandria, where Athanasius still lived, and Caesarea in Cappadocia, which at this time had Saint Basil as bishop, were its principal centres. Several churches in Asia had united in sending their deputies to Rome to bring about an agreement between Eastern and Western Christendom.[2]

This movement occasioned anxiety to Valens, and, to counteract it, he caused himself to be baptized by the Arian bishop of Constantinople. This public declaration of the sovereign's faith indicated

---

[1] Saint Chrysostom, *Homily* 38, upon the *Acts of the Apostles.*

[2] They had been furnished with letters to Liberius, "our brother and colleague." These letters were said to be addressed "by the Orthodox bishops of Asia to you and the other bishops of Italy and the West." And Liberius replied: "Liberius, bishop of Italy, and all the bishops of the West, to our very dear brothers and colleagues. . . . The bishops of the East are now in harmony with the Orthodox bishops of the West." These letters, condemning the Council of Rimini, and establishing the Nicene Creed as the sole rule of faith, established "communion;" that is to say, community of belief between the churches which interchanged them. This was a very ancient and useful custom. Cf. Socrates, iv. 12.

to all men connected with the court what their belief should be; and the indication became plainer still when they saw sentences of exile begin again. The persecution this time had alternations of severity and of indecision which took from it the gloomy grandeur of the great struggles in matters of belief.[1] It is a history which we have already related in the reign of Constantius, and we are reluctant to return to it. Mention also should be made of the disturbances in the churches, of competitions between the bishops, of elections obtained by bribery or by popular violence, of unworthy priests " who made merchandise of the Word of God," [2] and ordained for money. Saint Basil writes: " Will the bishops renounce their wickedness? God only knows. . . . Here, all is full of grief." [3] He himself, in order to make sure of the revenues of his episcopal estate, — devoted, it is true, to the relief of the poor, — broke with Gregory Nazianzen a friendship of thirty years; and the latter says: " It is now by intrigues that men attain the office of bishop." [4] However much allowance we make for the exaggeration natural to fault-finders, there yet remains in these accusations so much truth that history has no right to conceal troubles which were one of the elements of the political situation,[5] and explain, without justifying, the violent acts of the Emperors. In respect to the religious policy of Valens, we shall mention two facts only, showing how, after transports of rage, he sank into feebleness and inaction, — the worst possible habit of mind for a ruler. Athanasius, driven out of Alexandria for the fifth time, was obliged to conceal himself for four months in a tomb; after inflicting this useless punishment on the brave old man, Valens

---

[1] In respect to this persecution, see the fourth book of Socrates. A constitution (*Codex Theod.* xii. 1, 63) calls the monks *ignaviae sectatores*, and orders the Count of the East to restore them to their municipal senates, that they may bear the local burdens (*munia*). A law of 364 (*ibid.* ix. 16, 7) forbade nocturnal sacrifices. Upon the representations of Praetextatus, proconsul of Achaia, Valens made exception in the case of the mysteries of Eleusis, which were celebrated by night (Zosimus, iv. 3).

[2] Καπηλεύοντες (Basil, *Letter* 103).

[3] *Letters* 48, 53, and 57.

[4] Gregory Nazianzen, i. 335, edit. Billy.

[5] With his lofty soul and his tender heart for the poor, Basil had the malady of his time, — he was of an irascible temper. We find him at war with his uncle, with almost all the bishops of Pontus, and later we shall see what his conduct was towards the Pope. Gregory Nazianzen was equally hot-headed. These men had a most lofty ideal, and they gave way to recriminations all the more violent because they did not find this ideal realized in the men about them.

authorized him to return to his metropolitan church, where he found, in 373, by a tranquil end, that repose which in life he had never known. Saint Basil, threatened with death in his archiepiscopal city of Caesarea, maintained his position against the praetorian prefect, and even against the Emperor; and Valens, fearing an outbreak of the population, left them their bishop. With this Emperor all was petty, even wickedness.

Themistius asserts that he reduced the taxes by one fourth.[1] It would seem that certain fiscal reductions, probably temporary, were exaggerated by the official orator until they became, to an imagination over-excited by rhetoric, an abatement which an emperor of that time could not have made.

Upon a body whence life is departing, swarm injurious insects, hastening the work of destruction. Africa, Italy, Gaul, and Britain had been ravaged by robbers as well as by the Barbarians; Pannonia and Dacia Aureliana had suffered from inroads of the Quadi and Sarmatae; and the Gothic tribes will shortly make a permanent lodgement in Thrace. The province of Asia was in no better condition, the Isaurians incessantly plundering the territory adjacent to their mountains. Audacious brigands spread terror in Syria, the Saracens in Palestine and Phoenicia, the Blemmyes on the borders of Egypt. Saint Basil wrote, in 373, that from Cappadocia to the shores of the Bosphorus the whole land was full of enemies; Rome even was, so to speak, besieged by robbers, and Symmachus dared not leave the city to go to his estates in Campania. "It seemed as if the Furies were throwing everything into confusion," says Amm. Marcellinus. Against these unworthy enemies the army exhausted its remaining strength.[2]

With disorder like this at home, a foreign war was sure to be feebly carried on. Jovian had stipulated that the Armenian Arsaces, Julian's ally and, in some respects, his dependant, should be included in the treaty of 363; but had pledged himself not to assist Arsaces

---

[1] Themistius, *Oration*, 8.

[2] . . . *Adjumento militari marcente* (xxxii. 9). Concerning the valor of the Roman soldiers of this time, see Zosimus, iv. 40. In Amm. Marcellinus (xxx. 1) a legion takes flight before a small troop of Armenian cavalry, who, however, have done no more than show a determination to fight. Others refuse to quit the shelter of a fortress in order to drive away pillagers; their commander only succeeds in persuading them to do this by rushing out alone against the enemy (Zosimus, iv. 40).

if any hostilities should break out between him and Persia. This was in effect to give up Armenia to the intrigues and the open attacks of Sapor. The intrigues began at once, and' from the year 364 had been a cause of anxiety to Valens. But the Persian king hesitated to entangle his cavalry in the Armenian mountains; he preferred intrigue, and was successful in it. Arsaces, invited to a festival, was seized, loaded with silver chains, and then put to death. It was not, however, so easy to obtain possession of the country. Sapor followed another method: he invested two Armenian nobles, pledged to his interests, with the government; and the same thing was done in Iberia. Valens attempted to arrest the advance of Persia. He was not an impetuous soldier, and Sapor — who had been on the throne for sixty-three years — had exhausted his warlike ardor in innumerable campaigns. Accordingly, the two empires

LARGE GOLD MEDALLION OF VALENS.[1]

did not rush against each other with tremendous energy; it was more like two infirm old men who, from habit, strive feebly with each other. Count Trajan and Vadomar — once a king of the Alemanni, and now a Roman general — obtained some slight advantage in 373 over a corps of the enemy; this blow being struck somewhat softly, a truce suspended the inglorious hostilities. Later, in 380, the disturbances which followed the death of Sapor,

---

[1] Valens wearing the diadem. This medallion, which, with its ring, weighs nearly 15 oz., was worn around the neck, as (p. 90) Julian was required to wear the likeness of Constantius (Cohen, vol. vi. pl. 14). Cabinet of Vienna.

complicated with a war on the Eastern frontier, led the Persians to desire peace with Rome, and an ambassador came to seek it from Theodosius, bringing the Emperor rich presents, — silk stuffs, gems, Indian elephants, and other objects of value.[1]

The widow of Arsaces, daughter of that prefect Ablavius who had perished in the great Constantinian massacre of 337, had a son named Para. This young prince, sheltered in the territory of the Roman Empire, finally succeeded in recovering his ancestral kingdom, but was constrained to pursue the policy imposed upon the kings of Armenia by their situation: namely, to keep on good terms both with Persia and the Empire. Valens, feeling that the young king leaned too much to the Persian side, persuaded him by kind messages to come to the imperial residence at Tarsus; and when Para arrived, Valens made an attempt to keep him prisoner. Warned of his danger, the Armenian escaped. But with a confidence unusual in an Asiatic prince, he fell soon after into another snare by accepting an invitation from Count Trajan, the commander of the Roman forces in Armenia. The repast was sumptuous, and the music of lyres and lutes filled the hall, when suddenly a Barbarian soldier rushed in with a drawn sword, fell upon the young king, who fought bravely for his life, but perished under repeated blows (374).[2]

Valentinian had dealt thus with an Aleman chief, and the governor of Pannonia with the king of the Quadi. All these men, notwithstanding their Christian zeal,[3] were unscrupulous, and the morality of the time had fallen very low.

The war against the Goths prevented Valens from deriving any advantage from this crime, which proved profitable to the Persians only.

The Germanic invasion, arrested by Julius Caesar, Augustus, and the Antonines, had in the third century been very near succeeding. The brave Emperors who succeeded the Thirty Tyrants repulsed it, and for a century these Barbarians remained powerless.

---

[1] This embassy arrived in Constantinople in 384, sent by Sapor III., son of Sapor II. and successor of Ardeschir. He reigned but four years, and was perhaps dethroned.

[2] *Exquisitae cuppediae et aedes amplae nervorum et articulato flatilique sonitu resultarent jam vino incalescente* (Amm. Marcellinus, xxx. 1).

[3] The piety of this Count Trajan has been much extolled by the ecclesiastical writers of the time; he was in correspondence with Saint Basil.

In the West the Alemanni and the Franks, enfeebled by numerous attacks from the Romans, had also lost many of their soldiers, attracted into the Roman army or established as colonists in depopulated regions. On that side, therefore, invasion seemed unlikely, although the Empire had abandoned two important positions, giving up to the Alemanni the Decumatian lands, and to the Franks Toxandria. But nations coming from the North had accumulated in formidable masses behind the Danube and the Euxine. The most powerful of these, the Goths, ruled the country from the banks of the Don to Transylvania ; they were divided into the Ostrogoths, or dwellers in the steppe, on the east, and the Visigoths, or dwellers in the woods, on the west, in the vast forests and rich plains which descend from the Carpathians to the Danube.

Since their disastrous expedition in 270,[1] and especially since Aurelian had abandoned to them Dacia, these warlike tribes had almost renounced their raids across the Danube and in Asia Minor. Their relations with the Empire, facilitated by their neighborhood and by the propagation of Christianity among them, had brought them out of barbarism without as yet really making them a civilized nation.[2] They had furnished auxiliaries to Galerius for the Persian war, to Constantine against Licinius, and the Empire now kept in its pay, under the name of *foederati*, a corps of forty thousand Goths, which the Emperors endeavored to keep always at its full number.[3] Either from fidelity to treaties, or more probably from fear of the Empire, which since Claudius Gothicus had been almost continually in strong hands, the Goths had turned their warlike ardor

[1] Vol. VII. p. 224.

[2] Ulfilas (311–381), who is considered the first bishop of the Goths, translated the whole Bible, with the exception of the books of Kings, into the language of his people. This was the first time that the language was written. The evangelization of the Gothic nation, — which he actively carried forward, if indeed he did not begin it, — the translation of the Bible, and the invention of the letters necessary to represent the sounds of the language, testify that Ulfilas was a remarkable man. Philostorgius (ii. 5) represents the bishop as the son of a Cappadocian captive carried off by the Goths, and living among them. Fritigern, the principal chief of the Visigoths, seems to have been favorable to the Christians (Socrates, iv. 33); while his rival, Athanaric, was hostile to them and persecuted them. Upon the spread of Roman civilization among the Barbarians, see above, page 96, note 2. But we must reject the opinion that the mythology of the Germans predisposed them to embrace Christianity. Odin and Thor have nothing in common with Jesus, and the delights of Valhalla (the endless banquets and battles) are completely opposed to the ascetic conception that the Christians formed both of the present and the future life.

[3] Jordanes, *History of the Goths*, p. 21.

against their Barbarian neighbors, and the beginnings of culture
received by them, together with a certain spirit of discipline which
made the whole nation accept the sway of a single chief, secured to
them continual successes.

A great number of Scythian and Germanic tribes yielded obedience to the Ostrogothic king Hermanric, of the venerated family
of the Amalungs. The Visigoths, under their chief, Athanaric,
extended from the Dniester to the middle of ancient Dacia. Some
of their warriors profited by the confusion which followed the
death of Julian and of his successor to venture into Thrace, and
Procopius attracted three thousand of them into his service.[1]   On
the refusal of Athanaric to make any reparation, Valens crossed
the Danube twice, and ravaged the left bank ; and he even promised
a reward for every head of a Goth brought to him (367–369).
Wearied out by these incursions, which laid waste their fields, and
by the war, which interrupted their commerce with the Empire,
the Visigoths begged for peace. A treaty was made at an interview between Valens and Athanaric on boats anchored in the
middle of the river, for the Goth, suspicious of treachery, had
refused to cross to the right bank. He asserted that he had
sworn to his father that he would never set foot on Roman soil.
The Emperor continued his pension, but stopped that of the other
chiefs, and authorized commerce, hitherto carried on all along the
frontiers, only at two cities on the Danube.[2] " This was something
new," says Themistius, " to see the Romans grant a peace, not
buy it "[3] (369).

For many years peace reigned along the Danube ; but great
events were going on in the heart of Scythia. The plains of upper
Asia, where whirlwinds of sand sometimes bury all the cultivated
lands, fill up or divert the channels of rivers, and destroy cities, have
also their whirlwinds of human beings,[4] which, gathering slowly, far

---

[1] This is the number stated by Amm. Marcellinus; Zosimus (iv. 7) says ten thousand.

[2] We have seen Marcus Aurelius and Commodus make like conditions with the Marco-
manni and Quadi, and Diocletian attempt to impose the same on Narses. This is a principle
of policy.

[3] The historian was present at the interview between Valens and Athanaric. See his
Oration X.

[4] . . . Ruens ut turbo montibus celsis (Amm. Marcellinus, xxxi. 3). In the last century
six hundred thousand Kalmucks left the banks of the Volga and crossed half Asia, returning
to the western provinces of China, whence they had originally come.

from view of the civilized world, sweep upon it at certain epochs to destroy it. The Huns were one of these devastating cyclones. They were unknown to the ancients, and later tradition represents them as born in the desert, the children of demons and witches. They appear to have been of Mongol or Finnish origin; according to Amm. Marcellinus, who very probably saw some of them, their appearance was repulsive. "They are of great size, and short-legged," he says; "so that you might fancy them two-legged beasts, or the stout figures which are hewn out roughly with an axe on the posts at the end of bridges. As soon as they are born, the cheeks of their infant children are deeply marked by an iron, in order that the usual vigor of their hair, instead of growing at the proper season, may be withered by the wrinkled scars. . . . They are so hardy that they require neither fire nor well-cooked food, but live on the roots of such herbs as they find in the fields, or on the half-raw flesh of any animal, which they merely warm by placing it under the saddles as they ride. They never shelter themselves under roofed houses, but avoid them as people ordinarily avoid sepulchres, as things not fitted for use. Nor is there to be found among them a cabin thatched with reed; but they wander about, roaming over the mountains and the woods, and are accustomed from infancy to bear frost and hunger and thirst. There is not a person in the whole nation who cannot remain on his horse day and night. On horseback they buy and sell, they take their food, and there they sleep. . . . When provoked, they fight; and when they go into battle they form in a solid body and utter all kinds of terrific yells. . . . In one respect you may pronounce them the most formidable of warriors; for when at a distance they use missiles of various kinds tipped with sharpened bones instead of the usual points of javelins, but when they are at close quarters they fight with the sword, without any regard for their own safety; and often while their antagonists are warding off their blows, they entangle them with twisted cords so that their hands are fettered. None of them plough, or even touch a plough-handle; for they have no settled abode, but are homeless and lawless, perpetually wandering about with their wagons, in which they live, — in fact, they seem to be people always in flight. Their women live in these wagons, and there their children are born and reared. . . . They have no respect for any religion or superstition whatever, and they are immoderately

covetous of gold." These last words of the historian would be surprising, did we not know how, even in the nomad life of the desolate
steppe, the Barbarian is always attracted by the glitter of the yellow
metal.   Concerning the Huns one thing is most clear, — that they
loved to destroy; and we read that Attila, their great chief a few
years later than this time, was wont to boast that where his horse's
hoofs had trodden, the grass never grew again.

What may have been their primitive abode, and what cause
determined their migration, we cannot with certainty say.   It
appears that about the time when the German and Scandinavian
tribes moved southward, to draw nearer to the Roman world, the
Asiatic hordes struck their tents and advanced westward towards
the great prey which was to be the share of the bravest.   With
its ill-defended wealth, the Empire was an immense centre of
attraction, drawing upon itself the Barbarians surrounding it.   In
the time of Valens the Huns crossed the Ural Mountains and the
River Volga.   Beyond this river and on the two slopes of the
Caucasus dwelt the Alans.   Many peoples have taken
the axe as a symbol of command, and even of divinity;
the god of the Alans was a sword driven into the ground.
Their cavalry was formidable; they scalped the conquered
foe, and hung around their horses' necks the scalps of
those whom they had slain.   For them, to die of old age
was disgraceful; to fall in battle, a glorious fate.   However, they were either conquered by the Huns, or formed
an alliance with them to attack jointly the Ostrogothic
kingdom, which presented a rich prey (375).[2]

ROYAL OR
SACRED AXE.[1]

At the approach of this innumerable horde, Hermanric, notwithstanding his hundred and ten years (?), resolved to fight.   But the
tribes under the Ostrogothic sway showed much reluctance towards
this formidable war.   Two Roxalan chiefs, whose sister, Swanhilda,
had been trodden to death by Hermanric's horse because her husband
had refused to take up arms for him, attempted to kill the Ostrogothic

---

[1] See p. 266, note 2.
[2] . . . *Ermenrichi late patentes et uberes pagos* (Amm. Marcellinus, xxxi. 3).   The bulk of
the Alan nation continued to inhabit the Caucasus.   The Arab historian Maçoudi (tenth
century) estimated that the Alans could bring three hundred thousand horsemen into the field.
The number is not certain; but the fact is well known that the Alans were regarded as the
best cavalry in the Byzantine armies.

king; others refused him obedience, and Hermanric, in despair, fell upon his sword. His successor, Vithimir, was defeated and killed. This king left an infant son, Viteric, who was protected by two Gothic generals who had long served in the Roman army, Alatheus and Saphrax. While the larger part of the nation submitted to the conquerors, these two generals made their escape with the boy, and fled into the interior. Advancing westward, the Huns then encountered the Visigoths, whose king or chief magistrate, Athanaric, attempted to defend the passage of the Dniester. The Huns, however, crossed the river by night, and Athanaric, narrowly escaping capture, was compelled to fall back upon the Pruth. He

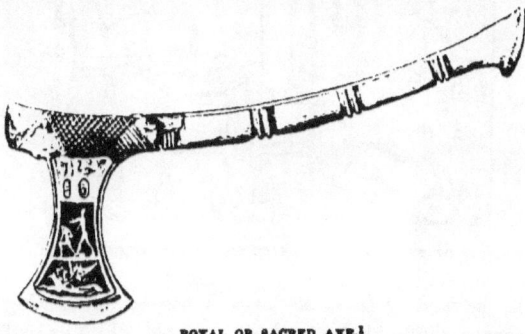

ROYAL OR SACRED AXE.[1]

made a stand on the right bank of this river, and it was his plan to make a line of defence along the Pruth from the Carpathians to the Danube, after the manner in which the Romans had so often done; but his discouraged people preferred to go, under the command of Fritigern, to beg shelter within the Empire. The brave Athanaric refused for himself this disgrace, or it may be that he distrusted the hospitality of Valens; and with a few faithful companions he took shelter in the rugged mountains which separate the Wallach plain from the plains of Hungary (376).

When the bishop Ulfilas arrived at Constantinople to negotiate for the admission of his people into the Roman provinces, Valens saw only a once-dreaded nation extending to him suppliant hands, and his flattered pride caused him to forget all prudence. He opened

[1] See p. 266, note 2.

the Empire to this multitude, which according to a writer of this time contained two hundred thousand fighting men,[1] and believed himself to have done all that was needful for the security of the provinces in stipulating that the Goths should give up their weapons, and a certain number of their children as hostages, whom he dispersed among the cities of Asia Minor. In return, the Emperor promised provisions. He believed that he should thus, at one stroke, accomplish two excellent things, — he should render his army

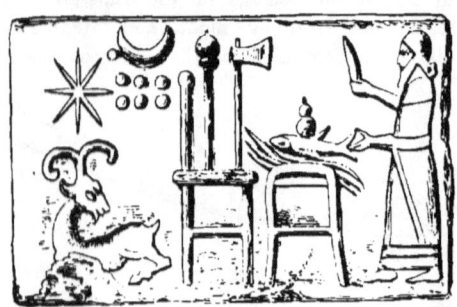

WORSHIP OF THE AXE REPRESENTED ON A BABYLONIAN CYLINDER.[2]

invincible, by adding to it so large a number of fighting men; and he should add to his treasury all the gold which he could now require from the provinces, instead of the soldiers they would no longer be required to furnish. The sum due for each soldier they were excused from furnishing, was raised to eighty solidi. "From that time forth," says Socrates,[3] " Valens neglected to make recruits and despised the veterans."

[1] Eunapius, *Fragm.* 42. But this seems a large estimate, and is not justified by subsequent facts. Amm. Marcellinus (xxxi. 4) and Socrates (iv. 34) say only a great multitude.

[2] De Longpérier, *Œuvres*, i. 170, 220. Behind the symbol of the god are the Sun and the Seven Planets. In Egypt, in Assyria, and even in Asiatic Greece (coins of Tenedos and of Mylasa, for example) the axe is a symbol of royalty or of divinity. In the magnificent tomb of the queen Aah-Hotep, which is one of the most valuable treasures of the Museum of Boulaq, was found, among other objects, a gold-edged hatchet, incrusted with lazulite, turquoises, and other gems. In hieroglyphic writing the axe is the character signifying " god ; " this word makes part of the royal titles, and, repeated nine times, signifies all the heavenly powers. See Arthur Rhône, *L'Égypte à petites journées*, pp. 112, 113. In Poland the same symbol of royalty is retained in the escutcheons of great families which were formerly royal.

[3] *Hist. eccl.* iv. 34.

The Goths had agreed to everything; happy in escaping from a great peril, they entered the Empire as a refuge, which they themselves would have an interest in defending (376). But all was rendered worthless through the fault of the imperial agents, whose venality we have so often had occasion to mention in the history of this period. It was not easy to provide for the subsistence of a multitude which must have numbered a million, if to the two hundred thousand fighting men mentioned by Eunapius we add the women, children, and slaves. The Roman officers speculated upon famine, or were powerless to prevent it; from day to day food became more scarce, and the Goths were obliged to buy it themselves. When their resources were exhausted, they sold their slaves, their wives, and the most beautiful of their children.[1] When they had nothing left, they took by violence what was kept back from them. Either they had secretly retained their weapons, or had purchased the right to keep them; they made themselves others, and pillaged the rich plains which lie at the base of Mount Haemus. It soon appeared that the Roman generals, by their improvidence and avidity, had brought a serious war upon the Empire.[2]

Valens, who had been able neither to foresee nor repress, assembled an army to repair the injury done, and called to his aid his nephew, the Emperor of the West, who sent to him the Frank Richomer, with some troops, to be followed by Frigerid with the Pannonian and Transalpine legions.[3] While, however, Gratian was making preparations to send a large force, and Valens called home from Mesopotamia the legions sent to fight the Persians, time slipped away, and the danger grew more serious. The Barbarians who were established as colonists, or had been sold as slaves in the adjacent provinces, and others who served in the imperial army, hastened to join their brothers.[4] The laborers in the Thracian mines escaped from the miseries they endured; and, as always happens in

---

[1] ... γυναικῶν εὐπροσώπων ... καὶ παίδων ὡραίων εἰς αἰσχρότητα θήρας (Zosimus, iv. 20).

[2] Saint Jerome says in his *Chronicle: Per avaritiam ... ad rebellionem fame coacti sunt.*

[3] Amm. Marcellinus says (xxxi. 7) that most of the soldiers sent from Gaul deserted on the way.

[4] Synesius wrote some years later: "There is scarcely a Roman family which has not Gothic servants; in our cities the masons, the water-carriers, the porters, are all Goths."

these times of disturbance and devastation, many peasants who
had lost all their little possessions joined the pillagers, serving
them as guides in order to share with them in the spoils. When,
at a later period, Alaric besieged Rome, forty thousand slaves
joined his army.[1]

A first and very sanguinary engagement took place near Salices.
Fritigern, having called in by fiery signals the detachments which
were absent on foraging expeditions, emerged from behind his rampart of wagons and attacked the Romans, who were encamped
upon a hill. The Barbarians advanced, shouting the praises of
their ancestors, with many discordant outcries; the legionaries re-
sponded with the *barritus*, which first ran along the ranks as a
gentle murmur, increasing gradually until ended with the full
strength of the men's voices. The losses were heavy on both
sides, and the fortune of the day remained undecided; the Goths
fell back behind their wagons, and the Romans sought shelter in
the neighboring city of Marcianopolis. A few of the dead were
buried; but most of them were left to be devoured by birds and
beasts of prey, and years later the ground was still in many
places white with bones (autumn of 377).[2] Reinforcements received
by the Romans made them strong enough to drive back the Barbarians into the gorges of the Haemus; the roads leading into the valleys were then closed with earthworks, and it was hoped that the
enemy, thus shut in, would perish with hunger. This had been the
successful strategy of Claudius II. But the Goths fell back into
the mountains only to await the arrival of other Barbarians, who
were constantly crossing the Danube, now left without defence.
Alatheus and Saphrax soon joined them with a strong force of
Ostrogoths; Taifales, Huns, and Alans all hastened to fall upon
their prey; those who had just been in arms against each other
became friends in prospect of the enormous booty awaiting them.

Count Saturninus, who was placed in charge of the defiles,
aware of the great masses of men accumulating in the mountains,
perceived that he could not arrest their advance if they should fall
upon any one of the points of the long line that it was his duty
to defend. He fell back on the Thracian fortresses; and Frigerid,

[1] Zosimus, v. 42.
[2] *Indicant nunc usque albentes ossibus campi* (Amm. Marcellinus, xxxi. 7).

the leader of the corps sent by Gratian, on his side retreated as far as Beraea, and even farther, to the pass of Succi, which he fortified, to preserve from invasion at least the Illyrian provinces.[1] Then from the Haemus to the Rhodope, and from the Rhodope to the Bosphorus, all the level country was given up to the most frightful devastation.

Meantime Gratian did not arrive. A young Aleman of the Emperor's guard, being at home on leave of absence, had revealed to his fellow-countrymen that several cohorts had set off for the East, where a formidable invasion was threatened, and that Gratian, with the main army, was about to follow, the advance-guard having already reached Pannonia.[2] The temptation was irresistible; forty thousand Alemans fell upon upper Germany, which they believed to have been left entirely unprotected. Gratian in all haste recalled the legions which were on the way to Valens; and to the forces in Gaul he added numerous Frankish auxiliaries, commanded by a gallant soldier, Merovaud, who was at the same time count of the body-guard and king of the Franks.

The battle of Argentaria (Colmar or Neuf-Brisach) was disastrous to the hostile army, which perished completely,[3] with the exception of five thousand men. Gratian followed the fugitives across the Rhine and drove them as far as the mountains of the Black Forest.[4] To obtain peace, the Alemanni gave up a number of their young men, who, according to the dangerous custom of the time, were enrolled in the Roman army.

This expedition being successfully terminated, Gratian turned towards the East; and from Sirmium, where he arrived ill, he wrote to Valens, then at Hadrianople, begging him to wait till he himself should arrive, that they might then encounter the Goths with the united forces of the two Empires. On receipt of this communication, a council of war was held. The master of the cavalry,

---

[1] . . . Ad societatem spe praedarum ingentium adsciverunt (Amm. Marcellinus, xxxi. 8).

[2] Frigerid destroyed a body of Goths who had ventured as far as the banks of the Margus, and sent his prisoners as colonists to cultivate the lands of Parma, Modena, and Reggio (Amm. Marcellinus, xxxi. 9).

[3] In the same way the accounts given by a scutarius, who had deserted, decided the Aleman kings, in 357, to fight the battle of Strasburg (Amm. Marcellinus, xvi. 12).

[4] A passage in Amm. Marcellinus seems to imply that the Alemanni were attacked at the same time by the Gallic army and the troops that Gratian was bringing back from Illyria; hence the extent of the disaster.

Victor, a prudent general, although a Sarmatian, the Frank Richomer, and the majority of the officers present, desired to await the arrival of Gratian. Valens, jealous of his nephew, wished for a victory which should be entirely his own; he decided that the battle should be fought at once, and on the 9th of August, 378, he set out, on a burning day and over a dusty road, to seek the enemy, whose forces were not yet all collected. Fritigern gained time by feigned negotiations; and when he knew that the troops he was waiting for had arrived, he began the fray. Amm. Marcellinus describes the battle in the last pages of his History.[1] The narrative is lacking in clearness, and the exact causes of the great disaster are not discernible. The Romans were overwhelmed with the heat, he says, devoured by thirst, and suffering with hunger. But the August sun must have been much more insupportable to the Goths, and the legions came from Hadrianople, where there had been no lack of provisions. We detect disorder in the march of the Roman troops,[2] and desertions, for entire corps disappeared without fighting;[3] on the part of the Goths an impetuous attack of their cavalry, hurled by Alatheus and Saphrax at a favorable moment upon the left wing of Valens, which had advanced in disorder as far as the rampart of wagons; and then the crushing mass of a multitude of men rushing with fury upon the imperial army.[4] The Emperor, wounded by an arrow as he was endeavoring to escape, was carried into a hut, to which the Goths, surprised that it was so strenuously defended, set fire. Valens perished in the flames, and no trace of him was ever found. Two thirds of the Roman army, almost all the generals, and thirty-six tribunes were killed; it was another battle of Cannae.

On the following day, notwithstanding the advice of the able Fritigern, who wished "to be at peace with walls,"[5] the Goths

---

[1] He withdrew to Rome, where he read aloud his History in public, to the great admiration of the Romans (Libanius, *Letter* 983).

[2] Zosimus (iv. 24) says: τὸν στρατὸν ἅπαντα σὺν οὐδενὶ κόσμῳ . . . ἐξήγαγεν.

[3] Amm. Marcellinus frequently speaks of *proditores et transfugas* guiding the Goths to the attack on Hadrianople the day after the battle, and to that made on Perinthos and Constantinople. These deserters gave the Goths information as to the interior of these cities, and even of houses.

[4] . . . *Sicut ruina aggeris magni oppressum atque dejectum* (Amm. Marcellinus, xxxi. 11). In respect to this battle, see also Socrates, iv. 38, and Sozomenus, vi. 40. In regard to Fritigern, Alatheus, and Saphrax, Jordanes (26) says: *Vice regum gentibus illis praeerant.*

[5] *Pacem sibi esse cum parietibus memorans* (Amm. Marcellinus, xxxi. 7).

MAP FOR THE GOTHIC INVASION UNDER VALENS

attacked Hadrianople, where Valens had left the treasure of the
army and the wealth of the palace. But for an assault they had
nothing except their courage. The inhabitants, and those who had
been able to take shelter in the city the night before, defended
themselves with the courage of desperation. They blocked up the
gates inside the city with huge stones, they strengthened the weak
parts of the walls, and planted engines to hurl javelins or stones
on all convenient places, and provided an abundant supply of water.
The assault lasted all day, and the Goths retired at night, having
suffered great loss, and made no impression upon the well-defended
walls. The second capital of Thrace had escaped, but Thrace itself
was in the hands of the Barbarians.[1] They now wandered over
the country, ravaging and burning everything as they passed,
avoiding the walled towns, plundering those that were unde-
fended, and finally, as they drew near Constantinople, marching
with speed for fear of ambuscades, and being very eager to obtain
possession of its ample wealth.[2] But the city was strongly fortified; behind its walls was an immense population, whom the Goths
feared as being of the same resolute temper with the men of
Hadrianople, and the Empress Dominica lavished gold in exciting
the zeal of the defenders of the city. Only a bold and lucky
stroke could give Constantinople to the Goths. They were, on the
contrary, themselves surprised and driven back by a furious sortie
made by a body of Saracens who had lately been introduced into
the city.[3] The fair-haired, blue-eyed children of the North recoiled
in surprise and alarm before these men bronzed by the Arabian
sun, with their short crisp hair, and dark flashing eyes. One of
these savage warriors of the desert, naked to the waist, a dagger
in his hand, had plunged into the midst of the Gothic host, uttering a kind of howl like a beast; and, striking down a man, had
applied his lips to the wound, and eagerly drank the other's blood.
This was the first encounter between the two Barbaric powers who
were to divide the Empire between them.

[1] . . . *Itineribus lentis, miscentes cuncta populationibus et incendiis, nullo renitente, pergebant*
(Amm. Marcellinus, xxxi. 16).

[2] . . . *Copiarum cumulis inhiantes amplissimis (ibid.).*

[3] Socrates (*Hist. eccl.* iv. 36) speaks of a treaty concluded by Valens with their queen,
Mavia, who stipulated that one of her Saracens, a hermit, should be consecrated bishop. The
monks of Mount Sinai preached to the Arabs.

Here we might well stop, for nothing more is left of Rome. Beliefs, civil institutions, military organization, arts, literature, — all have disappeared, and the invasion has begun. Fritigern has advanced as far as the walls of Constantinople; in a few years Alaric will make himself master of Rome. But the religious question, which has occupied so many pages in this volume, is not yet settled; Arianism holds almost the entire East; in many places paganism still endures, even in those great centres of Orthodoxy, Rome and Alexandria; and an Emperor is yet to come who, striking the last blows at the ancient religion, will establish the unity of the Church, and for a few months will reign sole master in both capitals of the world. Our task, therefore, is not yet ended.

¹ Rome and Constantinople (reverse of a gold medallion of Gratian).

ROME AND CONSTANTINOPLE.¹